SOUND of L

"Stand back!" Dazzler said, hitting play on her phone. A raucous rock song filled her ears. She cranked the volume and closed her eyes as she absorbed the sonic goodness that the thundering drumbeat and crunching guitars provided. She felt her veins spark and come alive with her light powers, and focused hard, drawing the energy down through her legs and pooling it entirely into her feet. Her soles began to glow brightly, and she ran toward the dead-end wall, at speed.

Just as she was about to crash into the wall, she leapt up and slammed her left foot against it, kicking off. Moving left to right, wall to wall, to the power of the song, she bounced higher and higher toward the top of the building. With one last push off the dead-end concrete wall, she finally bounced herself up onto the roof, landing with a glowing skid.

ALSO AVAILABLE

SCHOOL OF X
The Siege of X-41 by Tristan Palmgren

MARVEL CRISIS PROTOCOL
Target: Kree by Stuart Moore
Shadow Avengers by Carrie Harris

MARVEL HEROINES
Domino: Strays by Tristan Palmgren
Rogue: Untouched by Alisa Kwitney
Elsa Bloodstone: Bequest by Cath Lauria
Outlaw: Relentless by Tristan Palmgren
Black Cat: Discord by Cath Lauria
Squirrel Girl: Universe by Tristan Palmgren

LEGENDS OF ASGARD
The Head of Mimir by Richard Lee Byers
The Sword of Surtur by C L Werner
The Serpent and the Dead by Anna Stephens
The Rebels of Vanaheim by Richard Lee Byers
Three Swords by C L Werner
The Prisoner of Tartarus by Richard Lee Byers

MARVEL MULTIVERSE MISSIONS
You Are (Not) Deadpool by Tim Dedopulus
She-Hulk Goes to Murderworld by Tim Dedopulus

MARVEL UNTOLD
The Harrowing of Doom by David Annandale
Dark Avengers: The Patriot List by David Guymer
Witches Unleashed by Carrie Harris
Reign of the Devourer by David Annandale
Sisters of Sorcery by Marsheila Rockwell

XAVIER'S INSTITUTE
Liberty & Justice for All by Carrie Harris
First Team by Robbie MacNiven
Triptych by Jaleigh Johnson
School of X edited by Gwendolyn Nix

SOUND OF LIGHT

AMANDA BRIDGEMAN

FOR MARVEL PUBLISHING

VP Production & Special Projects: Jeff Youngquist
Associate Editors, Special Projects: Caitlin O'Connell and Sarah Singer
Manager, Licensed Publishing: Jeremy West
VP, Licensed Publishing: Sven Larsen
SVP Print, Sales & Marketing: David Gabriel
Editor in Chief: C B Cebulski

First published by Aconyte Books in 2022

ISBN 978 1 83908 178 1

Ebook ISBN 978 1 83908 179 8

Cover art by Christina Myrvold

Distributed in North America by Simon & Schuster Inc, New York, USA
Printed in the United States of America
9 8 7 6 5 4 3 2 1

ACONYTE BOOKS

An imprint of Asmodee Entertainment Ltd
Mercury House, Shipstones Business Centre
North Gate, Nottingham NG7 7FN, UK
aconytebooks.com // twitter.com/aconytebooks

To those whose lives never quite fit that of society's expectations – I see you. Keep doing you and never let anyone dim your light. Shine it for the world to see.

CHAPTER ONE

Dazzler, eyes closed, belted out the crescendo of her low tempo rock song. The veins in her neck swelled with exertion as every ounce of oxygen left her body and, when she finally ended the note, the crowd went wild. As her band moved into the instrumental break of the song, she opened her eyes again, saw the crowd rocking out and grinned, happy they liked her new tune. Swinging her long blonde hair around, she grooved her way over to the lead guitarist, Tommy, who shook his pink mohawk about and made his axe wail with delight. She turned her smile to Kirk, who pounded the drums, then to Paul on bass, and then to Eddie who fleshed things out on rhythm guitar. Her grin grew wider as every chord and beat of the music sank deep beneath her skin and surged through her entire body. To say the feeling was electric was an understatement.

She danced back across the stage in her fitted white jumpsuit, her mirrored wrist cuffs sparkling as she clapped her hands in time to the beat. As she moved, she subtly released a little of her mutant energy, flaring lights over the band in time to the music, then she grabbed the mic, ready to sing another chorus.

"*You won't ever knock me down…*" she sang, her vocals husky yet powerful, as Tommy's guitar riffed in response. "*I'll always be around… If you try to break me down… I'm gonna take you out…*"

As the song transitioned toward the outro, she scanned the dancing crowd before her. Erratic movement toward the back of the room caught her attention. She squinted against the spotlight to get a better look. It didn't look like dancing.

"*You won't* ever *take me down!*" she continued singing. "*'Cause I'm* here *for the count!*"

She made out that the erratic movement was a fight. A nasty one. There were three or four guys pummeling each other and parting the crowd like the Red Sea. She scanned the bar for security.

"*I'll run you to the ground…*" she sang. "*I'm here to claim my crown…*"

Two doormen made their way through the crowd to the unruly mob. Dazzler counted at least seven involved now. There was no way the doormen were going to be able to control the rapidly escalating situation.

"*Whoa-oh! You won't ever take me down… You won't ever!*"

She closed her eyes and pooled the sonic energy inside her body. Rolling it through her arms and down into her palms, she shot out a burst of light.

"*WHOA-OH!*" she sang.

The room flared with brilliant white light, stunning everyone and making them collectively cover their eyes. She pulled her power back, then sent it out again in small sharp bursts of light. To those in the room it would look like shards of light reflecting off a mirror ball – or in this case, her mirrored wrist cuffs – only Dazzler aimed the shards of light with perfection at the brawlers, blinding them into submission. It was all the doormen needed to gain advantage over the men and start hauling the worst of them out of the bar.

She raised her right fist in victory, and she screamed the final note of the song that ended in time with the music. "*WHOOOOOA-OH!*"

The crowd erupted into cheers, whistles, and applause. Some even began chanting, "Dazzler! Dazzler! Dazzler!" She beamed and waved to the crowd.

"Thank you. You guys rocked tonight!" she said into the mic, and then she and the band gave the crowd an applause of their own.

"Let's give it up one more time," Benedict, the bar manager's voice sounded over the speakers, "to Dazzler and the Casablancas!"

The crowd roared, the band gave one last wave, and then left the stage.

Dazzler stepped off the stage to see Benedict standing with his hand raised ready to high five her.

"Great show, Dazz," he said with his thick Cockney accent. "You rocked it, love!" Here in New York, Ben was a long way from home, but he'd spent most of his life traveling around as a roadie for many of rock music's greats, names that left Dazzler in awe. This pokey little rock bar was his version of retirement.

"Thanks, Ben," she said, high-fiving his waiting hand.

She made her way through the stage door, down the dimly lit

corridor to the band's tiny, minimally furnished dressing room, complete with graffitied walls and stained carpet, where she collapsed into a worn chair.

"That was awesome!" Tommy said, moving to a small tub full of bottled water and throwing one to Dazzler, which she caught.

"Did you see that fight breaking out at the back of the room?" Paul asked, as he stroked his goatee.

"No," Dazzler lied, shaking her head, and then gulping her water.

Eddie slumped into the worn chair opposite Dazzler, tying back his sweaty, straggly long hair. "Man, I thought World War Three was about to break out."

"Ah, security had it under control," Tommy said.

"I couldn't see anything from the drum riser," Kirk said. "Those lights were blinding at the end. What was the lighting tech doing?"

"Who knows?" Dazzler shrugged, standing to grab her bag, which sat on the small dressing table before a cracked mirror. She pulled out a towel and patted the sweat from her face. Her waterproof makeup was holding well: the black of her eyeliner that made her blue eyes pop, the pale pink sheen of her lips, and the large glittery blue wing painted over her left eye, forehead, and cheekbone.

"Hey, you coming to Katy's party?" Tommy asked her.

"Not tonight, guys," Dazzler said.

"Why not?" Kirk asked.

"I promised myself a quiet weekend," she said, strapping on her rollerblades.

"You'll be missing out, Dazz…" Tommy teased.

"You can tell me all about it at our gig next weekend," she said, hiking her bag over her shoulder. "Later."

Dazzler exited the club and began rollerblading down the street, the lights of the tall Manhattan skyscrapers filling in for where the stars should be. The cold night air felt refreshing, as she was still warm from her performance, but she suspected she'd find it too cold soon enough and would be wanting a jacket.

Her mind ran over the gig, happy with how things went. She'd had so many starts and stops in her career, but it felt like her music was finally moving forward again. The bar tonight was small and run down, but it was an indie favorite, and if they could sell out that venue, which they did, they'd be moving on to bigger clubs and concert halls soon enough. The new band was solid and held real promise. She felt bad lying to them about the stage lights, but she wasn't ready to let them in on that part of her life just yet. From what she could tell they were all humans, and until she knew how they felt about mutants, she didn't want to blow a good thing.

Normally she would've gone to the party with them, but tonight was no ordinary night. And that was something she wasn't ready to share with her bandmates yet, either. Besides, the band was on a high from the gig, and she didn't want to kill their vibe. Today was the anniversary of something very personal that always made Dazzler melancholy: the day her mother walked out on her and her father when she was just a child. Ever since it had happened, for whatever reason, Dazzler preferred to be alone on this day. Gigs were the only exception. So, as was her tradition, all she wanted to do was go home, curl up in bed, and cocoon herself from her feelings.

A black SUV with tinted windows suddenly pulled onto the sidewalk right in front of her, forcing her to brake abruptly on her rollerblades and jolting her out of her musings.

"Hey, you jerk!" she yelled.

The rear door opened, and a black man in his thirties, dressed in a smart suit, white shirt, and black tie, stepped out.

"You wanna look where you're going?" Dazzler berated him. "You almost cleaned me up!"

"No, we didn't, Alison Blaire. Your reflexes are too sharp for that," he said.

Her body stilled. Dazzler went by her stage name these days. No one called her Alison anymore and hadn't for a long time. But he knew her real name.

"Who are you?" she asked, eyeing him and the car.

"My name is Markis Bennett," he said. "I need a word with you." His eyes darted to a couple walking hand in hand along the sidewalk, who paused to glance at both them and the SUV. "In private," Bennett added, motioning to the vehicle.

"Yeah, I don't think so, buddy," Dazzler said, hiking her bag higher over her shoulder as she began to rollerblade around him and the car.

He moved to intercept her, cutting off her path. "I work for S.H.I.E.L.D.," he said quickly, quietly.

She halted again, then rolled backward, putting some distance between them. "No, you don't. S.H.I.E.L.D. has been disbanded."

"Things change," he said, eyes deadly serious. "And we need your help."

Dazzler stared at him for a moment, then laughed sardonically. "Yeah, right." Her face hardened. "Get out of here, before I make you disappear." She turned and continued blading past the car, along the sidewalk, and away from Bennett.

"I understand your reservations," he said, following her on foot as the SUV reversed and began to tail them along the street.

"My reservations?" She spun around on her blades, braking suddenly, and looked at him. "I have no reservations at all. I want nothing to do with you. S.H.I.E.L.D. is dead and buried to me. You want help, go find some other sucker you can use. You'll get no help from me." She bladed off again.

"Not even to help your father?" he called after her.

Dazzler rolled onward as the words sank in, before she slowed to a stop.

Did he say her *father*?

She heard the low rumble of the SUV idling beside her on the street, then the scratching, rolling sounds as a skateboarder whizzed past on the sidewalk.

"Judge Carter Blaire has been reported missing," Bennett said from behind her as he caught up. "He's been gone four days now."

Dazzler slowly turned to look over her shoulder at him.

"Let me brief you," he said, motioning to the SUV. "If you still want to walk away at the end of it, so be it. Just hear me out."

She rolled her blades around to face him. "You're lying. It's a trap."

He reached into his jacket, and she tensed, raising her hands, ready to light him up like the Fourth of July.

"Whoa!" he said, holding his hand out peacefully. "I'm just getting my phone to show you something."

"Slow moves or you fry," she said.

He pulled out his phone and stepped toward her, bringing something up on the screen. "His secretary reported him missing. This is her call." He held the phone out and played the recording to her.

"This is the Manhattan Police Department," a woman's voice said. "How may we assist your call?"

"Hello, I need to report a missing person, please." Dazzler recognized the voice as her father's long-time assistant, Maria. She'd often cared for Dazzler as a child when she'd been left waiting at her father's office while he finished meetings. Knowing her mother was gone, Maria had always been kind to Dazzler. "It's Judge Carter Blaire," Maria's voice warbled on the recording. "He hasn't shown for work, and he's not answering his calls. I went by his house, and no one is home. This is not like him at all. I'm worried. *Very* worried."

Bennett stopped the recording and put his phone away. "Just hear me out," he said calmly. "That's all I'm asking."

Dazzler's mind raced. Her shoulders were tense, her breathing rapid, her palms sweating. That was definitely Maria's voice, so this wasn't a S.H.I.E.L.D. trick. Could her father really be missing?

A group of young people walked past chatting and laughing. One of them recognized her and called out, "Hey, Dazzler! Great show!"

The group all smiled and chimed in with, "Yeah!" and, "Rockin'." Dazzler pasted on a smile and waved a thank you to them as they passed.

"We can't talk out here on the street," Bennett said, eyeing the group, then motioning to the SUV again. "Please."

Dazzler studied the idling SUV. Her whole body buzzed with stored light energy, as though it zapped from conduit to conduit, ready for anything. Bennett studied her, noticing the sparks of light glittering beneath her skin.

"I just want to talk. That's all," Bennett said. "I mean you no harm."

Dazzler stared at him. He sounded genuine, but that meant nothing. She'd trusted people like him before and she'd paid the price for it. A price that came with nightmares, anxiety, and a whole lot of mistrust.

Still… her father was missing. She had to know more.

"Make any sudden moves," she said threateningly, "and I *will* mean you harm. Understand?"

Bennett nodded. "Understood."

He moved slowly back to the SUV, where the back door remained ajar. He climbed inside. As she carefully neared the door, she peered inside to see a modified layout: two long seats faced each other, with a TV screen positioned at one end. Bennett was alone, aside from the driver up front, and it made her feel a little better.

She took one last look around the Manhattan streets, then climbed inside.

CHAPTER TWO

Bennett watched her carefully as she took the seat opposite his. The door automatically locked behind her, and Dazzler tensed, balling her fists.

Bennett eyed those fists then looked back to her face. "As I said earlier, my name is Markis Bennett. I'm an agent working on a special assignment for S.H.I.E.L.D."

"How is that possible when S.H.I.E.L.D. has been disbanded?" Dazzler demanded.

"A small contingent of us have been reinstated, informally, for this specific assignment."

"Informally?" She folded her arms. "So, is it black ops or have you gone rogue?"

Bennett ignored her comment. His face showed no emotion, but his eyes were sharp and analyzing. He wasn't a junior. This guy had experience. "The assignment involves something you're very familiar with. MGH."

"MGH?" Dazzler couldn't stop the way her face screwed up,

nor how her body tensed further, or how she pressed herself back into her seat, as though trying to move away from his words.

"We understand this is a sensitive topic for you," Bennett said, calmly, eyes darting to her balled fists again, "but you know the Mutant Growth Hormone better than anyone. That's why I'm here."

Dazzler stared at him, her face fierce and her blue eyes burning – a self-defense mechanism to cover her fear. She knew MGH, all right. It was a dark part of her past that she'd rather forget. A past that had seen her held prisoner by Mystique, and her DNA forcibly extracted to create the MGH steroid that would be used by others longing to be drunk with power.

Mutant power.

"What the hell has this got to do with my father?" she asked.

"We're still trying to figure that out," he said, eyes narrowing briefly with accusation. "All we know so far is that there appears to be a new supply of the steroid on the streets, and early tests have shown it's the same MGH that was derived from you. High profile missing persons tend to flag in our systems. When we learned that your father was missing and that the MGH derived from you had resurfaced, well, we have to assume the two are related. Do you know if your father was having any financial trouble, or any problems that might've led him to become involved in the distribution of MGH?"

"No." Dazzler automatically shook her head. "There's no way." First, her father didn't know she was a mutant. Second, her father would simply never do anything criminal. "If there's one thing my father takes a hard line on, it's upholding the law," she said. "He's a man rigid in his intent, and he won't bend on that for anyone."

"Well, right now he's disappeared, and there are no signs of a struggle." Markis did little to hide his skepticism. "It very much looks like he just left and doesn't want to be found. Your father is a smart man who knows the law, knows the loopholes, knows what can take a criminal down. If he was in trouble, if he needed help, wouldn't he leave some clue for us to find?"

"If he had time to, sure. But if he was taken by force–"

"There were no signs of a struggle," Markis repeated.

"That doesn't mean he wasn't taken by force," she countered. "Check my father's career history. It's impeccable."

"You want to find out what happened and clear his name? Then help us."

"Help you how?"

"There are mutants involved. That's how this all started. They contacted us to see if we knew anything about the new batch of MGH that had surfaced. We didn't, but we agreed to assist and investigate things on our end. As you can imagine, the information exchange has been very one-way. Since S.H.I.E.L.D. was disbanded, the relationship between us and the mutant community has been non-existent. It's... *difficult* for us to access information from the mutant world now. Given we've linked your father's disappearance to this, we'd like you to step back into your role as Mutant Liaison."

"You want me to work for S.H.I.E.L.D. again? You want me to put a target on my back again? Everything that happened to me last time, happened because Mystique and her mutant allies thought I was betraying the mutant community by working with S.H.I.E.L.D. What do you think is going to happen if they find out I'm working with you again?"

"This MGH could be a real problem if it spirals. Do you

understand what the consequences could be if the steroid becomes widespread? For humans *and* for mutants. No one would be safe."

Dazzler turned to look out the window at the late-night Manhattan streets. Across the road on the opposite sidewalk, she spotted the guys from her band laughing and talking as they headed toward the subway, on their way to the party. She felt a huge stab of regret for turning down the invite now. Still, she knew deep down it wouldn't have made any difference. Bennett would have still found her. Her father would still be missing. This problem wasn't going to just go away. The Mutant Growth Hormone was a powerful steroid that could indeed prove an exponential threat in the wrong hands.

And she knew that better than anyone.

Flashbacks suddenly invaded her thoughts. Memories of lying prisoner in that bed, drugged and having her mutant DNA extracted… DNA that her enemies used for their own gain. In mutants, the steroid would enhance their powers. In humans, MGH would improve speed, agility, and strength, or even unlock powers the humans never knew they had. It made her feel sick to think of people using her "essence" without her consent, and worse still to think of them using it to hurt others.

She watched her band turn the street corner and disappear from view. She turned her focus from them to her reflection in the window. Highlighted by the SUV's interior lights, she saw the glittery blue star over her left eye and the hardness of her face, framed by waves of long blonde hair. Her stab of regret for not being with her band turned into a sadness that sat deep within her. A sadness that made her long to be a normal human without such mutant troubles.

"Is Mystique involved?" Her quiet voice was razor sharp as she turned back to Bennett.

"We don't know," he said. "So far, we've found no trace of her involvement. But, of course, we can't be sure. She did escape from our custody, so anything is possible. That's why we need you. No one will become suspicious if *you* ask around about MGH among your kind–"

"My *kind*?" she cut him off. She didn't like the way he used the word.

"Mutants," he said. "You understand this is not information we want getting out. If people know they can get their hands on MGH, our problem will only grow larger. We need you to make some quiet inquiries among your people."

Dazzler's face hardened further. "Stop saying 'your people' and 'your kind' like we're some kind of other, like we're second-class citizens. You humans are so quick to forget everything mutants have done for *your* kind."

"And you mutants are quick to forget the damage that some of your kind have unleashed on the human population." Bennett's face turned mean for the first time. "We've lost a lot of innocent people because some mutants felt the need to dominate us and treat us like bugs to be squashed."

"And some humans have felt the need to hunt down innocent mutants like dogs and exterminate us because we might *one day* pose a threat!"

Bennett took a subtle breath and regained his calm composure. "So how about we work together to stop this from spiraling and any more of *our* people getting hurt. Let's find out who's behind this and shut them down. The clock is ticking."

The silence sat for a moment as she studied him. Dazzler

tried hard to stay strong and in control, but she couldn't stop her throat from giving an involuntary swallow. "If the MGH on the street is from me then Mystique must be behind it. She's the one who took the steroid from me originally. She must have stored stock somewhere or recreated it from a sample."

"Possibly," Bennett said, "but without proof nothing is for sure."

"So what exactly do you think I'm going to be able to do to help you?" she asked. "Some mutants still hold a grudge against me and don't trust my loyalty to them."

"Like I said, this started with the mutant community. They contacted us, and other powerful mutants were aiding us."

"*Were*? As in, past tense?"

For the first time, Bennett's steady face flashed concern. "We've lost contact with those mutants. Now, there is a chance their absence could be intentional, but we do not believe this to be the case. We believe they are missing. That's why we're talking to you now. Our mission status has been elevated to the highest level. We have no choice but to involve you."

Dazzler straightened a little. "Who's gone missing? And why do you keep saying *we*? Who else is involved?"

Bennett turned to the small screen embedded in the SUV wall and turned it on. Dazzler recognized the face that appeared: the cropped brown hair, the chiseled cheekbones, the sharp eyes fixed directly upon her. It was ex-S.H.I.E.L.D. Director, Maria Hill.

Dazzler instantly scowled at the woman. If she'd been a cat, she probably would've hissed at her.

"It's good to see you too, Dazzler," Hill said.

Dazzler turned back to Bennett. "You didn't say *she* was involved."

"Of course he didn't," Hill said frankly. "You wouldn't have got into that car if he had."

"No, I wouldn't have!" Dazzler spat and shuffled toward the car door.

"Magneto and Cyclops are missing," Hill said quickly, urgency lacing her voice.

Dazzler, gripping the door's handle, paused. She looked back at Hill.

"Along with your father," Hill added, and arched an eyebrow. "You still want to walk away?"

"Magneto and Cyclops are missing?" Dazzler asked.

Hill nodded.

"Well, you don't exactly have a great history with Cyclops," Dazzler said. "You tried to hunt him down once, remember? He's probably hiding from you."

"It's true we haven't always seen eye to eye," Hill said, "what with Cyclops trying to stage a mutant uprising and me being forced to defend the human population, but that's in the past now. Besides, Magneto was the one who contacted me about the MGH. He was the one who brought us in on this."

"Why would he do that? What did he say?" Dazzler asked.

"He found the MGH on some young mutants and inquired whether we had any intel on it. It was news to us. We suggested he speak to the scientist who assisted us previously, to find out what type of MGH it was. Both he and Cyclops were investigating it from their side, while we looked into things on our side, but they played a lot of things close to the chest. We agreed to check in with each other at regular intervals. They made their first check-in fine, told us they wanted to keep this issue contained and not alert the rest of the mutant community.

Magneto headed to New York, and Cyclops was in Vancouver to speak with the scientist. However, they both failed to meet their second check-in. We haven't been able to locate them since. They've disappeared, like your father, and we need to know why."

Dazzler turned to Bennett. "And you still don't think Mystique is involved?"

"We can't be sure," Hill answered for him. "All we know is that you have links to the three missing parties, and the MGH that's been tested contains your DNA. This has firmly become a mutant issue now, one that involves you whether you like it or not."

"So, you need me on the inside." Dazzler nodded to herself as she considered the possibilities.

"I know you have reservations about working with me again," Hill said, "but if you care at all for your father or these mutants, then you'll help us get to the bottom of this. No one in the mutant community will speak with us willingly."

"How do I know I won't be betrayed again?" Dazzler couldn't help the snarl that curled her top lip.

"I never betrayed you," Hill said.

"No, you just never cared enough to notice that Mystique was posing as me and that I was missing. I was kept prisoner *for months*, being bled dry of my DNA! You can't expect me to forget that."

"I don't," Hill said frankly. "But I do expect you to direct your anger in the appropriate place. At Mystique. She's the one who took you. She's the one who pretended to be you and infiltrated S.H.I.E.L.D. Don't forget, I was the one who gave you the opportunity to come back and help take her down. I gave you the closure you needed."

"And then she escaped from your custody. How am I supposed to get closure from that?"

"You want closure, then help us," Hill said plainly. "Magneto saved you from Mystique. He was the one who freed you from being her prisoner. You don't want to return the favor and help find him now? Even Cyclops took you in afterward when you needed it. And your father? You really don't want to find him?"

Dazzler looked out the window again, anything to avoid their eyes. Hill was a great emotional manipulator.

But this time, she was also right.

Dazzler owed Magneto a debt. Cyclops, too. And how could she possibly walk away knowing her father was missing? Despite all the strained years with him, despite him turning his back on her, he was still her father. He was the only family she had left since her beloved grandma died.

"Every second they are missing is another second they could be dead," Hill said. "Meanwhile, MGH is beginning to spread into the streets. We need to move on this. If you won't help, we'll do it our way, but my guess is it's going to take us a lot longer from the outside than it would with you on the inside. So, what's it going to be?"

Dazzler glanced briefly at Bennett, who looked as though he questioned whether she was up for the challenge, then she stared at Hill's uncompromising gaze. Dazzler did not want this nightmare to resurface in her life again. If her father was missing, if Magneto and Cyclops were missing, if someone was leaking her MGH onto the streets, then she wanted to stop them.

And she didn't trust anyone but herself to do it.

"All right," she said. "But I work alone. You stay away from me."

"No can do," Hill said.

"We need to work together," Bennett said, pulling another phone from his pocket and holding it out to her. "We stay in contact via this. All the information we have so far is uploaded on there, along with your new S.H.I.E.L.D. credentials." He also handed her a credit card. "These funds will support your investigation."

"We'll need regular updates," Hill told her. "You pass us information, and we'll do the same. We'll cover the human side. You find out what you can from the mutant side."

Dazzler eyed the phone and credit card, then took them from Bennett. "Fine. But I still work alone. If I see you guys sticking your nose in or getting too close, it's over. The mutant community won't trust me if they sniff S.H.I.E.L.D. involvement."

Dazzler opened the door and climbed out.

"Blaire," Hill called.

Dazzler looked back at the screen.

"Be careful," Hill said in a slightly softer tone. "If someone managed to take Magneto and Cyclops prisoner, or worse, kill them, that wouldn't have been an easy feat. They must be powerful or have a powerful network around them."

"Yeah, well, I have a powerful network too." She stared at Hill. "They're called mutants."

CHAPTER THREE

Dazzler sat in her apartment, scrolling through the phone Bennett had given her. The information she'd been furnished with wasn't much more than what they'd already told her. She had the name of the scientist that Cyclops was going to meet in Vancouver, but aside from the official S.H.I.E.L.D. credentials that she could use, the phone was of little value. She knew it was simply a tool for S.H.I.E.L.D. to track her movements. They'd mistaken her blonde hair for stupidity.

She was used to being treated as a "dumb blonde." Though, sometimes, it was useful to lean on her blonde bombshell looks, most of the time it just angered her. She was once on her way to becoming a lawyer and following in her father's footsteps. There was no nepotism involved. She had the brains for it, pure and simple. But then she realized that she didn't want to be a lawyer, and that music was her calling, much to her father's disdain. Like her "deadbeat" mother who walked out on them, Dazzler had longed to be an entertainer. She knew deep down that was why her father was so against it. His heart had been utterly broken when her mother had left, and then his daughter was planning on following in her footsteps, instead of his. What a blow that must've been to him, to his ego. He was the one who had done the right thing and raised her, and that was how Dazzler repaid him. By wanting to be just like her mother, instead.

The irony struck her deeply. Here she was on the anniversary of her mother's abandonment, discovering that her father was now missing. She felt guilt slash her heart for all the empty years between them. He'd refused to speak to her after she followed her dreams. Despite their strained relationship, she owed her old man this at least. She had to find him. She had to help him. He did the right thing by her once, not abandoning her; now she had to do the right thing and not abandon him.

Using her own personal phone, she took a careful photo of the S.H.I.E.L.D. credentials and the information from the case file, then threw the organization's phone onto her bed. There was no way they could be allowed to track her movements. First, she was still suspicious about the true motivation behind this S.H.I.E.L.D. operation. Was it truly to stop the MGH, or was it a ploy of Hill's to track Cyclops down for another reason? She didn't want S.H.I.E.L.D. predicting her next steps, which might give them the upper hand to interfere in whatever she did.

Second, she knew full well that her first move would be to visit the mutant school Magneto ran with Cyclops, where she figured the MGH must have surfaced. However, she could not allow S.H.I.E.L.D. to discover the school's location. The New Charles Xavier School was a closely guarded secret, even in the mutant community, and only certain mutants knew its location. If she inadvertently led S.H.I.E.L.D. to them, then she would be ostracized from a large part of the mutant community, and she couldn't afford to have any more mutant enemies. Especially when she owed Magneto a debt. She would do everything in her power to keep the school's location a secret, as he and Scott desired.

Staring at her personal phone, she realized she'd need to swap it out for a burner phone, too. There was much work to be done, and she had to move fast. It was just after two AM but, despite the hour, she grabbed her packed bag and left her apartment. If she'd had the option she would've left this journey until the morning, when she could've hidden among the early rush of people, but knowing how far she had to travel, she had to leave now. Every second wasted might affect her father's life.

That is, if he wasn't already dead.

She swept the thought into a dark recess of her mind, not wanting to consider it. She had to stay focused. She had to believe she would find him. She had to believe she could fix whatever mess he had gotten himself into. That thought alone puzzled her, though. The word "mess" was not something she would normally associate with Judge Blaire, a man who never strayed outside the boundaries. Had he somehow crossed paths with Magneto and Cyclops? Had he been drawn into something unsuspecting? Or had her father, for the first time in his life, made an error in judgement? Had he fallen into something he couldn't get himself out of?

She stepped outside, and the chill hit her like she'd stepped into a fridge. Though she'd changed into her black leather jumpsuit and black flat-heeled boots, she still zipped a jacket over the top for extra warmth and pulled the hood low over her face. Though her mirrored cuffs kept her wrists warm, she really could've used her gloves, but they were packed in her bag and she didn't have time to find them. She settled for shoving her hands into her pockets, instead.

She started making her way toward the subway station and felt an overwhelming sensation that she was being followed. She glanced around the streets but didn't see anything suspicious. Was it just paranoia from all she'd been told? She kept walking, eyes alert, then suddenly heard a noise that made her look up into the sky behind her.

A drone, black and almost invisible against the night sky, but sleek enough to reflect the shine of the city's lights as it passed them, followed her.

"Nice one, S.H.I.E.L.D.," she muttered to herself. "Real subtle." She shook her head and kept walking, placing her earbuds in and loading some music on her phone to fuel her. While the music poured through her, she started thinking about how to get rid of the drone.

As she made her way toward the subway, she took the most complex route she could think of, suddenly scooting around corners, cutting through alleyways, climbing over fences, and making every attempt to lose the drone. But every time she thought she'd lost it, there it was again. She had to assume it wasn't manually controlled by a S.H.I.E.L.D. agent, but that it automatically read her body heat and used facial recognition software. Given there weren't many people around in the area, the drone had no trouble tracking her... and would most likely calculate her route if she did try to disappear down to the subway.

What she needed now was people. Left with no other option at this time of night, she headed to a place where she could be guaranteed of a crowd: Times Square.

When she arrived at Times Square, she was happy to see there were still plenty of people around, given it was a Saturday night. They were mainly tourists checking out the flashing signs, or others spilling out of clubs and making their way through the square to other destinations. She found an ATM and checked the balance of the card S.H.I.E.L.D. had given her, having memorized the PIN provided on their phone. Her eyes nearly popped at the number of zeros on the balance. She'd never had that much money in her own account. It made her nervous that S.H.I.E.L.D. believed she might need all those funds to furnish her investigation, and more nervous still, wondering just where S.H.I.E.L.D. received such funding in order to hand it over to someone like her.

That said, she was fine with spending it. She started entering different figures into the ATM to see how much she could take out in one withdrawal. When she finally found the limit, she stuffed the cash inside her leather jumpsuit.

Her next stop was to buy a burner phone. As soon as she did, she navigated toward the thickest part of the crowd, standing below a large lit billboard currently featuring an advertisement for some expensive perfume. She stood among the crowd, her hands hidden as she stopped the music running through her earbuds and transferred the information from one phone to the other, including all her music, of course, then tossed her old phone into a nearby trash can.

She heard music start up and saw a nearby street performer dancing to some loud beats, popping and locking his body in ways that would make most breakdancers weep. She regretted that she didn't have the time to stop and watch his performance.

She sought out the drone and spotted it perched atop a billboard opposite where she stood. It still had her locked in its sights. The billboard behind her played a different ad, this one for a soft drink, which had some serious sci-fi vibes to it with all those strobing lights and quick-cut cinematography. She stood still, studying her surroundings and planning her escape, as several rotations of ads played out on the billboard behind her. Before she knew it the perfume ad was playing again, which meant the soft drink commercial was next, and that, Dazzler decided, was when she would strike. She soaked up the beats from the street performer's stereo.

The soft drink commercial began to play...

As the strobe lighting commenced, Dazzler quickly raised her hands and shot out a succession of focused light energy at the drone. She hit her target with the series of intense beams, aimed at frying its electronics. The drone sparked and smoked against its dark backdrop, then crashed down behind the billboard.

No one seemed to have noticed, and with a bit of luck not even S.H.I.E.L.D. would be certain of what had happened. With that knowledge, Dazzler seized the moment, ducking low as she moved through the crowd, and slinked off into the night. As she walked away from Times Square, she looked over her shoulder to check whether the drone would rise again or whether a new one would take its place. She saw neither.

Keeping her head down, she ran in the direction of Grand Central Station, flaring her light energy into the lens of every street security camera she passed to avoid detection. She did the same inside the station, knowing it wouldn't be long before S.H.I.E.L.D. picked up her trail, but hopefully she would have the head start she needed.

In the station's bathroom she quickly removed her jacket, stuffed it into her bag, and tucked her long blonde hair up into a beanie, then made her way to the nearest train and stepped aboard.

After an intense journey that involved several subway changeovers, flaring more lenses to keep herself hidden and to ensure she'd lost S.H.I.E.L.D.'s trail, she finally found herself on an overland train, making her way out of the city and heading for the US–Canadian border.

Dazzler awoke with a start.

"Whoa, now!" the man said. "I didn't mean to startle you. But this is where you said you wanted to get out."

Dazzler looked around to see that it was around midday and the farmer's vehicle was pulled over on the side of the road beside a thick pine forest, the scent so strong it permeated the closed windows. She looked back at the man's friendly face, adorned with gray whiskers.

It had been a long journey to this point. First evading S.H.I.E.L.D. and escaping New York, then catching a train close to the Canadian border, hitchhiking across the border, then making her way to an airfield where she paid a pilot in cash to fly her to Alberta, only to hitchhike again to this point to ensure she was close to the school's location, but not too close. To say she'd been exhausted was an understatement.

"I didn't mean to fall asleep," she said, rubbing her face awake.

"You must've been tired," he said, concerned. "You sure this is where you want to get out? There's nothing around here for miles."

She nodded. "Yes. Thank you. I'm going camping in the forest."

"In there?" He seemed perplexed. "I don't see a tent, and I doubt you've got warm enough clothes in that bag. You won't last a night."

She smiled, grabbing her bag. "I'm meeting a friend. They have all that for me." She pulled out some bills and offered them to the man. He waved her money away.

"You just take care of yourself, you hear?" he said. "This wilderness looks beautiful, but it can be real unfriendly, let me tell you."

Dazzler smiled again. "Thank you."

She got out of the vehicle, waved goodbye, and watched him drive away. As soon as he was out of sight, she turned to the tall pine trees, felt the chill kiss her cheeks, then entered the dense forest.

After trudging for over two and a half hours, Dazzler pushed past more thick emerald green pine branches, to finally see the New Charles Xavier School before her. At least, to see the few buildings that were visible above ground. Housed in the old Weapon X facility, she knew the bulk of the school actually lay deep below the surface.

The first dusting of snow littered the landscape. The river nearby crawled along slowly, as though contemplating whether it was ready to freeze. It had been a while since she'd been here, but she remembered it had been warm and sunny last time. She couldn't help thinking how the change of season reflected the turn of events that had led her back today. Without Magneto and Cyclops, the school would not be in a good place. The warm sunshine that had kept the students safe had turned cold. And if Dazzler didn't move fast, the oncoming freeze might kill them all.

She started walking toward the Institute, watching her footing on the rugged ground, and as she neared, she suddenly felt a slight pressure inside her skull. At first, she thought it was her ears readjusting to the altitude, but when she looked back up, she saw the blonde-haired form of Emma Frost standing in front of the school, her long white coat flapping in the breeze.

"Get out of my head," Dazzler said, quietly but firmly.

The pressure eased off, and Dazzler continued forward.

"I wasn't expecting you," Frost said as Dazzler neared, scanning the surroundings behind her carefully.

"Relax," Dazzler said. "I'm alone. No one followed me."

"Why are you here?" Frost's blue eyes narrowed in suspicion.

"We need to talk," Dazzler said.

"About?"

"Magneto and Cyclops," Dazzler said, noticing a slight furrow crease Frost's perfect brow. "Heard from them lately?"

Frost didn't answer, but the older woman's eyes pierced Dazzler's, clearly wanting to know more. Movement at a window into one of the buildings caught Dazzler's attention, and she saw several students watching them curiously.

"Let's talk somewhere private," Dazzler said. "I don't have much time."

Frost analyzed her a moment more, before snapping a turn, white coat flapping in the breeze as she headed inside.

CHAPTER FOUR

Dazzler stared across the desk at Frost, who sat poised in her chair not so much like a headmaster, but more like a queen on a throne. Dazzler knew Frost had once been the White Queen of the Hellfire Club, but Dazzler felt ice queen was probably a better description. If Dazzler was more polished and less rock 'n' roll, they could almost be sisters. Frost's features were flawless, her skin ageless, her eyes sparkling like blue diamonds beneath a sheet of silken blonde hair. Unlike many others, however, Dazzler wasn't drawn in by Frost's beauty. She knew it had been a trap to many and was wary of it. To have power over the mind was a very dangerous thing, and Dazzler did not want Frost going anywhere near hers.

As she thought that, she felt a slight pressure inside her skull again.

"I said, stay out of my head," Dazzler said firmly.

"You want to tell me why you're here or are you just going to sit there and admire my beauty all day?" Frost asked nonchalantly.

Dazzler paused. *Had Frost just read her mind?*

Frost smiled at her. "I don't have to read your mind to know what you're thinking. Some people wear their thoughts on their face, in their body language. And you, Dazzler, are one of them."

"Something to work on, I guess."

"You mentioned Magneto and Cyclops."

"When did you last see them?"

"What business is it of yours?" Frost stared at her.

Dazzler was at a loss for words. She figured honesty was best right now. If she wasn't upfront and Frost found out the truth by other means, it would become much more difficult to gain mutant cooperation. She pulled out her new burner phone that she'd transferred all the necessary files and her music onto and displayed the special S.H.I.E.L.D. credentials.

Frost studied it, tensing as those ice blue eyes locked with Dazzler's. "S.H.I.E.L.D. has been resurrected? By who?"

"Maria Hill is involved. My point of contact is an agent called Markis Bennett."

"So, you're working for them again."

"It's just a one-off case," Dazzler said. "Relax. I told you no one followed me here." She held up her phone. "This is a burner phone. I've taken every precaution to ensure your school remains a secret."

"What's this got to do with Magneto and Scott?"

"You tell me."

Frost remained calm, barely moving a muscle. "No, I think *you* had better tell me. You came here. I didn't invite you."

Dazzler analyzed her, sensing hostility beneath the calmness.

"Forgive me, Dazzler," Frost said, as though reading her mind again, "I know you were once a resident here, but then you left. Something you've done time and time again to the

X-Men. Every time you feel that pull to return to the stage, you leave. You can't just be a mutant when it suits you. There's no such thing as a part time X-Man. You're either in or you're out. And if you're not in with us, then you are out. So, tell me now, why have you come back here?"

Dazzler reluctantly conceded a nod to acknowledge Frost's words. She guessed she deserved the mistrust, the questioning. Dazzler had learned long ago that most people did not understand the creative urge she felt, how it wasn't something she could bury and forget existed. Like being a mutant, it was part of her, part of her very DNA. Music wasn't something she could live without.

But her decision to pursue a musical career was not why she was here.

"What do you know about the MGH running through your school?" Dazzler asked, getting them back on track.

Again, Frost remained still as a statue, smooth as ice.

"MGH is not running through our school," she said coolly.

"Isn't it?" Dazzler challenged.

"No. It is not. So why don't you tell me what you want and why you're here before I rip it out of your brain myself?"

Dazzler knew she didn't have much of a choice to tiptoe around the topic. Time was of the essence. "Did you know Magneto and Cyclops are working with S.H.I.E.L.D.?"

For the first time, she saw Frost's right eye give a slight twitch. This was news to the White Queen.

"You didn't," Dazzler answered for her.

"They left on business three days ago," Frost offered, clearly wanting more information from Dazzler. "Said they'd be back soon and would explain it then."

"You didn't question what it was?"

"No. I trust Magneto and Cyclops. I understand that may be a foreign concept to you. Trusting your fellow mutants."

"It is," Dazzler said plainly. "Especially when a mutant like Mystique did what she did to me."

"Like I said, I understand." Frost sat back in her chair. "So? I assume you're going to tell me what this is all about. Is Mystique involved then?"

"You really didn't know there was MGH in your school?"

Frost considered her answer before giving it. "I knew there had been an incident, but I didn't know the details. Erik and Scott left soon after, and I was put in charge of the school."

"I need to speak with whoever is involved. Now."

"Why the urgency?"

"Because S.H.I.E.L.D. has lost contact with Magneto and Cyclops. They're worried. And it takes a lot to worry S.H.I.E.L.D."

For the first time, Dazzler saw the ice maiden's face crack with concern.

"How long ago?" Frost sat forward. "When did they lose contact?"

Dazzler checked the notes on her phone. "About thirty-six hours ago now. They were supposed to check in, and they didn't. S.H.I.E.L.D. claims they can't find any trace of them."

"Well, I'm not S.H.I.E.L.D. I have better facilities at my disposal." Frost closed her eyes and touched her fingers to her temples. Dazzler watched as her eyeballs began to move back and forth beneath her closed lids. She knew Frost was trying to telepathically connect with them, so she sat quiet and still, letting Frost do what she did best.

Dazzler noticed the eye movement had become more rapid. *Had she found them?*

Moments later, Frost opened her eyes slowly, and Dazzler saw the concern within them had deepened.

"You didn't find them?" Dazzler said, concerned herself.

"No." Frost stood. "But I have something else I can try."

"Cerebra?"

Frost paused. Silent, on guard.

"I was an X-Man once, remember?" Dazzler said. "I know it exists. So does S.H.I.E.L.D."

"S.H.I.E.L.D. knew Cerebro existed, but Cerebro was destroyed. They don't know about Cerebra." Frost walked around her desk and headed for the door, throwing a dark look back at her. "And it better stay that way." Dazzler noted the veiled threat in her words but stood and followed her out the door.

Dazzler followed Frost into an elevator, and then down into the subterranean depths of the Institute, past highly secured doors that she knew few were allowed to pass. Though Dazzler knew of Cerebra's existence, her knowledge of it was limited. She knew its name and vaguely what it could do, but she knew nothing beyond that. And she certainly had never seen it before. She was actually surprised that Frost was going to allow her to witness it.

Dazzler wanted to question her further but thought better of it. Maybe Frost's mind was too caught up in not being able to trace her fellow mutants telepathically. If that was the case, Dazzler didn't exactly want to draw attention to her presence. Regardless, her skepticism and mistrust flared up, despite the fact that she'd never had any conflict with Frost before. But

Dazzler was smart enough to still be wary. After all, mutants were missing. Maybe she was walking into a trap. Maybe once she saw the subterranean depths of the New Charles Xavier School, she would never see the light of day again. The thought sent her pulse racing in fear.

They finally arrived at a set of gray metal double doors, the only doors in an isolated corridor at what Dazzler imagined was the lowest point of the Institute, but she couldn't be sure of this. All she knew was that it was deep below ground. Very deep.

At the doors, Frost submitted to an iris scan. The doors opened, and she entered. Not once did Frost turn to look at Dazzler. Yet Frost did not stop her from following either.

Dazzler stepped through the doorway and saw an expansive room, packed heavily with numerous cables, monitors and equipment, and at its very center sat a large metal orb with a circular opening. Inside the orb was a cabled chair and large, domed helmet. Frost entered the sphere, sat in the chair facing Dazzler, and pulled down the helmet, which covered her entire skull and the top half of her face. It looked a little like Frost was in an electric chair. Knowing what she did about Cerebra, however, Dazzler knew the only execution that would occur was Frost executing an amplified telepathic search for the missing mutants.

Curious and somewhat nervous as to what might happen, Dazzler stood back against the wall by the now sealed doors to the room, watching silently as Frost, several meters away inside the dome of Cerebra, commenced her search.

The lights in the room suddenly dimmed, throwing a red hue across Dazzler as she felt the machine come to life, its vibrations beginning to thrum across the floor and massage the soles of her flat-heeled boots. Through the circular doorway into Cerebra, Dazzler saw the curved ceiling and internal walls around Frost project what looked like a global map of Earth. Soon sparks of light shone here and there across the map like twinkling stars. It was breathtaking and utterly fascinating, drawing Dazzler closer for a better look.

She moved forward carefully until she stood at the circular doorway, eyes fixed on the internal domed walls and ceiling. Her mouth fell agape as mutants emerged from the sparks of light, coming in and out of focus in the form of faces, as Frost's mind jumped from spark to spark, mutant to mutant, city to city, country to country, searching for Magneto and Cyclops. The thrumming was much louder now. Dazzler felt a surge of energy within her body as Cerebra operated at full capacity, vibrating not just the floor but what felt like the whole room. She heard the mutant voices, in snatches and grabs, the chatter becoming a muddle of sound as Frost's mental movement became more rapid. She saw Frost's chest and shoulders moving up and down in time with her increased breathing and wondered whether that was normal.

The vision on the sphere's internal walls was now a complete blur, the voices nothing but a loud cacophony, and the heavy vibration through the floor ran right up the length of Dazzler's legs so that she felt as if she stood on the engines of an X-Jet. Her body, being what it was, absorbed every decibel of the sonic energy like a sponge.

Frost's movement increased further in rapidity. Was this normal? Or was she being impatient? Desperate? Was she struggling to find them?

It made Dazzler nervous as her legs physically shook from the vibration now.

"Frost," she said, but her voice was lost to the noise. Her chest rattled with Cerebra's vibration, and the light energy buzzed inside her. "Frost!"

The rumbling beneath the floor intensified. Dazzler struggled to look at the sphere's inside walls as everything spun, but she was sure she saw faces and places repeating. Which meant one thing.

Frost couldn't find them.

"Frost!" she yelled, holding onto the sphere's curved doorway, trying to suppress the energy surging within. "FROST!"

"Quiet!" Frost hissed back from *inside* Dazzler's brain.

Dazzler shot out her hand and sent a jolt of concentrated light energy at the woman. Not enough to hurt her, but certainly enough to get her attention.

Frost instantly jerked back to reality. The vibration immediately dulled, and the sphere's inside walls stopped spinning. She pulled off the Cerebra helmet, glaring, as a sharp headache like an ice freeze suddenly stabbed Dazzler's brain.

Dazzler groaned then shot another jolt out at Frost, who flinched and rubbed her shoulder at the point of contact, where a singe mark now dirtied her white coat.

"This isn't going to help find them!" Dazzler barked, before Frost could retaliate.

The ice maiden stared at her, breathing heavily, blue eyes angry.

"And you can't find them with Cerebra, can you?" Dazzler said, more calmly, rubbing her pained forehead.

Frost looked away, then eventually relented, and shook her head.

"So, how about we talk to whoever at this school was involved in the MGH," Dazzler said as the headache faded away, "and find our answers there? S.H.I.E.L.D. has no information in their files about that. I need to know what Magneto and Cyclops knew before they left the school."

Frost took a moment to compose herself, then stood, ever the ice maiden again, and flicked the tail of her coat aside before walking past Dazzler to the door.

As they stepped back into the corridor and the door sealed behind them, Frost paused and placed her hand on Dazzler's shoulder.

"You will forget everything you saw in there today." Frost's blue eyes burned into Dazzler's. "Former X-Man or not, no one from S.H.I.E.L.D. will ever know the true workings of Cerebra."

Dazzler felt a strange sensation in her brain. It was fuzzy for a moment, like the fresh carbonated fizz of a soda before it dies down. She saw Frost walking off down the corridor, coat swishing behind her. Feeling lost and confused, and a little dizzy, Dazzler suddenly glanced around and wondered why she was standing in the corridor.

"Do you want to speak to the students or not?" Frost called.

Dazzler shook her head to clear the fuzz and moved after her. As she did, she glanced back over her shoulder curiously, saw a set of closed doors, and wondered what was inside.

CHAPTER FIVE

Dazzler tailed Frost as they made their way back up through the subterranean levels of the Institute to where the main school classrooms were. Every now and then Frost would pause, her mind projecting and seeking direction. Finally, Dazzler sensed she had picked up on something, as she made a direct path toward one of the classroom doors.

Frost stood at the door, looking through the observation window as Dazzler peered in over her shoulder, receiving curious looks from the students inside. At the front of the class stood an athletic woman with long dark hair, dressed in a Lila Cheney T-shirt, leather pants, and motorcycle boots. Dazzler noticed that she wore Goth-like makeup down her face too. She looked like someone Dazzler would see at one of her gigs, not teaching a school class.

The woman glanced at them, then at her class. She stood before a large monitor showing media coverage of the event every mutant knew all too well: M-Day. The day the Scarlet Witch cast a spell sealing the fate of many and creating the darkest day in mutant history. The day when the majority of the mutant population lost their powers. Some had even died as a result.

Sorrow filled Dazzler and she glanced down at her own boots, partly in guilt. She had no idea why she'd been one of the lucky few to have been spared that day.

Frost opened the classroom door.

"Mutant numbers were decimated during this event," the teacher told her class, with an accent Dazzler placed as being from somewhere in eastern Europe. "You are all very lucky to be here at this school, working on your mutant gifts, when so many others cannot."

At this point the teacher looked questioningly at Frost.

"Sage, apologies for the interruption, but I need to speak with Fabio," Frost said to her.

Sage glanced at a hefty teenage boy with shaggy brown hair, sitting at the back of the class. "Fabio," Sage said, "come."

"Er, sure." Fabio stood tentatively, trying to avoid the curious stares of his classmates.

"Uh-oh, what'd you do?" a large young man made of rocks with a baritone voice said.

"Santo," Sage said plainly. "No."

As Fabio made his way toward the door, Frost turned to Sage. "I think you should join us for this."

Sage gave a nod. "Class, I will play this documentary on M-Day for you now. Please watch carefully. I will have questions for you at the end." She set the film playing, then followed Fabio out into the hall to join Dazzler and Frost.

"Is everything OK, Ms Frost?" Fabio asked, tugging nervously at the black shirt he wore, imprinted with three golden orbs across his stocky chest.

"No, it's not," Frost said bluntly. "What do you know about MGH?"

Fabio's face turned ashen.

"MGH?" Sage asked, arching a perfect dark eyebrow with curiosity. Her eyes were a blue-gray mix, like a misty morning over the ocean, and up this close, Dazzler saw that it wasn't Goth makeup on her face, but instead, strange tattoos. Two black lines ran down her face from beneath her eyes, like angular brackets that accentuated her cheekbones.

"Er…" Fabio stalled.

"Who else is involved?" Frost demanded. "Tell me now."

"I- It was just me," he said, before touching his hands to his forehead and wincing in pain.

Frost studied him fixedly for a moment, then looked to Sage. "Bring Benjamin Deeds to my office."

"Morph?" Sage asked, before heading off down the corridor.

"Is there anyone else?" Frost asked Fabio.

"No. No." Fabio shook his head. "It was just us. I swear."

He raised his hands to his head again as Frost gave him another mental pat down, then satisfied, she eased off again.

"He's telling the truth," Frost said, for Dazzler's benefit. She looked back to Fabio. "Let's head to my office. You've got some explaining to do."

Dazzler stood to one side of Frost's chair, arms folded, while Sage stood on the other, as the two nervous students, Fabio Medina and Benjamin Deeds, sat before them.

"Tell me everything you know about the Mutant Growth Hormone steroid," Frost said firmly.

The two young men exchanged a hesitant glance. Benjamin

was smaller than Fabio, meeker, and dressed in a collared long-sleeved shirt and tie like he was headed out to a job interview or maybe a date. He looked at them from behind a long dark fringe as though it would offer him some protection.

"I already know you're involved," Frost said, impatience setting in, "and I know Cyclops and Magneto knew about it, too. So, tell me. *Now.*"

Morph looked at Fabio. "Magneto knows?"

Fabio shrugged his shoulders.

"Which one of you brought it into the school?" Frost demanded. Dazzler sensed an anger rising in her beyond the impatience. An anger stemming from the fact that everyone else seemed to know more about what was going on than she did.

Fabio darted his eyes to Morph, who hung his head a little lower.

"Spit it out, Benjamin," Frost ordered.

The teen swallowed hard. "I- I heard these guys talking about it in town. One of them said his dad has access to this special substance that could give normal humans powers, like super strength and stuff. He said they could use it to defend themselves or maybe pick up dates." He swallowed again. "Then they started talking about what it could do to those who already had super-powers… and… and it sparked my interest."

"What interest?" Frost asked.

Morph shrugged nervously. "I can transmorph into people who are in close proximity to me, but… I wanted the ability to shapeshift into anyone. Whether they were close by or not."

Frost nodded. "So, you bought some."

"Not right away," Morph said, glancing at Fabio. "I came

back to school and saw Fabio. He was feeling down. Some of the kids had been teasing him, calling him Goldenballs–"

"I go by Egg now," Fabio interjected firmly, making sure the women understood that. Dazzler studied the orbs on his shirt and figured the kid's mutant power had something to do with those "golden balls."

"We both wanted to be more than what we are," Morph said quietly. "Especially after Magik accidentally transported us into Limbo that time, and we had to face those demons… So, we decided to try some."

Frost sighed. "Tell me you didn't buy it as you are. Tell me you morphed into someone else beforehand."

Morph nodded. "I took on the physical attributes of another kid nearby."

"How long have you been taking it?" Sage spoke up.

"We only did it once. Before practice," Morph said. "I managed to morph into Hijack. He wasn't part of the class. He was on the other side of campus at the time."

"And I made the biggest golden ball I've ever seen," Fabio said, unable to stop the smile that slid across his face. "It knocked Santo right off his feet."

"Cyclops knew something was up," Morph said. "He pulled us aside and made us tell him what was going on. He made us hand over the remaining MGH, then he left."

"Why are you asking us about this?" Fabio asked.

"Has something happened to Cyclops and Magneto?" Morph asked, his eyes popping wide behind that long fringe of his.

Frost considered her answer. "We've… lost contact with them."

The two young men shot each other a surprised look.

"And that's why *you're* here?" Sage asked Dazzler.

Dazzler gave her a single nod.

"Are they in trouble?" Fabio asked, his face turning ashen again.

"We don't know," Frost said. "We've just lost contact."

"You need to give us the details of who sold you the MGH," Dazzler said firmly, "so we can trace their footsteps."

"Sure." Morph nodded emphatically. "It was at Gamercade, on the main street in town."

"And the name of the kid who sold it to you?" Dazzler asked.

"I don't know his name," Morph said, "but I can identify him."

"Wait outside," Frost ordered them. "And do not breathe a word of this to anyone."

Seeing her stare, they nodded in acquiescence and quickly left.

Dazzler turned to Frost. "Why didn't Magneto and Cyclops share this information with S.H.I.E.L.D.? It's not in their files."

"S.H.I.E.L.D. is involved?" Sage asked, darting her eyes between the two women. "They're back?"

"I'm afraid so," Frost said, then turned to Dazzler. "Knowing Scott and Erik, they would've been protecting the school. If they gave S.H.I.E.L.D. the name Gamercade, then S.H.I.E.L.D. would have suddenly narrowed down the location of our school."

"Well, I need to retrace their footsteps and find out what they discovered," Dazzler said. "I'll head to Gamercade now."

"No," Frost said firmly. "Leave that to me. As you said earlier, time is ticking. Where did S.H.I.E.L.D. last trace Scott to?"

"They said Cyclops was in Vancouver."

"Then you go there and retrace *those* footsteps," Emma said. "I'll let you know what I find out here."

"And why should I trust you?" Dazzler asked, placing her hands on her hips.

"Why should I trust a mutant working with S.H.I.E.L.D.?" Frost countered.

"I may have a history with S.H.I.E.L.D., yes, which you know is not all roses," Dazzler said, "but I also have a history with Magneto and Cyclops. Magneto saved my life. If it wasn't for him, I'd still be Mystique's prisoner. I owe him a debt."

"Yeah, well, I have a few debts of my own to them," Frost said. "So, I guess we're even. We'll have to trust each other. In fact, I'm going to trust you so much that I'm releasing Sage from the school to go with you."

Dazzler eyed Sage, then looked back at Frost. "You trust me so much you're sending a spy to accompany me?"

"I'm not a spy," Sage said firmly, folding her toned arms, as her tattooed face gave Dazzler a plain stare.

"That may be, but I prefer to work alone. Thanks," Dazzler told her.

Frost swung her chair around to face Dazzler. "Working solo is not the X-Men way, you know that."

"I don't care. I may have been an X-Man once, but working alone guarantees I won't be betrayed again. By S.H.I.E.L.D. *or* mutants."

"You'll get yourself killed," Frost told her. "You need help."

"You underestimate my power."

"And you underestimate mine," Frost fired back.

"So, we've established that we're all kick-ass mutants," Sage said with a hint of boredom.

Dazzler glanced at her. "I'll take my chances alone," she said, walking around her desk toward the door.

"Magneto and Cyclops have disappeared," Frost said. "I can't find them with Cerebra, which means they might well be dead. They are Omega-level mutants, Dazzler. You are *not*!"

Dazzler paused and turned back to her.

Frost's blue eyes pinned hers. "One day, yes, you might have the potential to become an Omega-level mutant, I won't deny that, but you're not there yet, Sparkles. Don't let your rock star ego get to your head. If someone has taken both Cyclops and Magneto down, they are powerful. I'm concerned about this, and so should you be."

Dazzler looked away from her intense stare. "We don't know they're dead yet. They could be in hiding somewhere."

"Until they surface, we assume the worst."

Dazzler turned back to meet Frost's serious gaze.

"Sage has brilliant memory recall," Frost continued. "Her mind is like no other, and she has expertise in many fields that will be of use to you. She's what you would call an all-rounder. Trust me, you need her."

As much as Dazzler hated to admit, Frost was right about her not being at Magneto's or Cyclops's mutant level. And if someone had bested *them*? Though her every instinct wanted to fight this, wanted to do this alone, Dazzler was starting to think that maybe she might need help after all.

She looked Sage up and down, studied those face tattoos again, then rested her eyes on the woman's Lila Cheney T-shirt.

Dazzler gave a reluctant sigh. "Well, I guess you have good taste in music."

A smile curled the corner of Sage's mouth.

"Let's get going," Dazzler said, moving for the door again.

"Hold up," Frost said. "I said, don't get ahead of yourself, Sparkles. You're going to need more than just the two of you. This has become an X-Men mission now, especially with some of our own missing. You need a team."

Dazzler, frustrated, put her hands on her hips. "Yeah? And who else do you have in mind?"

Frost looked to Sage. "Fire up the X-Jet. You're going to meet them now. I'll send you the coordinates. With Magik away I can't afford to leave the school unattended, so I'll join you via video call."

Sage gave a nod and headed for the door, as Frost looked back at Dazzler.

"Your ride's leaving, Sparkles. I'd catch up if I were you."

CHAPTER SIX

Dazzler followed Sage into the subterranean cavern where the sleek and sophisticated X-Jet awaited them. She didn't generally get excited by cars, boats, or planes, but she had to admit the X-Jet was a work of art. Dark gray in color, its state-of-the-art design enabled high-speed and high-altitude flight with a number of defensive countermeasure devices at the pilot's disposal, including a repurposed alien cloaking device that allowed it to become virtually invisible when faced with any conventional means of detection. It was as stealth as stealth could get, and it could hold its own in any firefight with its powerful weapons capability.

They climbed aboard, stowed their bags in passenger seats, and then Sage, now dressed in a black leather X-suit and wearing a pair of wraparound mirrored glasses that appeared to be cybernetically enhanced in some way, settled into the pilot's chair. Dazzler strapped in beside her, watching Sage carefully as she ran through her preflight checks. The mutant seemed comfortable and adept at the controls. It gave Dazzler reassurance that she wasn't about to crash and burn in this bird with her at the helm.

"So where are we going exactly?" Dazzler asked.

Sage brought a small monitor to life, displaying the coordinates issued by Frost. From what Dazzler could see it was in the middle of nowhere, Canada, close to the US border but far from their current location.

"What's there?" Dazzler questioned.

"Nothing," Sage said. "That's the point."

"Why do we have to meet them there? Oh…" Dazzler realized the answer to her own question. "These mutants can't know where the Institute is?"

Sage didn't answer.

"So, are they friendlies or not?" Dazzler asked.

Sage glanced at her. "Do you think Frost would intentionally set you up with possible enemies?"

"If there's one thing I've learned it's that just because someone is a fellow mutant does not mean they are an automatic ally," Dazzler answered.

A tunnel opening yawned before them, drawing their attention. From where Dazzler sat, it seemed far too small for the aircraft. She knew how fast the X-Jet was and suddenly wondered just how straight Sage could fly. With the engines fired up, the jet began to move quickly toward the tunnel. Dazzler clasped hold of her chair's armrests, and within moments they zoomed through a concrete cylinder and shot through the open air, over the slow-running river, and up into the vast blue sky.

As soon as the X-Jet found its optimum altitude for the journey and leveled out, Dazzler looked back at Sage: the schoolteacher who could fly the X-Jet, had brilliant memory recall, and was apparently an "all-rounder."

"So, how long have you worked at the school?" she asked Sage, killing the silence.

"A few years, off and on," she answered.

When Dazzler realized Sage wasn't going to expand on her answer, she tried a different avenue of conversation. "You're a Lila Cheney fan, huh?"

Sage nodded. "I've seen her in concert many times. Even the tour she did with you."

Dazzler was surprised. Sage knew who she was…

"Any plans for a reunion?" Sage asked.

Dazzler gazed out at the endless blue sky. "I don't know. I guess it depends if she ever comes back from touring the space ways." A moment passed, and she looked back at Sage, unable to hide her curiosity. "Interesting tattoos." She motioned to her face, to where the tattoos showed beneath Sage's cybernetic glasses. "What inspired them?"

Sage, face emotionless, stared straight out the windshield. "Ask the man who gave them to me."

Dazzler paused, confused. "You… didn't have a choice in those?"

Sage kept her attention on the flight console, giving no response. Though Dazzler's curiosity was running wild, she chose to drop it. Sage did not look like a woman she wanted to cross, but also, if there was something Dazzler understood more than anything, it was that some things were better left in the past. Some things were too traumatic to talk about.

With the X-Jet's speed, it didn't take long to reach their destination. When they arrived, Sage landed the aircraft ever so delicately in an empty field, partially covered in snow. An empty field that doubled as neutral territory for the two groups of mutants about to meet.

"They're not here yet," Dazzler noted as she glanced around.

"They won't be long."

"Why all the mystery?"

Sage removed her headset. "Why do you think?"

"Because of S.H.I.E.L.D.," Dazzler said with a knowing sigh.

"You must understand, we need to be sure you're not setting us up," Sage said bluntly.

"Magneto saved me when I was captive on Madripoor," Dazzler said. "Why would I be trying to take him and the school down when they've been good to me in the past? I've kept the school's location secret for this long, haven't I?"

Sage shrugged. "Who knows why people do the things they do? Trust is a two-way street. You don't trust us, but we're expected to trust you? Take a look in those mirrored cuffs of yours, Dazzler. Tell me what you see."

Sage turned back to the console, removed a tablet, and contacted Frost. The ice queen's face appeared on the screen.

"Are they there yet?" Frost asked.

Sage looked up through the windshield, and Dazzler followed her line of sight to see a dark dot in the distance. "They're on approach."

"Go meet them. Let them see you come in peace."

Dazzler and Sage alighted from the jet and stood in the field while the air around them whipped into a frenzy as another jet landed a small distance away. When the jet's door yawned open, Dazzler recognized the mutant who exited, dressed in his yellow and black X-suit.

"Logan?" she said aloud.

Wolverine was followed by two women, who appeared to be in their twenties. One had long green hair and wore a green trench coat opened over what looked like a green and black X-suit. The other had short, styled red hair that matched the red leather X-suit she wore.

"So, this is the reason for all the secrecy," Dazzler said. "When will this rivalry between the Jean Grey School and the Charles Xavier School ever end?"

"Too much baggage between the headmasters." Sage shrugged. "Let's meet them halfway." She began to walk toward them, getting farther away from the X-Jet.

The two groups came closer and finally to a stop in the field, standing a few feet apart. While Sage stood to Dazzler's left, Wolverine's two companions flanked him. Up close, Dazzler noticed the one with long green hair had vibrant green eyes and green lipstick to match, while the redhead bore a hard expression that mismatched her soft green eyes.

"Dazzler," Wolverine said, eyebrow arched as he gave a slight nod of acknowledgment. "You back with Cyclops and Magneto?"

"No," Dazzler replied. "This is just a visit."

Sage held up the tablet to show Frost.

Logan scowled. "What's this about?"

"It's good to see you, too, Logan," Frost said.

"I'd prefer not to see you at all," he said.

"I'd prefer not to see you either, but we have a problem."

"So you say. I did agree to this meeting, after all. Now, what's going on? This better be good."

"If he'd told me we were coming to see you," the redhead said to Frost, "I wouldn't have come."

"It's about your fathers," Frost said, ignoring her comment.

"Our fathers?" the green-haired one said with surprise.

"Their fathers?" Dazzler echoed the surprise.

"Meet Lorna Dane," Frost said. "Also known as Polaris. She's Magneto's daughter. The one in the red is Rachel Summers. Scott's daughter."

"It's Grey," the redhead corrected. "Rachel *Grey*."

Dazzler studied the two young women. She saw a little resemblance in Rachel to Cyclops but saw none of Magneto in Polaris.

"And she is?" Rachel asked Frost, her head tilting toward Dazzler.

"This is Alison Blaire," Frost said. "You might know her as Dazzler."

"I thought you looked familiar." Polaris narrowed her vibrant eyes.

"We're here to meet a pop star?" Rachel said with a good dose of snark.

"That's *rock* star, honey," Dazzler said. "There's a difference."

"What's this got to do with my father?" Polaris asked Frost impatiently.

"I'd like to know that myself," Logan said, folding his muscular arms that threatened to bust the stitching of his X-suit.

"Both Cyclops and Magneto are missing," Frost said, bluntly. "As in we've lost contact with them. And when I say lost contact, I mean I can't even find them on Cerebra."

The thick muscles across Logan's shoulders eased off a little, as he glanced to Polaris and Rachel, checking their reactions. The two women mostly contained their responses to the news.

Mostly. Dazzler detected some emotion flare in Polaris's eyes, while Rachel's jaw tightened.

"They disappeared while trying to trace a new supply of MGH," Dazzler told them. "You know what MGH is, right?"

Logan nodded.

"Magneto made contact with Maria Hill," Frost said, "and now S.H.I.E.L.D. is suddenly back in action. S.H.I.E.L.D. brought Dazzler in because they knew I wouldn't talk to them."

Logan's eyes turned curiously back to Dazzler. "You're working for S.H.I.E.L.D.?"

Dazzler nodded. "A temporary Mutant Liaison. As I'm sure you can understand, I want to crush anyone pushing that stuff."

Logan looked back to Frost on the tablet. "You say they're off Cerebra… could that be intentional? Could they be in hiding somehow?"

"I guess anything's possible," Frost said. "When Erik left, he took his helmet with him. That could account for why I can't trace him on Cerebra, but that doesn't account for Scott. I don't see how they could evade it. If they were in trouble, they would've contacted me. They haven't. They've just vanished."

"So, they're dead," Logan said, thinking aloud, as the young women on either side shot him a startled glance.

"I don't know," Frost said. "All I know is that someone is pushing MGH again, Erik and Scott went to investigate its appearance, and now they're missing. If whoever is pushing the MGH took them down or somehow captured them… They're either very smart or very powerful. This could be a problem for both of us, Logan."

"It doesn't sound like my problem at all."

Frost's eyes suddenly narrowed.

"Hey!" Logan said, warningly, raising his hand to his temple. "Get out!"

"So," Frost said with a smug smile, "the MGH is at your school as well."

"It is?" Dazzler asked, then looked back at Wolverine. "Then I guess this is your problem, too, Logan."

Dazzler studied the three mutants before her, each processing what they'd just been told, as a thought suddenly occurred to her – the reason why they'd come here in the first place. She looked back to Frost's form on the tablet. "You want me to take their daughters to find out what happened to Magneto and Cyclops?"

Logan straightened a little, mistrust darting through his eyes.

"Yes," Frost replied. "We've been over this. You're not strong enough to do this alone. Whether this is a just a smart dealer or something else, we need to be prepared. Besides, if there's any mutants you can trust, it's them. You all have something in common. All your fathers are missing, and I'm sure" – she looked to Rachel and Polaris – "deep down, you all want them back."

Dazzler paused, feeling a shiver run down her spine. "I never told you my father was missing."

Frost gave a shrug. "Sorry, Sparkles."

"I told you to stay out of my head!" Dazzler snarled.

"Who's your father?" Polaris asked, eyes narrowed curiously.

"No one you'd know," Dazzler answered. "He's not a mutant."

"Wait a minute," Logan said. "You want to send these three out there to find them? Why is *she* leading this?" He motioned to Dazzler. "No offense, but there are others more equipped to lead an X-Men team."

"Because," Dazzler said, offended, "I know S.H.I.E.L.D., and

I know mutants, and the MGH substance we think is linked to their disappearances was created from me. And, like *Frosty* here says, my father is missing too. If anyone wants to get to the bottom of it, it's me."

"Wanting to do something and being able to execute are two different things," Logan said.

Dazzler's eyes flamed with anger, but before she could speak, Frost cut her off.

"She's best suited to investigate this, Logan, for the reasons she said. *You* may not care about Scott and Erik, Logan, but I'm sure their daughters do."

"I wouldn't be so sure about that," he replied. "Why do you think they're at *my* school and not theirs?"

"A blood tie is not something easily forgotten," Frost said.

Dazzler decided to push the conversation along in case the White Queen and Wolverine came to blows. "If we're going to work together, I'd like to know what powers you have," she asked Polaris and Rachel.

"Polaris's gifts are like her father's," Frost answered for them, when silence was their response. "There's not much she can't do with metal and magnetism."

"True," Logan jumped in. "But M-Day messed up her control. She's still getting that back."

"I can handle myself," Polaris said, perhaps not wanting to look weak in front of the others.

"Grey is like her mother," Frost continued. "Having a telepath on your team will be very useful, Dazzler. Take it from me. Add that to your light energy and Sage's talents, that makes a strong, well-rounded team."

"Wait a minute. I haven't released them yet," Logan said.

"Logan, someone is selling MGH," Frost said, exasperated. "You know what problems that can cause us. We need to find out who is doing this and how they got the better of Magneto and Cyclops. What's to say they're not coming for us next? Or our students?"

"Then I'm going too," Logan said to Frost. "You can't send them out there alone."

"And who will take care of your school?" Frost asked.

"There are others–"

"Someone has made Magneto and Cyclops disappear," Frost repeated. "How do we know this isn't a trap? We can't leave our schools vulnerable to attack. Those kids need us, Logan."

The scowl lines in Logan's face deepened. "Well, this group need us too. They're still working on their powers since the M-Day fallout."

"My powers are fine," Polaris reiterated firmly. "I can handle myself."

"If Lorna's powers are even half as strong as Magneto's, she will be an asset," Frost told him. "Rachel, too. I have no doubt that she will soon be as strong as her mother."

"Don't talk about my mother," Rachel said in a threatening voice. "Don't even say her name!"

Logan squeezed Rachel's shoulder. Dazzler wasn't sure what their history was, but Rachel was clearly not a fan of Emma Frost.

"Look," Frost said, "we all want to stop whoever is behind this. You mutants are our best option to do it. Why? Because, in case you forgot, since M-Day our numbers are down. Our strongest must stay and protect the schools. We need to send mutants out there who are not only capable but who care enough to see this through. And who better than the daughters of the disappeared?"

"Cyclops is my father in DNA only," Rachel said coldly.

"That may be." Frost stared hard at her. "But he's still your father."

Rachel scoffed a laugh. "In whose reality?"

Dazzler had only just met Rachel, and although she seemed almost as cold as Queen Frosty there, Dazzler did feel a pull of empathy toward her.

"I know the feeling," Dazzler said to Rachel. "I haven't spoken to my father in years."

Rachel turned her pale green eyes to Dazzler's. For the first time, Dazzler glimpsed that Rachel's battle shield had lowered. "But," Dazzler continued, "he's still my father, and if he's in trouble I need to help him."

"And if they're already dead?" Rachel asked, reiterating Logan's earlier sentiments.

"We'll soon find out. But if there's a chance they're still alive, every moment we stand here talking is another they're in danger."

"If you won't do it for your fathers, then think of the future," Sage said firmly. "Think about the young mutants out there being sold this MGH steroid. With our numbers reduced, they feel the pressure to step up and perform. We have to stop whoever controls the source of this, and who is tapping into their fears."

Dazzler nodded. "And not just for the mutant kids, but we have to stop it before the streets are filled with MGH-jacked humans, causing all sorts of problems that, let's face it, we'll be called upon to fix."

"I still don't like this," Logan said, placing his hands on his hips, spreading his already broad shoulders wider.

"Neither do I," Frost said. "But it's the only way. I'm not leaving my school open to attack if this turns out to be something more sinister than some dealer who got lucky with Omega-level mutants. We cover the schools, while Dazzler and her team dig up information. If they find Cyclops and Magneto, and they need help, then we round up every mutant we can spare and we take care of it."

Logan seemed to ponder Frost's words before he looked at Polaris. "You really think you're ready for this?"

Polaris took in a deep breath of pride, clenched her jaw, and nodded resolutely. "Yes. If it were me missing, my father would come find me. I'll do the same for him."

Logan looked to Rachel and arched an eyebrow in question. She hesitated but then relented a nod too.

"All right," Logan said, "so what's the plan?"

"They get on our X-Jet, and Sage flies them to Vancouver where Scott was last seen," Frost said.

Logan turned to Rachel. "Is this legit?"

Rachel studied Dazzler carefully. Dazzler noted Rachel's pale green eyes had whitened, and she felt pressure at her skull. Though her instinct was to fight it, this mind pushing into hers, she relented and let the mutant probe. If this won her trust, then so be it. Dazzler had nothing to hide. Rachel turned her whitened eyes to Sage. Her brow furrowed in concentration, but eventually the mutant's eyes turned green again and she nodded. "They're telling the truth."

"I'll have them report to me, and I'll keep you updated," Frost told Logan.

He ignored her and turned to Polaris. "You check in with me regularly. Got it?"

Polaris nodded, and he rounded on Frost. "Anything happens to them..." He held up his fist, and three long blades shot out between his knuckles. "We'll be having words."

Frost stared back, unaffected.

"Let me know what you find out from the Gamercade," Dazzler said to Frost. They needed to move things along. She was anxious to get to Vancouver and follow their lead.

"Will do, Agent Blaire."

Dazzler gave her a steely smile. "That's *mutant* Blaire, thank you."

"I'll be in touch." Frost ended the video call. Sage tucked the tablet under her arm. "Ready?" she asked Dazzler.

She looked at her new team and nodded. "Let's do this."

CHAPTER SEVEN

Dazzler stood with her mutant associates on the side of a road just outside the metropolitan area of Vancouver, waiting for their transport to arrive. Sage had flown the X-Jet as close to the city as she could with its cloaking capability engaged, then landed in a clearing bordered with tall trees, informing them they would need to walk to the nearest road and call ground transport from there. Dazzler hated these delays but knew they were necessary. Where possible they needed to avoid detection or interference from S.H.I.E.L.D., or any other government agencies or law enforcement.

Or from whoever was behind the MGH revival.

The atmosphere around the women was stilted to say the least. They were four strangers suddenly thrown together to solve a mystery, with very little information to go on. Due to the speed of the X-Jet, their journey had been short, so by the time Dazzler had filled them in on everything she knew to date, Sage was preparing to land. There'd been no time for small talk or getting to know each other.

When their ride arrived, the young, heavily pierced driver looked at them curiously as Dazzler climbed into the passenger side of the vehicle, while Sage sat behind her and the other two filled the rest of the back seat. The driver introduced himself as Brayton, the piercings through his bottom lip rattling as he did, then he started to make friendly conversation, asking if they were in a band or something. Dazzler guessed they probably looked like they could be, dressed in their various leather jumpsuits as they were, but they each had their own defined look, which she doubted would ever mesh together as a cohesive band. Where Dazzler had her standard rock look, Sage looked like she'd be right at home in a metal band. Polaris appeared entirely alternative, and Rachel could have belonged in a punk band. These thoughts only made Dazzler think of her own band, the Casablancas, which gave her another pang of regret for not being with them now.

Dazzler answered Brayton with a simple no. Given they were trying to fly under the radar, she didn't exactly want to make conversation with this guy. When she returned one-word answers to his next set of questions, he soon got the idea to close his mouth. After all, it was a long ride and a hefty fare they'd be paying, so he didn't want to disgruntle his customers. From that point on they drove in silence.

As they journeyed toward the city, Dazzler looked in the rearview mirror and studied Sage in her cybernetic glasses, wondering again what her capability was, and more to the point, just what else Sage could do that made Frost think she would be valuable to her. Obviously, Sage could pilot the X-Jet, but Dazzler was more curious about her memory skills. What exactly did excellent memory recall mean? Was it just facts, figures, and statistics? Or could she recall entire conversations?

As her mind turned over these thoughts, a slight smile crossed Sage's lips. Dazzler wasn't sure whether the smile was for her – or at her – as the mirrored glasses meant that she could not see the direction of Sage's gaze. Dazzler stared at her a moment longer, studying the glasses and the tips of her facial tattoos the glasses didn't cover, then with an even face, she turned away.

Snow began to gently fall, adding another layer to the city's picturesque backdrop of dusty white mountains. The beautiful view should have granted Dazzler peace and tranquility, but instead she felt weird and on edge. The last day and a half had been a whirlwind. There she was on her way home from a New York gig, and now suddenly she was in Vancouver looking for her father. She felt uneasy working for S.H.I.E.L.D. again, uneasy that the MGH on the streets contained her DNA, and uneasy that her trust in Frost and her three mutant companions was still pending.

Whether she liked it or not, Frost was right. If someone managed to kidnap Cyclops and Magneto, they were either powerful or had a powerful team around them. Even a two-bit dealer could have a small army of street soldiers at their disposal jacked up on MGH that might have outnumbered or surprised the mutants.

Dazzler couldn't help but wonder whether she would be powerful enough to defend herself if she came under attack, and whether the three women in the back would be enough to assist her. Or whether they would *want* to assist her, especially if it risked their own lives in the process. They were strangers after all, with no loyalty between them. Dazzler was a loner, and the others from opposing mutant schools.

She may have company on this investigation, but she would soon find out if she had the true support of an X-Men team.

Brayton dropped them off outside a modest hotel, where they quickly dumped their bags and headed back onto the street.

"So where to first?" Polaris asked, snowflakes dotting her long green hair and coat.

"According to S.H.I.E.L.D.," Dazzler said, scrolling through the notes on her burner phone, "Scott's last known location was in University Hill. He went to meet with one of their consultants, Doctor Simon Reid, who helped S.H.I.E.L.D. with some initial studies on MGH when it had first surfaced some time ago. Cyclops went to him to have the new batch studied and identified. Reid must have been the one to confirm that the MGH was derived from me."

"How would that help him find out who is putting this on the streets?" Rachel asked.

"He would be looking to identify the trace ingredients," Sage answered the question confidently, "to perhaps identify if it was the same supplier as last time."

"Mystique," Dazzler said, eyes narrowed.

"You really think it's her behind all this?" Rachel asked.

"The MGH on the streets was derived from my cells," Dazzler explained. "She's the one who used me to create it. It *has* to be her behind this. She must've kept stock from last time and hidden it, or maybe she's somehow replicated it and is now mass-producing it. I guess this Doctor Reid will tell us which one it is."

"But S.H.I.E.L.D. caught Mystique, right?" Polaris asked.

"Yeah, they had her for a while," Dazzler said, "but you can only keep her for so long. She's a slippery witch."

"Then let's go to this Doctor Reid," Sage said, lifting a muscular arm and hailing another ride, "before he disappears on us too."

Dazzler and her team stood in the plush white reception of Cameron and Cote, a company known for manufacturing pharmaceutical goods, including a variety of steroids to assist in the treatment of various diseases. Though their manufacturing plant was elsewhere, this office was their official headquarters and where Doctor Reid was based. Reid was considered the foremost expert on steroids, hence why S.H.I.E.L.D. had approached him for assistance after the MGH was first discovered. According to S.H.I.E.L.D.'s files, Reid had been the one to study the original MGH and break it down into its various components, identifying the link to mutant DNA.

She was about to meet the man who had studied her cells, the very DNA that had been harvested from her. This scientist probably knew more about Dazzler's own body than she did. That made her uncomfortable. More to the point, she wondered just what this Reid had done with her cells once the study was over. Had they been destroyed? Or were they being stored somewhere? Or worse, had they been transferred into S.H.I.E.L.D.'s custody? That thought alone terrified her most. They were *her* cells, and she had no idea where they were or who was using them.

"I'm sorry," a young, neatly dressed man at the Cameron and Cote reception told them, "Doctor Reid is not available today."

"We need to see him, please." Dazzler gave him a pearly smile and fluttered her eyelashes a little, showing her S.H.I.E.L.D. credentials. "It's important."

The young man blushed, studied the credentials briefly, before pushing his glasses further up his nose and looking back at her. "I'm sorry, but that won't be possible."

"Make it possible," Sage said, pulling her cybernetic glasses down to make eye contact with him. "Please."

"I'm afraid I can't." He shrugged.

"Why not?" Dazzler asked.

"Because he's not in today," he said apologetically. "He called in the day before yesterday to say that he would not be in for the rest of the week."

"Is he sick?" Dazzler asked, noting the time aligned with when Reid would've met with Cyclops.

"No…"

"Then call him," Dazzler said. "He'll want to speak with us." She flashed another pearly smile, which must've worked, because although the young man hesitated, he eventually walked over to a desk where he collected a handset and made the call.

"How convenient that he's not here," Polaris said under her breath.

"He's not answering," Rachel said, staring at the young man, her pale green eyes now white.

Dazzler looked at her curiously. "Is he telling us the truth about what he knows?"

Rachel flicked her white eyes to Dazzler. "I'll soon find out."

The young man hung up the call and walked back to them. "I'm afraid he's not answering. I'll take your details, and if he calls back, I'll pass your name on to him."

"Where does he live?" Sage asked.

"I can't give out that information."

"How about his cell number?" Dazzler asked.

"I'm afraid not." Irritation began to thread its way into the young man's voice now.

"You did see my credentials, right?" Dazzler showed him her phone again.

"Those credentials don't hold weight anymore," he said, then smiled politely. "But listen, maybe if I took your number…?"

Rachel smirked, as a bang suddenly sounded behind the young man. He turned to see a metallic bottle had fallen off his desk to the ground and the lid had rolled away, spilling water. No one stood near the desk where it had fallen. He looked at it, confused.

"Oh. I… I must've knocked it when I put the phone down." He reached across his desk, grabbed some tissues, and bent down to mop the water up. As he did, a metal tablet lifted up off the desk and whizzed toward Dazzler. She grabbed it and glanced at Polaris, who gave her a satisfied look. Sage took it from Dazzler's hands and stood behind her in cover as she scrolled the tablet for Reid's contact details.

The young man stood again. "Ugh. I'll need a towel for this…" He looked back at Dazzler. "Er, leave your details, and I'll have Doctor Reid call you. OK? That's the best I can do."

"No," Dazzler said, plucking a business card from a stand on the reception counter. "I'll call you."

Sage gave Polaris a nod, and suddenly a container of paperclips fell off the desk.

"What is happening?" The young man bent down and started picking up the paperclips. As he did, the tablet flew back across to the desk to where it rested before.

"Thank you for your help." Dazzler beamed.

The young man looked up at her and blushed again. "Sorry I couldn't do more."

As they stepped outside the building, Dazzler turned to Rachel. "Was he telling the truth?"

Rachel nodded. "He doesn't know where Reid is. But I tell you something, that kid ain't right."

"Why do you say that?" Dazzler asked.

Humor twitched at Rachel's lips. "Because he likes you. He wasn't taking that number for Reid."

"Yeah, thanks, I don't need to know any more," Dazzler said, before turning to Sage. "I take it you got Reid's home address?"

Sage nodded and tapped her temple. "It's all up here."

"So where do we go?" Polaris asked.

"I'm looking it up now," Sage said, staring ahead at the street as she pulled a thick grey glove from her jacket pocket. As she put it on her right hand, Dazzler saw the inside was lined with wires and microchips. Dazzler looked at her quizzically, then realized Sage was staring into her cybernetic lenses. Sage raised her gloved hand and began tapping and swirling the air – it was a haptic glove. "Reid's home is just under an hour from here," Sage eventually said. She waved her hand as if to remove the data from her sight, then walked to the street, raised her arm, and hailed another ride.

Dazzler watched curiously as Sage, Polaris, and Rachel climbed into the vehicle. She glanced back at Cameron and Cote and uttered a huff of amusement.

Maybe these mutants would be useful to her after all.

CHAPTER EIGHT

Emma Frost sat at her desk, eyes closed, as she connected her mind to Morph's. The young mutant had just entered Gamercade, seeking the human who had sold him the MGH steroid. Morph had wanted to go in alone without Frost inside his brain, but she wouldn't allow that to happen. With Magneto and Cyclops gone, and Magik away on an assignment with Doctor Strange, Emma couldn't leave the school and accompany Morph to the store personally. This was the best she could do – to keep an eye on both Morph *and* the school at the same time.

Besides, she hadn't let him go in alone at all. Fabio, Santo, and Hijack waited down the street from Gamercade, ready to spring into action if Morph needed. But if Morph played things the way Frost instructed him to, their help would not be required.

"Do you see him?" Emma asked aloud to her empty office. She had instructed Morph to simply think his response and she would pick it up.

"No." His answer came back inside her mind. "No, wait. Yeah. He's at the back of the arcade."

"Is he alone?"

"Yeah."

"Well, go make friends."

Emma waited patiently. Though she could read Morph's every thought, she could not see with his eyes. Thus, she'd instructed the transmorpher to picture whoever he spoke to in his mind, so she could "see" them. And it was working. She had a series of visions flash through her mind. She then sensed Morph absorbing the physical attributes of those he passed, constantly but subtly changing his appearance to cloak his true identity.

A picture of a young man settled before her. She assumed this was the kid they were after. He was blond, relatively handsome for his age, and wore expensive clothes. Perhaps he was making good money from his illegal dealings?

"Caleb," she heard Morph think. "He's wearing a name tag."

"So, he works there," Emma said. "We need a surname."

"I'll try," Morph replied. She listened carefully as Morph processed their conversation. She sensed hesitation and defensiveness from the young man, which was to be expected. Morph was a new face to this kid, and given he was selling an illegal steroid, he was bound to be wary.

"Make him feel at ease," Emma instructed Morph. "Just like we practiced."

She sensed Morph advising Caleb that he'd been told about the steroid from another boy. Caleb started to relax as Morph not only took on some of Caleb's physical attributes, but also as Morph's transformative psychochemical influence began to work on him, causing the young man to like and trust him.

Still, Emma sensed a certain underlying level of anxiety, but she soon she realized that it came from Morph himself.

"You're doing good, Benjamin," she reassured him.

"He wants me to meet him in the alley out back," Morph thought to Emma.

"Be careful," she said, then pulled her mind back from Morph's and tuned into Fabio's. "Be ready," she ordered the mutant backup.

"Yes, Ms Frost," Fabio replied.

She pulled her mind from Fabio's and pushed back into Morph's, the feeling akin to submerging her face into a pool of water. The silence sat for a moment as Emma detected Morph thinking about how cold it was outside and how he was glad the others waited for him down the street. A few more minutes passed before Morph made a direct thought comment to Emma.

"He's coming."

"Is he alone?"

"Yes," Morph thought.

Emma concentrated hard so she could pick up every little thing that ran through Morph's brain. She detected the exchange taking place, could tell Morph was making small talk, could tell Caleb gave him no additional information or leads in return. She saw an image of a vial of MGH in Morph's hand.

Then things went quiet. The seconds passed.

"Morph?" she said aloud.

The silence sat a moment more, before she saw an image of Caleb walking away down the alley.

"He gave me nothing," Morph eventually said. "Except the MGH."

"Go back inside and hang around for a while," Emma ordered him. "See who else is there and who he talks to."

Soon enough, Emma detected Morph playing a video game. A giant dragon hurled fireballs at a wizard. Morph was concentrating on the game and not on the people at Gamercade.

"Are you looking around?" Emma asked impatiently.

"Yeah," Morph replied, his thought heavily weighted with guilt.

"Check the walls," she said. They needed to tweak the plan. "Are there any signs stating who the proprietor is?"

"No," he answered. "Can't see any."

Emma sighed. "You might have to wait and follow him home."

"That could be hours!"

"Well, lucky you can morph into other people, huh?" Emma said. "He won't know it's you."

She detected that Morph worried about the exertion it would take to stay morphed as other people for long stints of time. The kid was still learning just what his powers could do. She felt his anxiety and detected that he considered taking the MGH he had just bought to boost his stamina.

"Don't even think about it, kid," Emma said. "You touch that stuff, and I'll teach you a lesson on tiredness. You'll be tired from cleaning the floors of the school for the rest of the year. Understood?"

"Yes, Ms Frost."

Emma felt his disappointment. "You're doing good, Benjamin," she reassured him again. "You're doing important work. Scott will be very proud of you, the way you're stepping up. We'll make an X-Man out of you yet."

She sensed his disappointment lifting, and a sense of pride flowing in.

"Go wait in the car with the others and rest for a bit," she ordered, "then you head back in and transmorph into a new person."

"Yes, Ms Frost."

Again, there was silence before Emma sensed Morph climbing into the car with the other students. Knowing he was safe for the time being, she ended the connection between them, and sat back in her office chair.

She, too, would give herself a rest.

Although she had been one of the lucky few to retain her powers after M-Day, those same powers had nearly been depleted after the Phoenix incident. And the truth was, the Phoenix incident had rocked her to her core more so than M-Day. The incident had seen a Phoenix-induced Scott do the unthinkable and kill Charles Xavier. As devastating as that had been, it had affected all their powers, too. While Emma had hers back now, she knew Scott and Magneto were still struggling with theirs. Had this been the reason they had gone missing? Had their powers failed them in their time of need?

Or worse, what if Scott still had the Phoenix within him? What if *he* had been the one to cause Magneto to disappear? She dreaded to think this. She knew the Phoenix incident had left scars upon their alliance, cracks in the foundation of their friendship. What if those cracks had caused their allegiance to crumble?

She knew the torment Scott had suffered. If anything had happened with the Phoenix again, or even to the students, she knew he would never forgive himself, could not live with the burden of another allied mutant's death at his hands. Could Scott have caused Erik to disappear? Could Scott have ended his own life in anguish?

She closed her eyes, took a deep breath, and told herself to focus. To think all this was foolish and only sent her down a spiral of uncertainty. She had to focus on the present, and she sent her mind out in search of the missing mutants once more. Her telepathic powers were like tendrils, probing a darkened room for any sense of them.

But once more, she found nothing.

It was like she stood alone on a deserted wasteland highway, calling out their names into the void. It was like they no longer existed.

And, quite frankly, it terrified her.

She took another deep breath to steady herself. Right now, she had to concentrate on what she could control. Her strength could not falter. She had to find out where that MGH came from and hoped it would lead her to Scott, or at least provide answers to where he had gone.

Dazzler sat with Polaris inside a quaint café by the window with a clear view of Doctor Reid's apartment. The team had split into two and were waiting for him to arrive home, each furnished with a recent photo of Reid from Dazzler's S.H.I.E.L.D. profiles. While Dazzler and Polaris took position in the warm café snacking on poutine, Sage and Rachel were located on the corner near a bus stop, pacing to try to stay warm.

While they established their stakeout of Reid's apartment, Sage hacked into the city's security cameras which captured footage of the street where Cameron and Cote was located, relaying the feed through to the phones they carried. If Doctor Reid suddenly showed up at his office, they would know about it. When Sage had access to the security footage, she and Dazzler began scrolling through the past few days to try to locate any trace of Cyclops. So far, they had not been able to find him.

"This is a waste of time," Polaris said, breaking the silence. "We can't just sit here and do nothing."

"We need information in order to move forward," Dazzler said. "Right now, all we know is that Cyclops and Magneto went missing. Without information, without direction, we're chasing shadows."

"Yeah, well… maybe those shadows are their ghosts," Polaris said quietly. "It's been too long already."

Dazzler felt an unexpected pain in her chest, like Polaris had plunged a hand inside and put her heart in a viselike grip. She hadn't really had time to consider the possibility that her father might be dead. She'd thought the words but hadn't really entertained what those words actually meant, felt the true weight of them. Her brain had accepted that he was missing, but it hadn't yet accepted the possibility of anything else. What if Polaris was right? What if her father *was* dead? She hadn't spoken to him in years. There were so many things left unsaid between them.

She heard a child's laughter and turned to see a young girl sitting in her mother's lap receiving cuddles. A man joined them, placing cake and coffee on the table before them, beaming at the child and tickling her chin. The child giggled in response. Dazzler turned away from the scene, numb. It was alien to her: the happy family dynamic; the mother and father still together, raising their child together, not walking out or turning their back on her.

Polaris seemed to detect a drop in her mood. "Something wrong?"

"Just thinking about what you said. About our fathers being dead." Dazzler studied Polaris's face and saw genuine concern. "Do you have a good relationship with your father?" Dazzler asked, gently.

Polaris's vibrant green eyes looked away. "It's complicated."

"What do you mean, complicated?" Dazzler asked.

Polaris studied her as though trying to gauge whether there was an angle behind her question. "He wasn't around for a large part of my life," Polaris said, "but... he's been trying lately. As much as someone like Magneto can." She seemed to think her next words through carefully. "I don't hate him."

Dazzler analyzed her. "The way Rachel seems to hate Cyclops?"

Polaris sighed. "She says she hates him, but I don't think that's true. She's just angry, that's all."

"Why?"

Polaris shrugged. "That's her story to tell. Not mine."

Dazzler nodded. "Well, we have that in common, I guess. Complicated relationships."

Polaris glanced at her again before turning to look back out the window. "I think my relationship with Magneto is different from yours and Rachel's. I say my relationship is complicated because we... actually care about each other, but we just don't know how to move forward. It'll take time to heal the distance that was between us and... I don't know. I'm very much a reflection of him, his gifts, and he's not sure how to deal with that. He's an Omega-level mutant. Who knows, maybe I could be one day too. I'm not sure how to deal with that myself. On the one hand we're an absolute mirror copy of each other, but we're also strangers." Polaris took a delicate bite of poutine. "Like I said, it's complicated."

Dazzler sighed and looked back out the window, too, watching people and cars go past. "A complicated mirror, I could handle. My father is the complete opposite of me. He has no mutant gift, and he never understood me or my desire to be a singer. He *wanted* me to be his mirror, but life as a lawyer wasn't for me. He refused to support my music, so I went it alone. I thought I had some idea of who he was and what he stood for, but now? I don't know. I'm not sure I ever knew him at all."

"Is your mother still alive?" Polaris asked.

"Somewhere," Dazzler answered, feeling another unexpected slash across her heart as the remnants of the recent anniversary swirled inside her mind. "She left us when I was a child. She was an entertainer too. She… fell in with a guy who wasn't so good for her. They got into all kinds of things they shouldn't have. I hear she eventually left him and she's past that now, but… we're strangers."

"Siblings?" Polaris asked.

"She had a daughter with the other guy. I've not met her yet." Polaris nodded, vibrant eyes studying her carefully.

"You?" Dazzler changed the topic of conversation.

Polaris gave a sardonic laugh. "If there's one thing I can say about my father, he was *very* good at having children. I've lost count of the half-siblings I have out there."

"Oh. Do you get along with any of them?"

"Some I do." She shrugged before her face fell. "Others… I can't stand. Others, I'm ashamed to be related to."

"Why?" Dazzler's brow furrowed, before she felt a sudden sensation of pressure inside her head.

"Any sign?" Rachel's voice sounded within Dazzler's mind.

She winced, then scowled. "No. And stay out of my head!"

"Getting inside people's heads is why I'm here," Rachel replied. "So, get used to it, Dizzler."

"It's Dazzler," she said, as the pressure eased off. Polaris looked at Dazzler strangely. "Grey," Dazzler explained. "Forgive me but I have a real problem with anyone taking control of my body like that."

Polaris inclined her head. "Understandable."

"So, you were talking about your siblings?" Dazzler said, curious to finish their conversation.

"No, *you* were," Polaris said. "I'm done with that conversation."

Dazzler retreated at Polaris's sudden shift in mood and turned her eyes back to Reid's apartment. "Fine."

Emma Frost concentrated hard, tuning into Morph's thoughts as he followed Caleb down the street. When Caleb had finally left Gamercade, Benjamin transmorphed into an old lady he'd passed on a street corner and continued tailing him, transmorphing into two other different personas along the way in his pursuit. Frost could tell Morph's energy was waning, though. Where his thoughts had once come through clear and rapidly, now they were few and far between, and of the few he had, one in particular began to repeat: "Man, I'm tired…"

"Hang in there, Benjamin, you're doing well," she said, hoping some encouragement would see him through.

"He's entering a building," Morph thought.

"What is it?" Emma asked.

A moment of silence passed before Morph answered. "Looks like a real estate company." Emma could tell Morph was looking at the houses listed in the windows, expensive prices flowing through his head. "He's talking to someone inside," Morph projected.

"Who?"

"A woman," he answered. "She's one of the agents. Wait… Her photo is in the window… She's Jane Rosenthorpe. She just hugged him. Maybe she's his mom?"

"Jane Rosenthorpe." Emma opened her eyes and looked at another of her students who sat on the opposite side of her desk, Christopher Muse "Triage", whom she had summoned. The young man with dark brown locs stared back at her now, fingers poised over a laptop as he waited for her command. Earlier, Emma had him search for information on Gamercade. It was owned by a larger chain of amusement stores, and so far, nothing stood out as unusual or warranting further exploration.

"Jane Rosenthorpe?" Triage asked. "That's who you want me to look into next?"

Emma nodded. "See if she has a son named Caleb." Then she closed her eyes again. "Morph? What's happening?"

"They're leaving," he replied. "But, Ms Frost, I need a break."

"All right," she said. "Join Fabio and the others. Get them to follow the suspects at a distance. If they're heading home, I want an address."

She opened her eyes again and saw Triage engrossed in his laptop, clicking through various screens, and occasionally tapping at the keys.

"Anything?" Emma asked.

Triage nodded. "Jane Rosenthorpe is a real estate agent who specializes in high-end property sales. Her bio says she is a mother of two. Let me see if she has any social pages." Triage began tapping away as Emma rolled her head trying to ease the tension she felt in her neck. "Yes, she does," Triage said. "From her photos it looks like she has two sons."

"Show me," Emma said. Triage turned his screen to her, and she scanned the photos until she saw the boy Morph had pictured in his mind. She quickly read the caption beneath. Caleb's name was there. "Is there anything on Caleb's father?"

Triage turned the laptop back and continued scrolling. "I don't see any photos of him. Maybe they're divorced?"

"Check Caleb's social media. Assume he has the same surname as his mother."

Triage nodded and began his search. Emma waited patiently, her mind turning over this new information. His mother worked in high-end real estate, so she likely had important connections. So far it seemed this kid, Caleb, came from money and privilege. So why would he be distributing MGH? It didn't look like he needed the money. Was it some form of rebellion? Or a youthful, misaligned play for power?

"I found a picture of him with his dad," Triage said, "but there's no name. Wait… He's tagged him in another photo… His name is Rick Rosenthorpe."

"Show me his profile."

"I can't." Triage showed his screen again. "His profile is set to private."

"See what a web search brings up on that name."

Triage set to work again, while Emma took a sip of coffee.

She was mindful not to go down any unnecessary rabbit holes, but right now she had no choice. It could take days of following this kid until they discovered who was suppling him with the MGH. They didn't have that long. She just had to dig and hope they found something useful.

"OK!" Triage said excitedly. "Looks like his father lives in New York. He's the VP of a company called Sanderson Holdings." Triage showed her the photo of Rick Rosenthorpe. He looked to be late forties with short, styled hair and wore an expensive suit.

"What does Sanderson Holdings do?" she asked, as Triage enacted yet another search, clicking through various screens.

"Seems like they own a transport company," he told her. "Ships, trains, trucks."

Emma sat back in her chair, curious. The transport industry was something she knew very well as it had been the foundation of her company, Frost International. Still, she had not come across the name Sanderson Holdings before. "A transportation company…" she thought aloud. "Sounds like the perfect front for the distribution of an illegal steroid."

"Illegal steroid?" Triage stared at her. "Why are we involved in that?"

"We're not involved in it," Emma told him. "We're trying to stop it."

"There's…" Triage began, tentatively. "There's some talk going around school."

"What talk?"

"That something big is about to go down. You pulled Fabio and Sage out of the classroom, and then Rockslide and Hijack left too. And no one's seen Magneto or Cyclops for days. We're all on edge, thinking we might get called on a mission. Does it have something to do with this?"

"It does," Emma said confidently. The last thing she needed was for the inexperienced mutants at the school to panic. "But you have nothing to fear because we will get to the bottom of it."

"When will Magneto and Cyclops be back?" Triage asked.

Emma thought through her answer carefully. "I'm not sure yet."

Triage stared at her with a slight furrow in his brow. The mutant had healing powers, and it was part of his nature to want to help people.

"That's why you're here," she added. "I need your help."

Triage nodded, his dark eyes analyzing hers carefully. "Whatever you need. Just say the word."

Emma motioned to the laptop. "Keep searching on Sanderson Holdings. I want to know everything about them."

CHAPTER NINE

Dazzler wasn't sure what to do next. It was now dusk, and Reid had still not shown his face, not at his home, not at his workplace. She was wondering whether it was intentional. If he was avoiding them, then why didn't he want to speak with them? If it wasn't intentional, then something else was going on. Maybe someone made Reid disappear too?

Sage had confirmed she'd found no sighting of Cyclops on the street security footage outside Cameron and Cote over the previous days, which led them to believe that he'd met Reid elsewhere. It was possible that Cyclops wanted to investigate this quietly to protect the reputation of his school and his students. If word got out that mutant kids were messing with this steroid, then it would stir up all sorts of trouble. They didn't need that kind of backlash against the mutant population.

Dazzler had discussed possible theories with her new team, but nothing seemed clearer to them. For all they knew, Magneto, Cyclops, and her father could be in hiding, their own disappearance intentional, though how they managed to evade Cerebra was another matter. But if it wasn't intentional, then yes, it meant they were in trouble, or worse, they were dead. Her mutant team was hoping for the former, but Dazzler realized with each passing hour that she might need to prepare herself for the latter. She felt the pressure starting to build within her.

"We should rest," Sage suggested. She and Rachel had left the bus stop and joined them inside the café. "Two stay on watch, two rest. I'll tap into the street security feed for his apartment, too, and those on guard can watch both."

Dazzler considered this. Sage appeared steady and confident, and Dazzler was strongly getting the impression that the woman had undertaken many missions like this before. In a way, it made Dazzler feel useless. It had been a while since she'd done something like this. She was supposed to be leading this investigation, but was she actually a leader?

"So, what's it gonna be, Blondie?" Rachel asked, the impatience clear in her voice.

Unsure, Dazzler busied herself with her phone to buy herself time to think, unplugging it from its charging brick in the café's wall. She tapped the screen to confirm it was fully charged and the S.H.I.E.L.D. credentials popped up. It felt like a sign, or a reminder at least. She was running this mission because she was S.H.I.E.L.D.'s Mutant Liaison. This was a joint initiative, but she was the lynchpin. She had a foot in both worlds and also a distrust of both worlds. She was the one who would decide who could and could not be trusted. She was the one who would ensure the good were kept safe, and the evil taken down.

At least, she would try to.

"Sage, Grey, go rest," she said firmly, then dialed Bennett's number that she had stored in the phone. She knew she had to check in with S.H.I.E.L.D. soon, and no matter where she checked in from, whether a payphone or this burner phone, they would have her location pinpointed within seconds. If they hadn't already located her via security footage, that is. Now that she wasn't near the school, it was less important. Besides, she'd swap to another burner phone after this call, just to be safe.

"I thought we had a deal," Bennett answered, as Sage and Rachel left the café, and Polaris headed to the bathroom. "Where are you?"

"I'm sure you're tracing this call and will find out soon."

"What's your update?"

"We can't find any sign of your scientist, Reid," Dazzler said, "but we're watching his known locations and hoping he shows."

"Sounds like he's spooked. If he is, he won't show. And what do you mean by we? I thought you wanted to work this alone."

"Yeah, well, it turns out mutants are more persuasive than S.H.I.E.L.D."

"Who? Which mutants are involved?"

"I'm sure you'll figure that out soon enough."

"Alison, I'll remind you that we agreed to share information. You're working for us, remember?"

"No, I'm working for me. I'm just using your credentials every now and then."

"Those credentials can be revoked," Bennett growled.

"They can, but if you want my help, we do this my way. Now, unless you have a new lead for me to follow, this is the best I can do right now. So, do you? Have a new lead?"

"Not yet," Bennett told her. "We've uncovered a new trace

of the MGH in the human population, and we're looking into links as we speak."

"How did you uncover the trace?"

"We've tapped into the hospitals' data systems. Anyone who presents with a steroid overdose will flag on our system. Any bloodwork will too. There are certain markers that identify mutant DNA. If we get a hit on both the steroids and the DNA, it means we have the MGH and we zero in."

"And you had a hit? Where?"

"New York. The day before yesterday, an adult male presented to one of the hospitals, and his condition raised both flags. The data is pushing through to your phone whenever we upload to our master files. But wait," he said sarcastically, "I guess that won't do you any good when you seem to be in Vancouver and your phone is still in New York."

"Oops. I must've left it behind by accident."

"Sure you did. Just like our drone had an accident."

"I told you I work alone."

"So, you don't want or need any information on this guy in the hospital, then? Oh, I'm sorry. My bad." Bennett hung up on her.

Dazzler sighed. Then re-dialed his number.

"Oh, so you *do* want our information?" Bennett answered.

"Stop the dramatics," Dazzler said. "I had my reasons for losing your drone. It's not exactly subtle, you know."

"Maybe not, but it might just save your life. Remember that."

"Or it could draw unwanted attention that could get me killed."

Silence was his response. She'd take that as Bennett ceding her point.

"Can you send me through those updated files?" she asked.

"This will be the last time I do," Bennett said, before hanging up again.

Dazzler saw the green reflection of Polaris in the café's window as she emerged from the bathroom, sliding her own phone into a pocket of her coat. Dazzler figured she must've checked in with Wolverine.

"The café's closing," Polaris said as she approached. "What do you want to do?"

Dazzler looked out to the street. The lights were now on, highlighting the falling snow. It looked quite pretty and felt a bit like Christmas. Memories of toasted marshmallows, the scent of pine, and hugs from her grandma flooded in. But the warm fuzzy feeling soon faded. Her grandmother had passed away, and she suddenly wondered whether she would ever spend another Christmas with family again.

"How about a walk?" she said, desperately wanting to shake her thoughts and the conversation with Bennett.

"In this weather?" Polaris looked at her like she was crazy.

Dazzler smiled and headed for the door. "The fresh air will do us good."

They stepped out into the falling snow as Dazzler zipped up her black leather jacket over her jumpsuit, while Polaris belted her long green coat and stuffed her hands in its pockets. They walked slowly along the sidewalk, passing other pedestrians occasionally, mostly folks on their way home from work. Dazzler checked their faces carefully to ensure none were Reid in disguise.

They reached the bus stop where Sage and Rachel had been before and pretended they were waiting for a ride. They both intermittently checked the security feed on their phones, taking it in turns to keep an eye on things.

Dazzler's phone suddenly rang. She didn't recognize the number but answered in case it was Bennett.

"Hello?"

"Sparkles, it's Frost," the ice queen said.

"Frosty," she responded. "How'd you get this number?"

"Sage."

Dazzler nodded, noting she needed to pay close attention to their relationship moving forward. "Do you have something?"

"Is there anything in your S.H.I.E.L.D. files about a Rick Rosenthorpe or Sanderson Holdings?"

"Let me check," Dazzler said. "I'll call you back."

"It would be faster if I could just jump into your brain."

"You'd like that, wouldn't you? I'll call you back." Dazzler hung up and noticed a message from Bennett containing the link to the S.H.I.E.L.D. files. Dazzler thought twice about clicking it, but by now they'd have tracked her exact location, so what did it matter? She'd kept the school's location hidden, and that was the most important part. She opened the secure link and searched through the new information for both names. Though S.H.I.E.L.D. had added the name of the person at the hospital, Dennis Stanton, there was nothing on Rosenthorpe. She called Frost back. Polaris kept her face turned away, giving Dazzler an appearance of privacy.

"What have you got?" Frost answered.

"Rosenthorpe isn't in their files. Nor is Sanderson Holdings. Where'd you get these names? From the Gamercade source?"

"The kid who sold Morph the steroid is Rosenthorpe's son. Rosenthorpe is the VP of a transport company, which would be a nice cover if he is the one trafficking it, don't you think? I'm about to hack into both their brains and find out more. What about you? Any trace of Scott?"

"Not yet. The scientist he met with is proving elusive. But he has to show up some time."

"Unless he's dead."

"Yeah," Dazzler said. "Let's hope that's not the case. Listen, while you're poking around in Rosenthorpe's brain, see if you come up with any link to a Dennis Stanton."

"Why's that?"

"He presented to a New York hospital with a steroid overdose that also flagged in S.H.I.E.L.D.'s system for mutant DNA."

"He took the MGH, and his little human heart couldn't take it," Frost said, as though thinking aloud. "All right. Talk again when one of us has something."

Dazzler hung up the phone.

"Frost has a lead?" Polaris asked.

Dazzler shoved her hands into her pockets. "Maybe. She's following up on a name. Some guy called Rosenth–"

Polaris suddenly looked down the street past Dazzler, eyes narrowing. "What are they doing back?"

Dazzler looked over her shoulder to see Sage and Rachel walking quickly toward them, eyes fixed with intensity.

CHAPTER TEN

Dazzler turned fully, her body tensing at the look on Rachel's face.

"He's here," Sage said quietly as they neared.

"Reid?" Dazzler asked, glancing around.

"I think he's been watching us the whole time," Rachel said, her whitened eyes not quite looking at them.

"How do you know it's him?" Dazzler asked.

"As we were heading back for a rest," Sage explained, "we passed an alleyway, and Rachel picked up his thoughts. Ever since she's been locked on to him."

Dazzler looked at Rachel, puzzled, and saw the redhead's pale eyes focus back on hers.

"Every now and then I've been casting my mind out to brush against those in the vicinity, testing to see if he was here, if I could pick up anything. He was lucky enough to be outside my range. That is, until I walked right past him."

"How long has he been watching us?" Dazzler asked.

"A while," Rachel said. "He's on edge. We have to be careful not to alert him."

"If he spoke to Cyclops, why won't he speak to us?" Polaris asked. "What's he so afraid of?"

"I don't know," Dazzler said, "but we're mutants. If I was human, I'd be afraid of us too." She turned to Rachel. "Where is he now?"

Rachel stared out at the darkened street, her eyes blanching white again as her mind felt for him. "Behind me. He's still in the alleyway. He's watching us."

Sage raised her hand to tap the side of her cybernetic glasses. "I have night vision. Follow me."

The four women walked casually down the sidewalk, which was empty except for a woman with a stroller, and further along, a suited man.

They spread out, watching all sides in case of a surprise attack. Dazzler pulled her earbuds out of her pocket and placed them in her ears.

"He knows we're onto him," Rachel said, quietly. "He's panicking."

A man dressed in black suddenly shot out from the mouth of an alleyway up ahead, narrowly missing the woman with the stroller, and racing away from them.

"That's him!" Sage said, as the four instantly gave chase.

Dazzler ran at speed after the man, wishing she'd brought her rollerblades with her. The man was fast. Dazzler seemed to be the quickest among the women as she led the pack, though Sage was not far behind, with both Polaris and Rachel bringing up the rear.

"Doctor Reid!" Dazzler called after the man. "We just want to talk!"

He turned abruptly into the mouth of another alleyway, accidentally knocking down the suited man. Dazzler didn't stop to help him, though. Instead, she leapt over him as she kept pace, chasing after Reid. He had to know something. That was why he was running. She had to get to him and find out what it was.

As they tore down the alleyway after him, Dazzler noted a dead end up ahead, relieved they now had him cornered. At least that's what she thought until she saw Reid jump up to pull down the fire escape stairs of the adjoining apartment block and quickly climb them as though he were a chimpanzee.

"How does he move like that?" Sage wondered aloud, just steps behind Dazzler.

"Polaris!" Dazzler called over her shoulder and pointed up. "Can you stop him?"

"On it!" Polaris called back, coming to a halt and holding out her hands. They watched as Reid continued to climb and Polaris's hands shook in his direction, but nothing happened.

"Polaris!" Dazzler called anxiously. "The stairs!"

The green-haired mutant grunted as she made a tugging motion. The bolts suddenly shot out from the stairs' structure, as Polaris destabilized it in an attempt to stop him or at least slow him down. The man looked panicked as the stairs groaned and swayed, before he dove across to an apartment's window ledge, took hold, then began to pry the window open.

Polaris concentrated hard, her temperature rising, melting the snowflakes that fell onto her forehead, as she pulled the stairs away from the wall, then separated the individual handrail bars and sent them over to the apartment window to cage the man.

But she was too late.

By the time the metal bars reached Reid, he was already inside, pulling the window shut.

"Damn!" Polaris spat, lowering her arms and allowing the rails to plummet to the ground with a crash somewhat dampened by the snow.

"Go around the front of the building, cut off his escape!" Dazzler called quickly to the others, as she pulled her phone out, and opened her music app.

"No!" Rachel said, her eyes whitening. "He's headed to the roof."

"How do we get up there?" Sage asked, scanning for a solution now that the stairs were ruined.

"I've got this," Dazzler said, hitting play on her phone. A raucous rock song filled her ears. She cranked the volume.

"Stand back!" she said, tucking her phone away and closing her eyes as she absorbed the sonic goodness that the thundering drumbeat and crunching guitars provided. She felt her veins spark and come alive with her light powers, and focused hard, drawing the energy down through her legs and pooling it entirely into her feet. Her soles began to glow brightly, and she ran toward the dead-end wall, at speed.

Just as she was about to crash into the wall, she leapt up and slammed her left foot against it, kicking off. The momentum, fueled by the concentrated energy released through the soles of her feet, pushed her toward the apartment wall adjacent on the right. She kicked out her foot and swiftly bounced off that too. Moving left to right, wall to wall, to the power of the song, she bounced higher and higher toward the top of the building.

With one last push off the dead-end concrete wall, she finally bounced herself up onto the roof, landing with a glowing skid. As soon as she steadied herself, panting, she muted the song on her phone and scanned the rooftop. She suddenly felt a strong breeze and turned to see Polaris landing gracefully, amid the fluttering of her long green hair.

"You're not the only one who can move through the air," Polaris said with a grin.

"Good to know," Dazzler said, then turned back to the rooftop.

They heard a door slamming open and immediately took cover behind a boxy storage shed fixed to the roof unit, hiding some mechanical plant. Dazzler snuck a peek and saw it was Reid. He was panting, agitated, unsure where to go. She turned back to Polaris and held a finger to her mouth. They sat still, waiting for him to near, and as soon as he was close enough, they sprang out.

Reid had the scare of his life and fell backward, but he scrambled up fast and was on his feet in no time. Dazzler swooped forward and tried to grab him, but he dodged her grasp. His movements were swift and far exceeding what any normal human should be able to do.

"We don't mean you harm!" she said.

He started running back toward the door, but Polaris quickly waved both her hands and with a grunting effort pulled part of an air-conditioning unit from its bracket and sent it flying to block the doorway. Reid pulled up just in time before he slammed into it, then pivoted swiftly around the doorway and raced across the rooftop away from them.

"Where's he going?" Polaris asked, breathless, as Dazzler ran after him, unmuting the song on her phone.

A wailing guitar blared in her ears amid screaming vocals as the cold night air scraped her cheeks, and Reid very quickly ran out of rooftop. Panicked, he glanced around at Dazzler, who was ready for him. Hands raised, palms outward, she flicked her wrists and shot out a blinding flare of light, stunning him. Reid called out in pain, raised his hands to his eyes, and fell to his knees, skidding to a stop in the layer of snow that dusted the rooftop.

Dazzler muted the song again and continued to race toward him. She was soon upon him, grabbing his wrist with one hand while leaving her other hand raised and glowing, ready to stun him with another burst of light energy if he tried anything.

Polaris was soon by her side, panting and eyeing her curiously. "So, that's why Frost calls you Sparkles, huh?"

"Something like that," she answered. "Let's get him off this rooftop."

They each took an arm of Reid's and helped him stand as he tried to blink away the glare from his retinas. He was taller than them both and lean like a greyhound. They led the partially blinded man toward the stairwell that would lead them back inside the building. When they reached the doorway, Polaris waved her hands to move the heavy mechanical plant away to give them access, but it didn't move. Polaris exchanged an embarrassed glance with Dazzler, then gritted her teeth with effort to try again and successfully moved it aside. They heard footsteps racing up the stairs and soon saw Sage and her cybernetic glasses staring back at them and their catch.

"Where's Rachel?" Dazzler asked.

"Watching the entrance," Sage answered, motioning them to follow her back down the way she came. Dazzler and Polaris followed, guiding Reid as they went, as he still blinked wildly, his footing unsure.

"I can't see!" Reid muttered. "You blinded me!"

"Nah." Polaris gave a green-lipsticked smile. "She just Dazzled you."

Dazzler smirked in amusement and asked Reid, "Where's Cyclops?"

Reid groaned and muttered, still blinking his eyes but doing so less now as his vision returned.

Dazzler tugged on his arm. "Where is he?" She noticed now that his arm felt unusually muscular and strong.

"Who?" he asked.

"Scott Summers. Don't play dumb. He came here to meet with you."

Reid glanced at her out of the corner of his eye, his mind calculating, but he gave no response.

"You know something," Dazzler said, still guiding him forcefully down the stairs, "and the less you say, the more guilty you appear. I told you we don't mean you any harm, we just want to know where he is."

"I don't know," Reid eventually offered.

"Yes, you do," Dazzler said, studying the lean arm she gripped. "No human moves that fast. You've taken some, haven't you? You've taken MGH."

Reid suddenly looked nervous. A sheen of sweat glistened across his brow. "I don't know what you're talking about."

"Tell us where he is," Polaris said, "or we hand you over to S.H.I.E.L.D."

Reid scoffed. "S.H.I.E.L.D. is obsolete. They have no power anymore."

Dazzler showed him her S.H.I.E.L.D. credentials. "Yeah, they do. And they are supported by mutant power. So, you better tell us what you know, or we'll hand you over. Not to S.H.I.E.L.D., but to mutants. Would you like that?"

Reid looked agitated.

"You used to work for S.H.I.E.L.D., Doctor Reid," Sage said, as she glanced over her shoulder at him. "What changed?"

Reid shrugged. "S.H.I.E.L.D. died. I was no longer beholden to them."

"So, you kept playing with the MGH on your own," Dazzler said, squeezing his arm tighter. "You replicated it? Are you selling it? On the street?"

Reid looked at her. "Why would I do that?"

"Why else? Money."

"MGH isn't something you share around," he said. "It's something you keep for yourself. It's like lightning in a bottle. You capture the original, and it's incredibly potent. You can replicate it, but it isn't the same. It's weaker. I won't share what I have with anyone."

"I knew you were using it!" It made Dazzler's skin crawl to think her DNA was flowing through the man's veins.

"Could someone have stolen the steroid from you and replicated it?" Sage asked.

Reid glanced at her. "No one stole it from me."

"Well, the same MGH you have is now on the streets," Polaris said. "Care to explain how that happened?"

Reid shrugged nonchalantly. "Guess that's your problem to solve."

"Tell us where Scott Summers is," Dazzler hissed. "You met with him. We know you did. And we know you tested the

MGH and confirmed it was linked to my DNA. So, tell us, what happened next?"

"I don't know," Reid said, coldly, as they finally reached the ground floor. Sage held open the doorway into the foyer, and Rachel turned around to face them. "Scott Summers got the results, then he left. That's the last I saw of him."

"So, why were you hiding from us then?" Dazzler asked as they spilled out into the foyer and Rachel fixed her whitened eyes on the man.

"Because," Reid said, "I don't trust *mutants.*"

"Stop him!" Rachel blurted out.

Reid suddenly shoved Dazzler hard into Sage with his amplified abilities. They lost their footing, and Dazzler saw Reid body-slam into Polaris before barreling past Rachel for the doorway. Polaris threw her hands out to pull the doors closed, but she was too slow, closing them only after he'd fled with Rachel on his tail.

Dazzler quickly got to her feet and burst through the doors to see Rachel paused on the sidewalk, eyes pale, with one hand at her temple and the other reaching out in Reid's direction. Reid glanced back at them, wincing and clasping his temples, as he raced erratically into the street…

…straight into the path of an oncoming bus.

The impact was hard and loud. Tires screeched as Reid's body cracked the windshield, then landed on the road and fell under the wheels.

Dazzler gasped and threw a hand over her mouth. Rachel dropped her hands, eyes now green and set wide in shock.

"Oh my god," Polaris said, coming to stand next to Rachel. "Is he dead?"

Sage nodded, looking at Reid's limp body, which lay on the street several feet from where the brake lights of the bus glared angrily into the night. The bus driver exited the vehicle shakily as a pedestrian nearby started screaming, "Someone call an ambulance!"

Dazzler automatically raised her phone, but Sage pushed her hand back down.

"We need to get out of here," she said. "Fast!"

Dazzler stared at her in a daze, then nodded as the ramifications made their way through into her brain. "Let's go. Hurry!"

She, Polaris, and Sage strode quickly away, but Rachel didn't follow. Dazzler turned around to see she remained fixated on the sight of Reid's body. Dazzler grabbed Rachel's arm and tugged her to go with them. It seemed to break the freeze in Rachel's brain, and she acquiesced, quietly lost in her own thoughts.

CHAPTER ELEVEN

Emma Frost was exhausted. After Morph and the others had followed Caleb and his mother to their house, she used the location information to home in on Caleb's mind and infiltrate it.

It was an art form to enter someone's mind without them knowing, especially from a distance. The subtlety took a lot of effort, but Emma was very adept at this now after decades of practice. Usually, she didn't care if someone knew she was inside their mind, but at times like this, secrecy was key. Like a burglar undertaking a daring heist, she had to be careful to take what she needed without tripping the sensors of this kid's mind.

She shouldn't have feared, though. The kid was currently doing three things at once – eating dinner, watching TV, and reading a comic – so his mind was tied up elsewhere, jumping his attention between the three. Emma concentrated to filter out the teen sitcom, the monster comic, and the disgusting way the kid ate, and she burrowed down into his subconscious, zeroing in on thoughts and memories triggered by keywords like MGH, steroid, and sales. When she had hits on these, she tugged on those threads gently to see what they revealed. It was akin to being a librarian and moving through rows of books; the memories she sought drew her attention like gold gilded book spines catching the sunlight. She plucked them from their shelves, opened the books, and scanned the memories before her.

She found the memory of Caleb's sale to the disguised Morph. Not the one she'd witnessed today, but the original one – the one that had started all of this. She knew it was Morph from the way he was dressed, from his posture, his face slightly lowered, his eyes looking upward as though staring through an imaginary fringe. Morph may have had the ability to change his appearance, but he had not yet learned to fully become the person he mimicked. It made Emma sad to know that the mutant, despite his abilities, still felt like he wasn't enough and needed the MGH to improve himself. He *was* enough. Every mutant kid was enough, just as they were.

Though Emma wanted to continue watching that memory, time was of the essence. She continued to scour through the memories, while every now and then the canned laughter from Caleb's sitcom sounded through her ears, flashes of a comic monster eating people appeared, or the kid's loud burping caught her attention. As the disruptions inched forward, she carefully pushed them into the background.

Soon enough, she found a memory that caught her interest. She saw Caleb, in an expensive house with views over Manhattan. She heard a man's voice, saw Caleb peer around a doorway into what appeared to be his father's home office.

His father, dressed in another expensive suit, had his back to the door, looking out the window at the expansive views. He spoke on the phone and held a vial of MGH. She heard Caleb's father speak words like "super strength," "special steroid," and "invincible." Caleb's father ended the call, then placed the steroid in a safe among many more vials, which he then locked. Caleb slunk away and hid, waited for his father to leave, then entered his father's office and took what he was not even supposed to know existed.

At this point Emma retreated from Caleb's mind. She had her answer as to where he got the MGH and how the steroid found its way into her school. It was an accident of sorts, not intentional and certainly not targeted. She hoped the appearance of the steroid at Wolverine's school was just as accidental. If Morph hadn't heard Caleb talking about it that day at the Gamercade, it might never have spread to the mutant school. But then again, perhaps it was only a matter of time. Either way, this was simply a case of a bored rich kid rebelling and creating mischief, probably wanting to push boundaries to get his father's attention.

The real problem, and therefore the real focus for Emma now, was to infiltrate Rick Rosenthorpe's mind. He was the key. The man had stock of MGH in his house, so either he was the one distributing the steroid, or he could lead her to whoever was. She needed to find the source of his supply, find out why it was suddenly being created now, and most importantly, see if this would lead to information on Erik's and Scott's whereabouts.

She took a deep breath then sipped a fresh coffee. It had been a long day of using her telepathic powers, and she was starting to feel drained, as Morph was earlier. Mutants were gifted, but they were not invincible. At their very core they were still humans, and like humans, they could falter and grow tired. And the truth was, since the Phoenix incident, Emma still worried that her powers weren't quite as strong as they'd once been. Could they suddenly flicker in and out again like a candle in the breeze?

Like an untrained muscle, she had to keep working it to keep it in shape.

"Just one more mind," she told herself. *Willed* herself. "Just one more."

Though she knew how tricky it would be. Rick Rosenthorpe was an adult, and he was farther away in New York. She had to be very careful not to trip his sensors.

But if anyone could do this, it was her.

Dazzler paced her hotel room. It was tiny and housed two single beds. Polaris sat on one, while Sage stood by the door, arms folded. Rachel stood at the window, staring out into the night, a permanent crease in her brow.

"It's not your fault," Polaris reassured Rachel.

Rachel turned her face a little but then looked back out the window. "I'm fine."

"No, you're not," Polaris said. "I may not read minds like you, but I can read yours now."

Rachel didn't respond and continued to stare out into the night.

"Were you..." Polaris paused. "Were you in his mind when he...?"

Dazzler stopped pacing, watching Rachel carefully. Again, Rachel didn't respond, but she squeezed her eyes shut briefly.

"It's not your fault," Polaris said again firmly. "I should've shut those doors faster. Sometimes it just takes a bit for my powers to fire up. They've been glitchy since M-Day."

Rachel ran a hand over her face, then through her short red hair. "He was planning to run. He kept thinking it."

"And you warned us," Sage said.

"Yeah, right as he ran," Rachel said. "I should've said something sooner."

"And I should've kept a tighter grip on him," Dazzler said. "He was stronger than expected."

"And I should've held my feet, instead of falling down," Sage said. "There. We are all guilty. Now let's move on. What do we do now?"

Dazzler studied her. There was Sage leading again. It made her think of Bennett. "I need to check in with S.H.I.E.L.D.," she said. "Let them know what happened."

Sage gave a nod. "I will get us some food. Our bodies need fuel."

"Here." Dazzler threw the S.H.I.E.L.D. credit card to her. Sage caught it, then she left the room, as Dazzler pulled out her phone and called Bennett.

"I saw the news," Bennett answered without formalities. "Doctor Reid was hit by a bus? Tell me you weren't involved."

Dazzler hesitated. "We had him, then he ran. It wasn't our fault."

"Our only lead on Cyclops's whereabouts is dead."

"I said it wasn't our fault."

"Did you get any information from him before he died at least?"

Dazzler sighed. "Not much. He claims he doesn't know what

happened to Cyclops. He also claims that he wasn't selling the MGH to anyone. He was keeping it for himself."

"What do you mean, for himself?"

"He was a user. That's how he got away from us. He was incredibly fast. No human can move like that."

"So, an innocent man is dead, and we have no further information."

"I wouldn't call him innocent," Dazzler said. "When S.H.I.E.L.D. shut down, did they shut down Reid's studies of the MGH?"

"I can't answer that," Bennett said.

"Well, if they did, he kept the studies alive and used the steroid for himself. Which means S.H.I.E.L.D. failed in its duty of care to ensure the MGH was contained. If S.H.I.E.L.D. *didn't* shut down the study, then that means you knew full well the risk of what could happen, of the MGH leaking out and falling into the wrong hands. Which means, S.H.I.E.L.D. failed in its duty of care to ensure the MGH was contained."

"We are not your enemy, Alison. It was S.H.I.E.L.D. who brought you in on this. Would you rather we hadn't?"

"I'd rather S.H.I.E.L.D. be honest with me. I'm sensing some big blind spots here and blind spots will get us killed."

"You may be Mutant Liaison, but your credentials will only give you so much clearance. You *cannot* and *will not* be privy to that which does not affect your clearance level. That does not mean we wish you harm. It simply means you are not of a high enough status to know."

"Reid was using the steroid. We could've used a warning on that!"

"We didn't know he was using it!" Bennett snapped.

Dazzler sighed with frustration. "Well, now you do. I guess we all have to live with his death now."

Rachel looked over at Dazzler, locking eyes, before she turned back to look out the window again.

Bennett was quiet a moment. "Did anyone see you?"

"I don't think so, but I can't be sure."

"You need to stay low. In fact, I think you should probably leave Vancouver."

"But we still don't know what happened to Cyclops."

"No, but we have a new lead on Magneto in New York."

"Magneto?" she said, as Polaris straightened with interest. "What is it?"

"We tracked down some street footage that shows Magneto entering an alleyway in Manhattan the night he disappeared. Drone surveillance leads us to believe he entered a doorway down that alleyway. It turns out that doorway leads to a private bar, called *The Gilded Arrow*. Not just anyone can enter. It requires a membership and not one you can just apply for. It's by personal invitation only."

"Who was he with?"

"He was alone, but we did pick up a person of interest on the street security footage, entering the alleyway not long afterward. Toby Squires, legal counsel to Senator Clive Earnest. From what we've been able to ascertain, the two are associates who go back a long way."

"Squires or Earnest?"

"Squires. Magneto has never been seen with the senator."

"Did Magneto and Squires leave together?"

"We don't know. Some kids came along and took out the street security cameras after he entered the alleyway."

"How convenient."

"Isn't it?"

"Why would Magneto be meeting Squires?" Dazzler asked, as Polaris's brow furrowed.

"Well, the senator is obviously well connected and is a staunch advocate for supporting US businesses."

"So?"

"So, Squires, who would be privy to a lot of the senator's information, might have contacts that could help Magneto find out who could be making money off the distribution of the steroid."

"So, you don't think a two-bit dealer is behind this, then? Is the senator a person of interest?"

"Not yet," Bennett said, "but he has links with several other POIs on our list. It makes sense that he could be involved too. If he is, we need evidence."

"What other POIs? You only listed the hospital guy in the file."

"We just pushed through an update," Bennett said. "Dennis Stanton, the guy who wound up in hospital with heart difficulties, is a successful Wall Street broker. He held a dinner party at his house the night he wound up in hospital. Among the guests that we've uncovered from security footage so far is Squires. Now this may just be a coincidence. The two were college roommates back in the day. We're trying to track everyone who had contact with Stanton in the weeks leading up to his dinner party."

"It's no coincidence. Squires was at the dinner party where Stanton had MGH. Then Squires meets with Magneto, and now he's missing. We need to talk to Squires."

"We approached his office," Bennett said, "and they said he's currently on vacation and is not contactable. We've traced him to a small island in the Pacific to confirm this."

"So, are you going to question him?"

"No. Not yet."

"Why?"

"We need to be careful before leveling accusations at people in office, Alison. We want to gather more information first. Evidence."

"We need to visit this bar, then," Dazzler said.

"You do, but you're not just going to be able to walk in off the street. It requires an exclusive membership. You need to find a way inside."

Dazzler's mind spun. "Hill was right. There's a powerful network behind this, isn't there?"

"It's looking that way," Bennett said gravely.

"Send me the address of that bar. We'll head back to New York and find a way inside."

Rachel looked back at Dazzler again. "What about Cyclops?"

"What the…" Bennett suddenly said. "Turn on the news!"

"The news." Dazzler motioned to Polaris who sat by the remote. "Turn on the TV."

Polaris ignored the remote and instead waved her hand, and the TV switched on. They saw footage airing from someone's phone of the aftermath of the Reid accident. Footage that clearly showed Rachel standing on the sidewalk staring at Reid's body. Suddenly an image of Rachel's blown-up face was displayed along with a number for people to call if they had information on her whereabouts. She was wanted for questioning.

"This is bad. You need to pull back now," Bennett ordered. "I

swear, if you draw attention like this again, you will be cut off from this case. You're lucky I don't rip you off it now and put you out of harm's way."

"Oh, yeah?" An anger suddenly swelled within Dazzler. "Like a dungeon where you can extract some MGH from me?"

"Look, Alison–"

"No, you listen to me! This wasn't our fault. We are doing our best with what we have. You withheld information about Reid, so you're lucky we don't cut *you* off."

"I'm not going over this argument again," Bennett hissed. "Keep Rachel out of sight and pull back from Vancouver. Cross the border. *Now.*"

Bennett hung up. Dazzler threw the phone down in frustration with a small spark of angry light.

Sage re-entered with an armful of food and looked at their faces. "What did I miss?"

CHAPTER TWELVE

Dazzler and the team exited the hotel with their bags and walked down the sidewalk.

"We can't catch a ride," Sage said. "We'll need to steal one."

"You want me to break into a car?" Polaris asked.

"No," Sage said, pulling a long wire from the zipper of her X-suit. "I can do that." She turned down a side street and chose a car parked in the darker space between streetlights. Dazzler watched as she took the wire, bent it, jimmied it in the lock, and had the door open in seconds.

"You *are* multi-talented," Dazzler said.

"Get in," Sage said, popping the trunk and throwing her bag inside. The rest followed suit and they were soon on their way.

Their drive out of the city center was smooth, until suddenly it wasn't. The main road out of the city that would lead them back to the X-Jet, was blocked by a series of police cars, lights flashing red and blue, and cars lining up to be checked.

"This is a problem," Sage said. "Especially in a stolen car."

"Is there another way?" Dazzler asked Sage, who sat behind the wheel.

"Not unless we want to walk a long way," Sage said, her mind analyzing something. "This is a big response for the incident involved."

Dazzler considered the roadblock ahead. "Maybe this isn't related to Reid's death."

"It's all over the news," Polaris said. "I like the positivity, though."

"Someone doesn't want us to leave," Sage said. "Someone with reach to shut down a major road out of town that just so happens to lead to our jet." She looked at Dazzler. "Could this be S.H.I.E.L.D.?"

"What?" Dazzler said, surprised. "No. Bennett wanted us to leave immediately."

"And immediately there are roadblocks," Rachel said from the back seat.

Dazzler stared at her mutant associates, unsure how to respond. *Had she been played?* Bennett would've been looking for her after she escaped New York. Had they tracked her down *before* Vancouver? Did they know where the school was now? Did they know where the X-Jet was? But how? Sage had cloaked the jet.

Sage suddenly turned the car around and headed back the way they had come.

"Where are you going?" Dazzler said. "We need to get to the X-Jet."

"We need to cross the border, so that is what we're doing."

"If they have roadblocks here, they'll have them there, too," Polaris said.

"The border is a roadblock, that's true," Sage said, "and they'll be hard to convince, but I'd rather face one man in a booth than several police. Wouldn't you? It's the lesser of two evils."

"And what do we do when we cross the border?" Dazzler asked.

"Call Logan," Rachel said to Polaris. "Ask him to send us his jet."

Polaris nodded and made the call as Sage headed for the border.

Emma Frost thumbed through the recesses of Rosenthorpe's mind. It had taken some effort to get to this point, as the adult Rosenthorpe was much more intricate than that of his teenage son, and as the man was relaxing on his couch with a glass of scotch, listening to music, his mind was less distracted than his son's had been. Emma had to move more carefully and avoid many more "sensors" as she waded through a lifetime more of memories. But she finally found some that were useful – memories triggered by the keyword MGH.

She saw Rosenthorpe in her mind, standing in a warehouse, studying a shipment of MGH. She froze the memory, reached for a pen, and scribbled down the consignment note she saw, then unpaused the memory and let it play out among the faces of his employees as he took a handful of vials, placed them in his pocket, and the cargo was sealed.

She found another memory. Rosenthorpe was at a dinner party in someone's home. They were rich, the house spacious and generously decorated. Rosenthorpe walked into a separate room with another man she didn't recognize, handed the man one of the vials, and she heard him say: "Try before you buy."

Emma suddenly wondered whether this was the man who wound up in hospital with heart troubles. She rewound the memory, went back to that dinner table, and studied the faces sitting around. She didn't recognize any of them.

Intrigued, her mind wandered back to Rosenthorpe's memory of the cargo. She wanted to figure out where it was being kept. She glanced around at the faces, then looked at the consignment note again, reading the shipping address. It was addressed to Sanderson Holdings in New Jersey. It must be their warehouse.

She suddenly saw Rosenthorpe, in real life, in his bathroom brushing his teeth. He was getting ready for bed, which meant her time was running out. When someone was awake the channels in their mind were open, but when they slept, they were closed and harder to enter. It was akin to locking a public aquarium at night. The public couldn't enter, but the fish still swam. At night, a person's subconscious, though active in their brain while they slept, was closed off from normal telepathic energies. Given Emma's mutant skill level, this wasn't normally a problem, and she could still enter their minds, but since the Phoenix incident she'd found it more difficult. If the doors and windows to a person's brain were closed, it was harder to enter without tripping their senses.

She began to move more quickly, desperate to find out what she could.

Her mind began trawling for Cyclops and Magneto, but she found no memory of them, other than the occasional news article on their deeds that Rosenthorpe had read in times gone by. From what she could see, Rosenthorpe did not appear to have physically crossed paths with them at all.

Rosenthorpe, it seemed, had not been responsible for their disappearances.

But he was definitely involved in the MGH...

Tiredness suddenly swept over her as Rosenthorpe in real life yawned and climbed into bed. She needed more time!

She quickly searched for Dazzler's father, the judge. Wanting to see if there were links.

And he appeared.

Though, not as the judge he was now. Emma saw him when he was just a young lawyer. Rosenthorpe sat across from Carter Blaire who pushed legal papers toward him, pointing where to sign. Rosenthorpe signed the papers... representation papers. Dazzler's father was once Rosenthorpe's lawyer. Was he still involved with the man?

Despite Rosenthorpe's tiredness pulling at her, Emma still felt alert, wondering what this memory meant. Dazzler's father had a direct link with Rosenthorpe, who had a direct link with supplying the MGH. It made her wonder, now, about Dazzler's involvement.

Another memory flew her way. She suddenly saw Rosenthorpe at an event for Carter Blaire's law firm. Dazzler was young, maybe thirteen. She smiled up at Rosenthorpe as Carter introduced them. Next, she suddenly pulled a memory of Dazzler performing a concert. Rosenthorpe was in the crowd...

Did that mean something? Emma had a thousand questions, desperate to dig further, but she paused suddenly when Rosenthorpe appeared in her mind, looking confused.

He was staring at Emma.

She'd tripped his sensors.

She instantly pulled back, her eyes wide with shock.

Did he realize what had been happening, that she'd infiltrated his mind? Did he know who she was?

Had she just put a target on her back?

She stared at her empty office, her body drained from the day's activities and her mind utterly shot with exhaustion.

It would seem Dazzler's father was more involved than Dazzler had let on. Did Carter Blaire have something to do with the disappearances of Scott and Erik? Could Dazzler and S.H.I.E.L.D. be laying some sort of trap for Emma and her school? Or was something else going on?

A knock at the door sounded.

"Come in," she said, rubbing her face.

Triage entered. "Did you find anything useful in Rosenthorpe's mind?"

Emma contemplated her answer. She didn't have any answers right now. Only more questions. "Useful, yes, but conclusive, no. I think I connected with Rosenthorpe too well. He was about to fall asleep, and I was about to do the same."

"You look tired," Triage said. "You've been at it all day."

"What about you? Did you uncover anything else?"

"Yes, we did."

"We?"

"I found out there were a bunch of companies connected to Sanderson Holdings. I asked Tempus to help me."

"And you told her this was confidential, right?"

"Yes. Of course."

"OK. Send me a list of the companies."

"I did." Triage nodded, pointing to Emma's laptop.

"Thank you. Go get some rest."

"You should too." Triage nodded and left.

It sounded like a great idea, but Emma needed answers first. She phoned Dazzler. It went unanswered, which annoyed her. Next, she called Sage.

"Frost," Dazzler answered the phone, her voice sounding on edge. "Sage is driving."

"Blaire?" Emma said, curious. She heard the sound of traffic in the background. "What's going on, you're on the move?"

"We are. You didn't see the news?"

"No. What happened?"

"Well, let's just say that Reid is a dead end."

"You found him dead, or you made him that way?"

"He made himself that way, but now Rachel's face is everywhere, our passage back to the X-Jet is blocked, and we need to cross the border."

"You need to head to New Jersey."

"Let me call you on my new phone." Dazzler hung up before another call sounded on Emma's phone.

"Why the number change?"

"The usual. I don't fully trust S.H.I.E.L.D., so I switched burner phones. Save this number."

"Turn the other one off and remove the chip."

"Oh, it's back in Vancouver. So, you said New Jersey? What did you find out?"

"The Gamercade kid, Caleb, stole the MGH from his dad, the VP of Sanderson Holdings. Their office is in Manhattan, but they have a warehouse in New Jersey. Trawling Rosenthorpe's brain I saw images of a shipment of MGH there. It was a large shipment. You need to get to that shipment before they can distribute it or move it elsewhere, especially if they see Reid's death and he's connected to them somehow."

"How big was the shipment?"

She heard trepidation in Dazzler's voice. Emma had to remind herself how personal this was for the light transducer, given the MGH was made from her mutant DNA, and especially given what she'd been through before.

Then again, Dazzler was a performer. Could Emma trust her reactions?

"Big," Emma said. "Big enough to worry me."

"S.H.I.E.L.D. found security footage of Magneto entering an alleyway where there's a hidden club, and Senator Earnest's legal counsel, Toby Squires, entered not long afterward. The cameras were destroyed after he entered, so we have no way of knowing what happened after that. Did Magneto ever mention a bar called *The Gilded Arrow* in Manhattan?" Dazzler asked.

"It doesn't ring a bell."

"He never mentioned Squires?"

"Not to me."

Dazzler sighed down the phone. "All right. I think we should keep the warehouse quiet from S.H.I.E.L.D."

"I agree. But, Blaire, there's something else."

"What is it?"

She heard the exhaustion in Dazzler's voice at yet more possible revelations. Emma was particularly interested to see how she reacted to *this* news.

"Trawling through Rosenthorpe's brain, I discovered something else. Something about your father."

"Tell me," Dazzler said quickly.

"Your father, back when he was a lawyer, was on retainer to Rick Rosenthorpe. They have a past together."

"S- so?" Dazzler stuttered defensively. "He represented a lot of people back then. It doesn't mean anything."

"*You've* also met Rosenthorpe before."

"What? When?"

"When you were thirteen or so. He's also been to see your shows."

"What? I... I met him when I was thirteen? How am I supposed to remember that?"

"You never talked to him after your recent shows?"

"No. Just what are you suggesting?"

"I'm not suggesting anything. I'm stating facts. Your father used to be Rosenthorpe's lawyer, and now he's disappeared. Rosenthorpe has been to see your concerts. Rosenthorpe has a large shipment of MGH in his warehouse in New Jersey. MGH that's apparently derived from you."

"So? I don't know where he got it from."

"Why do you think S.H.I.E.L.D. brought you in on this? They think your father is involved and taking his cut, don't they? He's probably on an island somewhere by now."

"He's not," Dazzler said adamantly.

"Does your father know you're a mutant?" Emma asked. "Does he know the MGH was derived from you?"

"No!" Dazzler's voice was hard as nails. "He doesn't know, and he *wouldn't* do this."

"Are you sure about that?"

Silence filled the line. Emma knew what that silence meant. That silence meant doubt.

"Yes, I'm sure," Dazzler eventually said. She sounded adamant, but Emma knew she was definitely performing now.

It left Emma feeling conflicted.

She knew Dazzler had been traumatized by what had happened with Mystique. She also knew that sometimes trauma caused people to do things they ordinarily wouldn't. Some turned bitter, some did rash things, some closed themselves off from the world at large. Dazzler was younger and still had some learning to do. Emma knew what Dazzler had been like before the Mystique incident, knew that Dazzler had once been quite a trusting soul. So, the question was, was someone taking advantage of her? Was S.H.I.E.L.D. or someone else using her as a pawn for their own gain? Or had Dazzler turned bitter and vengeful? Was Dazzler performing innocence to achieve another goal? With S.H.I.E.L.D. or with someone else?

Well, Emma could perform as well. She could show support for the singer, while investigating things beneath the surface.

"If you're sure your father's innocent," Emma warned her, "then you need to be careful. Because someone might be setting a trap for *you*. Maybe that's why S.H.I.E.L.D. wanted you to lead this so badly. Your father is the bait to trap you, and you're the bait S.H.I.E.L.D. is using to trap whoever is involved."

There was a long pause over the phone.

"Send me the warehouse details," Dazzler said, coldly, before she hung up.

CHAPTER THIRTEEN

Dazzler's mind raced as fast as their stolen vehicle cruised down the freeway, a thousand conspiracy theories churning her thoughts. She rubbed her temples, feeling a headache setting in.

"What did Frost say?" Sage asked, glancing at her from the driver's seat.

"She's located a shipment of MGH in a warehouse in New Jersey. We have to find it before it disappears."

"She knows who's distributing it?" Polaris said from the back seat.

Dazzler nodded. "Rick Rosenthorpe, VP of Sanderson Holdings is involved. It's their warehouse."

"And?" Rachel asked, her voice low with intent, or perhaps accusation. "Tell them who else is involved." Dazzler glanced into the rearview mirror at Rachel's reflection. She rubbed her temple again, noticing the headache was gone.

"You were inside my head?" Dazzler asked, feeling a shiver run down her arms.

Rachel didn't answer. Dazzler glared at her, angry she'd let her guard down.

"Who else is involved?" Polaris pushed, looking between the two.

"Someone Dazzler knows *very* well," Rachel said.

Dazzler gave a short sharp laugh. "That's where you're wrong, Grey. I don't know my father well at all."

"Your father is involved with Rosenthorpe?" Polaris asked.

"No," Dazzler said. "He just represented him once."

"But Frost thinks he's helping Rosenthorpe now?" Sage asked.

"Frost doesn't *know* anything," Dazzler said. "Let's not forget my father is missing, just like your fathers are. Missing does not mean guilt. If anything, I'd say it's the opposite."

"Guess we'll soon find out," Rachel said quietly.

Dazzler glanced briefly at Rachel again, then turned to look out the passenger window. Anything to remove herself as much as possible from these mutants. She wasn't sure what to think or who to trust now.

It worried her immensely that Magneto walked into a bar and was never seen again. He was there to meet with someone, she was sure of it, which meant he must've been betrayed by someone he trusted. And if he couldn't trust his allies, then who could *she* trust? S.H.I.E.L.D. was clearly withholding information from her and she didn't like that one bit. And Frost? She *had* been sharing information, but Dazzler didn't like the accusation she made against her father or herself, and their history with Rosenthorpe. How was she supposed to remember someone she'd met when she was thirteen? And plenty of people saw her gigs. She couldn't possibly recognize everyone in the crowd with the stage lights in her eyes.

She didn't like the warning Frost had given her either. Was she feigning concern? Or was she taunting her? Something bothered Dazzler about her visit to the school, and the strange feeling she'd had in that underground hallway, wondering what was behind those metal doors. The way Frost had looked at her. Could she trust the woman who would be in the perfect place to betray Magneto and Scott? She suddenly wondered whether Frost had any history with Mystique. Could she be helping her exact revenge on Dazzler and Magneto? What could Frost gain from the betrayal? More power over the school?

And what of these mutant teammates of hers that she barely knew? Sage had a mysterious history and an alliance with Frost, and she seemed eager to steer the team in certain directions. Was Sage leading her into a trap at Frost's command? When she'd left the motel room to get the food, had she been the one to set up the roadblock?

Rachel seemed to hate Frost. What if she was somehow trying to undermine the White Queen, to weaken her by helping someone take Magneto and Cyclops away? Would Rachel, and Logan for that matter, team up with whoever was behind this to get back at Frost and Cyclops for whatever the reason was she hated them? Was it because of the Phoenix incident and what Cyclops did? Frost took Cyclops's side and supported him afterward, when not many did. After all, Cyclops had killed the beloved Professor Xavier and alienated himself from much of the mutant community. Logan in particular despised Scott. And Rachel's allegiance was to Logan's school.

With Rachel's mind skills, could she have known that bus was coming for Reid? Did she purposely send Reid into its path? Did she want to kill him before he could tell them what they wanted to know? Was Rachel playing them?

And what of Polaris? Her powers conveniently acted up when they were chasing Reid, allowing him to get away. She said her relationship with her father was complicated. What did that mean? Their gifts were very similar, which meant she would know his weaknesses. Could she have betrayed her father for some reason? Or maybe she was she working *with* her father. Was *he* behind this? Perhaps they were working to undermine Frost. Magneto's relationship with both Frost and Cyclops had been strained after the Phoenix incident. Despite their differences over the years, Charles Xavier had been Magneto's friend, and he'd been murdered by the Phoenix-influenced Cyclops.

Or could Magneto just want the MGH for himself? Was that why he rescued Dazzler from Mystique? Simply to wrest control of the MGH for himself and take over Mystique's empire. Mystique, who had once been Magneto's ally…

A memory flashed inside her mind, of Polaris exiting the bathroom of that café in Vancouver and sliding her phone into her coat pocket. Had she been calling Logan to report in? Or had she been calling Magneto? Or warning Reid?

There were too many questions. Too many people in play.

Dazzler looked into the back seat to see Polaris's vibrant green eyes studying her… and if Dazzler wasn't mistaken, those eyes were a little threatening.

"What are you going to do if your father's involved?" Polaris asked her.

"What are you going to do if yours is?" Dazzler shot back.

"Excuse me?" Polaris's brow furrowed.

"My father's a human. He wouldn't have the power to make people disappear. Your father would."

"Your father is a judge," Rachel countered. "I'd say he'd have the connections."

"And so would yours." Dazzler turned around in her seat. "He'd have the connections, *and* he'd have the enemies, given the Phoenix incident and the little mutant uprising he tried to make happen afterward."

"Yeah, weren't you a part of that?" Rachel shot back.

Dazzler paused. She had been staying at the school when Scott had grown bitter and mistrustful of humans, and no longer believed an alliance between mutants and humans was possible.

"I was around because your father gave me somewhere to stay," Dazzler said, "but I was in a dark place at the time."

"Yeah? So was Cyclops," Rachel said.

"So, you're defending him now?" Dazzler challenged.

Rachel looked away, out the window.

"I thought you were here to repay a debt to our fathers," Polaris said to Dazzler. "So, why are you questioning their motives?"

"I was repaying a debt, but even Frost warned me that this could be a setup planned by someone working with Mystique, or someone wanting control of the MGH, or someone just wanting to take me or the Xavier school down. And, right now, I'm thinking it's a mutant. Who else could make Magneto and Cyclops disappear? Unless, of course, their disappearance was voluntary... because they're the ones behind this."

"They wouldn't do that." Polaris's whole face was screwed up now. "Finding out who is behind this is the whole point of us being here."

"Magneto and Cyclops are strong. Either a mutant took them down, or Magneto or Cyclops themselves are behind this, and they're trying to stop us from getting close to the evidence." Dazzler's mind quickly waded through the possibilities, wondering who could want to hurt them. Cyclops had many foes after the Phoenix incident, and Magneto had gained many enemies over the years, especially from his younger, more extremist days. A sudden thought struck her. She looked back at Polaris. "Who are your siblings?" she asked her.

"What?" Polaris asked, confused by the turn in conversation.

"I know some of Magneto's children but not necessarily all of them," Dazzler said. "You said you're ashamed of some of your siblings. Is Magneto, too? Could they be behind this?" Dazzler's mind flew with conspiracy theories that set her pulse racing with despair.

"This has nothing to do with–" Polaris began.

"It has everything to do with it!" Dazzler cut her off. "Who are you ashamed of?"

"Dazzler," Sage cautioned.

"What?" Dazzler snapped. "Everyone can throw accusations at my father, but I can't throw accusations back? If Magneto and Cyclops are innocent, then someone betrayed them, and if someone betrayed them, that someone will betray us, too. Look at that roadblock back there! Someone knew we were going to take that route back to the X-Jet." She looked back at Polaris. "In the café you made a call. Who to?"

"Stop trying to turn this back on us," Rachel said.

"It's convenient, don't you think, that her powers kept acting up and enabling Reid to get away," Dazzler said.

"That wasn't on purpose!" Polaris said, anger flushing up her cheeks now. "You can't think *I'm* behind this?"

"If not you, then who? Who would betray your father?" Dazzler pushed. "Who are these siblings that you're ashamed of? Someone made your father disappear. Could it be them?"

Polaris's eyes simmered with green fire as she considered the accusation.

"Well?" Dazzler shouted, unable to contain her frustration and anger. "Give me a name!"

"You want to know who I'm ashamed of?" Polaris yelled back, as the car began to vibrate with her anger. "The *Witch*! That's who."

"The Witch?" Dazzler asked, confused, as the car shook violently around her.

"Polaris!" Sage warned. Rachel placed a hand on Polaris's arm.

"Yes, the Witch!" Polaris yelled at Dazzler, eyes blazing green fire now. "The one who brought M-Day upon all of us!"

"S-she's your sister?" Dazzler said in shock as the car's windows rattled and she held on to the car's dashboard amidst the vibration.

"My half-sister!" Polaris said. "Are you happy?"

"Polaris!" Sage yelled again, her biceps bulging as she struggled to control the car. It shook and swerved left and right. Rachel, eyes whitened, quickly clasped Polaris's shoulder to calm her.

"The Scarlet Witch is your sister?" Dazzler asked, her voice soft with sympathy now.

The vibration of the vehicle eased off as Polaris calmed, thanks to Rachel's help.

"Yes," Polaris said, tears staining her eyes. "It was *my* sister who tried to kill us all. Are you happy now?"

A wave of shame washed over Dazzler from her outburst, followed by a wave of sympathy. "Could she be behind this?" she asked, softly.

Polaris stared at her a moment, then turned her eyes out the window. "With her, anything is possible."

"You happy now?" Rachel said, venomously to Dazzler.

"No. Are you?" Dazzler said, mind turning over again, studying the resentment burning in the telepath's eyes. "You seem to hate your father and you hate Frost. Why are you sitting there so quietly?"

"Who can get a word in with you having a *paranoid* break in front of us?" she said.

Dazzler snapped and reached for her, light energy surging through her body, but Sage swiftly shot out a hand and pushed her back into her seat.

"You're one to talk!" Dazzler spat at Rachel. "Isn't your mother famous for her mental breaks?"

Rachel lunged forward now, reaching for her, but again, Sage thrust a muscular arm out and pushed her back, and Polaris joined in too, pulling Rachel back into her seat.

"Enough!" Sage barked, shooting them each a hard glance. "All of you!" She turned back around and motioned up ahead. "We're approaching the border. *Don't* draw attention!"

Through the windshield, Dazzler saw the lines of cars, red brake lights flashing on and off, as they lined up for the crossing. She shot Rachel another glare, then adjusted herself back in her seat, and caught her breath.

Unable to trust S.H.I.E.L.D. and unable to trust her mutant

team, Dazzler found herself in the exact position she expected to be. She couldn't trust anyone, human or mutant. Both sides were involved, she felt it in her bones.

The only way to ensure she didn't disappear like the others was to only trust herself. If her walls had been up before, they were now reinforced with steel.

CHAPTER FOURTEEN

Dazzler, earbuds in and head resting back against the car seat, listened to music as she waited patiently for their turn at the border. The song was calming but also preparing her in case she needed to use her powers at the crossing. It was nearing nine PM, and they were all out of conversation as the suffocating tension from their earlier argument sat in the car with them.

It was not a great team atmosphere, and being the leader, Dazzler felt a mixed bag of emotions from her outburst: anger, shame, terror, sadness, righteousness, loneliness, guilt. Rachel's words about a paranoid mental break had stung her. Maybe Dazzler wasn't ready to face what this mission was bringing up in her. She'd worked so hard to move past her trauma, to drown it, but it was bubbling to the surface. And she couldn't let it. Not yet, not now. If she couldn't face what lay ahead, what did that mean for her father? Who would care if he lived or died, if not her?

But she was in a difficult and precarious position, not

knowing who she could trust. And yet, she had no choice but to work with these women for now. But how to keep her guard up? Would she need to sleep with one eye open? Could she never turn her back? It exhausted her just thinking about it. And if she was exhausted now, how could she see the rest of the investigation through like this?

As their vehicle moved ever closer to the US checkpoint, Dazzler fixed her eyes on the large, white Peace Arch, illuminated in the dark, marking the border between the two countries. She read the inscription along the top of the Canadian side as they passed:

Brethren Dwelling Together In Unity.

As they passed, she looked back to read the inscription on the US side:

Children Of A Common Mother.

She thought it ironic to see those phrases now. Essentially, the mutants in this car had something in common in that they sought their fathers, and they were brethren of the mutant kind, dwelling together for the sole purpose of this mission, but certainly not in unity.

What a mess…

The next song started playing through Dazzler's earbuds, and it was one of her own. Again, she felt a pang of sorrow that she wasn't with her band right now, innocently playing music to a bar full of fans or rehearsing in Tommy's jam room.

"Shoot!" she hissed. She muted the music and immediately called Tommy's number, which she'd memorized because she'd called it so much over the past few months.

"Hello?" he answered.

"Hey, Tommy," she answered. "It's Dazzler."

"Hey!" he said cheerfully. "New phone, who dis?" He laughed.

She smiled. "Yeah, it's my dad's phone."

"You need a lift to rehearsal?"

"I'm sorry, man. Something's come up, and I can't make it tonight. You guys go ahead, and I'll see you at the gig this weekend."

"Everything all right?" He sounded concerned.

"Yeah. It's just something with my father. Sorry."

"It's all good. Let me know if you need anything. Otherwise, I'll see you Friday. Rock on!"

"Bye, Tommy." Dazzler hung up the call.

"You sound so sure you're going to make that gig," Rachel said.

Dazzler glanced into the rearview mirror again. *Was that just snark or a threat?* "I never miss a gig," she said. "The show must go on."

Rachel chuckled sardonically and shook her head, but the words resonated with Dazzler.

The show must go on...

Dazzler had to pick herself up, dust herself off, and perform the mission. She had to be a team player, at least on the outside.

"I spot several cameras," Sage said, tapping the side of her cybernetic glasses. "Polaris, when we get near, can you turn them away from us so they don't pick up Rachel?"

"Tell me where they are," Polaris said, and Sage handed the glasses to her. Polaris put them on, studying what Sage had seen, then nodded. "Got it."

"I can run interference," Rachel offered. "With the guard. I can confuse him. Run a little static inside his brain."

"Do it," Sage said. "Run the interference."

Dazzler looked at Sage. There she was taking the lead again.

"Yes, you do that," Dazzler reiterated, "and I'll run some of my own."

"How so?" Sage asked.

"I'll sparkle a little light into his eyes so he can't see Rachel properly," she answered.

Sage gave a nod, then glanced into the rearview mirror at Polaris. "Hide the glasses."

Polaris nodded and tucked them inside her coat.

When it came their turn to meet with the crossing guard, each member did as they'd planned. Polaris subtly turned the cameras away as they drove into position, and while the guard talked to Sage, studying her face tattoos, Rachel rested her elbow against the car door, fingers to her temple and eyes white but hidden by her hand.

As he examined their passports, the guard began to sound muddled and shook his head as though trying to clear his mind. When he came to Rachel's passport and tried to examine both her and her photo, Dazzler, with one earbud in, sparkled light his way, making him wince. The guard looked up at the checkpoint lights, thinking they were acting up. Between the mind interference and the light in his eyes, he must have been getting a migraine. He gave in, waving them through while rubbing his forehead.

Sage drove across the border, then smiled. "Nice work, team."

Dazzler shot her another look, then turned to Polaris. "Better put those cameras back in place. We wouldn't want *real* criminals crossing the border now."

Polaris, though still clearly angry with Dazzler, waved her hands over her shoulders, seeing it done.

An hour past the border in another clearing, they found Logan's X-Jet empty and waiting for them.

"Thanks, Logan," Polaris whispered as they climbed aboard. Sage took the pilot's chair while the rest of them strapped in behind her.

"What are you going to do about your X-Jet?" Dazzler asked Sage.

"It's cloaked for now. I'll pick it up later," Sage told her, getting them on their way to New York.

As much as Dazzler loved Canada, she was glad to be on her way home, though she had to admit, being strapped in opposite Polaris and Rachel felt incredibly awkward right now. Despite her trust issues, she knew she had to smooth things over from her outburst in order to continue on with her mission. It was a means to an end. She could play nice and still not trust anyone.

She swallowed and cleared her throat. "I'm sorry about before," she said to them. "In the car."

The two mutant women stared at her, emotionless, but their very presence was anything but: the fiery red of Rachel, the intense vibrant green of Polaris.

"I'm sorry the Scarlet Witch is your sister," Dazzler said gently to Polaris. "*Half*-sister. That must be hard to deal with."

Polaris offered no words in return but seemed to accept her apology before she looked away. Dazzler turned to Rachel.

"I know you don't like me," Dazzler said, "but don't assume that I align with Frost on whatever you hate her for. I'm Switzerland here. I don't align with either school, and I don't align with S.H.I.E.L.D. I'm an independent party."

"Yeah, that's what bothers me." Rachel stared at her. "You have allegiance to no one but yourself."

Dazzler stared back. "Maybe that's because no one has ever shown allegiance to me."

Silence filled the jet as, for once, Rachel did not have a snarky comment to return.

Dazzler broke eye contact, and that silence surrounded them for the rest of their journey.

Dazzler rode the subway with her fellow mutants. Given they were headed to the bar that S.H.I.E.L.D. had told them about, secrecy wasn't required, so they could travel freely. The jet had been fast, they'd landed just outside New York City after midnight and, continuing in their bubble of silence, Dazzler had them drop their bags in some cheap hotel rooms. She certainly wasn't going to invite these mutants to her apartment and into her life. Once they'd checked in, they headed into central Manhattan, to try to figure out a way inside this bar.

They arrived at the location of *The Gilded Arrow* and hung around on the street. As Bennett had said, the bar was located down an alleyway, and it was one that Dazzler hadn't even known existed. Their plan was simple enough: while Sage tested the venue's security with her glasses and haptic glove, Rachel read the minds of the few entering and exiting the alleyway, trying to scrape membership details or anything that would help them gain entry.

Dazzler noticed Polaris standing a few feet away on the street, staring down at her hands. She approached cautiously.

"Everything all right?" Dazzler asked.

Polaris shoved her hands into her coat pockets.

"Your powers," Dazzler said. "Tell me about it. It just comes and goes?"

Polaris looked at her, eyes still angry and on guard.

Dazzler knew she had to make amends. "I don't know what it's like. I don't know why, but my powers remained intact after M-Day."

"Guess you're lucky then," Polaris said, a coldness to her voice that matched the night air around them.

Sensing Polaris was not going to share, Dazzler turned and began to walk back to the others.

"They work just fine," Polaris said to her back. Dazzler turned around again to face her. "When I don't think about it," Polaris continued. "When I just react, they work. If I think about it too much… my own thoughts get in the way."

Dazzler nodded, then gave a sympathetic smile. "Yeah, sometimes my thoughts get in the way too."

Polaris's cold eyes warmed slightly, sensing Dazzler was offering another sort of apology.

"Their security is tight," Sage said, putting her haptic glove away.

"You can't break in?" Dazzler asked, turning her attention back to the task at hand.

"I never said that," Sage said with an air of offense, "but it will take some time."

Dazzler nodded and looked to Rachel, who was focused intently on a woman entering the alleyway. Once the woman had passed and Rachel's pale-eyed intense look eased off, Dazzler spoke. "Anything?"

Rachel looked back at them. "There's a daily password that needs to be spoken to the doorman."

"What is this, high school?" Polaris said.

"It's sent through an encrypted system daily," Rachel said.

"They have layers of security," Sage nodded. "They want those who attend to feel protected and safe."

"Yeah, so they can plot their nefarious deeds together," Dazzler said.

"Well, I have the password for tonight," Rachel said to them. "We could go in there right now."

"How many are inside?" Dazzler asked, rubbing the tired muscles of her neck.

Rachel moved over to the wall of the building, placed her hand against the brown bricks, and closed her eyes in concentration. After a moment she opened her eyes and looked back at them. "It's a full house."

"Give me a number?" Dazzler said.

Rachel shrugged. "Maybe fifty or sixty."

Dazzler looked at her watch. It was nearing two AM. She felt exhaustion tugging at her shoulders. She wasn't sure she was ready to face more trouble if things turned bad inside.

"I think we should come back tomorrow on opening, when there's less people inside. We want to talk to the owner, not some random bar-goers."

"And if our fathers die in the meantime?" Polaris asked.

Dazzler sighed. "And if we die because we're shot with exhaustion and not thinking clearly?" She looked to Rachel. "Are you up for scraping fifty minds for information right now?"

Rachel looked down at her feet and didn't respond.

"She's right," Sage said with finality. "We rest. Tomorrow, we crack the bar, then we crack the warehouse. We save our strength for that."

Dazzler could see that Polaris wanted to object, but even she was showing the signs of weariness, having used her powers several times in the past day.

"We rest," Dazzler said firmly. "We'll be back in a few hours, and we'll bring our A-game then."

CHAPTER FIFTEEN

Emma Frost stood in one of the abandoned Weapon X buildings at ground level, looking out at the almost frozen river in the morning light. Her mind was turning over rapidly. She'd needed to come up here to get some fresh air, to let her thoughts breathe and roam. After Dazzler had asked about the bar where Magneto had last been seen, *The Gilded Arrow*, she'd decided to do some digging.

She had called a number that had proven fruitful over the years, but it was one she used sparingly. They had never exchanged their names, only large sums of money or important favors. Her contact asked no personal questions and neither did she. All she ever did was give this person a name and pay them, or undertake a mutant favor, and they would trace detailed information and all online activity of the name requested: bank records, travel records, and the like, to help locate the target or at least provide information as to who the person was, their purchasing history, and their latest movements. This contact had the ability to dig deep without restriction. She didn't know how, and quite frankly she didn't want to know. All she wanted was the information.

And when she'd asked for details on *The Gilded Arrow*, she'd been intrigued by the data returned to her.

The Gilded Arrow was owned by a company called The Bronzed Wing. The Bronzed Wing was one of the companies that Triage and Tempus had found connected to Sanderson Holdings, which meant there was now a direct link between the MGH and the bar from which Magneto had gone missing.

Emma's source had provided ownership details of The Bronzed Wing, which was headed up by a woman named Cassandra Walsh. Emma had never heard of this person, so she'd arranged a secondary search on this name. And it was the response to this search that had left her intrigued, and quite frankly, stunned.

Walsh herself had a series of companies in her name, and Emma's contact had supplied a detailed listing of each company's board members. Having enacted searches for Emma over the years, this contact knew which names might be of interest to her, and sure enough they found one linked to Walsh that left Emma on high alert – a name that Emma was all too familiar with.

Shaw.

Sebastian Shaw.

Emma knew deep within her bones it had to be the Sebastian Shaw she knew, but she had to be absolutely sure. She immediately requested a third, specific search to confirm whether Cassandra Walsh was indeed linked to the Sebastian Shaw Emma knew.

The Sebastian Shaw of the Hellfire Club.

The man who called himself the Black King.

And it was this response she now waited for.

She paced the derelict building, her mind mulling over the possibilities. Could Sebastian Shaw, her old business partner and nemesis from the days of the Hellfire Club, be involved in this? And if so, what on earth was he up to?

Emma searched her own memories, wondering whether Shaw had ever mentioned Cassandra Walsh before, but she struggled to find any. Was this really the Shaw she knew? Was he involved, working deep in the shadows and staying out of sight? Or was this a crazy coincidence? Was Cassandra Walsh running her own game, alone?

Emma's phone rang, startling her. She quickly enabled the signal scrambling she'd uploaded onto the phone, ensuring anonymity, then answered it.

"Yes?" she said expectantly, noticing her heart beating faster than normal.

"I managed to trace details to confirm his identity," the computerized voice said. Her contact made every attempt to ensure they were untraceable. "It wasn't easy. I had to do a lot of digging, but, yes, this is your old business partner. Sebastian Shaw, son of Jacob Shaw. It's him."

Emma stared at the near-glacial river.

"Anything else you need?" the computerized voice asked her.

Emma, much like the river, was frozen in shock.

"Is there anything else you need?" the voice asked again.

She blinked and managed to get her mind moving again.

"Yes," she said. "I have one last trace for you to enact. I need to know where they are now and what they've been up to. I need to know everything about them."

"I bet I can guess who it is."

Her hand tightened around the phone. "Sebastian Shaw."

Dazzler managed to sleep a few hours out of exhaustion, but somehow still found the time to stare at the ceiling and think about all the ways she'd screwed up the previous day and all the mistrust she still had for everyone, wondered whether her father was dead and whether there was anything she could've done differently to avoid it, and contemplated how her life would never feel the same again if he was gone forever. Guilt weighed upon her heavily.

The thing that haunted her most, though, was Rachel's comment on the X-Jet.

"You have allegiance to no one but yourself."

She was right.

Part of Dazzler felt ashamed of this, but part of her knew she'd had no other choice. It was her base survival instinct. Her mother had abandoned her as a child. Her father had disowned her. She'd been used and mistreated by mutants, by S.H.I.E.L.D., by ex-boyfriends, by ex-bandmates and ex-band managers. She had good reason to be the emotional island that she was.

And yet, deep inside, she desperately longed to connect to the mainland.

To be like everyone else.

She wanted the friendships, love, and loyalty that others seemed to have. The happy families. But it felt so alien to her. With each betrayal and disappointment, she had learned to cage her heart. Despite being a strong mutant, the truth was she was just a fragile human underneath who hid behind her music. And if she didn't protect that fragile human, there would be nothing left of her. All the light energy in the world could not revive her shattered heart if it was broken one more time.

She had to protect that at all costs. But it was easier said than done. The biggest enemy she faced right now, the dark shadow that followed her everywhere, was mistrust. The fear of being betrayed. By humans, by mutants, by everyone. Mistrust was an enemy greater than any she'd faced before. And since waking, thanks to a dream she'd had, it was terrorizing her once again.

The dream had been strange. She just stood in that corridor in the subterranean depths of the New Charles Xavier School staring at Frost. Dazzler had been confused as to why she was there, and Frost merely smiled at her like the cat that got all the cream. And once Dazzler awoke, it was all she could think about: standing in that corridor, and Frost's smile. What was it about that space that haunted her so?

When she got sick of thinking, she decided to get out of bed and get to work. She contacted both Frost and Bennett to see if there had been any other updates overnight. There was none from either, but something felt off about each conversation, like they were holding back. And Dazzler hated that. Was her paranoia getting the better of her? Could she trust her own mind?

When Bennett asked to confirm her next steps, Dazzler simply said they would infiltrate and investigate the bar. She didn't mention their planned warehouse visit. In a way it was a test. The information on the warehouse had come from Frost, so it was assumed that S.H.I.E.L.D. wasn't aware of this connection. But Dazzler wasn't sure she believed that. Frost did scrape the information by mind-reading, so it could be possible that S.H.I.E.L.D. didn't know about the shipment. But then again, if Frost had discovered that Dazzler's father had a connection with Rosenthorpe, Dazzler had to assume that S.H.I.E.L.D. with all its technology, data mining, and spies, would eventually stumble across this fact too. Especially if Rosenthorpe hung in the same circles as the man Dennis Stanton, who wound up in the hospital. Could S.H.I.E.L.D. have somehow traced the MGH to Rosenthorpe's warehouse already?

But if S.H.I.E.L.D. knew this, Bennett hadn't mentioned it. She couldn't put it past them to have discovered the link and then intentionally excluded this information from her. Maybe they pushed an update through to her old phone, which was now back in Vancouver. Which was another strange thing because Bennett had not mentioned this to her at all, about her being back in New York, calling from a new number, and her old phone being in Vancouver. Was S.H.I.E.L.D. testing *her*? Her loyalty? Testing whether she would share information with them?

But what if they legitimately didn't know about the warehouse? It would not be perceived well by S.H.I.E.L.D. if they discovered she intentionally withheld this information. She would burn the trust they had with her as Mutant Liaison. Was it smart to make an enemy of S.H.I.E.L.D.?

But trust had to be earned, and S.H.I.E.L.D. had not earned it yet.

She heard the door of the next room close, and she looked out the peephole to see Sage, wearing her cybernetic glasses, walking toward the elevator. Dazzler's mind raced, wondering where she was going, and wondering whether those glasses had hearing capability. Could Sage, with her technology, be

listening through the walls to Dazzler's conversations? She tensed, suddenly wondering how much Sage was reporting back to Frost.

Or to someone else…

With Sage reporting to Frost, Polaris and Rachel reporting to Logan, and Dazzler reporting to S.H.I.E.L.D., they were most definitely a team of fractured alliances.

Which made it a difficult team to try to lead.

She turned away from the door, squeezing her eyes closed and taking a long, calming breath. She had to steady herself. She had to remain calm. Paranoia would keep her safe, but too much would screw up her mind and force mistakes. She had to find the middle ground, the balance in between the two.

Dazzler and her team arrived at *The Gilded Arrow* right at opening hours – eleven AM. Twenty minutes passed before the first guest arrived that Rachel could scrape the password from – a man in his mid-thirties, dressed in an expensive suit and styled very city-chic. As soon as Rachel had the password she gave it to Sage, and they set forth to infiltrate, having cobbled a ragged cover story together from bits and pieces Rachel had obtained the night before.

They located the bar's rusted iron door, hidden from view of the street by some dumpsters and almost camouflaged against the surrounding brown brick. Unsurprisingly, they found the door locked.

Sage knocked, and a few seconds passed before a peep slot slid across and two brown eyes stared back at them.

"Can I help you?" a man's voice asked. The words were polite enough, but his tone was gruff.

"The arrow flies south today," Sage told him.

He stared at her a moment, then the others, then shut the peep slot. Dazzler looked at Sage questioningly before they heard bolts scraping on the other side of the door. It opened, and a large, barrel-bellied man with four-day growth stared back at them.

"Haven't seen you here before," he said, eyeing them suspiciously.

"No. We've been out of town," Sage said, applying her Eastern European accent thickly. "But I'm very much looking forward to my visit."

"Your membership is local?" the man asked.

"No," Sage smiled. "I am with the London club, but I was told courtesies would be extended here for me and my guests. Was I informed wrong?"

He eyed them for a moment, then shook his head. "No. Of course not. Come in." He stepped back and ushered them through.

They stepped into the dimly lit bar that looked like it was right out of the 1920s. With mosaic tiled floors, dark wood bar and booths, gilded lightshades and tap fittings, it was a rich man's dive bar. Behind the bar itself, the walls were mirrored and lined with row upon row of bottles, and at the far end was a straight staircase, leading to the second floor. Based on the security to enter and its hidden location, Dazzler wondered just what was up that staircase. And more to the point, she was starting to wonder whether this place was more than a membership-only, exclusive bar. Was this place some kind of secret society?

The ultimate question, though: was Magneto a member?

Or was he merely a guest on the night he disappeared? And if Squires was a member, who else might be? Who was inside the night it happened?

As they moved across to the bar, Dazzler noticed smooth jazz playing through the speakers, the sound of trumpets tingling her veins. The bar was empty except for the doorman, an attractive, expensively dressed barmaid, and the guest they'd followed inside, who sat in a booth alone, reading a tablet.

They ordered a round of sodas from the barmaid, who stared back at them. "Just soda? That's all you want?"

Dazzler nodded. "We're here for a meeting."

"Oh." The barmaid smiled, glancing at the guest in the booth. Like the doorman, her eyes were suspicious of the new faces.

"Is the owner around?" Dazzler asked brazenly. "That's who we're here to meet."

The barmaid glanced to the doorman. "Davis? She says she's here to meet the owner."

"Well, that can't be," Davis said, stepping forward. "Because they tell me when they're expecting someone, and they didn't mention you."

"It was a last-minute thing." Dazzler gave her bombshell smile. "May we speak with them?"

He studied her carefully. "You're here for a meeting and don't know their name?"

"It was recommended I speak with them," Dazzler said. "Time was of the essence. I was only given the bar name."

"And yet you're supposed to be members?" he said accusingly to Sage, who smiled back, but her face was otherwise vague. Dazzler figured she was already looking at something through her glasses.

"May we speak with them?" Dazzler asked him.

"You can't waltz in and expect their time," Davis said, mistrust flaring in his eyes now. "If you knew them, you'd know that."

"We don't know them personally, no," Dazzler said, "but you could say they're a friend of a friend."

"And who's the friend?" he asked.

Dazzler leaned her elbows back on the bar, as a saxophone poured through the speakers now, warming her veins. "Magneto."

The barmaid stilled. Davis stared at her in silence.

"I take it you know who that is," Dazzler said.

Davis took a deep breath, and then he looked to the guest in the booth. "Excuse me, sir, but would you mind adjourning upstairs for a moment?"

The guest looked at him, then the women, then collected his tablet and did as asked, disappearing up the stairs.

Dazzler watched him go then turned back to Davis. "Let's cut to the chase. Magneto's missing, and I think you know that. He was last seen entering your bar. Did you think that no one would come looking for him? I mean, it's Magneto we're talking about."

"What makes you think you'll find him here?" Davis asked.

"Oh, we don't think he's still here," Dazzler said. "We just know that he was last seen here. So, you know, we'd like to find out what happened here that night."

"If you're members of this bar, then you know we offer discretion," Davis said. "So, I'm afraid we're legally bound to confidentiality."

"The law would suggest otherwise in the circumstance of a missing person," Dazzler said.

Davis chuckled as he ran his eyes over her leather jumpsuit. "Well, see, you don't look like law officers, so we don't need to say squat."

Dazzler gave another bombshell smile. "Don't let this jumpsuit fool you. I know a thing or two about the law."

"Until you can show me a badge, sweetheart, you got nothing."

Dazzler displayed her S.H.I.E.L.D. credentials. "Heard of these guys?"

He looked at it. "Yeah, they were powerful once," he said, then smiled, "before they were disbanded."

"Heard of mutants?" Polaris said, slicing her hand through the air and scraping a metal table against the door, blocking it.

Davis spun around at the sound, saw the blocked door, then looked back at Polaris. He quickly regained his carefree composure. "Well, you're definitely not members of this bar then, because we don't allow your kind here."

"No, we don't," a woman's voice said from the top of the stairs.

They turned to see a woman in her forties, expensively attired, caramel-blonde hair, her face cast in shadow from the overhead lights. Dazzler couldn't see her eyes but noted her sharp cheekbones.

"Magneto was here. He's a mutant," Polaris said.

"And the person who brought him inside has been penalized," the woman said.

"Who brought him inside?" Dazzler asked.

"Our membership information is private," the woman answered. "Regardless, if we don't allow mutants here," she continued, her voice polite but threatening, "that means you used illegal methods to gain the access phrase for today's entry.

Which means" – she smiled – "if anyone is going to get in trouble with the law, it's you."

"How much does Senator Earnest pay for his membership?" Dazzler asked, leaning off the bar and turning toward the woman. "He's a member, right? Like his legal aide, Toby Squires."

The woman stared back silently from her shadows, no smile visible now.

"He was the one meeting with Magneto here the night he went missing." Dazzler shrugged again. "If he or your bar were to be publicly implicated in the disappearance, well… that would not be a good look, would it?"

"What happens after someone leaves my bar, is none of my business," the woman said.

"Maybe," Dazzler said, "but still, you want to keep this place secret, don't you? I mean, that's how you get your clientele, right? You've created an exclusive hideaway here. It won't be so secret if the press gets hold of it. Imagine the tabloids hanging around out front."

The woman smiled again. "What makes you so sure that Magneto is the victim here?"

"You tell us," Polaris blurted, stepping toward her. "We're all ears."

The woman grimaced. "Tell the redhead to stop trying to get inside my head. I wasn't born yesterday."

Rachel shifted uncomfortably, her whitened eyes turning green again.

"Just tell us one thing," Dazzler said. "Who did he leave with?"

"I can't tell you that," she said. "Now go or I'll have you thrown out."

Polaris laughed. "By who? Your *lone* doorman?"

They heard footsteps, and suddenly saw more large men lined up behind the woman at the top of the stairs. Dazzler counted five of them, but who knew how many more were obscured from her view.

Dazzler sized them up then looked back at the woman. "We just want a name. Did he leave with Squires?"

"Get out," the woman said with disinterest and walked away.

"Last chance," Davis said, punching a fist into his palm. "Before me and my buddies get to work."

"Hey, what are you doing?" the barmaid asked Sage. Dazzler saw Sage's hands were behind her back, her haptic glove on and her fingers moving about. "Davis–"

"We can take these guys!" Polaris said, adamantly, overriding the barmaid while Rachel's eyes went white again. "We need answers."

Dazzler glanced at Sage who gave a subtle shake of her head. Dazzler wasn't sure what she'd been doing with the glove, but she must've found something, and Dazzler wanted to know what it was. If they went into battle with these guys, she might not. She'd save the fight for another day.

She looked over at the doorman and flashed another smile. "Sure thing, Davis," she said. "Come on girls, let's go. This bar sucks."

Davis gave a smug laugh. Dazzler wanted to wipe the smile of his face but held herself back.

They moved to the door, and Polaris angrily shoved the table aside with a flick of her hands, then flung the door open wide.

CHAPTER SIXTEEN

Dazzler watched as Polaris strode ahead, green coat flapping in the late autumn air.

"Polaris!" Dazzler called after her.

She whipped around in a ball of fury. "We could've beaten them! Why did we leave?"

Dazzler looked at Sage. "I think Sage has something."

Sage stared ahead, absorbed in her cybernetic glasses.

"Sage?" Dazzler prodded her.

Sage's attention came back to them. "I managed to access their security footage inside the bar. Squires left Magneto in a booth. Soon after, Magneto looked weary. He went to leave and collapsed. I think his drink was spiked."

"So, it was Squires," Polaris said, her cheeks and nose turning pink against the cold, or perhaps the anger that still flushed through her.

"The bartender poured the drink," Sage explained. "The waitress took his order. At no time was Squires involved."

"It had to be him!" Polaris said.

"It sounds like the footage doesn't prove that," Dazzler said. "And we need proof."

"But if the bartender spiked his drink," Polaris argued, "he did so at the orders of someone in that bar. We need to go back and see that woman!"

Dazzler turned to Rachel. "You couldn't access her mind?"

Rachel shook her head. "It was weird…"

"Was she was blocking you? Is she a mutant?" Dazzler asked.

"No," Rachel shook her head again. "She wasn't blocking me. I felt nothing. It was like… like she wasn't actually there."

"She wasn't," Sage said. "She was a projection. You couldn't access her mind because she wasn't there to access."

"Then where was she?" Polaris asked.

Sage shrugged. "I don't know. But I used my glasses to scan the place and read her heat signature. She wasn't there. Neither were her security men. They were holograms."

"So why did we leave?" Polaris said, outraged.

"There was no one else in the building involved with Magneto's disappearance," Sage told her. "And the footage showed Magneto being carried out the back door."

"By who?" Polaris asked.

"By the bartender and doorman, not Davis, another man. Both came back inside the bar moments later."

"So, they either dumped him in the back alley behind the bar to sleep it off," Dazzler said, "or they handed Magneto over to someone else."

Sage gave a nod. "And now we've shown our faces, I doubt we'll ever see that bartender or doorman at this bar again. They won't let us near them to ask the question."

Polaris cursed as she turned and kicked a small pile of snow.

Dazzler looked back at Rachel. "What I don't get is, how did that woman know someone was trying to infiltrate her mind?"

"My eyes go white," Rachel said. "It's not exactly subtle."

"Their security was next level," Sage said. "I detected all sorts of scanning systems. Perhaps they picked up on abnormal brain activity in Rachel." She placed her hands on her hips, shoulders softening a little in defeat. "They knew we were mutants before Polaris pushed that table against the door."

Polaris kicked the snow again, growling.

Dazzler understood her frustration. Magneto had been there just days ago. He'd walked in and been carried out, and Polaris wanted to know who was responsible. Dazzler looked back at Sage. "Can you find out who she was?"

"I'll try." Sage walked ahead as she made a call. Dazzler noticed Rachel watched Sage carefully, following her. Dazzler turned back to Polaris, who still steamed in the snow.

"At least we know what happened now," Dazzler said softly.

"He was betrayed, his drink spiked, and he was carried out like a piece of trash," Polaris said, brow furrowed. "Is that supposed to make me feel better?"

"At least you know," Dazzler said. "I don't know what happened to my father and Rachel doesn't know what happened to hers. You have some answers at least." Dazzler began to follow the others. "Come on," she called over her shoulder, ditching her burner phone in the trash and switching to a new one she'd purchased earlier that morning. "Let's prepare to hit that warehouse."

Emma Frost sat in her office, unsure as to what her next move should be. Her contact had been unable to provide her with any tangible information on Sebastian Shaw. His bank accounts, hidden under the veil of his many decoy companies, had shown a large withdrawal, then no movement for a couple of months now. The man himself was a ghost online. His tax records erased, no social media presence, and he didn't even have an email address. If there was one thing she had to give Shaw credit for, it was that he was smart and knew how to operate his many enterprises off the record. Years working with him at the Hellfire Club had taught her that. If there was a loophole, Shaw would find it. And if he couldn't find it, he'd employ someone who could. Shaw always had the best people around him. After all, Emma had been one of those people once. That was until she realized Shaw was a cancer that had to be cut out of her life.

Curious about this lack of digital presence, Emma had visited Cerebra and attempted to undertake a search for him.

And just like Magneto and Scott, Shaw was nowhere to be found.

Which only left her perplexed.

Like herself, Magneto had a long history with Shaw. Could the two be reacquainted? Was this why Magneto and Scott had told her little before they'd left the school? Were they up to something she was not to be a part of?

Emma didn't want to believe Scott or Magneto would betray her, but she hadn't survived this long by being naïve, either. Her history with Magneto was long, and her history with Scott had been deep, but just like the seasons, things could change. They certainly had with Scott. Their relationship hadn't been the same for some time.

And nothing had been quite the same since M-Day. Nor

had they been the same since the Phoenix incident, when Scott had taken Emma's portion of the Phoenix and had killed Charles Xavier in the battle that had ensued. Afterward, Scott and Magneto had rescued her from the custody of the New Avengers, and though she had been angry with Scott at the time, for taking her portion of Phoenix, she'd agreed to join the two and had been with them ever since. She knew Scott carried a deep regret over the death of Charles and had been forever changed by the events, and not for the better. Could she be entirely sure that the Phoenix did not still possess a part of him?

But how did this tie in to the MGH? Or Shaw?

There was a chance, however slim of course, that like Magneto and Cyclops, Shaw, too, had somehow become a victim in whatever was going on. Perhaps Magneto had reached out to him for help when trying to figure out who was distributing the MGH? Shaw had a long history in the business world, and he had powerful contacts, many a legacy from the days of the Hellfire Club.

But how did this explain the involvement of Cassandra? Could she be behind the disappearances? Had she somehow risen up and bested her business partner?

Something didn't sit right with Emma. She struggled to reconcile the thought of Shaw being innocent or a victim. If there was one thing she'd learned over the years it was that the self-proclaimed Black King was not to be trusted. He was a powerful mutant who, though once an ally, had soon turned on her. Though the truth was, it was *she* who had turned on him first. She had betrayed him by helping his fiancée to escape the life of the Hellfire Club, faking her death. Frightened of Emma's capability, Shaw had wanted her out of the way where she did not pose a threat to him and his business. Try as he might over the years, he had failed to get rid of her. It had been a long time since she'd heard his name, and it bothered her that she heard it again now. She thought those days were over, that Shaw had disappeared into history, and she'd moved on. But now?

Was Shaw back?

Was he angling at another way to get at her by making Magneto and Cyclops disappear? Or could Shaw have turned over a new leaf? Could she give him the benefit of the doubt and think him a victim like Magneto and Cyclops? Why were these mutants disappearing? Why could she not locate them on Cerebra?

Were they dead?

Or were her powers failing her?

She needed to know the truth, and time was running out.

Desperate times called for desperate measures. There was one last thing she could try, but it was a risk. If she did what she was planning to do, and Shaw *was* involved, it would expose that she was on to his game. But what else could she do?

It was problematic, as it would mean leaving the school, but if she called Magik back and left her in charge, Emma hoped that the sorceress alone would be enough to protect the young mutants.

Emma Frost knocked on the large oak door of the expensive house. She was in upstate New York, at the home of Cassandra Walsh. It was another favor she owed her contact, who'd given her the address.

A butler answered the door, though if Emma was to hazard a guess, she'd say he was more of a security guard. Either way, like Shaw, Cassandra had wealth and resources, and no doubt the power that came with the two.

"Yes?" the man asked. He was in his early forties, fit and toned, and his eyes sharp and alert.

"Hello." Emma smiled, softening her blue eyes as she did. She'd made sure to wear her fitted white leather X-suit. "I'd like to see Cassandra Walsh, please."

"And you are?"

"A friend of a friend," she said, tucking her long blonde hair behind her jeweled ear.

The man smiled with amusement. "I'm afraid she's busy."

"Tell her I would've gone to see her at *The Gilded Arrow*, but I wasn't in the mood to speak with a hologram today," she said, using the information Sage had passed to her earlier.

"How did you get this address?" he asked.

Emma smiled again. "Like Cassandra, I have my ways. Now, please. Tell her I'm here. I think she'll want to see me."

"And why is that?" he asked again, not budging from the doorway.

She stared at the man, her smile in place, as she gently pushed a thought into his mind.

"Because I'm a mutant like her associate, Shaw."

The man stepped back in surprise.

"I just want to talk," Emma said, calmly. "That's all."

The man stared at her a moment, alarmed, then closed the door in her face, locking it. Pressing into his mind again, however, she could tell he was on his way to tell Walsh of her arrival.

Emma waited patiently at the door, glancing around the rich neighborhood. She noticed a man sitting in a parked car nearby, watching her carefully as he spoke into a comms piece.

Another member of Walsh's security, she guessed. Emma waved and smiled at him, wondering how many more there were. Sage had told her there'd been several in the bar, but they may have been holograms. Emma had to play this carefully. She was good at what she did, but even she couldn't best an unseen bullet or a knife.

Eventually the door opened, and the man stood there again. He said nothing but ushered her inside. She smiled and quickly scraped his mind for a name.

"Thanks, Steve," she said, and he blanched in response.

She stepped into an ornate living room decorated in shades of white and pastels, with exotic flowers and expensive sculptures and artwork. When she turned back to Steve, she saw Cassandra Walsh standing beside him. Her caramel hair was set in a stylish bob cut, and she was adorned with diamond jewelry and an expensive dress suit.

"May I help you?" Walsh asked with the charm of a practiced politician. Her voice was deeper than she'd expected, and though her tone was nice enough, Emma still caught a threatening undertone.

"I want to speak with you about your associate, Sebastian Shaw."

"I don't know any Sebastian Shaw."

"Yes, you do. That's why you came running down here so fast when I mentioned him."

Walsh stared at her.

"When did you last hear from him?" Emma asked, glancing casually around the room.

"May I ask what business it is of yours?"

"You may." Emma smiled. She could also muster up the

charm of a greasy politician. "Some friends of mine have disappeared. Mutants. Sebastian's name is associated, and I can't find any trace of him. So, either he's in hiding because he's up to something, or he's disappeared like my friends. So, the question is, do you want to help me find him?"

"No, I don't," Walsh said bluntly. "Whatever he's involved with, it's got nothing to do with me." She turned to walk away.

"You met some friends of mine earlier today." Emma stopped her. "At your bar. They were searching for Magneto."

Walsh turned back to face her.

"They weren't given a warm reception," Emma said. "So, I was forced to come here."

"They made accusations that were unfounded. And now you're here, harassing me. I ought to call the police."

"Do it." Emma smiled. "I'd very much like to get to the bottom of why Magneto was drugged in your bar and why no one's talking about it." She moved casually over to Walsh's white leather couch and sat down, crossing her legs. "I'm happy to wait."

"Get out of my house," Walsh said, eyes like iron marbles as any charm completely evaporated.

"*Make me,*" Emma pushed into her mind.

Walsh's hard exterior twitched. "Stay out of my head."

"*Make me,*" Emma pushed again, studying her nails.

Walsh gave a flick of her head to Steve, and he grabbed Emma by the arm and yanked her up from the couch. As she got to her feet, she quickly engaged her diamond form, her skin morphing into solid glass, and ripped her arm back. Steve stumbled, staring at her smooth, silvery-grey form, unsure how to deal with her. Walsh, too, was ruffled.

Emma smiled at them both. "That's no way to treat a lady."

"I have nothing to do with Sebastian, so get out!" Walsh said.

"But I think you do," Emma said, still in diamond form. "Magneto is an old acquaintance of Sebastian, and he disappeared from your bar. That's too much of a coincidence for me. You're involved. So, what is he up to?"

"I told you, I don't know," Walsh said.

Emma had had enough of the games now. She turned her face to Steve's and thrust her mind at his so fast it was like clapping his head between two symbols. He instantly fell unconscious and onto the couch. She looked back at Walsh who tried to run for the stairs, but Emma thrust her mind at hers too, though not as hard. Walsh fell to her knees, gripping her head in a daze.

Emma walked toward her casually, stepping off the plush carpet of the living room and onto the expensive tiles of the foyer, her heeled boots tapping with each step. Walsh rolled over to sit on the floor and tried to push herself away, but it was useless because Emma's mind was still connected to hers as though tethered with invisible tentacles. Tentacles that began to probe and scrape her brain.

"You can tell me, or I can take it from you," Emma said, with a low warning voice. "Now, I normally believe in a woman's choice" – she came to a stop by Walsh's side, staring down at her, still in her diamond form – "but when I take on this form, I lose all empathy. So, I'll only give you this opportunity once."

Walsh looked at her, eyes shining with resistance. "I'll tell you nothing, *mutant*." The way she said "mutant" was akin to speaking of vermin. Emma did not like that one bit. She knelt down beside the woman and pressed her hands either side of her face.

"Fine," Emma said, coldly. "I'll take it then."

The woman tried half-heartedly to fight Emma, but every hit or scratch slid right off her diamond form. Emma tuned her out like a buzzing fly, as the information from Walsh's mind flowed into her own. She moved quickly through the banks of Walsh's memory, plucking them out, one by one. She saw Sebastian, saw him meeting with Walsh, saw bank accounts filling with money, saw the bar opening, saw all manner of important names and faces in the bar. She saw another night at the bar where Judge Carter Blaire drank with another man. Yet another night, she saw Magneto drinking with the same man.

Emma pulled back from Walsh's mind as she realized this man must be Toby Squires. The man, it seemed, also had an affiliation with Dazzler's father. Just like Rosenthorpe.

She thrust her mind further into Walsh's, scoured and scoured, came across a phone conversation between Shaw and Walsh, heard Shaw saying: "You work for me now. I'll ensure your success."

Emma saw them raise a toast and heard Walsh say: "To the future." Then Emma was back at the bar, saw Walsh meeting with Rosenthorpe, saw the two of them toasting to something–

A gunshot sounded, and glass smashed. Emma pulled her mind back and ducked low. She saw the man from the vehicle out front trying to get inside. Emma looked back at Walsh and gave her mind a thunderclap like Steve's, knocking her out, then let her go, standing as the man broke the door down and fired at her again.

The bullets ricocheted off her diamond form as she strode angrily toward him. Realizing the gun was useless he tossed it aside, and for some reason thought his brute strength would take her down instead. He charged at her like a gridiron player, but she quickly stepped aside, thrust her arm out, caught him across the shoulders, and sent his dumb human form flying backward into the tiled floor, where he knocked himself out cold.

She looked at him and shook her head. "As I told your friend, that's no way to treat a lady."

With that, Emma strode out the front door, deciding what to do next. She couldn't just leave Walsh and her guards there. No doubt a nosy neighbor heard the shots and was calling the police right now. That wouldn't do at all.

She decided what to do quickly, focusing her mind hard on that of Maria Hill's.

"Frost," Hill's terse voice sounded inside her mind. "Breaking and entering someone's mind is a criminal offense, you understand that?"

"I have a suspect for you to interrogate in the MGH case you're working with Alison Blaire," Frost projected back, turning to look at the street name and number, and project that too. "I just gave you the address. I'd hurry before they wake up or the police take them."

Frost severed the connection, then calmly got into her car and drove away.

She didn't know if she could trust S.H.I.E.L.D., but she couldn't leave Walsh free to go about her business and warn Shaw either. This way, S.H.I.E.L.D. would take her off the street for at least twenty-four hours to enable Emma time to find him.

CHAPTER SEVENTEEN

Dazzler squatted low behind a clump of trees, eyeing the warehouse. Located off the New Jersey Turnpike and not far from the Port of Newark, it was a white-walled, rectangular, modern building, surrounded by lush green landscaping and many parked semi-trailers, waiting to be filled and sent on their way the next morning. The building was large, and Dazzler knew there was going to be some ground to cover inside.

Polaris and Rachel were to her left, and a few feet away, in a more elevated position, Sage scanned the building with her cybernetic glasses.

After a few moments, Sage ran low back toward them.

"There are two guards on patrol at the entrance, six security cameras on this half of the building, and from my scans I detect the warehouse is guarded by an Axxon-43 alarm system," Sage said.

"What does that mean?" Dazzler asked.

"It's a secure system with several failsafe backup measures in place."

"So how do we get inside?" Polaris asked.

"I'll try to hack it," Sage said. "If I fail, you and Dazzler will need to destroy it, the whole electrical system, back-up generators, everything. But that in itself will trigger an alert with an external security company, which means we won't have long to look around inside before the cavalry come."

"So, we need to get inside legitimately without any damage," Dazzler said.

"How strong is your mind?" Sage asked Rachel. "Could you control one of the guards?"

Rachel considered this. "I can try. But wouldn't it be easier if we just knock them out and take their passes or whatever we need to get inside?"

"We'd need their fingerprints and irises," Sage said. "Probably access codes too."

"I'll dazzle the guards," Dazzler said to Rachel. "That should make it easier for you to control them. Once we're inside, we send them to sleep."

"And what about the guards inside?" Polaris asked.

"I didn't detect any," Sage said, tapping her glasses.

"You can X-ray with those things?" Rachel asked.

Sage gave a nod. "I'll start the hack and see if I can put the security cameras on a loop." She raised her haptic glove and began tapping the air before her, while the others waited patiently.

Dazzler scanned the warehouse again, wondering what they would find inside, and wondering again about Rosenthorpe's connection with her father. It creeped her out to know that Rosenthorpe had been to see her perform, this man who was possibly distributing MGH derived from her. Had he seen her perform just the once, or had he been stalking her intentionally? Had he known she was a mutant? Had he known the MGH had been derived from her? Did that mean her father also knew she was a mutant? She felt a cold chill run through her body that wasn't from the night air. She'd worked so hard to keep her mutant abilities secret from her father, and the chance that he might now know scared her to her core. What would he think of her?

"Done," Sage said, looking back at Dazzler with triumph. "The cameras are on loop."

"OK," Dazzler said, shaking out her long blonde hair. "My turn."

She began walking down the road that led to the guardhouse out front of the warehouse, placing an earbud in one ear. She hit play on a great pop-rock song on her phone, the kind she would shake her booty to on a dancefloor.

It didn't take long for the male guards to notice her. A young, lanky one stood by the gate, mouth agape, while the older, rounder and bearded one sat inside the guard booth.

"You lost?" the older one asked, looking her up and down.

"Wait. You know who that is?" the younger one asked him, then looked back to her in awe. "Are you … are you Dazzler?"

She gave her best bombshell smile. "I sure am, honey."

She raised her hands and shot bubbles of iridescent light toward them.

"What the … ?" the older guard said, utterly mesmerized by the balls of light floating around his head. They both stumbled back as though drunk, while her mutant team swiftly flanked her.

"Which one?" Dazzler asked Rachel, as she paused the music in her ear.

"The younger guy," she said. "He'll be easier to manipulate."

Dazzler nodded, then gave the older man a strong blast of light energy, which hit him between the eyes, knocking him out. She quickly swooped inside the guard booth to catch his fall and lay him on the ground.

"Confirming the cameras are still on loop," Sage said. "Let's move."

Dazzler and Polaris each took an arm of the younger, dazzled guard and began to move him toward the thick metal gates, while Rachel followed, hand to temple, eyes whitened, as she focused on controlling his mind.

They reached the gate and the guard stood there, dazed.

"Open the gate," Rachel ordered him.

They watched with bated breath as he swayed and stared at the gate's bars.

"*Open* the gate," Rachel said again, firmly.

This time he raised his hand to punch in an access code on the keypad. Sage swooped in close to watch the numbers as he did.

"Got it," she said, swooping back out and scanning their surroundings with her glasses.

The thick gray metal gates began to slide apart. As soon as the gap was big enough, Dazzler and Polaris pushed the guard through, and they made their way toward the warehouse entry doors.

"What if there's cameras inside?" Dazzler asked Sage as they made the doors. "You'll need to loop them too."

Sage nodded. "I'll try."

The young guard seemed to be coming out of his forced reverie, blinking and looking at Dazzler with a big starstruck smile.

"Not yet, honey." She smiled and waved her hand over his face, sending more mesmerizing bubbles of light at him. "Rachel?"

Rachel moved up behind the guard, hand to temple, as her whitened eyes bore into the back of his skull. "Open the door. Let us in."

The guard stared at the door with his intoxicated sway, bubbles of light floating around his face.

"I could get us through that door," Polaris said impatiently.

"We can't risk tripping anything," Sage said, her back to them as she continued to scan their surroundings.

"Open the door," Rachel said firmly to the guard. "Raise your palm to the console. Place your eye to the scanner. *Now*."

The guard looked at both the console and the scanner. Dazzler leaned in and whispered in his ear.

"If you open the door, I'll sing you a song."

The guard gave her a goofy grin.

"*Open* the door," Rachel demanded, sweat beginning to shine across her forehead.

The guard raised his hand to the console plate, and it scanned his print. Rachel grabbed the back of his neck and moved his eye toward the scanner. It read his iris, then seconds later they received a message on the console.

Access approved.

As soon as the door unlocked, they entered, looking around carefully. The warehouse was in darkness. The only light came from outside the door they had just entered.

"Rachel," Dazzler whispered. "Sense anyone?"

The redhead stepped forward and scanned the dark cavernous space before her. After a few moments, her body relaxed and she turned back to Dazzler. "It's clear," she said, then glanced curiously at Sage. "I sense no one, outside of us."

Sage locked eyes with Rachel and gave a nod. Something was going on between those two, and as soon as they were out of this warehouse, Dazzler was going to find out.

Dazzler turned to the guard.

"Thanks, honey. It's time for a rest now." She shot a burst of light energy that instantly rendered him unconscious like the guard out front, then she and Polaris laid him on the ground, and dragged him out of sight.

"Any chance we could get some non-blinding light?" Polaris said. Though Sage had night-vision capability through her glasses, the rest of them were hindered by the darkness.

Dazzler unpaused the song on her phone and let it play, low, through one ear. Though she had the ability to store excess light energy, like any cache, it could run low, so at times like this, she preferred to keep her charge through music. She spread her arms wide, sending a soft pool of light from her fingertips.

Through the light they saw the warehouse was effectively one massive room filled with row upon row of stacked cargo, running east to west, and each row was at least five racks high. The cargo came in all shapes and sizes, each packaged in different ways.

"You go that way." Sage pointed off to the right. "Keep your light with them. I'll go this way." She began to head toward the rows of crates on the left.

"No," Dazzler said firmly, stopping her. "You stay with us."

Sage looked back at her. "There is much to search. We have to find concrete evidence linking Sanderson Holdings and MGH."

"I don't care. We stay together." Dazzler wasn't saying it for Sage's protection. She was saying it because she wanted to keep her eyes on all of them, at all times.

"I can take care of myself," Sage said, squaring her strong shoulders.

Dazzler lifted her glowing hand to shine the light directly on her, reflecting brightly in the woman's cybernetic glasses. "I'm sure you can, but like Frost said, we're stronger together." Dazzler wasn't sure how strong Sage's link to Frost was, but she knew Frost's words would carry more weight with Sage than Dazzler's own.

Sage relented and waved Dazzler forward. It was clear the woman didn't agree with the tactics, but they didn't have time to argue. "Let's move."

Dazzler took the lead as Polaris and Rachel walked behind her and Sage took up the rear, scanning the warehouse behind them.

"Keep projecting, Rachel," Dazzler said.

"I am," she said with a tinge of annoyance.

"So how do we find the shipment of MGH?" Polaris asked.

"I need to find a console," Sage said, glancing around at the roof before she spotted something. She moved ahead of them and pointed. "Head for the cables."

Dazzler turned her light in the direction Sage pointed and saw a metal pillar over the top of some nearby racks. The pillar was entwined with cables that led up into the ceiling space. They began to head for it, before Sage, now in front, stopped abruptly, holding out her hands to stop the rest of them too.

"Polaris, camera. Turn it away from us."

Dazzler made her light intensely bright and aimed it directly into the camera lens, as Polaris stepped forward with a look of determination, waved her hand upward, and turned it to focus on the roof.

They continued forward, quickly but carefully, eyeing their surroundings, as they made their way to the pillar. As Sage had predicted, they found a small console attached to it. Sage immediately set about trying to access the data, while the rest of them spread out to watch each entrance of the row.

Dazzler glanced at Rachel, whose head was lowered and eyes fixed in concentration.

"You're scanning for others?" she asked.

"No," Rachel said sarcastically, "I was thinking about what I'd have for lunch tomorrow."

"Scan this," Dazzler said, directing a specific thought to Rachel, one not best said aloud.

Rachel smirked, clawing her hand and mimicking a hissing cat.

"Focus!" Sage admonished them.

Dazzler watched as Sage, not having any luck with the console itself, slid on her haptic glove, tapped her glasses, then set to work finding another way.

"How are you going to find evidence?" Polaris asked. "I'm sure they didn't load the cargo description in the system as MGH."

"Frost wrote down a consignment number when she hacked Rosenthorpe's brain," Sage said.

"You have the number?" Polaris asked.

"AFSS-001-975381246," Sage recalled.

"When did she give you that?" Dazzler asked, prickling. "She didn't give that to me."

"This morning," Sage replied, getting back to work. Dazzler stared at her, wondering what else Frost had forgotten to mention to her. After a moment, Sage turned to Dazzler with an annoyed furrow in her brow, then looked down at her feet. Dazzler eyed her boots and realized she'd been tapping her foot to the music in her ears.

"Oops," she said, holding still.

Rachel shook her head at Dazzler dismissively, then turned away. Dazzler flared her light at the woman's back, then noticed Polaris staring at her, but her face was hard to read.

"What?" Dazzler asked.

Polaris looked away too. Dazzler wasn't sure whether it was in solidarity of Rachel, or like Sage, she wanted them to focus.

While they waited silently, Dazzler dimmed her light right down to a soft glow to conserve her powers.

"There!" Sage whispered excitedly, her cybernetic glasses alight. "Row J. Left segment. Slot 74."

Dazzler brightened her light again and looked around to see which row they were in. She found a letter on the nearest racking. "We're in row D."

"Let's head back to the aisle," Sage said, tucking her haptic glove away and striding for the row entrance. Dazzler moved swiftly with her, hands out front to light the way for Polaris and Rachel.

They hit the aisle and made their way to row J. Once they found it, they turned into the left segment that housed slots 50-100 and began searching for slot 74.

The song playing in Dazzler's ear ended, and a new one started. She groaned, quickly pulling out her phone and pausing it. The three women looked at her.

"This song reminds me of an ex I'd like to forget," she said, skipping to the next one.

The three women remained staring at her.

"What?" Dazzler asked, putting the phone back in her pocket. "He was a jerk."

They moved along to slot 74. It was positioned four racks high.

"Well…" Dazzler said, looking around for a way to get it down. She glanced at Polaris. "Over to you."

Polaris studied the pallet for a moment. "It's not metal. The cargo is made of a toughened plastic, so I can't pull it down. I could fly up there, but I'm not going to be able to carry it on my own. However…" Her eyes traced down the row to the aisle. "I have a better idea. See those rails?"

Dazzler noticed the racks were lined with metallic railing. Polaris extended her hand down the row, back toward the aisle. With an intense look of concentration, Polaris seemed to be feeling for something. Suddenly they heard a rolling sound in the distance, getting louder and louder, before a small metallic carriage on wheels came racing around the corner along the railing and stopped before them. Polaris raised her hand in an upward motion, but nothing happened. She furrowed her brow and tried again. This time the carriage rose up on its hydraulic system, then she waved it down again.

"Get in," she said.

"Are you going to be able to get us down again?" Rachel asked.

Polaris gave her a steely stare in response. Rachel waved an apology, and then she and Sage climbed in, while Dazzler continued to provide light. Polaris, concentrating hard, used both hands this time to raise the carriage up to slot 74, and the two mutants heaved and tugged the large crate into the carriage with them. Polaris carefully lowered it to the ground again, then all three pulled the crate out onto the floor.

"How do we open it?" Polaris asked, examining it.

Sage pulled a hidden knife out of her X-suit, but Dazzler stopped her.

"This will be faster." Dazzler extended her hand, pointed her index finger at the sealed plastic locks, and shot out an intense beam of light energy, melting the toughened plastic. Sage then took her knife and pried the lid open before the melted plastic could harden again. Inside, they saw a lot of packing material and began eagerly pulling it aside – only to find it devoid of contents.

"It's empty," Polaris sighed, as Dazzler stared at a foam tray with hundreds of empty vial slots. A spike of fear ran down her spine. All those vials of MGH missing. All those vials of her mutant DNA gone. Had they just been moved or sold already? Were there humans out there right now filled with her essence, wreaking havoc?

"Did they sell it already?" Rachel voiced her thoughts.

Dazzler clenched her teeth, her fear surging now as anger and adrenaline. "Or did they know we were coming?"

But who could've warned them? Dazzler's eyes turned hard as she stared at each of the women. Her so-called mutant team.

"What's that look for?" Polaris bristled.

"We were the only ones who knew we were coming here. Us and Frost," Dazzler said.

"So?" Rachel asked.

"So, someone must've warned them."

"That sounds like an accusation," Sage said, standing up and squaring her athletic body.

"Did Frost say the shipment was full?" Dazzler asked.

"You're the one she spoke to after scraping Rosenthorpe's brain," Rachel said to Dazzler.

"Yeah, and Sage has spoken to Frost about it further since."

"True," Rachel said, narrowing her eyes at Sage.

"She gave me the consignment number only," Sage said.

Dazzler turned her light onto the container, found the consignment note and studied it.

"AFSS-001-975381246," Dazzler read aloud. "Do the letters mean something?"

"Yes," Sage said warily and then looked uncomfortable. "A.F.S.S. is the Alpha Flight Low-Orbit Space Station."

Dazzler studied the consignment note again, then stood and cast her light on the woman. "How do you know this? And when were you going to mention it?"

Sage stared back at her. "I'm familiar with A.F.S.S., and I know the 001 in the consignment notice means that it's classified."

"I ask again, how do you know this?" Dazzler demanded.

"I have worked for them before. Briefly."

"When?" Dazzler asked, mistrust flaring again.

"Some time ago, but it was in another dimension." She motioned to the label. "I did not work for them in this dimension or on that particular space station."

"Why didn't you mention it before?" Dazzler asked.

"I guess you're not the only one with trust issues," Sage said. "I figured working for S.H.I.E.L.D., you already knew but weren't saying so."

Dazzler stared at Sage, a thousand questions suddenly flooding her mind.

"Who's up on this space station that we should be worried about?" Rachel asked. "S.H.I.E.L.D.?"

Dazzler shook her head. "No. The Alpha Flight Low-Orbit Space Station is home to S.W.O.R.D."

CHAPTER EIGHTEEN

Dazzler tensed significantly as adrenaline continued to flood through her body.

"S.W.O.R.D.?" Polaris said. "They're the ones shipping the MGH?"

"What's S.W.O.R.D.?" Rachel asked.

"The Sentient World Observation and Response Division," Sage answered, then eyed Dazzler, "once a division of S.H.I.E.L.D." Dazzler heard an accusatory edge to her voice.

"It can't be," Polaris said in disbelief.

Dazzler turned and walked away from them. She suddenly felt claustrophobic. Did S.H.I.E.L.D. know about this? Was this more information they were hiding from her, that her clearance level did not allow her to know? Was this why they wanted her as Mutant Liaison? S.W.O.R.D. was S.H.I.E.L.D.'s counterpart in space, dealing with extraterrestrial threats to world security. Had S.H.I.E.L.D. sent her to investigate this because they wanted her to handle the staff of S.W.O.R.D., who were largely made up of mutants and extraterrestrials, that regular S.H.I.E.L.D. agents may not be equipped to handle?

What was going on? What else weren't they telling her?

Dazzler's anxiety rose, her trauma clawing its way back to the surface and choking her, as memories of lies and betrayal flashed through her mind. Of Mystique and Madripoor. She pushed it back down to focus on the present.

Who betrayed Magneto in the bar, and who warned Rosenthorpe to move the MGH shipment?

"So, what do we do?" Polaris asked. "Confront S.H.I.E.L.D.?"

"No," Dazzler said firmly, turning back to the women. "I think they already know."

"How do you know that?" Rachel asked.

"How could S.H.I.E.L.D. not know? S.W.O.R.D. was their counterpart."

"We should tell Frost," Sage suggested.

"You didn't discuss this with her when she gave you the consignment note?" Polaris said. "Frost doesn't know this is related to S.W.O.R.D.?"

"No," Sage told her.

"Why not?" Dazzler asked.

"I wanted to be sure first. Now that I am, we should tell her."

"So, you withheld information from Frost?" Dazzler asked, unable to hide her tone of accusation.

Sage tapped the knife she held against her thigh. "I have learned along the way to be sure of something before taking action. Or making accusations."

"I think Frost already knows," Dazzler said, positive the pieces of this puzzle were beginning to fall into place, however raggedly. "She's been around long enough to know about S.W.O.R.D. She was the one looking into this warehouse. Someone warned Rosenthorpe that we were coming, and he had the shipment moved. We forget, Frost has a long history, and she hasn't always been on the right side of it."

"She wouldn't be involved in this," Sage said.

"How do we know we can trust her?" Dazzler questioned. "Magneto and Cyclops have disappeared. She was *their* counterpart."

"Frost wouldn't betray them," Sage insisted.

"Do you know that for sure?" Dazzler asked. "You'd trust her with your life?"

Sage considered this for a moment. "It depends on what hung in the balance. If she could save me, she would. If she risked many other lives to do so, she wouldn't. Like me, she will do what needs to be done."

"So, she'd sacrifice you," Dazzler said.

"If it meant saving many others from the MGH, yes."

"Do we know if she has links to S.W.O.R.D.?" Polaris asked. "We need to know for sure so we can figure out what to do."

"That would be easy if I knew who I could trust around here!" Dazzler said, unable to help the accusatory looks she threw at her companions.

"Hey, we're in this with you, aren't we?" Polaris said, offended. "You can trust us!"

"Can I?" Dazzler asked, anxiety rising up again and anger trembling her body.

"What's wrong with you?" Sage asked.

"What's wrong with me?" Dazzler's stored light energy pulsed through her clenched fists. "What's wrong with me is that I'm being lied to! And I've been here before. I'm *not* going back to someone's dungeon because I've been betrayed!"

"You need to calm down," Rachel said, eyes turning white.

"Who are you?" Dazzler demanded, waiting for the telepathic press in her mind.

Rachel's face screwed up. "Who am I?"

Dazzler turned to Polaris. "And who are you?" Then she turned to Sage. "And who the heck are *you*?" She looked at them all again. "Who do you work for? Whose side are you on? Because if you're going to betray me, let's get this over with now!" She jerked her hands and a bright ball of light emanated from each fist. The women shaded their eyes.

"What are you doing?" Sage said.

"Protecting myself!" Dazzler said through gritted teeth.

"Quiet!" Rachel said, snapping her head around and looking for something with her pale eyes.

"What are you doing?" Dazzler hissed, raising her hands up toward Rachel, ready for any tricks.

"They're coming!" Rachel said, staring off into the dark.

"Who?" Polaris tensed.

"People! Lots of them!" Rachel said, looking all around. "I can't get a lock on any one thought. There's too many!"

The overhead lights suddenly came on. The warehouse lit up as though it were in full sun.

Dazzler turned her balls of light around to the aisle as they heard footsteps headed their way.

"Get ready to fight," Sage said, knife still in hand, as Rachel moved behind them.

"Er, I'll do what I can but I'm not really a fighter," Rachel said.

The adrenaline continued to surge through Dazzler. She shoved her second earbud in, pulled out her phone and selected her favorite playlist, aptly titled *Songs for Butt-Kicking*, and she cranked it loud.

"Lucky for you," she said, unable to hear her own voice over the music in her ears, as her body came alive with light energy, "the rest of us are."

Four guards, dressed in black uniforms, sprang around the corner of the row, weapons raised. They shouted something, but Dazzler didn't give them much time to say anything. She sent a bright flare from her hands as though wielding a flame thrower, and they all reeled back, stumbling to the floor, stunned.

She saw Sage yell something and point behind them. Dazzler felt a thud and looked around to see a guard on top of Rachel and three more flooding into the aisle behind them. There was another thud, and Polaris went down. They were coming from the roof now. Dazzler looked up to see another just in time as he collided with her, slamming her down onto the floor and rolling away. Winded, she looked up to see two more guards swarming down on her. She greeted them with kicks and punches, knocking one of them over, but the other one pounced, grabbing her arms and heaving her over onto her stomach. Dazzler was a powerful mutant, but her power lay in transducing sonic energy into light energy. Her physical strength wasn't much greater than the average human woman.

She groaned in pain, as the soldier on top twisted her hands behind her back tightly, while nearby Sage fought another two. Channeling the rock 'n' roll screams in her ears, Dazzler flicked her wrists and sent an electric charge through each of her fingers at the man pinning her arms. Suddenly his weight was off her, and she looked around to see him writhing in pain from the shocks. She quickly looked back to Polaris and saw her on the ground, wrestling with two guards. Dazzler swiftly raised her hand, blasting one with light, then the other, to give Polaris the upper hand.

Dazzler moved to get up, placing her hands on the floor, as the first guard swooped back in and grabbed her. As she wrestled with him, she felt more thuds as some of the soldiers she'd stunned earlier were now on their feet and running her way.

They didn't get far, though.

The carriage the women had used to get the crate down earlier suddenly flew across the aisle, knocking them down like bowling pins. Dazzler saw Polaris gritting her teeth, her powers more efficient as she reacted without thought.

Dazzler pressed her hands over the eyes of the man she wrestled with, blasting him with light. He fell away stunned and screaming, though she couldn't quite hear it over the music. Dazzler and Polaris exchanged a quick glance, before Polaris turned to help a bloody-faced Rachel, whose hands were clasped on a soldier's head as she mentally tried to overpower him, while another tried to drag her away by her legs.

Dazzler moved in the opposite direction to aid Sage who was now overpowered by three attacking guards. Dazzler flared her lights, stunning one, then another, allowing Sage the time and space to lift her strong leg and kick the third away. The few soldiers who remained standing backed away.

"No, you don't!" she saw Sage mouth, as she ran after them, wiping her bloodied nose. Dazzler followed her. They couldn't let any guards get away. She needed answers. As they reached the center aisle between the racks, five guards in red uniforms suddenly stepped out, and she realized the others had led them into a trap. Dazzler quickly raised her hands and pulsed a blast of light out at them.

But they were too fast.

The guards ducked and weaved her blasts, two running at Sage and three running for her. She gave another pulse and again missed. One soldier swooped past swinging his fist. It connected with her face, and she stumbled backward. Another ran past landing a punch to her abdomen. She curled over as the third elbowed her in the back, sending her toppling to the floor. Her knees hit concrete, and she groaned.

These guards were not like the others. They were too fast and too strong.

Dazzler felt a pain at her scalp as one of the guards grabbed her hair and pulled her head back, ready to land another punch, but he was suddenly thrust aside by a metal crate, which sent him into one of the racks.

Then another metal crate went flying, then another, knocking the guards off their feet. Dazzler turned to see Polaris, her arms extended, swaying in a symphony of revenge. Dazzler took the opportunity to get to her feet, saw some of the black uniformed soldiers standing again and aiming for Rachel, who stood not far from Polaris. Dazzler pulsed her light, stunning them, before she felt another thud and saw the red sleeve of a soldier wrap around her neck.

She felt her throat crushing in his strong grip. She had no doubt now that these humans were jacked up on MGH.

She reached her arm back and slapped her hand against his

skull, sending a current of light energy through it. The man fell away limply. She spun around to see Sage lying on the floor, possibly unconscious, and being dragged away by her ankle. Two more of the red-suited guards charged Dazzler. She ducked and dodged, pulsing light at them as they passed, but she missed hitting them. They came back at her. One was taken out by another carriage thanks to Polaris, and the other dodged her pulses and rammed her into the rack wall, knocking one of her earbuds out in the process. Dazzler, though winded, clasped her hand on his shoulder and sent a sharp current through him. The man groaned and stepped backward, as Polaris charged in from the side, knocking him down to the floor.

"Dazzler, watch out!" Rachel yelled, staring past her toward the end of the row, hand to temples.

Dazzler spun around to see another red-suited soldier appear, this time with a gun in his hand. He moved to fire at Dazzler, but his face suddenly screwed up in pain, no doubt thanks to Rachel. He winced then raised his weapon and fired anyway. Dazzler dropped low, just in time, then quickly raised her hand to pulse light at him, stunning him. He stumbled back, firing aimlessly. They all ducked for cover. As soon as he hit the floor, Dazzler raced to him and kicked his gun away, then she knelt over him, hands over his throat, sparking intermittently in threat.

"Who are you?" she demanded. "Who are you working for?"

The man refused to answer as his face strobed in the light of her hand.

"What have you done with the MGH? Where is it?" she asked.

She darted a glance to the others. Polaris crouched in front of Sage who was awake now but dazed, and Rachel moved carefully toward Dazzler. The stunned soldiers around them were starting to groan and awaken.

"We need to leave," Rachel said, looking about.

"This was a trap," Dazzler said. "They knew we were coming."

"That's why we need to get out of here," Polaris said. "Before more come."

"Another!" Sage yelled, pointing down the aisle.

Dazzler saw a lone, red-suited guard with his gun aimed at her. The man fired, as something shoved her aside.

It was Rachel.

The mutant groaned and grabbed her arm as she rolled onto the floor. Dazzler and Polaris immediately raised their hands. Dazzler stunned him with a bright blast of light, and Polaris threw one of the metallic carriages his way. The man went flying, then skidded along the floor until he stopped, limp and unconscious.

Panting with effort, Dazzler looked back at Rachel, who held her arm and then brought the fingers away, bloodied.

"You're shot?" Dazzler said, moving to help her.

Rachel winced with pain. "It's just a graze."

Sage and Polaris were soon by their sides.

"Let's get out of here before they wake up," Sage said.

"We need answers!" Dazzler said, wanting to stay.

"Someone sent these men, and they could be sending more," Sage panted. "Like you said, this was a setup. We need to retreat. *Now!*"

"C'mon," Polaris said, hauling Rachel to her feet.

Dazzler hissed in frustration, but followed, as they quickly headed for the exit, on alert for further attacks.

CHAPTER NINETEEN

Dazzler watched as Sage stitched the wound on Rachel's arm, and Polaris kept watch at the window as they holed up in their cheap motel room. They'd managed to escape the warehouse with no guards following them, and thanks to Sage's glasses, no drones were detected either. This only made Dazzler even more concerned about what had transpired. The guards did not call on any external security forces to apprehend them like other warehouses would have. They'd wanted to handle this themselves and protect their MGH secret – something they didn't want outsiders to know about. Whoever was behind this had their own private little MGH army, ready to defend their rising empire at all costs. This was a big problem, and a terrifying one at that.

Rachel groaned as Sage tugged on the stitching.

"Almost there," Sage said, her hands steady as though she'd done this a thousand times before. The wound hadn't quite been a graze, but Rachel was lucky that it had merely cut through the side of her arm. The telepath looked a little pale but was handling the pain well enough. Dazzler wondered if she was just trying to look tough in front of the rest of them. She wanted to tell her not to bother, that it was OK to express her pain, but she couldn't find those words.

"Those men in red weren't guards," Dazzler said, gently pressing on her swollen and bruised cheekbone. "They were soldiers, amped on MGH."

"Maybe they took the MGH from the crate and used it on themselves," Polaris suggested. Her face was also bruised in parts.

"Maybe," Dazzler said, concerned. "Whoever is behind this probably has more out there somewhere. We need to know who betrayed us before more soldiers come and take us out."

"So, you don't think it was us now?" Polaris asked, shooting her a look that bordered on both accusatory and offended.

"I didn't say that." Dazzler folded her arms. Rachel scoffed and shook her head. Dazzler felt a slash of guilt. After the warehouse fight, she wanted to trust these women, but could she? If she allowed herself to trust again, and they ended up turning on her… she wasn't sure she could handle it. "But I do appreciate you saving my life," she added.

"Gee, thanks," Rachel said sarcastically.

"Let's focus on the facts that we know," Sage said, not taking her eyes off the stitches. "Who could've known we were going to the warehouse?"

"It has to be S.H.I.E.L.D.," Polaris said.

"They knew we were coming to New York, but they didn't know about the warehouse," Dazzler said. "But… they have eyes everywhere. They could've easily followed us without us knowing."

"Someone knew in advance, though," Rachel said. "That's why the MGH was gone when we got there."

"Or maybe they'd already sold it and we were just too late?" Sage said.

Rachel studied Sage. "No, I think Blondie's right," she said, eyes darkening. "Frost knew."

Polaris nodded. "She's the one who told us to go there. She had plenty of time to make arrangements."

"Frost is on our side," Sage insisted, finishing the stitches.

"Frost is only ever on her *own* side!" Rachel spat.

Dazzler felt a sting with those words, which were close to what Rachel had said to her on the X-Jet. Is that why Rachel disliked Dazzler? Because she reminded her of Frost? "Why do you hate her so much?" Dazzler asked Rachel. "If you know something, you should tell us."

"She's angry at Frost for personal reasons," Polaris said when Rachel didn't answer.

"What reasons?" Dazzler pushed. "I don't like blind spots."

"It's got nothing to do with this mission," Rachel said.

Dazzler stared at her, arms still folded, waiting for an answer. "You want me to trust you?" she asked. "Then we need to be honest with each other."

Rachel stared at her a moment, wincing again as Sage dabbed an ointment on the stitches, then gave in. "Emma Frost had an affair with my father. It happened while my mom was still alive, and it broke them apart. That's why I hate her, OK?"

"Oh," Dazzler said, her shoulders softening. Her mind ticked over. "I'm sorry."

Silence sat heavily in the motel room for a moment.

"Well, I say we call Frost and see what she says." Dazzler

broke the silence. "We don't tell her about what happened at the warehouse. Let's see if she gives anything away that means we can't trust her."

"Why do *you* distrust her so?" Sage asked Dazzler. The side of her mouth was swollen and bruised from the fight.

"Because," Dazzler said, mentally moving those puzzle pieces around, "I don't know where she really stands. She's polite, but she gives me nothing. I sense no loyalty. Not to me. And… there's something about her. Something happened when I visited her at the school. I can't put my finger on it, but… we were in her office, then suddenly we were below ground, and I don't know how we got there. It's like there's a gap in my memory." Goosebumps broke out across her arms as a realization washed over her. "And I think she put that gap there. I think she did something to me, and if she did, that makes her no better than Mystique. Mystique took my life for a while. Frost took a memory. And because of that I can't trust her."

"Sounds like something she'd do," Rachel muttered.

"She's on our side," Sage reiterated firmly.

"Then prove it," Dazzler said. "We call her, see if she gives anything up."

Silence sat in the room a moment before Sage nodded. "All right."

"Use your phone," Dazzler ordered her.

"Fine, but you call her." Sage threw the phone to Dazzler, then turned to clean up and repack her med bag. It was clear she wanted nothing to do with this test.

Dazzler called Frost's number and waited for it to connect.

"Sage," Frost answered. "How'd it go at the warehouse?"

"It's not Sage," Dazzler said. "It's your friendly Sparkles."

There was a pause before Frost answered. "What happened to Sage?"

"Nothing. She's in the bathroom."

"Why are you calling?"

"You sound surprised to hear my voice," Dazzler said. "Didn't think you'd hear from me again?"

"Well, you are calling on Sage's phone," Frost said.

"Any updates for us?"

There was another pause. "No. Nothing concrete."

"What does that mean?"

"It means when I have something concrete, I'll let you know. What did you find at the warehouse?" Frost asked.

"Nothing concrete," Dazzler replied.

"Put Sage on the phone."

"I told you she's busy."

"Why are you being cagey?"

"Why are *you* being cagey? What do you have that's not concrete?" Dazzler asked.

Frost paused, as if considering what to say. "I was looking into the bar, *The Gilded Arrow*, and found a tenuous link to an old associate who also has links to Magneto."

"Who is the associate?"

"No one you know."

"Who?" Dazzler demanded.

"Put Sage on the phone. *Now*."

Dazzler sighed angrily and tossed the phone to Sage who caught it. "She wants proof of life."

Sage held the phone to her ear. "Frost?"

"Put it on speaker," Dazzler ordered.

Sage ignored her, listening to whatever Frost told her.

"Speaker!" Dazzler demanded.

"Put it on speaker," Polaris chimed in. Dazzler's paranoia was becoming infectious now. Rachel stared hard at Sage, and her eyes paled. Sage suddenly turned to Rachel, whose eyes turned green again. Dazzler glanced between them both, wondering what kind of unspoken communication had just occurred. She recalled the strange look in the warehouse, and remembered when they left the bar and Rachel followed Sage curiously as she made her phone call.

"All right," Sage said, now staring at Dazzler as she spoke into the phone. "No, there's nothing to report. The warehouse was empty. We're deciding what to do next... Yes. We'll let you know when we have a plan." Sage ended the call and looked around at them all. "See, I told her nothing."

"But what did *she* tell you at the start?" Dazzler asked.

"She mentioned a guy named Shaw," Rachel said. "Told Sage not to mention anything yet."

"Oh, really?" Polaris said, folding her arms.

"Who's Shaw?" Dazzler asked Sage.

Sage sighed and stood, resting her hands on her hips. "He's an old acquaintance of ours."

"Is he going to help us?" Polaris asked.

"Probably not," Sage said. "Frost and Shaw have a long history, but he's not an ally."

"What does that mean?" Dazzler asked.

"Put it this way, the last time Frost saw Shaw he tried to kill her. Frost outsmarted him, got the upper hand."

"He's the tenuous link to the bar?" Dazzler asked. "So why wouldn't she tell me that?"

Sage shrugged. "Like I said, you're not the only one with trust issues."

"Speaking of trust issues," Rachel said, staring at Sage, "why haven't you mentioned your telepathic abilities?"

Dazzler looked from Rachel to Sage. "You're a telepath?"

Sage stared calmly at Rachel. "I don't use my abilities anymore."

"But you have them," Rachel said.

"Have you been scraping our minds?" Dazzler tensed again.

"We'd know, wouldn't we?" Polaris said.

"I told you," Sage said, "I don't use them anymore."

"Why didn't you say something earlier?" Dazzler asked. "So you could report back to Frost on us?"

"I told you, I don't use them and haven't for some time. I tend to keep them cloaked. Rachel must be strong to have detected them."

Rachel shrugged humbly.

"Has she been using them?" Dazzler asked Rachel.

The redhead considered Sage a moment, then shook her head. "No, she hasn't used them yet. I've been watching her."

"See?" Sage said to Dazzler.

"When did you find this out?" Dazzler asked Rachel.

"In the field when we first met. I sensed open channels in her brain. Only telepaths have these."

Dazzler nodded to herself, understanding now the odd behavior she'd witnessed between Rachel and Sage.

"You should've told us," Dazzler said to Sage.

"My brain is essentially a super-computer," Sage said. "There is much it can do, but my capabilities are divided. I don't have the same sole power that Rachel's mind does. Would you like me to tell you every single thing my brain can do? How about you tell me everything you can do, Dazzler? You can bounce up walls, you can make lasers, you can blast light, you can produce mesmerizing bubbles. What else? And you, Polaris? And you, Rachel? What are the limits of your abilities?"

Dazzler stared at her, conceding the point.

"My telepathic abilities are minimal," Sage told them. "I can read and project basic thoughts. That's it. But I haven't used them in years. There was no need for me to mention this because Rachel is far stronger and of far more use to us in this field."

"Why don't you use them anymore?" Dazzler asked.

Sage studied her a moment, then relented, sensing Dazzler wasn't going to let up. "I've been cloaking my telepathic ability as a means of survival," Sage told them. "The man I told you about, the one who tattooed me? He was a powerful billionaire. It's a long story, but I crossed him to essentially help Frost, though it also aided Shaw at the time. When the billionaire sought revenge on me, he found me by tracing my telepathic ability. He captured me and gave me these." She pointed to her tattoos. "I escaped with help, and since then, I have locked my ability away to remain hidden from him. So, you can be assured that I won't use it again."

Dazzler studied her, a sense of empathy filling her, yet she wondered again about Sage's relationship with Frost, this Shaw guy, and just what the information flow was between them. "So, this guy, Shaw, what does Frost know about this link between him and the MGH?"

"Like Magneto and Cyclops," Sage said, "she can't locate him on Cerebra. It could mean he is a victim like them."

"He's a mutant?" Rachel asked.

Sage nodded. "And a hard one to take down."

"Why?" Dazzler asked.

"Because he absorbs kinetic energy. Whatever you throw at him, he throws back at you. You cannot touch him."

"So how did someone manage to take him down?" Dazzler asked.

Sage shrugged. "Possibly the same way Magneto was taken down. Betrayed and drugged by someone he trusted."

Dazzler's mind raced. "It's kinda funny, don't you think? That all of Frost's associates are suddenly going missing?"

"That doesn't prove her guilt," Sage said. "It could mean someone is out to get *her*."

"Her associates are missing," Dazzler said, thinking it through, "and she didn't hesitate to send you away from the school. The same school where the MGH first surfaced..."

"So?" Sage's brow furrowed now.

"So, I don't know," Dazzler said, "but there are too many touch points in this case that link to Frost. She says she's all about protecting her school, but it seems to me she's the one weakening it."

"She would never intentionally hurt those kids," Sage said. "She's always wanted to teach, and she wants to help those mutants. You must've seen that when you lived there before."

"Yeah, but as I recall, for a while there she and Scott wanted to start a revolution, protecting mutants, yes, but at all costs, even if it meant turning their backs on humans."

Sage shrugged. "She followed Scott. They were misguided for a while."

"Misguided?" Rachel asked.

"Yes," Sage said, then looked at Dazzler, "and you were too, for a while, remember?"

Dazzler looked away, ashamed. After Magneto had rescued her, she had fallen into a dark place that she'd been stuck in ever since.

"Maybe she's trying to take the school from Cyclops and Magneto?" Polaris pondered aloud.

"She's on our side," Sage said, firmly, bristling with impatience.

"You said Shaw was an old acquaintance of hers," Polaris argued. "Maybe he offered her a deal too good to turn down."

"She wouldn't betray Scott."

"You forget that she no longer has a relationship with my father," Rachel said.

"They still have a friendship," Sage said. "Besides, he's not the only reason she wouldn't take Shaw's side."

"What other reason is there?" Dazzler asked.

The lamp positioned close to Rachel's arm for the stitching cast shadows across Sage's face. "Frost is a powerful mutant who rose to the top in a world full of male mutants. She's competitive and at times, ruthless, but there's one thing I know about her for sure. She's fought tooth and nail for everything she has. Every road she has walked, she had to lay the pavement herself as she went. We all walk along the path that she laid for us. She's fought many battles alone, but over time she has learned the power of allies and when to trust. She does not give away allyship easily, but when she does, she is fiercely loyal. And she expects that loyalty in return. You break that loyalty, and her gloves will come off."

"We haven't earned her loyalty yet," Polaris said. "Maybe you have, but we haven't."

"Well," Sage said, flicking her eyes to Polaris, "then maybe you should listen to me. *Me*, who *has* earned Frost's trust. I'm telling you, I don't believe she would sell us out. Not to whoever is peddling this stolen MGH."

"You mean hope," Rachel said. "Hope she hasn't sold you out. I still don't trust her."

"What happened with your father is irrelevant here," Sage said.

"What happened with my father is *exactly* relevant," Rachel said, raising her voice. "She got inside my father's head, and they had a mental affair before my mother died. She is sneaky and underhanded and can't be trusted!"

"Or she simply fell in love," Sage said. "Something few of us have control over, the who, the when."

"Please!" Rachel scoffed, standing up. "She fell in love, so she broke up his existing relationship? You don't do that to someone you care about!"

"Careful," Sage said, "you lost some blood."

"I'm *fine*!" she said, before pausing, then reaching out to sit on the bed opposite, still pale and now looking a little dizzy.

"I knew Frost before her relationship with your father," Sage said, "and I've known her since. And the person she is today is a better person because of him. She was a loner before, but Cyclops changed her, made her see differently. She has a sense of family now. Of community. She longs to protect those young mutants. She wants to give them something she never had."

"Just don't, all right?" Rachel said. "Stop trying to make her a martyr. I'm not buying it."

"All right, we need to decide what to do," Dazzler said, cutting through the personal drama. "What we know for sure right now is that the MGH came from A.F.S.S., which is S.W.O.R.D.'s HQ.

This is serious stuff. If they're involved ..." Her voice trailed off, not wanting to face the possibilities. "Who knows how far this goes?"

"What if you sound out S.H.I.E.L.D. to see what they know?" Polaris asked. "If they're watching us as you say, then they'll know we were at the warehouse, and if they're involved, they'll know we might've found out about S.W.O.R.D.'s involvement."

Dazzler considered this, her body throbbing where bruises formed at the sites of impact from the MGH-jacked soldiers. She looked in the motel mirror and rubbed her bruised cheekbone.

"I just don't know who I can trust," she said, leaning against the wall by the window.

"So you said before." Polaris glared at her. "But do we look like we knew any of this would happen? Look at us! We're bloodied and bruised. Rachel got shot! For *you*!"

Dazzler studied Polaris's disheveled appearance, then looked to Sage's bruised face, then to the bandaged bullet wound on Rachel's arm. She locked eyes with the redhead.

"I did mean it when I said I appreciate you saving my life."

Rachel stared back at her, face softening a little.

"We saved each other in that warehouse," Sage said. "So, would we bother to save each other if we were trying to take each other down?"

Dazzler considered her answer. "It depends whether your goal had been achieved yet or not. Sometimes you need people alive in order to use them."

"Oh, you're unbelievable," Polaris said, looking at her with pity. "What happened to you to make you so cold like this?"

Tears unexpectedly pricked Dazzler's eyes. "What

happened?" Her voice came out croakier than she'd expected. "I was drugged and held prisoner and drained to make MGH, while Mystique went about my life as *me*. No one knew I was missing. No one could tell she was me. No one cared enough to *notice* it wasn't me."

"No one noticed because Mystique is a superior mutant," Sage said. "She is brilliant at what she does."

A tear fell down Dazzler's cheek. She quickly wiped it away. "No one knew I was missing…" she said softly.

"Maybe that's because of the walls you've built around yourself," Polaris said gently. "Nobody knows the *real* you in order to detect the missing nuances. They just know Dazzler the rock star. If you let people in, if you let people be your ally…"

More tears slid down Dazzler's cheeks. She wiped the first few away but gave up on the rest. Her mother flashed inside her mind, the anniversary, the woman who walked out on her, the performer she never knew. Her father turning his back when she wanted to follow in her mother's footsteps… She slumped onto one of the beds, lowering her face into her hands. After a moment, she felt a light touch on her shoulder and looked up to see Rachel.

Dazzler wiped her cheeks and gave an awkward smile. "I guess this was the trauma that broke this camel's back."

"We all have trauma in our past," Sage said, the tattoos on her cheeks seemingly more visible than ever, making Dazzler wonder more about them. "Find me a mutant who doesn't have that."

"If we don't trust each other," Polaris said, "we might as well end this now. Because I'm not taking on S.W.O.R.D. or

S.H.I.E.L.D. or whoever is behind this if I can't guarantee that you'll have my back."

"She's right," Sage said, then gave Polaris a nod. "You can trust that I will have your back."

Polaris nodded at Sage, then looked to Rachel.

"You know I have your back," the telepath told her. Polaris nodded, then looked to Dazzler.

Dazzler stared at each of them. Despite the inner urge to push these mutants away, she couldn't deny the cold hard facts before her. Rachel, despite the snarkiness, had taken a bullet for her. Polaris had used her powers several times to help Dazzler against the soldiers. Sage's calm, experienced nature had offered Dazzler a lot of support. Their rocky ride so far may well have been a whole lot rockier if Sage hadn't been there to break up the fights and keep them together.

Again, she wondered whether Sage should be leading this team.

"Well?" Rachel asked, breaking her thoughts. "Don't keep us in suspense, Blondie."

Dazzler nodded. "All right. I'll trust you. And I'll have your back," she said, and their faces lightened in response. "But if any of you betray me, you will regret the day you did."

Sage smiled. "Ditto."

Polaris smiled too. "Ditto."

Even Rachel cracked a grin. "Ditto."

"So," Sage said, moving closer. "Now we're all friends and the sisterhood is strong, what's the plan?"

CHAPTER TWENTY

Sage was looking to Dazzler to lead them. Dazzler's mind raced, thinking about S.H.I.E.L.D. and S.W.O.R.D. It was time to lead this team.

"Can you find out if my S.H.I.E.L.D. credentials will be enough to get us onto the Alpha Flight Low-Orbit Space Station?"

Sage pulled out her haptic glove and tapped her glasses. "I'll try."

Dazzler looked at Polaris. "Check in with Logan." Polaris nodded and pulled out her phone. "Don't give any information away though," Dazzler warned. "We trust no one outside of the four of us. Not even Logan."

Polaris nodded in agreement and stepped outside.

Dazzler looked at Rachel as she examined her arm. She still looked pale. "I'll get you some food."

Rachel gave her a nod of appreciation, as Dazzler left the motel room and headed for a late-night café a few doors down. She spent the last of her S.H.I.E.L.D. funds, buying an armful of hot, hearty food and some water with the cash, then headed back to the room, where she planned to destroy the credit card for good.

When she got back to the room, Polaris was still out front on her phone talking to Logan. Inside, Rachel was taking a shower.

"Your credentials should certainly gain *you* entry," Sage said, as she walked in, "but as suspected, the rest of us will need to apply for visitor passes, and that would take time."

"We'll figure out a way around that," Dazzler said.

"How?" Sage asked.

Dazzler beamed her pearly smile as she set the food down. "Between our feminine wiles and Rachel's mind tricks, we'll Dazzle our way inside."

Sage arched an eyebrow. "This is S.W.O.R.D., not some bored guards on a warehouse gate. It will be dangerous."

Dazzler's smile faded. "I know."

"Lucky for you," Sage said, "I am very good at forging credentials." She started to pack the compact med kit she'd brought with her inside her neatly packed bag. Her movements were ordered, methodical, practiced. Everything about her screamed ex-military.

"You've done a lot of missions, huh?" Dazzler asked her, popping a french fry in her mouth.

Sage nodded. "Yes."

"And you've dealt with both S.H.I.E.L.D. and S.W.O.R.D. before?"

"A little."

Dazzler folded her arms. "You're being modest. Why?"

Sage shrugged. "Habit, I guess. If there's one thing I have

learned it's that it's not wise to advertise all your assets. The element of surprise is the more powerful tool to use."

Dazzler nodded to herself, realizing this may have been part of why Sage had not mentioned her telepathic abilities before. "Did Frost send you here to run this mission?" Dazzler asked, unable to hide her curiosity. "You're making me think I'm leading this, but you really are, aren't you?"

Sage studied her. "No. I am making calculated suggestions based on my knowledge, skill, and experience. That is why she sent me with you."

Dazzler glanced down at her feet. "You're the one who should be leading us. You know that, right?"

"No," Sage said firmly. "I am a soldier first and foremost. I will undertake my missions with precision, and I will achieve my goal. That is what I do. I am a mutant of action. My gift is information retention and processing, which enables me many skills. And I can fight." She smiled. "Put me on the battlefield, physical or political, and I will do what needs to be done, and I will advise you what course of action I recommend. *And*, if necessary, I will make sacrifices for the greater good. But I am not a leader."

"Everything you said sounds like leadership to me."

"No, it's not. I am a soldier who works best in the shadows. Leaders must be visible. Leadership takes passion and empathy. You have both. That is why you are an artist." Sage cocked her head to the side in consideration. "Though I must say, for a singer you lack confidence at times."

Dazzler nodded. "I used to have a lot of that, but it's been eroded over time."

"I get that," Sage said. "I know what it's like to have trauma, to have been in a position where you felt helpless at the hands of someone cruel." Sage pointed to the tattoos on her cheeks. "The man who gave me these didn't just mark my face but left a permanent stain on my soul that I will never be able to scrub off. But it's a stain I use to fuel me when I need to do the impossible. Someone did this to me, but I am alive and free now. And I will *never* let anyone do that to me again. You, Dazzler, whether you admit it or not, are moving to this place, too. Mystique did what she did, yet here you are, free. Because you are a survivor and because you won't let anyone break you down again."

Dazzler felt goosebumps tickle her skin. "It's funny, you know, I wrote a song about that."

Sage came close to Dazzler and clasped her shoulder. "You need to find your confidence again and fast. The way you are on stage, you need to do that with your mutant abilities. I'm not here to lead. I'm here to support. Rachel and Polaris are too young, too hot-headed, and are still figuring out who they are and how to fully embrace their gifts. You are healing from trauma, yes, but your base temperament is even and makes you better suited to lead. You are also experienced and relatively comfortable with your mutant abilities and know how to control them. You can empathize with mutants *and* with humans. Use that. Use the control of your abilities and the empathy you carry. And use your independence, the fact that you have no allegiance to either school, nor to S.H.I.E.L.D. But hear this. If you show weakness again, the team won't succeed. A team is only as strong as its leader. You are the thread that pulls us together. *You* are the star of this show, Dazzler. You were born to shine, so dazzle us with your brilliance."

Dazzler stared at her, watching a smile slide across Sage's lips. Dazzler couldn't help but smile back.

"Thanks for the pep talk," she said. "Sage is a very apt name for you."

Sage lifted her fingers to her temple and gave a salute. "Now where is that food? We need to refuel before we hit the Alpha station."

Emma stared out the window of her hotel, studying the Manhattan landscape in thought. She'd checked in with the school to say she would be returning soon, and Magik had confirmed that all was well. It was a relief to know, because right now so many other things were not OK.

Dazzler's behavior was odd, not to mention Sage's. She sensed Sage was lying but when she tried to access her thoughts, she'd hung up the phone and shut down her mind. Sage's brain was complex and talented, and penetrating it without her consent was something even Emma couldn't do. It very much gave Emma the feeling that Sage was undercover, that she was in a situation where she couldn't give up her position. It bothered her, but at the same time, she knew Sage was experienced and skilled, and had to trust that she would make contact when she could.

But what did this all mean? Was Sage in a precarious position? Was her life potentially in danger? Or was Sage shutting her out to hide things? But what things? What was she up to?

Emma had sensed a strong mistrust within Dazzler, so she'd decided to keep news of Shaw secret for now. Sage knew Emma's history with the Black King of the Hellfire Club, knew Emma had been the White Queen. Sage had lived through that era with her. But what would Dazzler and the others think if they knew some of the things the old Emma had done? Or had they somehow found out and that was why they were acting so evasive and wary? Sometimes after you throw out the trash the stink remains. She'd worked hard to erase that stink, but some people had a good memory and believed leopards couldn't change their spots.

And if they'd found out Shaw was behind this and knew of her link to him and the Hellfire Club, they may just expect her involvement now, especially with Magneto and Scott missing. Would people think she was making a play for control of the school?

So, she'd decided to keep this news to herself for now. She trusted only Sage to know.

Besides she had some mistrust of her own. She was still troubled by the images she'd scraped from Rosenthorpe's brain. Of Judge Carter Blaire having a drink in Walsh's bar with Toby Squires, the same man who had been drinking with Magneto the night he disappeared. Images of Rosenthorpe at Dazzler's concert, of him knowing her since she was a teen, resurfaced. Dazzler's father had to be the key to what was going on here. He would be a man who held certain power and would have powerful connections, given his career. It was just all too coincidental for her liking. The fact that the MGH on the streets was derived from Dazzler. The fact that her father knew the man who had probably drugged Magneto. The fact that he had once represented the man storing the MGH at his warehouse. The fact that the judge had a membership to Walsh's bar. Walsh, who was an associate of Sebastian Shaw.

But the biggest question was *why*?

Why would Judge Blaire do this? Or had Squires betrayed him too? Or blackmailed him? Had Blaire caught wind of the

MGH and was he trying to stop it? Did he know it involved his daughter? Or was Blaire just a lure in a trap to draw Dazzler in? Did someone want what Dazzler had? The current batch of MGH on the streets had been derived from her. Did they want more of the same?

Was Mystique behind this after all? Could she be working with Shaw?

Emma was suddenly curious to get back to Cerebra and track Mystique down. What if she had vanished like the others? But first, there was one more person she had to pay a visit.

Dazzler stared off into the distance at the speck that was the Alpha Flight Low-Orbit Space Station, some two hundred and fifty kilometers above the Earth. Thanks to Sage's piloting prowess and the high-altitude capabilities of the X-Jet, they were making good time and would be there soon. Just what they were going to do when they arrived was something Dazzler was still trying to figure out.

All she knew for sure, was that her mutant team had a basic level of trust between them now, and they had agreed to work alone without any outside help. This gave Dazzler a level of comfort that the opportunities for betrayal had narrowed down some. Between the X-Jet's cloaking capabilities upon leaving Earth, and them shutting out everyone external to the core team, Dazzler felt secure.

For now.

But she knew their head start would only last as long as it took for them to dock on the A.F.S.S. and show her credentials. After that, Bennett and S.H.I.E.L.D. would be all over them.

As the space station drew nearer and the Earth grew smaller,

Dazzler tried to steady her mind and strategize. If S.W.O.R.D. was behind the supply of MGH, they weren't exactly going to admit their activities – to her or S.H.I.E.L.D. Dazzler had two options. She either had to lie and say they were there on another matter and try to investigate things privately, or come right out and try to bluff, informing them that S.H.I.E.L.D. was closing in on their activities. It was a risk either way.

"Bennett is *not* going to be happy when he finds out what we're doing," Polaris said, staring at her fake S.H.I.E.L.D. credentials.

"Relax," Sage said from the pilot's chair. "Would you rather we said you were the cousin of S.W.O.R.D.'s commander, Abigail Brand? You have the green hair for it."

"No way," Dazzler said. "As soon as Brand sees her, she'll say it's a lie and we'll never reach the station."

"What about Magneto's daughter?" Sage posited. "No lie there."

"No," Polaris said. "I get that enough. And it really is enough."

"Why don't you like people knowing he's your father?" Dazzler asked.

"I don't like living in his shadow. He has a past that follows him. I'm not him. I'm me."

"Your parents are human," Rachel, sitting beside Polaris, said to Dazzler. "It's not something you'd understand. We live with everything our parents have done, good and bad. It follows us everywhere. When people look at us, they see *them*. Polaris has abilities similar to Magneto, so that's all people see, a mini-Magneto, even though Logan says her abilities are untapped. She could one day be more powerful than Magneto, and will use those powers for good."

"Rachel," Polaris said, quietly, clearly not wanting to talk about it.

"And my parents?" Rachel continued. "I look like my mother, so people look at me and wonder whether I'll go crazy and try to kill everyone. Or they see my father and know what he did to Professor Xavier. Even though that wasn't really him, it was the Phoenix. But they look at him and think he's a cold-blooded murderer. Do you know what that's like? To be the daughter of the man who killed Professor Xavier? And he's not even really my father anyway. I mean he is, but he isn't."

"What do you mean?" Dazzler asked, confused.

"She doesn't know where you're from," Polaris said to Rachel.

"Where you're from?" Dazzler was more confused now.

Rachel looked at her. "I wasn't born here in this dimension. I came from an alternate reality."

"Another dimension?" Dazzler asked, stunned.

Rachel nodded. "I stumbled into this dimension by accident and got stuck here. The Cyclops in this dimension didn't technically father me, but he's still my father. Kind of. He's my father in the other dimension. It's complicated."

Dazzler stared at her, open-mouthed. "Your relationship makes more sense to me now. That and the whole Frost affair thing. That's why you're at Logan's school?" she asked gently.

Rachel nodded. "Logan knew my mother, knew the *real* her. After what happened with Frost… Logan's been more of a father to me than Cyclops ever has. I stay at the Jean Grey School because that's where I feel my home is. With her memory. The good ones."

"Yet, you still came to help save Cyclops," Dazzler noted.

"If he's still alive," Rachel said coldly, before a look of guilt washed over her face. She turned to look out the observation window at the station growing larger and larger as they neared. "My mother loved him once. I'm doing this for her. It's what she would've wanted."

"You are the scions," Sage said. "The scions rising from the ashes of your parents. The next generation of mutants who will one day lead."

Dazzler smiled. "Scions rising… I like that sound of that. If we make it through this, I'll write a song about it."

The three women looked at her amused, as an alert suddenly sounded on the X-Jet's console.

"We're on our final approach," Sage said.

Dazzler turned to view the Alpha Flight Low-Orbit Space Station. It almost looked like a giant spinning top with large robotic legs jutting out. The main part of the station was star-shaped, and according to the notes Sage had provided her with, each point of that star was a module that housed a different functional station requirement. Whether it was the command bridge module, detention module, staff pod module, or the like, each module could easily be detached and moved around to suit the station's needs.

"Unidentified spacecraft, please identify," a voice sounded over the comms panel before Sage. Dazzler stood and moved toward her.

"This is a S.H.I.E.L.D. designated flight," Sage replied. "Request permission to board the station."

"We have no knowledge of your visit," the voice said. "Please turn around."

"S.H.I.E.L.D. Agent Alison Blaire is aboard," Sage replied. "Sending credentials now." She tapped at the console, sending the information packet, then motioned Dazzler to the console camera to confirm her identity to those on the A.F.S.S. command bridge.

"Agent Blaire," the voice said, "we've received no notification of your visit. Please explain."

"I apologize for that," Dazzler spoke into the comms mic. "This was not a planned visit, and time was of the essence. We are working on a missing persons case, and our intel has led us to your station. Request permission to board and speak with the commander."

Silence was their reply.

"I'm sending through a list of the agents working with me," Dazzler said. "Repeat, we request permission to board."

"Your vessel is not registered with S.H.I.E.L.D.," the voice said. "It has no designation whatsoever."

"No, it's a rental, but *I* am S.H.I.E.L.D. designated. Again, I request permission to board."

Silence filled the comms for a long moment, as Dazzler and Sage exchanged a glance, waiting with bated breath.

Finally, the voice replied.

"You are not permitted to board. Please turn around."

Rachel moved to stand behind their chairs. Dazzler saw her eyes were whitened, and she motioned for Dazzler to speak into the comms mic.

"Er, please check our credentials again. We have the authority to board."

"Please turn ar–"

"Please check again," Rachel said, firmly, her face frozen in concentration, as she took over the comms mic.

"Who are you?" the A.F.S.S. soldier asked.

"Confirm our authority to dock," Rachel said, her voice calm yet more forceful at the same time. "Lower your weapons and open the gates to the dock."

She leaned back, and they watched in suspense, joined by Polaris now, as the station grew in size before them.

And still the dock did not open.

"Do you think you can open those gates?" Dazzler asked Polaris. The green-haired mutant studied the station and paled.

"I- I don't know about that. They're pretty big."

Rachel leaned into the mic once more, eyes pale, brow furrowed. "You will open the dock for us now. We are permitted to board. Repeat. We are permitted to board."

Silence hung thickly over the comms system. Rachel's hand tightened around the comms mic. She leaned forward angrily, about to repeat her command, but stopped when they saw the station's dock opening.

"They're letting us board!" Dazzler smiled, relieved.

"Or they're about to blow us out of the sky," Sage said.

Dazzler's smile fell away as she stared at the yawning gates.

CHAPTER TWENTY-ONE

Emma Frost sat patiently in the foyer of Sanderson Holdings. She'd told the receptionist she was waiting for someone. When the woman asked who, Emma simply smiled and said he would be down shortly.

Sure enough, Rick Rosenthorpe did come down from his office, though Emma's mind tricks played a part in that. While she could have penetrated his mind from afar like she did last time, this time she wanted a more personal touch. Her powers would be stronger in person, face to face. Besides, now that she'd confronted Cassandra Walsh, she didn't have time to go slowly and avoid tripping any of his mind's sensors. It was time to be brutal and direct about things.

Rosenthorpe stood at the open elevator doors, staring at her with a slack face. She smiled, stood from the couch, and followed him into the elevator, where he pressed the basement floor on the console and sent them down into the building's parking garage.

Rosenthorpe remained slack-faced and under Emma's mind control as she made him lead her to his shiny black Mercedes. Sitting comfortably in the driver and passenger seats, Emma then had him lock the doors before freeing his mind from her hold.

Rosenthorpe suddenly blinked, realized where he was, and looked confused. He jumped when he saw her in the passenger seat. She smiled, as his brow slowly furrowed in recognition.

"You remember me?" Emma asked. "I was in your dream the other night."

He stared at her, his confusion morphing into anger.

Emma shrugged and continued, "I do that sometimes. Enter people's minds."

Rosenthorpe scowled. "You *mutants*!"

"You say that like it's a bad thing."

"Get out of my car!"

"I don't think so, *Rick*."

Rosenthorpe tried to open his door, realized it was locked, but before he could unlock it, Emma was back inside his mind.

"You're going nowhere until I have some answers," she said.

He slowly turned his face back to hers. The slowness wasn't intentional. It was all to do with the grip she had on his mind. She was no longer controlling his thoughts but limiting the functionality of his brain. He could move his body, but it was like it was trapped in a medieval gibbet cage – movement was difficult.

"What do you want?" he managed, eyes vengeful.

"Where's the MGH?"

"I don't know what you're talking about."

"Yes, you do. I accessed your memories. The MGH was in your warehouse, and now it's not."

"You're behind the break in."

"Not exactly. Where is it? The MGH cargo?"

"Somewhere you'll never find it."

"Where?" she demanded, tightening the gibbet cage around his mind.

His muscles tightened and strained as he fought the mental pull. He managed to spread a smile across his face. "It's been distributed far and wide. Our people are armed and ready."

"What people?"

He smiled wider. "Those who've had enough of your mutant reign."

Emma stared at him. "Where are Magneto and Cyclops?" she demanded in a low, cold voice.

A flicker of pleasure crossed his eyes. "They're dead."

"You lie!" She squeezed his mind tighter.

Rosenthorpe groaned as sweat beaded his shaking, straining body.

"Where are they?" she shouted.

"I told you, they're *dead*!"

Emma thrust her mind into his, making Rosenthorpe cry out, as she plummeted through his memories, swimming frantically looking for any new information on them.

And a memory rose up like a shark before her, baring its teeth.

She saw Rosenthorpe on the phone to another man, a man who said, "You have nothing to worry about. Magneto and Cyclops have been taken care of. We'll never see them again."

Emma couldn't help the gasp that escaped her as she relinquished her mind-grip on the man.

Rosenthorpe, free of her hold, looked at her with satisfaction, which quickly turned into a venomous threat. "And you're next!"

Emma's mind swooped back into his, swamping it like a tidal wave. Rosenthorpe cried out again as his body locked up.

"Where is Judge Carter?" she asked, reaching out and physically shaking him. "Where is he?"

"Mister Incorruptible!" he sneered. "Ha!"

"Where is he!" she demanded. "And where is Shaw?"

"Who?" His brow furrowed.

"Sebastian Shaw."

"I don't know who you're talking about!"

"You do!"

"All I know is that you're a dead woman. No, you're a dead *mutant*!"

"News flash! I'm the one with the upper hand here. Give me one good reason I don't take you out right now," Emma seethed, leaning right into his face.

"Look behind you." Rosenthorpe managed another satisfied smile.

Emma turned to see several men rushing toward the car, weapons raised in her direction.

Dazzler and her team stared at the yawning mouth of the low-orbit space station as they approached. They each held their breath as they scanned the inner dock, looking for any weapons that might blast them back out of space.

"Permission granted to dock," the voice from the station announced.

They gave a collective sigh of relief.

"Good work, Rachel," Dazzler said.

Sage held her hands up. "Let's not get excited. They could still shoot us on the dock. I calculate there is a fifty percent chance of this."

Dazzler, Rachel, and Polaris looked at Sage, who shrugged.

"My brain is a super-computer. I calculate such statistics."

"I have legitimate S.H.I.E.L.D. credentials," Dazzler said. "They can't just kill me."

"Depends on if they see you as a threat," Sage said. "We used mind control to gain access. They could lock us up for that."

Dazzler unplugged her phone from its charger and looked at Rachel again. "Be ready. We might need you to do some more of that inside."

Sage docked the X-Jet on the Alpha Flight Module of the station, which featured a hangar and mustering deck for the Alpha Flight Squadron Jets. At first, there appeared to be no one around, but as Dazzler, earbuds in, began to disembark from the X-Jet, she and her team suddenly found themselves face to face with an armed unit of S.W.O.R.D. soldiers – some human and some alien kinds that she hadn't seen before. Dressed in their forest green suits, bearing built-in armor across the chest, shoulders, knees and elbows, their weapons were large and their faces extremely unfriendly.

Dazzler held her hands up in a relaxed gesture. "We come in peace."

A human woman stepped forward in front of the soldiers. Tall and dark-skinned, with pretty but mistrusting eyes. Dazzler assumed she was in charge.

"I'm Agent Blaire," Dazzler said, extending her hand. The woman looked at it but didn't move to extend her own. "You're not Commander Brand."

"No," the woman said. "Commander Brand is off-station at present. I'm Acting Commander Valdana."

Dazzler gave a friendly smile and reached for her phone, but the soldiers quickly raised their weapons in her direction. Dazzler paused and held her hand out peacefully. "I just wanted to show my credentials."

"Your credentials are fine," Valdana said firmly, folding her arms across her chest, "but theirs aren't." She motioned to Dazzler's acquaintances.

"And I thought I did a good job, too," Sage said, offended.

"You did," Valdana said. "That is, until S.H.I.E.L.D. failed to confirm your status as anything other than mutants."

"They are mutants, yes," Dazzler said. "And so am I. As my credentials, and I'm sure S.H.I.E.L.D., have attested to, I am their *Mutant* Liaison, so it makes sense that my chosen team are also mutants."

"Your mutants don't have S.H.I.E.L.D. approval," Valdana said.

"Maybe not," Dazzler said confidently, "but they have mine." She noticed her three mutant companions shoot her a glance upon hearing this.

"You were not authorized to dock on our station, and yet somehow you were granted permission. Bring them to the Detention Module," Valdana said to her soldiers, then dropped her folded arms and walked away.

"Detention?" Dazzler said. "I have legitimate S.H.I.E.L.D. credentials, and these women are part of my team!"

Valdana didn't respond as the soldiers stepped toward the mutants. "Any weapons to the floor!" a big burly male guard yelled. "Now!"

"My weapons are in my DNA," Dazzler said. "I can't."

The guard wasn't sure how to respond to that. He looked at Sage. "Glasses to the floor now."

"They're not a weapon," she said.

"Now!" he barked and turned to Dazzler. "And you hand over those earbuds."

"They're for music," she said. He answered her with a glare and a tightened grip on his weapon. Dazzler stared back, testing how much "juice" she had in her system and whether she could risk handing her earbuds over. She felt the tingle of light energy within her veins. She'd have enough if it came to it. She sighed, took her earbuds out, and placed them in his palm. "I hope you washed your hands."

Sage relented also, took her glasses off and handed them to him, as the guards surrounded them and gave them a pat down. They quickly finished with Dazzler, Rachel, and Polaris, but took a little longer with Sage, removing one knife, then another, then a third, then a long piece of wire, then a bandolier of what looked like darts...

Sage shrugged at their surprised faces. "I'm always prepared."

Satisfied they had taken all of Sage's weapons, the soldiers ushered them toward a body scan device, leading onto the station proper. One by one they stepped through, and the machine remained silent. Dazzler saw Polaris eyeing everything metallic, calculating action, but Dazzler subtly shook her head at her. Polaris backed down.

Once scanned, they were led down a corridor past curious S.W.O.R.D. officers and into the Detention Module, where they were seated at an empty table in an interrogation room.

Finally, the door opened. A guard entered. He stood by the

door, fidgeting nervously, his eyes darting between Dazzler and the door.

"Everything OK?" Dazzler eyed him curiously.

He eyed the door again before quickly pulling out a piece of paper that was tucked inside his suit. He rushed over to her, unfolding it, and slapped it down on the table.

It was a poster of Dazzler.

"Could I get an autograph?" he asked, sweat breaking out on his brow as he kept glancing over at the door.

"Oh..." Dazzler looked at him, surprised, as her mutant companions stifled their amusement.

"Quickly," he said. "Before Valdana comes."

"Sure," Dazzler said, amused herself. "Got a pen?"

"Oh, yeah," he said, patting his pockets and utility belt. He plucked the writing utensil out and handed it to her.

Dazzler took the pen and signed the poster. The second she was done he snatched it back, quickly folded it and tucked it away again, standing back by the door as though nothing had happened. Dazzler stared at him, a little perplexed.

"Thank you," he said, darting his eyes to her. "I'm a big fan. Love your new sound."

"No problem." She laughed softly as the door opened and Acting Commander Valdana entered carrying a tablet-like device in her hands, with another two officers. The small room was feeling pretty crowded now.

Valdana sat down at the table, assured. She'd obviously dealt with mutants before and didn't appear to be afraid of them in any way.

"I'm Lieutenant Lauren Valdana," she introduced herself formally, "Acting Commander of the Alpha Flight Low-Orbit

Space Station." She turned her eyes to Dazzler. "You may have official credentials, Agent Blaire, but I've checked in with colleagues at S.H.I.E.L.D., and they have no idea why you are here. Care to explain?"

"We were following a lead on a S.H.I.E.L.D. case. I came here to ask you some questions."

"I'll be asking the questions, thank you," Valdana said, firmly. "Is it not S.H.I.E.L.D. protocol to check in with your case leads to clear the way before turning up at a place like Alpha Flight?"

"There wasn't time," Dazzler lied.

"Unlikely," Valdana said, without skipping a beat. She tapped her tablet-like device, scrolled through some information, then turned her dark eyes to the others. "Lorna Dane," she said to Polaris. "Magneto's daughter."

Polaris stared back at her. "I'm sorry, was that a question?"

"No," Valdana said, then turned to Rachel. "Rachel Summers."

"It's Grey," Rachel corrected her. "Rachel Grey."

"You're Scott Summers's daughter." Valdana ignored her. "Cyclops's daughter."

Rachel arched an eyebrow in response.

The acting commander turned to Sage. "You were hard to find information on. Certainly not any names."

Sage kept her face even. "I go by Sage."

"I'm going to need more than that," Valdana told her.

"Some people once called me Tessa."

"Surname?"

"That's the only name I have," Sage said. Dazzler shot her a curious glance wondering whether that was a lie, or whether

Sage really didn't know her given name. Knowing Sage's mysterious past, it wouldn't surprise Dazzler if Sage really didn't know.

"You must," Valdana persisted.

"I don't."

"We'll fingerprint you and see if that doesn't tell us your real name."

Sage shrugged. "Go for it."

Valdana tapped her device.

"One thing," Sage said, and Valdana looked up. "I'd like my glasses back please. They are not a weapon."

"Maybe not, but those glasses are akin to this," Valdana said, holding up her tablet device. "You'll get them back if and when I release you." Valdana turned her attention to Dazzler. "S.H.I.E.L.D. informs me that your father is listed as missing," she said, then turned her eyes to Polaris and Rachel. "As are yours."

"You did all that in the twenty minutes we've been here?" Dazzler asked, narrowing her eyes in suspicion.

"No, I've been doing that since you sent through your credentials en route. Now, tell me why you're here. I assure you your missing fathers are not on this station, so it can't have anything to do with them."

"Or," Dazzler said, "it has *everything* to do with them."

"As I said, your fathers are not here, nor have they been here. As you can see, we're very particular about checking who arrives on our station."

"Are you?" Dazzler asked. "You've never had Mystique or another shapeshifter here posing as someone else?" She smiled. "I guess you wouldn't really know, would you?"

"We do facial recognition scans, not personality tests. Why are you here?" Valdana said bluntly, her impatience seemingly sparked by her lack of a counterargument. "Why are you here?"

"I'm not sure I can tell you," Dazzler said. "Some things remain classified."

"You don't come here uninvited and expect to retain classification."

"You do if you have S.H.I.E.L.D. credentials."

"I've checked your classification level, Agent Blaire. It's low. *Very* low. That means S.H.I.E.L.D. doesn't trust you, and given they have no idea why you're here, you really should explain yourself."

"Well, there's that classification issue again. There're just certain things I can't tell you."

Valdana smiled. "I assure you my classification level is higher than yours."

Dazzler remained silent.

"Well," Valdana said, standing. "Clearly you wish to waste my time."

"You expect me to divulge classified things in front of a room full of foot soldiers?" Dazzler stopped her.

"You expect me to send the soldiers away and remain alone in a room with four mutants?" Valdana collected her device and turned for the door.

"We traced a suspect shipment of goods to Alpha Flight," Dazzler said quickly. "Meaning, the suspect goods came from here. Who do you suggest we talk to about that?"

Valdana stopped and turned around to her.

"And by suspect," Dazzler added, "I mean highly illegal and very dangerous."

"You're accusing S.W.O.R.D. of illegal activities?" Valdana asked, with a hint of incredulity.

"You wouldn't be the first organization affiliated with S.H.I.E.L.D. to do so."

"We run a tight ship, Blaire," Valdana said. "And your accusations are unfounded."

"You don't know the specifics of my accusations yet. You're not curious to know?"

Valdana stared at her a moment. "If it weren't for the incoming asteroid shower, I would put you back on your jet and send you away immediately. Luckily for you, I won't send you into a risky situation, so you will leave once the shower has passed. Until then, you will be confined within the Detention Module in the cells we've assigned you." She looked to one of the soldiers. "Take them."

"Wait," Dazzler said, sitting up. "You're locking us up?"

"Because of your credentials you are not being formally arrested with falsifying authority to dock on our station. Don't push it, Blaire."

Valdana left the room, and the guards stepped toward them.

CHAPTER TWENTY-TWO

Emma Frost carefully stepped out of the vehicle, her hands raised. Rosenthorpe got out the other side and moved around the vehicle toward her. He grabbed her arm and put his face in hers.

"You are going to regret what you did!" he hissed.

"Am I?"

The sound of screeching tires rang out. Rosenthorpe and his men looked around to see several black SUVs tearing into the basement parking lot.

Emma smiled at him. "I don't need a phone to call for help."

SUV doors flung open, and Maria Hill's voice rang out. "S.H.I.E.L.D.! Drop your weapons! *Now!*"

"Take them out!" Rosenthorpe yelled to his men, diving for cover.

Gunfire rang out, and Emma ducked low beside the car as glass rained over her. "You idiot! You think you're going to get away?" she yelled at Rosenthorpe.

"Yes!" he said, swinging a fist her way.

He screamed in pain as his knuckles cracked against her diamond form. She smiled as he cradled his fist and crawled backward from her as gunfire continued to crack and glass shattered. Emma crawled after him like a lioness in the African savanna, stalking her prey.

"You're going to regret what you did," she taunted him. "Sound familiar?"

With that, she thrust her mind into his, taking a firm hold and paralyzing all thoughts. Rosenthorpe tried to fight her, but it was futile. Soon enough his vacant face looked to his men.

"Drop your weapons!" he called to them. "Drop them!"

The men looked at him, confused.

"You just told us to take them out," a brawny blond said, hiding near a stairwell.

"Drop them!" Rosenthorpe yelled.

The men now shot each other confused glances.

"Now!" Rosenthorpe shouted.

The men relented and did as ordered, laying their weapons on the ground.

And with that, Maria Hill and her S.H.I.E.L.D. agents swooped in.

Dazzler stood alone in the all-white micro-cabin she'd been allocated, staring at the red light above her door that reminded her she was locked inside. Her mutant team had been separated, and she could only assume they were in similar cabins close by. The cell was so small there was barely room for a bunk and a miniscule bathroom. There was no entertainment or comms system, nothing but the plain white walls. What was she supposed to do to while away the hours until they were released? She turned in circles for a moment, her mind toiling, wondering if Rachel would be able to make contact with her in here.

"You rang?" Rachel's voice popped inside her head with a sense of pressure, startling her.

"God," Dazzler breathed. "You don't warn people before you just jump in?"

"You were just thinking you wanted me to connect. I took that as an invitation."

"Why didn't I feel any pressure before you jumped in? How could you tell?"

"Because I was projecting, feeling for whatever was out there. I caught my name on your mind. So, what is it?"

"Where are you?"

"In a similar cell to you, as are the others. I was the last one locked away. I guess we should be grateful they gave us nice cushy cells that don't dampen our mutant abilities, huh?"

"We need to get out," Dazzler said. "Sage doesn't have her glasses or weapons. Can Polaris work her magic and get these doors open?"

"You need to know the guard movements before you do that," Sage's voice sounded inside her head.

"Welcome to the party, Sage," Rachel said.

"I thought you said you don't use your telepathic abilities anymore?" Dazzler said, as that sense of mistrust threatened to creep up and take over her again.

"Well, now seemed a good time, don't you think?" Sage said. "I use it now only because I have to."

"Are you here, too, Polaris?" Dazzler asked.

"Polaris isn't telepathic," Rachel said.

"Well, can one of you ask her to open our cabin doors?" Dazzler asked.

"Like I said," Sage answered, "we need to know the guard movements first. The station is set to Earth time and has a twenty-four-hour light progression to align with a standard day on Earth," she explained. "Just like on Earth, at night they have a skeleton crew working. That'll be our best shot."

"How do you know this?" Dazzler asked.

"I told you, I once worked for S.W.O.R.D. in an alternate dimension. So far, my impression is that this station runs in a similar way to the other one."

"You have a long and mysterious history, Sage," Rachel said.

"Don't we all," Sage replied.

"No," Dazzler said. "I think you have us all beat."

"We still need to know the movements of the guards outside to continue our investigation safely," Sage said, ignoring the comment.

"How do we do that?" Dazzler asked. "Can you mind-read them for that?"

"Rachel is best placed for this," Sage said.

"Rachel?" Dazzler asked.

"I like how you hate me jumping into your head but constantly insist I jump into everyone else's," Rachel said.

"Rachel," Dazzler said.

"All right, all right, I'm on it."

Emma Frost watched as S.H.I.E.L.D. bound Rosenthorpe's men and packed them into their SUVs. Now the immediate threat was over, the news that Magneto and Cyclops were dead had time to resurface. She didn't want to believe it. Her whole body shook, rejecting the thought from every fiber of her being. But what if it was true? She hadn't felt so unsure about her next move before, and it bothered her. She preferred to be cool, calm, and collected. Not useless. Not helpless. And that's how she felt.

"Are you coming?" Maria Hill asked as she approached.

"I need to make a call first," Emma said, pulling out her phone and calling Sage.

Her call went unanswered. She stared at the phone a moment, then tried Dazzler's number.

It, too, went unanswered.

She closed her eyes and tried to connect telepathically with Sage, but she found it difficult. All she picked up was static and interference. She knew Sage's brain was unlike any other. It was complex and harder to manipulate than most, and right now it felt extra difficult, as though she had erected some kind of firewall to stop Emma from knowing what she was up to.

Emma's concern increased. She enabled the scrambling mechanism on her phone then made a third call.

"I thought you said *a* call?" Hill said, placing her hands on her hips.

Emma raised a hand to silence her, then turned and walked away.

"How nice of you to use a phone this time," Logan answered gruffly.

"Do you know where they are?" Emma cut to the chase.

"Who?"

"Who do you think? Sage isn't answering my calls."

"She's your acquaintance, so how would I know?"

"Did Polaris or Rachel check in with you?"

"A while ago. Said they'd been to some warehouse but found nothing."

"I was told the same thing, but I'm starting to think they're cutting us out of whatever is going on."

"So do your mind thing and find out."

"I tried. I can't make contact with Sage. I'm just picking up static."

"Sounds like she's running interference with you. What about Dazzler?"

"I don't want to go there yet. She's been acting cagey, and if I force myself into her mind, I know she'll definitely cut me out then."

"So, Sage is blocking you and Dazzler doesn't trust you," Logan said. "Why is that?"

Emma ignored the pointed question. "Do you know where they were headed?"

"No."

"And you're OK with that?" she asked, suspicious. Was Logan hiding something?

"No. But Polaris asked that I trust her. So, that's what I'm doing. She and Rachel are good mutants."

"Why are they hiding their movements from us?"

"If I was to take a guess, I'd say they're trying to hide their movements from S.H.I.E.L.D. The fewer people know, the less likely that information is to fall into the wrong hands. I've already had Maria Hill sniffing around here to offer me assistance should I need it."

"Hill was at your school?" Emma asked, turning back around and eyeing the former S.H.I.E.L.D. director, who stood in the distance, splitting her attention between watching Emma and checking her phone.

"Yeah. So, I'm thinking they're just trying to stay hidden."

"And if they get into trouble and we don't know where they are?" Emma asked.

"I thought you trusted Sage. Why are you so jumpy to know their exact movements?"

Emma was silent, considering how to answer. She wanted to mention Shaw but wasn't sure how the volatile Logan would handle that.

"I don't like it when I can't see what I need to," she said. "Listen, do me a favor, see if you can trace Mystique on Cerebro."

"Mystique? Why?"

"Just do it, Logan. I don't have time."

He growled, then she heard him give muffled instructions to someone off the phone.

"We're on it," he said. "Why are you being so uptight? What do you know?"

"Nothing. Yet. But I hope to soon. I have the owner of a shipment of MGH in custody, and I'm about to interrogate him."

"Where?"

"I don't know. It depends where S.H.I.E.L.D. takes him."

"*You're* working with S.H.I.E.L.D. now? Well, that's new." She heard more muffled voices in the background, before Logan came back. "Mystique's in some bar in Paris, lifting some guy's wallet."

"She is?"

"Yeah. And we couldn't detect Dazzler or her mutant team in Mystique's vicinity, so it doesn't look like they're on her tail."

"Right," Emma said, her mind turning over. "Keep an eye on her and keep me posted." She hung up the phone, exhaled subtly with frustration, aware of the S.H.I.E.L.D. agents in the vicinity. She didn't want to tell Logan that Shaw might be involved. Given her history with the mutant and her time at the Hellfire Club, Logan might be fast to mistrust her, and right now she needed an alliance with him.

So where did this leave her?

"You ready?" Hill asked, approaching her again, eyes narrowed in suspicion.

Emma nodded, tucking her phone away.

"You better be right about this guy," Hill warned. "We've got nothing on Cassandra Walsh so far, and if we don't find some evidence soon, we're going to have to let her go."

"You can't do that."

"Why?"

"Because someone is making mutants disappear, so I'm making his people disappear."

"His? Who are you talking about?" Hill asked, eyes piercing hers. "I assume you don't mean Rosenthorpe."

"I'll tell you when I have concrete evidence."

"If you know something, you tell me now," Hill demanded.

Emma stared back but remained silent.

"*You* contacted me, Frost," Hill said.

"And I'll tell you when I have evidence," Emma said, walking past her toward the SUVs. "That's what you need, right? Evidence."

CHAPTER TWENTY-THREE

Dazzler lay on her bed in the station's dim night lighting, humming a song and watching as her light powers manifested at her fingertips like glowing nail polish. She sang partly out of boredom and partly to add to her stores, however minor the sonic conversion was. She always got a stronger result when the sound came from an external source, like the heat produced from a fire burning out of control versus the warm coals of a dying fire. But there was also another reason she sang to herself. She was trying to distract herself from more thoughts about Frost, and that corridor at the New Charles Xavier School, and the gap in between. She was convinced now that Frost had wiped part of her memory. But why? What had been behind that door? What was Frost up to? What was she trying to hide?

She suddenly heard a bang on the external wall of her cell. Then she heard another, like a soft thud. She paused her singing and listened. She heard another thud and sat up.

"What is it?" she said aloud, thinking one of her team must be trying to get her attention.

"It's not us," Sage's voice sounded inside her mind. "It must be the asteroid shower hitting the station."

"Oh," Dazzler said, placing her hand against the wall. She heard more thuds but felt no vibration and realized the station had probably enabled a protective shield. Now she knew what the sound was, she realized the thuds were actually some distance away from her cell.

"I have the guard movements," Rachel said, popping into her mind. "One remains outside our cabins at all times while one patrols the surrounding hallways. The second guard is due to pass by our area on patrol soon. That's our chance to make a break for it. As soon as his thoughts wander away, I'll give Polaris the sign to start freeing us. While she does that, I'll distract the guard outside by jumping into his head and confusing him. We'll only have a short window before he might get edgy and shoot, so we need to move fast."

"All right," Dazzler said, standing up. "I'm ready."

"What's the plan for when we get out?" Sage said.

"We need to access the dock manifests and see what we can find out about the cargo," Dazzler said. "So, I say we head for the cargo hold."

"I need my glasses and weapons," Sage said.

"Yeah, and I need my earbuds. Rachel, can you find out where they are?"

Silence surrounded her for a moment as Dazzler flexed her hands. Her fingernails shimmered.

"They're in the guards' Security Room," Rachel finally answered. "That's what I pulled from the heads outside."

"Do you know where the Security Room is?" Dazzler asked.

"Rachel," Sage said. "Tap into the guard's brain and download a rough floorplan to this station and push it into my brain."

"Rachel, can you do that?" Dazzler asked.

"I... guess."

"Once data enters my brain, I never forget it," Sage said.

"I'll get the floorplan, then tell Polaris to start," Rachel said.

Suddenly Dazzler was in silence again. She stared at the door, waiting, as the energy sparked within her, and her heart raced to the beat of a new song.

The song of the scions.

Dazzler heard a clunk, then another, then a small commotion of footsteps and voices, then a click as her door's light went from red to green. She stepped forward and pulled the door open to see a guard unconscious in Sage's strong arms, Rachel at the corner of the hallway keeping watch, and Polaris motioning Dazzler out.

"Where's the Security Room?" Dazzler asked, as Sage removed the guard's comms then dragged the man's body inside Dazzler's room and locked him inside.

"This way," Sage said, moving toward Rachel. "We won't have long as there are security cameras everywhere."

"Tell me where they are and I'll move them," Polaris said.

"Or I'll blind them," Dazzler added.

They moved swiftly as a unit down the corridor, following Sage's assured steps, as though she knew these corridors like the back of her hand. With precision, she indicated the upcoming security cameras, and either Polaris would turn them away, or Dazzler would flare light into the lens as they passed.

Sage suddenly slowed, slinking up to a corner in the corridor. "The Security Room is through there," she said.

"There's guards inside," Rachel said, eyes whitened.

"Can you confuse them?" Sage asked.

"I'll try but there's several to hit at the same time," she answered.

"Leave this one to me," Dazzler said, moving ahead of them, and wiggling her fingers to loosen them up. "I've got enough juice in the tank to stun these guys."

She walked toward the office with her usual hip-swaying strut, and when she entered the Security Room, seven pairs of eyes turned to look at her.

"What are you doing out?" one asked, mouth falling open.

"Thought I'd come say hi." She beamed. "I hear some of you are fans." She raised her hands, and blasted them with light, knocking them unconscious. Their bodies slumped over tables and chairs, and one or two fell to the floor, spilling cups of coffee and chicken sandwiches.

Rachel, Sage, and Polaris swiftly spilled into the room behind Dazzler, closing the door behind them.

"Where's our gear?" Dazzler asked Sage.

"They're in there." Rachel pointed to a locker.

"Polaris?" Sage said.

Polaris raised her hand in a claw, in the direction of the locker, and yanked her hand back, ripping the door off. Sage instantly dove in, pulled out her glasses and weapons, then in swift movements, threw Dazzler her earbuds and phone, then whipped out her haptic glove and slid it on her hand.

"We need to get out of here before the patrolling guard comes back," Rachel said.

Dazzler nodded. "Let's move. How far is the cargo hold from here?" she asked Sage.

"It's close," Sage said, then motioned to the unconscious guards. "Let's put their uniforms on."

Dazzler followed Sage once more, this time playing a little Lila Cheney in her ears. It was one of Dazzler's favorite rock ballads about betrayal and revenge. It seemed appropriate given the circumstances.

As they neared the cargo hold, she felt her light powers crackling beneath her skin, thanks in part to Lila's angry vocals, but also thanks to the adrenaline coursing through her bloodstream. They walked with confidence, thanks to the stolen uniforms they wore over their jumpsuits, the swift and efficient camera turning movements of Polaris, Dazzler's hypnotic lights, and Rachel's mind interference on anyone who looked at them twice.

When they reached the cargo hold, Sage quickly located an unmanned console and got to work. As she tapped away on its screen, searching for the cargo records, the mutant team stood close by, scanning their surroundings.

Dazzler, feeling secure for the moment, pulled her earbuds out, watching in awe as Sage navigated through S.W.O.R.D.'s shipping system without any trouble and punched in the consignment number from memory. Though Dazzler figured Sage's time working for S.W.O.R.D. in the other dimension obviously helped with her moving so swiftly through a familiar software system, she still whistled, impressed.

"Frost was right. You really are useful."

A smile curled Sage's lips, as she continued working the

system. "Frost has an eye for talent, and if you stay on her good side, she'll help you develop it."

The mutant's words floated in Dazzler's mind as she recalled what Frost had said to her at the very start of this mission – that Dazzler might have the potential to be an Omega-level mutant one day. Did this mean she was on Frost's watch list? Dazzler had a pretty good grasp on her talents, but it was starting to make her wonder just what else she could do if her powers were nurtured and developed further. What level could she take her light powers to? She'd never really tried to do more than hypnotize or temporarily blind people before, or use her light energy as a protective shield, or channel it into a fine laser or light sword. But what if she could do more? Did Frost see potential that Dazzler hadn't? What could happen if she took in a large amount of sonic energy? With enough stimulation could she one day have the equivalent power of a nuclear bomb?

Quite frankly, the thought terrified her.

A flash of red caught her eye, and she came out of her reverie to see Rachel looking at her curiously. Dazzler's brow furrowed. Had Rachel been reading her mind again?

"You all right?" Polaris asked her quietly. "You seemed to vague out for a moment there."

"Yeah." Dazzler nodded, suddenly feeling a strange kinship with her. Polaris didn't know the full extent of her powers either. Nor did Rachel for that matter. If Lorna was as strong or even stronger than Magneto, and Rachel was as strong or even stronger than her mother, Jean, then all three of them had the potential to be powerful mutants. All three could one day have the potential for great good. Or great destruction.

She turned to look through a distant observation window at the asteroid shower all around them, the rocks bouncing off the station's protective shield, sparking light with each hit. It was a stunning sight.

Dangerous, but beautiful.

"I've tracked the cargo," Sage said, breaking her thoughts, "and accessed the security footage on the dock. We need to find this guy." She pointed to a paused image from the footage of a dock worker in a S.W.O.R.D. uniform with the suspect cargo. The man was tall and his face thin with angular lines, and there was something hard about his eyes too. Sage raised her hand to her glasses. "I'll record his image. He arrived with the cargo, then he sent it on to Earth, to Sanderson Holdings."

"How do we find him?" Polaris asked.

"I'll check the S.W.O.R.D. staff files," Sage said.

Dazzler noticed two officers talking at the entrance of the cargo hold and watching them. "We don't have long," she said.

"It's too late," Rachel said, eyeing the same officers. "They've put in a call to Valdana."

"Shoot," Dazzler hissed.

"I can't find him in the staff files," Sage said, shaking her head. "He's not listed as staff."

"So, who is he?" Dazzler asked. "And how did he manage to just walk around Alpha Flight without anyone noticing?"

"Wait," Sage said, "I found something."

"What is it?" Dazzler stepped closer. "Hurry, Sage."

"Guards!" Rachel warned.

They turned to see several soldiers flowing into the cargo hold, weapons raised and headed toward them.

Sage glanced at the soldiers, then to Dazzler. "This man,

Lieutenant Hask, he was transferred from a unit called A.R.M.O.R."

"Another acronym?" Polaris said.

"What's A.R.M.O.R.?" Dazzler asked.

Sage gave her a troubled look. "I don't know."

"Stop right there!" one of the guards yelled, as the rest of the squad spread out, surrounding them with their weapons aimed.

"Do we fight?" Polaris tensed, her hands ready.

"No," Dazzler said, concerned. They were outnumbered, and although she had no doubt the four mutants could easily clear the dock, she wasn't ready to use mutant powers on human guards who were just doing their job. At least, she hoped that was all they were doing. "There's nowhere to run, and our leads have dried up," she said. "We need to talk to Valdana again."

Emma Frost stepped out of Maria Hill's SUV and found herself in an abandoned airfield hangar not far from JFK airport.

"This is where you're working from these days?" Emma asked.

Hill ignored her, motioning to an agent who joined them. "This is Agent Bennett."

Bennett extended his hand, and Emma shook it.

"Where's Cassandra Walsh?" Emma asked.

"She's on the other side of the warehouse," Bennett said. "Up in the office space."

Emma watched as Rosenthorpe was pulled from another SUV, marched over to a single chair placed on the bare concrete floor, and pushed down into the seat.

As Rosenthorpe dropped into his seat, so, too, did a realization descend on Emma.

"S.H.I.E.L.D. aren't back, are they?" she said to Hill. "If you were, you'd have better facilities at your disposal."

Hill's gaze sharpened. "Let's just say if we expose a real threat here, then the keys to S.H.I.E.L.D. funding will return."

"Why are you allowing me to see this?" Emma asked.

Hill studied her a moment. "We once had an alliance, S.H.I.E.L.D. and mutants. If we get S.H.I.E.L.D. reinstated, we would like that alliance to return."

Emma smiled. "Because you need us."

"Because we need each other."

"No," Emma said. "Because *you* need us. The only reason I'm here now is because you want me to read their minds." She stepped closer toward Hill. "I don't mind being used, Hill, but do hate being lied to."

"I'm not lying to you."

"Care to let me read your mind to prove that?"

"No can do, I'm afraid." Hill tapped her temple. "This mind holds a lot of classified information. Besides, you forget, you're the one who contacted me. You invited me to get involved with Walsh and Rosenthorpe because you needed S.H.I.E.L.D.'s help. So, don't play hard to get, Ms Frost. We can use each other and both get what we want." Hill turned and walked toward Rosenthorpe, looking back over her shoulder. "You coming?"

CHAPTER TWENTY- FOUR

Dazzler suffered from a serious bout of acrophobia as she stood in the spacious commander's office surrounded by S.W.O.R.D. soldiers. She'd never feared heights before, but standing on the clear flooring and seeing the bodies walking around on the station level below was very off-putting. Not to mention that the whole office was essentially an expansive glass box that, although it offered amazing views of the Earth's curvature and the dying asteroid shower in the starlit space beyond, made her feel like if she didn't hold on to something she might float away into space or fall through to the level below. It was both stunning and terrifying at the same time.

"You wouldn't want to wear a skirt in here," Dazzler said, looking through to the floor below.

"The flooring has one-way vision," Valdana told her. "It's so the commander can keep an eye on things." She smiled. "Did you really think you'd be able to break out of your rooms and into our shipping system and not get caught?"

Dazzler shrugged. "Well, if you'd just spoken to us in the first place, we wouldn't have needed to do all that."

"Do you know how many charges I can lay against you?" Valdana asked.

"A few, I'm guessing, but I also have a few of my own I could throw at *you*."

"I don't think so. Your S.H.I.E.L.D. credentials are weak and of a low classification level, Blaire. You don't have the power you think you do."

"Maybe not, but the people I report to do have the power."

"Stop trying to distract from the fact that you broke into our systems, Agent Blaire. That is a *serious* offense."

"And it's also a serious offense to distribute a banned substance."

"Excuse me?" Valdana frowned.

"I told you before, we tracked an illegal shipment as having come from here. When we accessed your systems, we located that shipment on your security footage. Someone wearing a S.W.O.R.D. uniform brought it here to Alpha Flight, then sent it on to Earth. Care to explain that?"

"I need to explain nothing," Valdana said firmly, "other than the charges against you."

"The man who sent the shipment to Earth," Dazzler pushed on, desperate to get her message across before they were locked up again, "we can't find him in your staff profiles, which could mean you've been infiltrated." Dazzler intentionally left out Lieutenant Hask's transfer from the mysterious A.R.M.O.R. to test her.

"Impossible. You've seen our security," Valdana said. "No one infiltrates the Alpha Flight Low-Orbit Space Station."

"Then S.W.O.R.D. is complicit in the distribution of a banned substance–"

"That is a serious allegation–"

"A very dangerous substance known as MGH!"

Valdana paused, eyes narrowing. Dazzler glanced nervously at the guards in the room with them and mentally kicked herself for revealing the substance's name.

The acting commander's mind seemed to halt briefly, before she looked at the guards. "Leave us."

"Commander Valdana?" the lead soldier questioned. "They're mutants."

"I can handle them. Go. And don't breathe a word of this to anyone, or you'll find yourself flying out the nearest airlock. Understood?"

The guard nodded. Dazzler watched them leave the glass box, then turned back to Valdana, curious as to why she sent them away.

"Do you take me for a fool, Blaire?" Valdana asked. "I'm the Acting Commander of Alpha Flight, S.W.O.R.D.'s HQ. I know a lot of things–"

"Except what MGH is or the consequences of this getting out on the streets."

Valdana gave her a hard stare before conceding the truth. "What is it, this MGH?"

"It's a steroid made from mutant DNA. It can affect both humans and mutants. In the wrong hands…" Dazzler let her eyes finish her sentence.

Valdana understood her perfectly. "Well, I assure you, it has nothing to do with S.W.O.R.D. or this station."

"I beg to differ. There are both humans and mutants missing, and their disappearance is linked to whoever is distributing the MGH. We found a shipment that came from this station, sent by a man in a S.W.O.R.D. uniform." Dazzler looked to Sage. "Can you show her the image?"

Sage nodded and tapped the side of her glasses. The image of the man on the dock projected in holographic form.

"He's one of ours," Valdana said simply.

"No, he's not. He was missing from your staff profiles," Sage said. "He transferred from someplace called A.R.M.O.R. apparently."

Valdana stilled. "Let's just say he's on secondment. He's working for us but doesn't actually work for us."

"What's A.R.M.O.R.?" Dazzler asked. "Can you tell us anything about it?"

Valdana contemplated her answer.

"We know that shipment contained MGH," Dazzler said, "so you might as well tell us. Does S.H.I.E.L.D. know about this?"

"You tell me?" Valdana volleyed.

"Well, like you said, my credentials only unlock certain benefits."

"Then why should I tell you?"

"Because people are missing, and the MGH is starting to spill out onto the streets of Earth. If we don't stop it, there will be carnage. Humans and mutants alike will be jacked up on this stuff, and people will die. And S.W.O.R.D. will be the ones responsible for its release. Do you want that on your conscience? Do you want to be the fall guy for whoever is really behind all this?"

Valdana considered again, the seriousness of the situation beginning to settle into her features.

"Who is this guy," Dazzler asked, motioning to the projected hologram image, "and why is he shipping MGH from your station?"

Valdana sighed. As she did, Dazzler caught a falling star through the windows, in the distance. She took it as a sign. Valdana was about to give in.

"A.R.M.O.R. is the Alternate Reality Monitoring and Operational Response agency. They're an extra-dimensional security force that guard against contamination and conflict from other alternate realities."

"Alternate realities?" Polaris asked. "As in, other dimensions?"

Valdana nodded. "We're working on a joint initiative together. A new dimension was recently discovered, and a billionaire bought the rights to it."

"Sebastian Shaw," Sage said.

"Yes," Valdana said, surprised. "You know him?"

"We have history," Sage said, tapping her glasses and removing the hologram projection. "You?"

"I wasn't aware of him until recently," Valdana answered. "We initially thought he was setting up an extra-exclusive off-world Hellfire Club in this alternative reality, but we soon detected a lot of shipments going back and forth, mainly of scientific equipment. S.W.O.R.D. grew suspicious. The man you identified on our dock is an undercover A.R.M.O.R. agent, Lieutenant Hask, who's been working for Shaw and delivering us intel."

"Did Hask provide you with intel on this particular shipment of MGH?" Dazzler asked.

Valdana's face flushed with a mixture of concern and embarrassment. "No. He did not."

"So, he's working for Shaw," Rachel said with a scowl. "Not you."

"Where does A.R.M.O.R. fit in with this?" Polaris mused. "Whose side are they on? S.W.O.R.D.'s or Shaw's?"

"S.H.I.E.L.D., S.W.O.R.D., and A.R.M.O.R." Dazzler shook her head. "There's too many of you guys to keep an eye on."

"Answer me this. Why would Shaw want this MGH?" Valdana sat forward over her desk. It was clear she wanted answers now, wanted to know if S.W.O.R.D. had already been made a fool. "It can't be money. He seems to have plenty of that already."

"Power," Sage answered for her. "It's what Shaw thrives on."

"Well, I guess we've established that he's not a victim in this," Dazzler said.

"No," Sage said, placing her hands on her hips. "This does not surprise me."

Dazzler looked back to Valdana. "Do you trust A.R.M.O.R.? Could this guy, Hask, be a lone wolf working for Shaw?"

Valdana considered the possibility. "I trust A.R.M.O.R. But there's only one way to find out for sure. Let me speak with Hask's commander, see what he says about the evidence I present him."

Dazzler nodded. "While you do that, any ideas on where we can find this Hask?"

"Yes," Valdana said. "He's on station. Shouldn't be hard to find."

"Good," Dazzler said. "Don't announce our arrival. We'll bring him in. Tell your soldiers to stay out of our way."

"You're assuming I'm going to free you and absolve you of your sins, Agent Blaire," Valdana said.

Dazzler stared at her. "You need us. If you like alliances so much, then make an alliance with us."

"I'll have my soldiers bring him in." Valdana reached for her comms panel.

"No. Let us do this. On the quiet. You don't want to draw attention to this, do you? The fact that MGH was being shipped from your station and S.W.O.R.D. was unaware?"

Valdana studied her for a moment in consideration. "All right. But step out of line, and you'll find yourself back in the Detention Module so fast you'll feel like you're spinning in orbit."

Dazzler gave a single, sharp nod as she inserted her earbuds. She pressed play on Lila Cheney's angry vocals, sparked light from her fingertips, then headed for the door as her mutant team followed.

Dazzler stood with her team in a glass elevator as it descended to the floor below, visible from Commander Valdana's office. As it moved swiftly, so did Sage's haptic glove in the air, locking in to the station's security footage and running a facial recognition trace on their target.

Dazzler looked at Polaris and Rachel. "We need to be ready for this guy. If Hask is working for Shaw, I don't trust him or the tactics he may use."

"We can handle him," Polaris said confidently.

Dazzler studied her. Although Polaris's powers had been glitchy, when her life had depended on it, they'd been working full force just fine. Dazzler had to hope that their lives didn't need to hang in the balance in order for Polaris's magnetism to work properly.

"Just don't kill him," Dazzler said. "We need information."

"At least there're no buses here that he can run into," Rachel said, her voice a little distant.

"Yeah, let's not get ahead of ourselves," Dazzler said. "We don't know this station like he does."

"Found him!" Sage said. "He's in the Pod Module. The staff barracks."

"How do we get there?" Dazzler asked.

Sage smiled as the elevator doors opened. "Follow me."

They walked across the expansive floor of the station to a bank of elevators opposite that serviced the Pod Module. Thankfully, these elevators looked to have metal walls, which eased Dazzler's sense of acrophobia. Her mutant team didn't seem to be drawing attention, which added to her relief. Still dressed in the S.W.O.R.D. uniforms, they blended in nicely with those roaming around the station – all manner of humans and alien beings. Dazzler was utterly fascinated by those she had never seen before, but she didn't have time to study or try to meet any of them. They had to get to Hask before he knew they were on to him and he ran.

They stepped inside the elevator and began to ascend to level three. Dazzler cranked the music in her ears, feeling the electricity crackle all over her body. Maybe a little too much because the other three mutants scooted away from her, shooting her concerned looks.

"Sorry," she said, pulling her energy back and lowering the volume.

"Now I know where the light show came from during your gig with Lila Cheney," Sage smiled. "It was awesome."

Dazzler smiled back. "Thank you."

They arrived on level three, and the elevator opened. Sage was swiftly out of the doors, and the others followed her down white hallways, not dissimilar to the Detention Module, on their way to the traitor's cabin. Sage slowed as they neared their target's pod. She motioned for Polaris and Rachel to guard one side of the door and Dazzler to take the other, while she knocked.

There was no response, however.

Sage tapped her glasses and stared at the door, scanning side to side. "It's empty," she said, tapping her glasses again and turning around. "He's not here."

"So where is he?" Dazzler asked, placing her hands on her hips. "Could he have known and manipulated the security footage?"

Sage shrugged. "If he's a spy, anything is possible." Dazzler locked eyes with Sage curiously, who smiled. "Not that I would know."

Polaris pointed down the hallway. "Nope! There he is!"

Dazzler turned to see Hask paused in the hallway intersection, staring at the four strange women at his door. Then, he suddenly snapped around and raced back toward the elevators.

"Not another runner!" Dazzler groaned, sprinting after him.

"Rachel, go with her!" Sage said from behind. "Polaris, come with me, we'll cut him off via another route."

Dazzler chased Hask to the elevators, but she was too late. The doors closed, and no matter how many times she hit the button, they did not re-open. "Shoot!" She stepped back watching which level it went to as Rachel joined her side. "You need to keep up."

"And you need to be quiet," Rachel said, white-eyed and concentrating.

The elevator seemed to pause on level six.

"Tell Sage he's on level six," Dazzler said, as another set of elevator doors opened for them.

"He's not on level six," Rachel said, following her inside the elevator. "He just wants you to think he is."

"Where is he then? It didn't stop at any other floor."

"He's in the elevator shaft," Rachel said, still concentrating. "He's climbing down to level five."

Dazzler punched five on the elevator panel. "Make sure you tell Sage."

"Already done," Rachel replied, looking back at her as the doors closed. "I'm not completely useless."

"No," Dazzler said, her face softening. "You're pretty good actually."

Rachel studied her as though trying to gauge whether she was being sarcastic or not.

"Thanks again for taking that bullet," Dazzler told her.

Rachel returned a genuine smile, but as the elevator dinged on level five, she fell back into a concentrated business. They stepped out into the hallway, and Dazzler waited with anticipation as Rachel tried to get a lock on the guy.

"He's still climbing down. He's almost at our floor," Rachel said. "Want me to mind control him?"

Before Dazzler could answer, they heard thumping footsteps and turned to see Sage and Polaris running down the hallway toward them from their alternative route.

"Access panel is this way!" Sage said, turning a corner before the bank of elevators. Dazzler and Rachel ran after them.

Sage pulled up in front of a locked access door. "Polaris!"

Polaris extended her hand and jerked her hand back, but

nothing happened. She growled then concentrated, repeated the movement, and pulled the door open with force. Sage carefully leaned through the small doorway as she scanned for Hask, then hissed.

"He's already below us!"

Dazzler pushed her way forward to look inside. "Can I stun him from here?"

"Too risky. He may fall," Sage said.

Sage was right. Hask was climbing down the side of the walls. If Dazzler stunned him, he would fall many floors to his death.

"I'll go after him," Sage said. "Polaris, come with me. If he tries to flee through another access panel, I'll need you to close it for me."

Polaris gave a nod and Dazzler watched as the two mutants climbed into the elevator shaft.

"We'll go down to level four and cut him off from there," Dazzler said, closing the shaft door behind them and running back to the elevators.

Dazzler and Rachel made their way down to level four and found another access panel in a similar position to the floor above.

"Where's Polaris when you need her?" Rachel said, studying the locked door.

"Move aside," Dazzler said, raising her hand and pointing her index finger at the lock. She pooled her light energy into a long, thin configuration, then fired it out of her fingertip. The concentrated laser-like light energy drilled into the lock, burning a hole through the door.

"It's kinda cool that you can shoot lasers," Rachel said.

Dazzler smiled. "You should see me project a light sword." She pulled open the door, leaned in carefully and looked up to find Hask just a few feet from her, and beyond Sage and Polaris were on his tail. Hask looked worried, but as he saw Dazzler below and realized he was boxed in, his concern turned to pure panic.

"Careful," Rachel said, eyes whitened. "He's concealing a laser weapon of his own."

Just as she said that, Dazzler saw Hask reach into his jacket and pull out the weapon. "Sage! Look out!" Dazzler yelled, before retreating from the access door, as laser fire shot past the opening. They heard more shots but saw no fire go past the doorway, which meant he'd fired at Sage and Polaris. "What's happening?" she asked Rachel.

"They're safe," she said, white-eyed. "They took cover behind some elevator rigging."

Dazzler's mind raced, wondering how to catch him. She needed to disarm him, but everything she thought of involved stunning him in some way, which meant he could fall.

"OK, it's time to mind control him," she said.

Rachel clenched her fists in concentration, eyes still white.

They heard more laser fire.

"Rachel?"

The redhead was silent for a moment, before her eyes turned pale green again. "He's blocking me somehow. I just keep seeing pink cotton candy."

Dazzler dared another peep into the shaft. Hask aimed his weapon to fire at her.

"Elevator!" Sage yelled in warning.

Dazzler and Hask looked up to see the elevator cable, damaged from the laser fire, snap and the large metal box fall toward them with the speed of gravity. Hask flattened himself against the wall and Dazzler pulled back from the access panel again. They heard a collision, saw sparks, and heard a grinding, crunching sound as the unit moved past the shaft opening, before a loud squeal sounded and the floor they stood on rumbled. When it eased, Dazzler carefully peered back inside and saw the elevator below her, looking slightly mangled and sitting on an angle between the wall and another elevator opposite. She looked up the shaft to see Polaris with her hand out, straining as she held it in place.

"Tell Sage to shut down the elevators," Dazzler told Rachel, who nodded and turned away in concentration.

"She's on it," Rachel said, turning back.

Dazzler peered back into the shaft again. Hask was still in place, panting with fear from the narrow miss, while Sage and Polaris remained above him, near the damaged rigging. Polaris's hand was at rest now, so the elevator was staying put on its own.

And it gave her an idea.

"Tell them I'm going to stun him," Dazzler said. "Tell Polaris she needs to fly down and catch his fall. I won't have time to stun him and catch him. She'll have to do it."

Rachel stared at her for a moment in shocked consideration, then turned her face away to relay the message. Dazzler peeped inside again, and Hask fired his weapon at her. She pulled back, narrowly missing the laser fire.

"Does this guy have a death wish? He's really starting to annoy me," she said, pulling her phone out and cranking the volume on Lila again. "Did you relay the message?"

Rachel nodded.

"On the count of three," Dazzler said, and Rachel nodded. "One, two, THREE!"

Dazzler leaned into the shaft, hands first, palms outward, and pulsed a strong beam of white light energy at him. It hit Hask right in the face, and he fell from the wall like a ragdoll. Dazzler swiftly retreated from the shaft as his body flew past and Polaris rushed after him. In an instant, Dazzler climbed inside the shaft and jumped down after them, pushing her light power through her feet as she bounced from wall to wall. She saw Polaris grab the falling, unconscious Hask, and the two hung midair for a moment before she lowered his body onto the top of the stalled elevator, leaning on its awkward angle.

Dazzler bounced down to join them on the askew elevator roof, which shuddered and shook with her added weight. She paused Lila's vocals, waited for the elevator to stabilize, and looked at Polaris. "Nice work," she panted.

Suddenly the elevator dropped several inches, and Dazzler felt butterflies in her stomach. She held on as much as she could. The weight of the three of them and the elevator's odd angle did not mix. It paused briefly for another moment, before falling again, this time several feet, and Dazzler tried to find her balance, surfing the falling box. Polaris swung both hands out, arms straining as she stalled its fall, her face quickly turning pink.

Dazzler, eyes wide, peered over the side. She saw the doors to the next floor below. "Can you lower us to those doors? I'll get him inside and out onto the floor."

Polaris, laboring like she was lifting a ton, glanced over the side to the door's location. She looked back at Dazzler and gave a restrained nod, motioning to the access panel in the elevator's roof. "Get him inside."

Dazzler knelt carefully and opened the elevator's access

panel. She then moved to the unconscious man and dragged him to the opening, then dropped him inside as gently as she could. The elevator swayed and groaned, and Polaris swayed and groaned, but she kept her arms and power strong. Teeth gritted and sweat forming on her brow, Polaris motioned for Dazzler to get inside. Dazzler fed herself through the opening to the elevator's interior, careful not to land on Hask. Again, the elevator swayed with the movement, and Polaris grunted loudly but held things steady.

A few seconds passed, then Dazzler felt more movement.

Bit by bit Polaris carefully lowered the elevator down to the next set of doors.

"You're there," she called out with a tight voice to Dazzler, who pried open the doors of the elevator, then did the same with the external doors to the floor. When they opened, she saw the elevator was lower than the door opening. In fact, the floor was at her chest height.

"Hurry!" Polaris yelled. "I can't hold this all day!"

Dazzler grabbed Hask and heaved his body to the opening, pausing as the elevator swayed again. "OK, we're crossing over," Dazzler said, wanting Polaris to hold as still as she could. She grabbed Hask under the arms and tried to heave his body off the floor of the elevator, but it was difficult. Lifting this guy was easier said than done for her physical strength. She looked around, considering her options. She heard running footsteps and looked up to see Sage and Rachel headed toward them.

"Hurry!" she called to them.

They skidded to their knees before Dazzler, grabbed Hask's arms, and heaved him out onto the pod floor with them, then turned and pulled Dazzler out too.

Dazzler called back into the elevator, "We're out!"

"Stand clear," Polaris called back, her voice cracking with effort. Dazzler did so, watching as the elevator suddenly scraped past to a stop just below the opening, then a rush of wind blew around them as Polaris flew through the opened elevator doors to land softly beside them, a vision of flowing green hair.

"Great job," Dazzler panted, as Polaris collapsed on the ground, catching her breath.

"He's waking," Rachel warned them, as Hask began to stir.

"No, he's not," Sage said, lifting her fist and knocking him out again.

Dazzler stared at her in surprise, before suddenly breaking into laughter, joined soon by Polaris and Rachel, and even Sage herself.

"Good job, team." Dazzler smiled at them all. "Good job."

CHAPTER TWENTY-FIVE

Dazzler stood beside Valdana in the interrogation room, opposite a now conscious Hask who was cuffed and seated at the table. Her mutant team and a sprinkling of S.W.O.R.D. soldiers filled the room. Dazzler was glad to be one of the interrogators this time, and glad that Valdana had agreed to let her assist in the questioning.

"You were caught on camera arriving with this shipment and then forwarding it to Sanderson Holdings on Earth," Valdana said to Hask, showing him the footage on her tablet. "There's no denying it."

"I didn't know what was inside," Hask said. His eyes were brown and spotted with reflections of the white room around him, and the stubble across his cheeks made his gaunt face appear gray. "I was just asked to forward it."

"Who asked you to send it?" Valdana asked.

"Shaw."

"Where did it come from?" Dazzler asked. "This new dimension of his?"

Hask nodded.

"What is he doing with all the scientific equipment he's shipping there?" Valdana asked, slowing her pacing before the table.

"I don't know."

"But you've been there, right?" Dazzler asked. "To the new dimension? So, you've seen it."

Again, Hask nodded. "I've been there several times. I run his errands," he explained. "I escort his shipments. And I don't ask questions."

"But it's your job to ask questions," Dazzler said. "You're an undercover agent. It's *literally* your job to get intel on things like mysterious shipments."

"It's my job to fly under the radar and not get caught," Hask told her. "These things take time. Someone like Sebastian Shaw doesn't give his trust away easily, you know."

Dazzler stared at him for a moment. "If you're so innocent in all of this, then why did you run when you saw us? Why did you shoot at us?"

"Because four mutants were at my door, in uniforms I knew weren't theirs. What did you expect me to do?"

"Not run. And not shoot at us."

Hask shrugged. "I guess it's the hazards of being an undercover agent. You learn not to trust anyone."

"Oh, I hear that," Dazzler smiled. "And that's exactly the reason why I don't buy what you're saying now." She placed her hands on the table and leaned toward him. "That's exactly why I don't trust you. You knew what was in that shipment, and you knew what Shaw was up to, and that's why you didn't report it to Commander Valdana. So, save yourself a long prison sentence by cooperating and telling us what you know."

"I've already told you. I don't know." He stared at her with a glimmer of defiance in his eyes.

"But you somehow knew we were mutants," Sage said from where she stood at the back of the room, arms folded. "Despite none of us having any outward traits to identify us as such."

"Word gets around," Hask said. "I heard there were uninvited mutant women on the station. I put two and two together."

"What's the scientific equipment for?" Dazzler asked. "Is he mass-producing MGH in the other dimension and shipping it back to this one?"

Hask shrugged, disinterested.

"Why didn't you report the shipment to Acting Commander Valdana?" Dazzler asked, leaning on the table.

"I report to my superiors at A.R.M.O.R.," he said.

"You're also supposed to report to me," Valdana said firmly. "That was the deal, to let you operate from Alpha Flight. This is S.W.O.R.D. territory, and we have the right to know what's happening on our turf."

"I forwarded a shipment, so what?" Hask was getting angry now.

"Your superior at A.R.M.O.R. tells me you didn't report this to him either," Valdana said, "so that's three organizations you've upset now, Hask. S.H.I.E.L.D., S.W.O.R.D. and A.R.M.O.R."

"Do you realize who you're messing with?" Dazzler asked.

"Do *you* realize who you're messing with?" Hask shot back, burning with defiance.

"Tell us what you know!" Dazzler demanded.

Hask rolled his eyes now, like she was a dumb blonde bimbo, who wasn't worth his time.

And if there was one thing that could set her light energy on fire today, it was that.

"Did you just roll your eyes at me?" She leaned forward on the table again. "Did you forget what just happened in the elevator shaft? Did Sage knock some memory loss into you?"

"Shaw is a powerful mutant," Hask said. "More powerful than *any* of you. He's untouchable. Whatever you throw at him, he'll just fire it back at you. You won't win."

"Yeah, well, we can throw things too," Valdana said.

"He's referring to Shaw's mutant powers," Sage said. "He has the ability to absorb kinetic energy and metabolize it to enhance his own physical strength, speed, and stamina. He is hard to beat given those circumstances."

"There's a way to beat every mutant," Valdana said. "There has to be."

"Good luck with that," Hask said.

Rachel stepped forward. "We're running out of time. You tried it your way, now let's try mine." She walked slowly around to stand behind Hask, her eyes turning white as she did. Unnerved, the A.R.M.O.R. agent tried to look around at her. Rachel stood, fingers to her temple, as she attempted to break into his mind.

Hask suddenly pushed his chair back into Rachel, but Polaris swiftly thrust out her hand and scraped the metal chair back to the table, holding it there.

"We're not done with you yet!" Polaris spat.

Hask struggled, pulling at his cuffed hands, gritting his teeth, and shaking his head and torso about, trying to fight off Rachel's attack.

"Sage," Dazzler said. "Hold him." Breaking into his mind

made her uncomfortable, but with everything at stake, she knew it was necessary, given he was hiding vital information.

Sage moved to Hask and caught him in a headlock, but still he struggled.

"You might want to put your sun visor on those shades," Dazzler warned her. Sage quickly tapped the side of her glasses, sending the mirrored lenses to black, as Dazzler pooled her stored light energy into her eyes. She leaned forward and began to pour her soft, hypnotic light into his eyes, distracting him, so that Rachel could pull what they needed from his mind. Hask squeezed his eyes closed, swiping his cuffed hands out at Dazzler, but Polaris quickly pinned those cuffed hands to the table, with her free hand, while Sage took her fingers and forced his eyelids open. Dazzler aimed her hypnotic light into his eyes, and his body began to fall limp and peaceful, while Rachel remained a ball of concentration, whitened eyes moving back and forth as she searched for what they needed to know.

Rachel suddenly dropped her hands from her temples and stepped back, concern clear on her face.

Dazzler stopped the flow of her light energy and stared at her. "What is it?" she asked as Sage released Hask from the headlock, and Polaris lowered her hands.

"Shaw's planning to finish what the Scarlet Witch started," Rachel whispered. "He wants to wipe out all remaining mutants for his own supremacy. He's calling it S-Day."

Polaris's face paled as she stepped forward. "Does… Does that mean our fathers are already dead?"

Rachel shook her head. "I don't know. I didn't see them." She looked at Dazzler. "Or yours."

Dazzler's mind spun as though it raced away on its own pair

of rollerblades. "That's why he's producing the MGH?" she said, breaking the stunned silence in the room. "He's going to jack up human soldiers to help him, use it to boost his own abilities, so he can take us all out?"

Rachel nodded. "He's hiding in his new dimension and planning it all out." She looked back at Hask. "What's the N.E.A.?"

Hask glanced at her, concern washing over him. "If I tell you, he'll kill me."

"If you don't tell us, he'll kill us all!" Dazzler said.

"No." Hask shook his head. "Just you mutants."

Anger flashed through Dazzler, and light surged from her eyes again, this time a bright, harsh kind of flare. Hask groaned and squeezed his eyes shut as tears of pain fled down his cheeks. She pulled the light back from her eyes.

"Tell us!" Dazzler demanded.

Hask whimpered and stalled, blinking, so Dazzler flared her lights again, and he winced in pain.

"All right! All right!" he said. "It's the New Earth Alliance," he panted, as tears continued to run down his cheeks. "It's a secret society of humans who want mutants gone. They've made Shaw their leader."

"That doesn't make sense," Polaris said, brow furrowed in anger. "He's a mutant."

"The N.E.A. figures they can handle one of you, especially if that mutant helps rid them of all the others. He has money, he has connections, and he's feeding them the MGH, which makes them feel safe."

"Why would Shaw want to destroy other mutants?" Valdana asked them.

"Like Rachel said," Sage told her. "For his own supremacy. He thrives on power. He wants to take out his competition."

"When are they planning to kill the rest of us?" Dazzler asked, her voice deathly serious.

Hask shrugged. "As soon as they can. He's going to simultaneously pick you off one by one. He's not stupid enough to give you time to prepare a defense and start a war with all of you at once."

Hask's words haunted Dazzler. Her chest felt hollow. "Do you know if Magneto, Cyclops, and Judge Carter are dead?"

Hask shook his head. "I never saw them."

"Where is this new dimension," Dazzler asked, "and how do we get there?"

Sage raised her hand for quiet, then turned back to Hask. "Who or what is in this new dimension? Does he have an army of MGH soldiers there?"

Hask shook his head. "No. I only ever saw a skeleton crew guarding the dock."

"Can you get us in there," Dazzler asked, "to this new dimension?"

Hask's mind turned over, analyzing his options, but soon his face showed signs of relenting. He knew it was over and there was no other way out for him. "I can show you the way there, but I can't guarantee he won't kick you straight out again."

"Let us worry about that," Dazzler said.

Valdana stepped forward. "I think you should proceed with caution, Blaire. We don't know if we can trust him."

"I'm cooperating," Hask said quickly. "I know I'm caught. I get it. If I cooperate, you'll go easy on the punishment, right?" He looked desperately at Valdana.

"You say you're cooperating." She analyzed him. "But I guess we won't know until this is over, will we?"

"How long does it take to get to this new dimension?" Polaris asked him.

"Not long. But we'd need to hurry," he said. "I was due to escort a new shipment of supplies there. If I don't turn up or I'm late, he'll become suspicious."

"How soon?" Dazzler asked.

"Two hours."

"Two hours!" Sage said.

"If I make my regular run there, Shaw won't be suspicious," Hask said. "But we'll need to leave within the next twenty minutes."

"If you're going in, we need time to prepare a tactical offense," Valdana said to Dazzler.

"We don't have time," Dazzler said. "We can't let him do this run alone. He'll warn Shaw."

"She's right," Polaris said. "If Shaw finds out about us and our fathers are still alive in this dimension, he'll kill them."

Dazzler felt a slash of emotion across her chest. A slash of hope. Could they still be alive? Could she let herself believe it?

Sage looked at Hask. "How many soldiers are there? You said there's a skeleton crew, how many exactly?"

"M- maybe ten, twelve." He shrugged. "I- I never counted."

"Can you draw me a floor plan of Shaw's operations?" Sage said. "What does this dimension look like once inside?"

"He's on a station like this one when you enter the portal. I only saw part of it. Only the dock."

"We need more information," Valdana said firmly to Dazzler.

"We need to stop Shaw before he amasses any more MGH

or attacks more mutants," Dazzler said. "We need to stop this clandestine war before he gains more ground."

"We need to tell Frost," Sage said. "Get reinforcements."

"Are you positive she's not in this with Shaw?" Dazzler asked.

Sage gave her a confident look. "There's no way she'd want to wipe out her fellow mutants."

"But it'll take too long for her to get here," Polaris said.

"She knows Shaw better than anyone," Sage said. "We need to act smart!"

"We are," Dazzler said, the enormity of the situation washing over her. "Right now, Shaw doesn't know about us, so we have the element of surprise. But our window is small. We have to move, now. We can't wait for her."

Valdana relented with a sigh. "If you're going in, I'm sending S.W.O.R.D. and AR.M.O.R. soldiers with you." An alert sounded on her tablet. She looked at it, then showed Dazzler security footage from the dock. A bright light was flaring the lens, and once it receded, she saw a man walking along the dock with several soldiers following him.

"Who's that?" Dazzler asked. "And what was that bright light?"

"That's the A.R.M.O.R. team," Valdana told her. "That's how they travel. They dimension hop. I arranged for the unit to come when I spoke with Hask's commander."

"Well, tell them to get ready, because we're going in," Dazzler said, then looked back at Hask. "If you're lying to us…" She flared her light energy through her eyes and fingertips again in warning.

Then, she looked back at her team. "Let's prepare."

•••

Emma Frost stood in the abandoned warehouse with Maria Hill by her side, as they faced Rosenthorpe.

"Where's my lawyer?" he demanded.

"Cell service is really bad in this area," Hill said plainly. "I'm sorry about that."

"You can't keep me here."

"It's not just mutants who can disappear, it seems." Emma gave him a cold smile.

"So, why do we have this guy?" Hill asked her.

"He received a shipment of MGH that has since vanished from his warehouse," Emma said.

"And how do you know this?" Hill asked.

"A little birdy told me," Emma said.

"She *broke* into my warehouse. You should be arresting her!" Rosenthorpe said bitterly.

"I didn't do anything, Mr Rosenthorpe," Emma said. "The only guilty party here is you. So, tell us, what did you do with the MGH?"

Rosenthorpe refused to respond.

"You told me in your car that you had distributed it far and wide," Emma continued. "Where and to whom?"

Rosenthorpe stared at her with hateful eyes but remained tight-lipped.

"How does this connect to Cassandra Walsh?" Bennett asked.

"Walsh owns *The Gilded Arrow,* the bar that Magneto disappeared from. The same bar that both Judge Blaire and the senator's aide, Mr Squires, were members of. The same bar that Mr Rosenthorpe is a member of."

"It's a crime to be a member of a bar?" Rosenthorpe asked.

"No, but it is to be a part of an organized crime syndicate that includes the owner of that bar. Was *The Gilded Arrow* your meeting place?"

"Organized crime? Where's your evidence?"

Emma gave a laugh. "You're singing a very different tune to the one you sang before in your car, Mr Rosenthorpe. What's changed?"

"If I don't return to work, I will be reported missing. If that happens there will be consequences."

"For whom?" Hill asked, folding her arms.

Rosenthorpe didn't answer but fixed his murderous eyes on Emma again.

"Where is Sebastian Shaw?" Emma asked.

"Who?" Rosenthorpe asked.

"What's Shaw got to do with this?" Hill asked in surprise, unfolding her arms.

"Cassandra Walsh is Shaw's associate," Emma told her. "Shaw appears to be missing like the others. Either he's a victim or he's involved. Knowing Shaw like I do, I'd wager he's involved."

"In distributing the MGH?" Bennett asked.

Emma looked at Rosenthorpe. "That's for Mr Rosenthorpe to confirm."

"You will all be prosecuted for this," Rosenthorpe said. "I have powerful friends. *Very* powerful friends."

Emma leaned down to him. "So do I."

"Not for long," Rosenthorpe said menacingly.

"What does that mean?" Hill asked.

Rosenthorpe turned his glare to Hill. "It means we're everywhere, in all places, at all times, and you are all dead people walking."

Hill gave a surprised laugh. "I'm sorry, did you just threaten me?"

"I think he did." Bennett smiled in amusement.

Rosenthorpe looked away from them and stared straight ahead. "Now's the time to stand your ground for the New Earth Alliance, soldiers."

Hill's brow furrowed as she exchanged a glance with Bennett. A shiver ran down Emma's spine. She immediately thrust her mind outward like a spaceship's radar, searching for any asteroids that posed a threat.

And she found them.

One of the S.H.I.E.L.D. agents suddenly turned his weapon on her and fired. Another agent aimed at Hill and Bennett.

The bullets from the first weapon ricocheted off Emma's diamond form, then she swiftly stepped in front of Hill and Bennett and blocked those from the second weapon, too. Hill and Bennett dropped low, pulling their weapons, using Emma as a shield, as the remaining loyal S.H.I.E.L.D. agents took cover. Emma thrust her mind out again, hitting the attackers with such swift force that they were instantly incapacitated, dropping their weapons and falling to the ground.

Silence descended over the warehouse as Hill's and Bennett's heavy breathing could be heard. They swung their weapons around, searching for more threats.

"Anyone else?" Hill challenged.

"Everyone, drop your weapons! Now! *Everyone!*" Bennett barked. Their agents did so, raising their hands in the air.

"You can come out from mommy's skirts now," Emma said to Hill and Bennett still cowering behind her.

Hill shot Emma an unimpressed glance as she and Bennett

swiftly got to their feet and moved toward the traitorous agents, kicking their weapons out of the way.

Emma, now back in her human form, approached Rosen-thorpe.

"What's the New Earth Alliance?"

Rosenthorpe smiled smugly at her. "Your *end*."

CHAPTER TWENTY-SIX

Dazzler stood on the command bridge and stared at the leader of the A.R.M.O.R. squad who'd arrived on station. Handsome, toned, and meticulously coiffed, he'd introduced himself as Senior Lieutenant Jake Aspen, and proceeded to take command of their mission.

At least, he thought he was taking command.

"We appreciate your assistance, Lieutenant Aspen," Dazzler said, "but this is our mission and I'm in charge."

"Are we heading into another dimension?" he asked her.

"Yes, we are."

"Then that's our domain. We lead. You follow."

Before Dazzler could respond, Valdana intervened. "A.R.M.O.R. handles the other dimensions," she told Dazzler. "It's their jurisdiction. They have the necessary equipment and skills to handle things. Let them lead this."

"Shaw is a mutant," Dazzler said firmly. "We have the necessary skills to handle that."

"We've handled all kinds before," Aspen told her confidently, "and we have a thorough file on him and his abilities. We're prepared for him. We've procured weapons from other dimensions that are perfect for the Shaw scenario."

"How so?" Sage piped up.

Aspen waved one of his soldiers forward, and a lean but muscular woman wearing an eye patch and a name tag that said Lenny, stepped up. She hoisted what looked like a standard S.H.I.E.L.D. semi-automatic rifle. "This is a CAP-89," Aspen told them. "It shoots a projectile that entraps its target inside an impermeable bubble. It won't actually touch Shaw, so he can't absorb its kinetic energy and use it against us."

"I've seen them before," Dazzler said. "S.H.I.E.L.D. uses similar technology."

"Similar, yes," Aspen said confidently. "We acquired the technology, and S.H.I.E.L.D. adapted it for their use."

"What kind of dimension uses a weapon like that?" Polaris asked, studying it curiously.

Aspen glanced at her. "A peaceful one."

"The words 'peace' and 'Shaw' don't usually go together," Sage told them.

"Well, they do today," Aspen said, turning to Valdana. "Let's head to the dock for departure."

"I have Hask's ship waiting," Valdana said. "It'll take you to the location of the portal he uses to enter the other dimension. Good luck."

"Thank you, but hopefully we won't need it," Aspen said.

As the A.R.M.O.R. unit began to head out with Dazzler's team, Valdana pulled Dazzler aside.

"Good luck, Blaire. I'll inform S.H.I.E.L.D. of your mission."

"Don't," Dazzler said quickly. "The more classified we keep this mission, the better."

"I can't leave S.H.I.E.L.D. in the dark about this, you know that," Valdana said.

"I'm not sure who I can trust inside S.H.I.E.L.D. yet. You can report in when we return. Until then, no one else knows what we're about to do. If Hask, from A.R.M.O.R., was on Shaw's payroll, who knows who else is?"

Valdana studied her warily, analyzing the risk.

"The element of surprise is all we have right now," Dazzler said firmly. "If we don't return in twenty-four hours, you can alert whoever you want, but you give us those twenty-four hours."

"All right," Valdana said. "You have twenty-four hours before I call reinforcements."

Dazzler headed for the door, as a thought suddenly haunted her. Several thoughts, actually. Thoughts of mutants like Frost and Logan, and all the kids at their schools, and what would happen to them if Shaw succeeded in his plans. Though she was still unsure about Frost, she trusted Sage's judgement.

She looked back at Valdana. "If it does come to that, you'd better contact Emma Frost. I'm not sure S.H.I.E.L.D. and S.W.O.R.D. will be enough. You might need an army of mutants to clean this up."

Valdana gave a nod, and Dazzler left the room.

Acting Commander Valdana sat in her office and watched the dock footage as the mutants boarded Hask's small S.W.O.R.D. cargo jet, and shortly afterward, they disembarked. Seeing the dock was now empty, she logged into her secure portal and made a classified video call.

Ex-S.H.I.E.L.D. Commander Maria Hill appeared.

"Valdana," she said, eyes fixed and awaiting her update.

"Hill," Valdana said. "We have a problem."

Dazzler and her mutant team sat strapped in a small carrier jet as it departed from the Alpha Flight Low-Orbit Space Station. With them were Aspen's A.R.M.O.R. team and a unit of S.W.O.R.D. soldiers, headed up by a man in his early fifties, named Detson. That meant Dazzler was heading into this new dimension with her mutant team and sixteen soldiers. Based on the intel from Hask, that ought to be enough to handle Shaw's contingent of soldiers. Still, she felt on edge as her trust issues threatened to surface again.

With a little help from the mutant team, they'd had Rachel infiltrate Hask's mind one more time to check he was telling the truth, and she confirmed he was. Sage had warned them, however, that if Hask had only seen the dock that may have been an intentional move on Shaw's behalf. It meant Hask was not privy to the full workings of the station, so just because he'd only ever seen a dozen soldiers, did not mean there weren't others.

"So how do we do this?" Dazzler asked, looking at Hask, who remained cuffed as he sat with the rest of them, strapped into two rows of seats that faced each other.

"We travel to the coordinates I gave you. When we get there, I punch in my docking codes and the portal opens."

"You traveled to another dimension before?" Aspen asked Dazzler, as he sat opposite her in full combat gear.

Dazzler and Polaris shook their heads, but Sage gave a steady nod to him. His eyes then turned to Rachel.

"I came from another dimension," she said plainly, "but I've only crossed over once."

Aspen eyed Rachel curiously, then turned back to Dazzler. "Anyway, dimension crossings can mess with your head a little," he said to her, pointing to his temple. "It's like upon entry your brain stops then restarts in the new atmosphere, the new gravity, wherever you're going to."

"And does Shaw's dimension do that?" Dazzler asked Hask.

"Maybe the first few times," he answered. "But I'm used to it now."

"We have drugs to clear your head," Aspen told her. "If you don't feel right, let us know."

Dazzler gave a nod, then pulled out her phone and began searching for some music, wanting to prepare for what was to come.

"Tunes to calm the nerves, huh?" Aspen smiled a little condescendingly.

"No," Dazzler said, waggling her glowing fingers at him. "For this."

Aspen raised his brows, impressed. "Nice! Just don't use that on Shaw."

Dazzler pulled back the glow from her fingers. She turned to look toward the A.R.M.O.R. team's weapons. She hated that she was going to have to rely on others to stop Shaw, but she guessed this was what trust was all about. She was trusting her mutant team, and now she was going to have to trust the A.R.M.O.R. and S.W.O.R.D. cavalry. She had to let her ego and need for control go.

It didn't take them long to reach the coordinates Hask had given them. It was long enough that the Alpha Flight Low-

Orbit Space Station had disappeared from view, and there was no curvature of the Earth, making it appear as a flat sticker against a sea of black. Alarms began to sound. Aspen unstrapped himself from his seat, then both he and the lean muscular woman, Lenny, escorted Hask to the flight deck to enter the authorization codes, which he'd refused to give them until they'd reached the dimension doorway.

The team waited in silence. Well, the rest of the team waited in silence. Dazzler was nodding her head to the metal playing in her ears, thriving on the double-kick drumming, her body soaking up the sonic rhythms and transducing those beats into light energy that crackled over her entire body.

Sometimes she was so caught up in the feeling the music gave her that she forgot where she was. Rachel soon oriented her, though, shifting uncomfortably beside her, and trying to put a little space between them.

"Sorry." Dazzler smiled, turning the volume down at little. "Sometimes I get carried away and think I'm on stage or something."

Rachel glanced down at her clasped hands. "I'm kinda jealous in a way. Everything I do is so internal, no one would ever know I'm a mutant. I mean, unless they see my eyes."

Dazzler softened. "Sometimes I wish I could be more subtle like you."

Rachel smiled back in empathy.

"It's good to see you two not snarking at each other any more," Sage said.

"I don't know," Polaris said. "It was kind of amusing."

"I wish I could fly," Sage said, looking at the green-haired mutant.

Polaris smiled, then looked at Rachel. "I wish I could read minds."

Dazzler joined in, looking at Sage. "I wish my brain was a super-computer."

"We are a complementary team," Sage said.

Dazzler nodded. "We are."

"Aw, isn't that sweet?" one of the A.R.M.O.R. soldiers, a big square guy with a black crewcut, said sarcastically, as some of the other soldiers giggled at them.

Dazzler stared at him, raising her hand and sparking light from her fingertips. The soldier raised his CAP-89, tapped it, and winked at her, before suddenly his harness pulled him tightly back against his seat, almost choking him. Dazzler glanced at Polaris and saw her hand subtly raised.

Rachel chuckled, her eyes turning from white to green. "He's pretending to be a big dog, but he's secretly crapping himself."

"I am not!" he managed to say, struggling with the harness.

Rachel tapped her forehead. "Oh, yes, you are."

"I'd be nice if I were you," Sage addressed the soldiers. "According to my calculations, statistically speaking, heading into an operation like this with vague information, a powerful mutant, and plenty of MGH on hand, I predict only fifty to sixty percent of you will return alive. You'll need all the friends you can get."

The soldiers stared blankly back at Sage, and Dazzler smiled.

"OK." Aspen returned with Hask and Lenny. "Get ready. We're counting down, then heading in. Strap in and prepare for the crossing. Oh, and you might want to put some shades on. It tends to get bright."

The A.R.M.O.R. and S.W.O.R.D. crews pulled down helmet visors or slipped on lenses.

"Thanks for the heads up," Polaris said, sarcastically, as Sage tapped her cybernetic glasses, sending the lenses dark, and the rest of them closed their eyes and hoped for the best.

Emma waited for her call to connect with Logan.

"I'm looking forward to the day you stop contacting me," he gruffed.

"Oh, come on, Logan, you've always liked attention," she said.

"Not from you," he said bluntly.

"Keep telling yourself that," she said. "Listen, we've got a problem. A big problem. The MGH on the streets isn't some clever hustler. It's being orchestrated by a powerful crime syndicate calling themselves the New Earth Alliance. Heard of them?"

"No. Who are they?"

"We're still trying to figure that out exactly, but apparently they're everywhere. They seem to have infiltrated many top line organizations, including S.H.I.E.L.D."

"What? Is Dazzler involved?"

"No. But I think she might be walking into a trap."

"Laid by who?" Logan's voice lowered in anger.

Emma hesitated, took a breath, then came clean. "I think Sebastian Shaw is involved."

"Shaw? *Your* Shaw?"

"He's not *my* Shaw. I can't find any trace of him, but I have some of his associates here. This whole thing reeks of Shaw, Logan. This New Earth Alliance is planning on wiping all mutants out. If that's the case, Dazzler and her team will be first in line. We need to warn them!"

"They already know," Hill said, walking toward her with Bennett.

"Putting you on speaker, Logan," Emma said, then looked at Hill. "Where are they?"

"I just had a call from S.W.O.R.D. Dazzler's team was on the Alpha Flight Low-Orbit Space Station. They discovered Shaw is running the MGH operation from another dimension."

"Another dimension?" Emma said, her brow furrowing.

"They're heading in now to stop him," Bennett said.

"What? We need to get up there and go with them," Emma said.

"We won't make it in time," Hill said.

"You've got to stop them! They need our help," Emma said. "Tell them to wait for us!"

"The portal's opening, and they're just about to pass through." Hill shrugged. "It's too late. They're on their own."

Emma heard Logan's growl over the phone, before the line went dead. Emma turned and walked away from Hill and Bennett, her mind racing.

Another dimension? That had to be why she couldn't find Shaw on Cerebra. But if she couldn't find Shaw because he was in this other dimension, did that mean Magneto and Scott might still be alive in this other dimension, too?

Scenarios played out inside her mind. Was Dazzler and her team equipped to deal with Shaw? Should Emma have shared her suspicions earlier? Should she have warned them? Tried to stop them?

Had she just sent these mutant lambs to their slaughter?

Dazzler listened as the pilot began the countdown. She glanced over her shoulder through the observation window and saw nothing but a sea of black and gray with white specks of light sparkling here and there.

But then suddenly she saw it – a small dark gray swirl that appeared in the middle of nowhere.

And it grew, turning from a dark gray into a bigger, lighter swirl.

Soon it was almost the size of the ship. And bright. It was so bright that Dazzler had to squint her eyes against the glare.

As the ship careened at speed toward the growing swirl, she turned away and squeezed her eyes shut. The brightness grew, astounding her. Even with her eyes shut she felt as though they were open in bright daylight. Her closed eyes began to water, and tears rolled down her face.

The ship rumbled and vibrated heavily now as it neared the swirling portal, bright as a sun. The raucous sound, louder than the metal song in her ears, buzzed through Dazzler's entire body. She reached for her phone and stopped the music, wanting to soak up the immense natural sonic energy and bury it deep within her cellular stores.

She'd never felt anything so powerful before. It was like fifty Cerebras. Maybe a hundred.

Another countdown sounded.

"Three, two, one. Transference engaged."

The ship suddenly felt like it had flipped over sideways and then spun like a turning top, making her yelp in surprise along with Polaris. Sage and Rachel remained quiet, but Sage had no doubt done this many times before, and maybe Rachel knew what to expect from reading the others' minds.

Suddenly Dazzler's stomach was somewhere up by her throat,

as she felt a strong sensation of the ship falling before it suddenly flipped back up the right way. A bright flash pierced her retinas even through her closed eyelids, and a massive sonic boom sounded, making her gasp as the energy overwhelmed her body.

"Man, what a ride!" one of the soldiers yelled.

"It's such a rush!" said another. "It never gets old."

The ship seemed to even out then and seamlessly cruised along just like it had done before the crossing. Dazzler opened her eyes, panting, and feeling a little drunk from that sonic boom, to see everyone staring at her body as it crackled brightly with intense light energy.

"Whoa…" one of the S.W.O.R.D. soldiers said, looking at her in awe.

"Are you OK?" Sage arched her eyebrow.

Dazzler nodded, catching her breath and pulling her light back within. "I think I almost overdosed on sonic energy."

"Just make sure you stow it," Aspen said firmly. "Keep that away from Shaw or he'll kill us all."

"So you already said," Dazzler said, wiping the tears from her cheeks and feeling the fuzzy head he'd told her she'd experience. "You just make sure you trap him with those CAP-89s, and I won't have to."

Aspen looked over to their prisoner. "Hask? Get back to the controls, and radio that you're coming in to dock."

Hask nodded and headed for the flight deck under Lenny's guard, before Aspen grabbed his arm. "If you try to warn them, we will take you out."

Hask stared at Aspen, then continued on. Dazzler watched him go, then looked at Rachel.

"Can we still trust him?"

Rachel watched Hask leave, eyes whitened, then turned back to Dazzler. "I don't know. He's doing that thing again. All he's thinking about is pink cotton candy."

"Cotton candy?" Polaris asked, confused.

"I think he's trying to block his thoughts and the chance of me reading him," Rachel said.

"It's a meditation technique," Sage said and looked to Aspen. "Do you train your AR.M.O.R. soldiers with that?"

For the first time Aspen's confidence dipped. He nodded. "You never know what you'll find in these other dimensions. We have to be prepared for anything."

"If he's blocking us," Sage said, undoing her harness, "it means he plans to betray us."

"We don't have any other choice," Dazzler said. "We need him to get inside."

"Even if he delivers us straight to Shaw?" Rachel asked.

"Yes," Polaris said, unbuckling her harness and standing too. "We came here prepared to fight, so that's what we do."

"She's right," Dazzler said.

"No," Aspen said, stepping in front of her and cutting her off. "That's what *we're* here to do. You stay back."

"Aspen, you should let me go first," Dazzler said. "I can use my light energy as a shield. It will protect all of you until we can get to cover and know what we're facing."

"We can't risk it," he said. "If anything ricochets off your shield, Shaw might absorb it and use it against us. We do not want to fuel the enemy." He locked eyes with her to reaffirm his point, then followed Hask to the flight deck.

Dazzler stared after Aspen, flexing her hands, which still tingled with the overflowing energy inside her.

"I don't like this," Rachel said.

Sage locked cautious, steady eyes with Dazzler, then turned to the others. "Just be ready," she said.

Dazzler nodded confidently to her team. "We've got this."

CHAPTER TWENTY-SEVEN

Dazzler waited at the back of the ship with her mutant team, staring at the two units of soldiers before her, armed with the CAP-89s and various other weaponry, mainly stun guns. She glanced out the observation windows to see things in this dimension that, so far, looked exactly like the one she'd come from. All she saw was dark skies and the pinpricks of distant stars, before she noticed a floating, glittery white space station looming closer. From afar, it looked to be shaped like a curved disc, a soccer ball squished in half.

Silence filled the compartment holding the soldiers, as they listened to the radio comms between the ship and the dimension's docking station.

"Hellfire-Prime," Hask's voice sounded from the flight deck, "this is the good ship *Herald*, preparing to dock. Authorization codes have been sent. Hoping there's some champagne on ice."

"That's code," Rachel said quickly, eyes white. "He's warning them."

Dazzler's body tensed. "Aspen!" she called to where he stood at the front of the compartment. "He's warning them. Be careful!"

"Then we better be ready," he said, raising his CAP-89 and aiming it at the door.

"Get behind me," Dazzler told her team. "I'll shield us." She pressed play on her music, pulling one of her earbuds out and tucking it into the neck of her leather X-suit. Though her cells were absolutely brimming with stored energy, she didn't want to use it just yet. For now, she was going to run on rock 'n' roll alone.

Sage and Rachel didn't argue and immediately moved to stand behind her.

"If I can get my hands on some metals in this dimension," Polaris said, "I can make a shield of my own."

"Until then, get behind me," Dazzler ordered. "I admire your fighting spirit, Polaris, but for now we move as a team."

Polaris fell back with the others. The ship docked and the doors unlocked.

"Wait for my signal, S.W.O.R.D.," Aspen addressed that unit of soldiers. "You don't move until A.R.M.O.R. is in place."

"Understood," S.W.O.R.D.'s Detson answered, glancing at his soldiers to reaffirm the message.

Dazzler looked at Rachel, whose eyes were still white. "You picking up anything?"

Rachel's eyes focused hard on the ground. "I'm trying."

The ship's doors opened, and the A.R.M.O.R. soldiers pushed through, carrying CAP-89s, with their stun guns at their belts. As they spilled quietly onto the station with efficiency, the S.W.O.R.D. soldiers filled their void in the ship, and Dazzler's mutant team followed. The closer they moved to the doors, the worse her visibility got, however, as the observation windows ended, and all she saw was the ship's bulkhead.

Rachel looked up at Dazzler, concerned. "I'm sensing a lot of minds. Way more than our soldiers and way more than Hask said to expect."

Lieutenant Detson suddenly raised his arm, signaling for his team to move out.

"No! Wait!" Dazzler called.

But she was too late.

The S.W.O.R.D. soldiers rushed through the ship's doors, and Dazzler pushed forward into their void, desperate to see outside.

Laser fire suddenly struck the ship's doorway, and she ducked and pushed her fellow mutants backward, as mayhem erupted outside. The battle had already started. There was yelling, screaming, laser fire, and other strange sounds that were followed by soft blue glowing lights, which she guessed had to be the CAP-89s firing their bubbles.

Then another commotion caught her attention, coming from the flight deck.

"Hask!" Rachel said.

Sage surged past Dazzler to the door, but it was locked.

"He's killed the pilot!" Rachel told them.

"Move!" Polaris said, and they scattered as she reached her hands up and pulled the door off.

Inside, Hask looked up in surprise as Sage surged toward him. He raised a stun gun, stolen from the dead pilot, but Polaris ripped it from his cuffed hands. Sage landed a crunching blow to Hask's face that sent him toppling back into the flight desk.

"Careful!" Dazzler called. "We'll need him to get out of here."

"They're getting slaughtered!" Rachel said panicked, drawing Dazzler's attention back to the mayhem outside. "Shaw's soldiers have gotta be fueled by MGH! They're fast and strong."

Dazzler looked out onto the Hellfire-Prime dock and saw it was already littered with the groaning bodies of wounded and dying A.R.M.O.R. and S.W.O.R.D. soldiers.

"No!" Dazzler hissed through clenched teeth. She looked back to see Polaris twisting pieces of metal from the ship's storage compartments around Hask, to restrain him in his seat.

"Is he secure?" Dazzler asked.

Polaris nodded, Hask moaned, and Sage punched him again for good luck.

Dazzler raised both hands and surged her energy outward, forming a large, golden protective energy shield. "Let's go!" she said.

Dazzler stepped onto the dock as rock 'n' roll filled one ear, laser fire sparked off her shield, and the others fell in behind her. As they moved away from the ship, Dazzler got a good view of the station's dock laid out before her. It was smaller than Alpha Flight's, with no other ships docked, a whole lot of cargo stacked, and many more troops than they'd been expecting.

Many more.

She should've let Sage punch Hask a few more times.

The soldiers firing at them wore red uniforms just like those at the warehouse in New Jersey, and the wall along the back of the small dock was emblazoned with the words "WELCOME TO HELLFIRE-PRIME, HOME OF THE N.E.A." She counted four S.W.O.R.D. soldiers and only three A.R.M.O.R. soldiers left standing, who held their ground in pockets here and there, in ones and twos, hiding behind stacks of cargo and their loaders. Aspen lay badly wounded on the ground in the distance, and Dazzler feared the worst for Detson, who lay silent.

Dazzler and her mutants pushed further out onto the dock, protected by her shield. Which was all well and good, but they needed to start reducing the number of the Reds – red uniformed assailants firing at them, because she wasn't going to be able to produce this shield forever, and they needed to find Shaw.

"Polaris?" she called over the zipping sound of laser fire that sparked off her shield. "Anything you can do to take some of these jerks out?"

"Hold still a second," she called back, glancing around the dock. "Let me get my bearings." Dazzler paused her forward movement while Polaris quickly formulated a plan. The green-haired mutant gritted her teeth, then raised her hands. Biceps flexed to full extension, she lifted one of the cargo loaders and threw it across the dock, wiping out a row of Reds like a bunch of bowling pins.

"Stttttrrrriiiiike!" Rachel yelled in admiration.

They pressed forward again, but Dazzler counted at least twenty more soldiers still on their feet firing at them. As they passed a fallen A.R.M.O.R. soldier, Sage swiped his CAP-89, quickly studied it, then stepped out from the shield and fired at three Reds to their right. The projectile shot across the dock, expanding its light blue glow, and swallowed the Reds whole, despite the soldiers firing at it. Whatever that bubble was made of, it was impenetrable. Trapped inside the sphere, the soldiers yelled and banged on the curved walls, slipping over each other inside as the bubble rolled around with their movement.

Satisfied they weren't going to free themselves, the mutants continued to press forward.

They made their way to the nearest group of surviving A.R.M.O.R. and S.W.O.R.D. soldiers, which included the hardened Lenny. Dazzler took a deep breath, then expanded her shield to include them.

"We gotta get Aspen!" Lenny said, falling in behind the shield. "He's still alive!"

"Yeah, we gotta do a lot of things," Dazzler said through clenched teeth, as Lenny's two companions joined them.

"Cover me while I shoot Aspen with the CAP," Lenny said. "It'll protect him until we get this under control."

Dazzler admired her positive thinking. "How does he breathe in that thing?" she asked.

"There're tiny holes for oxygen. Cover me!"

Dazzler angled her shield, so that Lenny could get into position. She aimed, fired, and hit her target, the bubble quickly encapsulating Aspen. Then she aimed and fired at another two wounded soldiers, enclosing them too.

"I can't hold this shield all day!" Dazzler yelled at her. "You stay here, try to cover us as we press forward."

"Roger that!" Lenny said, leaving the shield and ducking behind another cargo loader, before turning and giving orders to the two soldiers with her.

Dazzler pushed forward again, leaving Lenny's ragtag group taking shelter, as the laser fire continued to spark off her shield. Polaris, close behind her, waved her hand across another group of Reds, ripping the weapons from their hands and sending them flying across the dock. Then she waved her hand in the other direction, targeting another group of Reds, disarming them with a roar of effort. Sage followed up by shooting the CAP and trapping the soldiers, weaponless, in several bubbles.

"Shaw!" Rachel suddenly said, eyes white. "He's here! He's close!"

"Where?" Sage asked.

Rachel suddenly gasped.

"What is it?" Dazzler asked.

"They're here…" Rachel breathed.

"Who?" Dazzler asked.

"Our fathers," she said. "They're alive!"

"Where?" Polaris asked quickly.

"Here!" a male voice boomed. They turned to see a tall, broad, bearded man standing on an elevated platform at the end of the dock.

"Shaw," Sage said, her face hardening.

Dazzler held her shield firm while Shaw reached back through a doorway and pulled Dazzler's father out, holding him in front as his own shield. Dressed in a business suit, her father appeared disheveled, stubbled, and blindfolded. He'd aged since she'd last seen him, his hair lighter with the gray of time. Dazzler's own shield began to recede in response to the shock of it all. With everything else going on she'd almost forgotten about her father. She wasn't sure she'd ever see him again.

"Dazzler!" Rachel warned as laser fire sparked off the edge of the shield. Dazzler quickly thrust her receding shield back out.

"Dad?" she called, eyeing her father. "Are you OK?"

Her father's blindfolded face showed signs of confusion. "A-Alison?"

The reassurance that he couldn't see her or her powers, made Dazzler grateful.

"Lower your weapons or I'll kill them all," Shaw threatened.

Dazzler stared at the two men, stunned, as Shaw turned his eyes to Sage.

"Sage," he said, his eyes turning dark. "It's been a long time."

"How do we know the others are still alive?" Sage asked him, cutting to the chase.

"Rachel just confirmed that to you," he said. "They're here, but you understand it would be a risk for me to release them from their cages, being the mutants that they are. Judge Carter was the only safe one to show you in the flesh." His eyes narrowed as he looked back at Dazzler. "And I feel the most important one of all."

The silence hung thickly as Dazzler's mind raced.

"Concede or your fathers will be killed," Shaw said. "Now."

"Is he bluffing?" Sage asked Rachel quietly.

Rachel was silent a moment, before shaking her head. "No. He'll do it."

"We can fight!" Polaris whispered.

"If we concede, will you let them go?" Dazzler asked, ignoring her.

"No," Shaw said. "But I won't kill you. Or them. You shall live. That is my promise to you."

"You expect us to trust you?" Rachel spat. "The whole aim of the N.E.A. is to wipe mutants out."

"Yes," Shaw said simply. "Eventually. But I can make use of you for now. You have my word that you shall live."

"We'd prefer to fight!" Polaris said, clenching her fists.

Shaw took hold of Dazzler's father roughly, pulling his arm right back as though he were about to break it. Judge Carter yelled in pain, and Dazzler flinched. "Surrender or he *dies!*" Shaw bellowed.

Dazzler stared at her father's anguished face.

"Don't listen to him!" Polaris pleaded with her. "We have to fight!"

"We can't give in!" Rachel agreed.

Dazzler felt her shoulders slump. "We have to."

"Why?" Polaris asked.

"Your fathers might be mutants, they might stand a chance at defending themselves, but my father's not. He's only human."

"We came all this way to give in?" Rachel asked, brow furrowed angrily.

"We'll find another way," Dazzler said. "I'm sorry, but I won't risk his life like this."

Sage stared at Dazzler, her super-computer mind analyzing the situation, before she relaxed her stance. "We'll find another way," she said in support. Polaris and Rachel stared at Sage in confusion, but then relented when Sage gave them an assured nod. "We'll find another way," she said again, firmly.

"All right!" Dazzler yelled at Shaw. "We'll give in. But if you fail to keep your word, there'll be no dimension strong enough to stop the pain we'll inflict on you!"

"I am a gentleman and a man of my word," Shaw said, giving them a slight bow.

Sage scoffed. "I know you better than that, Sebastian."

Shaw pulled harder on Judge Carter's arm, and he screamed in pain.

"All right! All right!" Dazzler slowly pulled her shield back, leaving them vulnerable. All four mutants tensed as they looked around, ready for what may come.

"That wasn't so hard, was it?" Shaw said, then nodded to his guards. Several stunners were raised in their direction.

Dazzler stared up at Shaw with hard eyes, then glanced at her father. Her gaze softened.

"I told you. I don't wish to harm you," Shaw said.

"Why is that?" Dazzler asked.

"Because" – he smiled – "you, my dear, produce some of the best MGH we've ever seen."

A cold chill shot down Dazzler's spine like a sharpened blade.

"I'm going to need all the MGH I can get," Shaw said, "and the MGH Mystique took from you was incredibly powerful. I've tried replicating it, but it's just not the same. I need the real thing. I'm going to add you to my little menagerie alongside Magneto and Cyclops. Just imagine what I could produce if I combine the MGH of the three of you." Shaw's eyes turned to her three mutant companions, and he smiled. "Perhaps all six of you."

Dazzler saw her father's blindfolded face look around, confused by their conversation. Her heart started beating rapidly as her panic spiked.

"You've kept Magneto and Cyclops alive for their MGH?" Polaris asked, while Dazzler's body rattled with terror as her past trauma flooded back like a tidal wave, crashing onto the rocks of her long-held mutant secret. The terror of her father knowing the truth. The trauma of being drugged, of being held prisoner, of having her very mutant essence stolen.

And it was about to happen again.

"Yes," Shaw answered Polaris, "but they also made a good lure to bring the three of you here, didn't they?" He gave a smug laugh. "Thank you for walking into my trap, Alison. I wasn't sure if your father would be enough bait given there didn't seem to have been any contact between you two for years, but having gained the intel about what happened on Madripoor, from a mutual friend…"

"Mystique," Sage said in a low venomous tone.

"…I did wonder whether you might want to return a favor to Magneto. And I was right." He laughed again before his face turned dark and he muttered, "And now that I have Magneto, Cyclops, and the three of you, Emma Frost will never defeat me again. Her strongest allies are gone, and once I have this new batch of MGH in my system, nothing will stop me."

Dazzler tried to manage her panic, breathing like she was gulping for air. So far, her blindfolded father had not witnessed her light shield, and she hoped he would be confused by all that Shaw had said. So long as things stayed that way, the mutant secret she kept from her father would remain. She couldn't handle it being unleashed right now on top of everything else.

"This was all to get back at Frost?" Sage asked, brow furrowed.

"This is for my *own* hegemony. If I am the only mutant left alive, nothing will stop me. But, yes, I've wanted vengeance for some time, and this is the perfect way to do it."

"Dazzler?" Rachel said, eyeing her with concern, noticing how her body physically shook.

Dazzler felt Rachel gently enter her mind but didn't have the strength to stop her. Her brain was numbing with fear, with the memories of what Mystique did to her, the fear of it happening again, the fear of her father finding out the truth.

"We won't let that happen to you," Rachel's voice said firmly in her mind.

Polaris, sensing something was up, touched her shoulder in support.

Sage did the same, squeezing her other shoulder.

"I don't think we can stop this," Dazzler said, her voice barely a whisper.

Shaw's guards fired up their stunners.

Dazzler looked back at her blindfolded father as a tear ran down her cheek. She heard the stunners fire. Her body crackled with light energy, and then everything went black.

CHAPTER TWENTY-EIGHT

Dazzler felt a tapping at her face and blinked her eyes open to see her father staring down at her.

"Alison?" he said in worry, as she suddenly remembered where she was.

She bolted upright, pushing him back, and glanced around the room for threats. Sage sat close by, but other than her father, they were alone in what looked like a padded cell. The only feature in the bare room was a black monitor screen placed high up on one wall.

"Where are the others?" she asked Sage, who leaned back against the soft wall.

Sage shrugged, rubbing her neck as though she hadn't been awake much longer than she.

The screen on the wall came to life. There was no sound, but the image was split between footage of Polaris and Magneto in one cell, and Rachel and Cyclops in another. Polaris and Magneto sat side by side, their body language awkward and uncomfortable, but they were talking. The footage of Rachel and Cyclops was very different though. Cyclops sat on the ground, his feet chained together and his hands restrained behind his back, probably so he couldn't remove his ruby quartz crystal visor and use his laser eyes. Rachel, too, was restrained and there was a drip feeding into her arm. Dazzler felt a spike of panic run through her at the sight. Was Shaw already taking MGH from Rachel?

She suddenly wondered why Shaw was allowing them to see into the other cells. Was it to torment them? Or was it a warning to behave, that any foolish moves could have repercussions on the others?

Dazzler looked back to the cell of Polaris and Magneto. They weren't restrained, but the walls of their cell seemed different. In fact, all three cells looked different. Dazzler glanced around her cell's padding.

"We're in a soundproof cell," Sage said, having already figured it out. Dazzler realized that Shaw was trying to inhibit her powers. She felt her ears, then checked her suit and realized her earbuds and phone were gone. Sage's cybernetic glasses were missing, and she suspected her various weaponry was, too. Dazzler looked back to the screen at the others.

"He must be keeping Polaris and Magneto in a non-metal room," Sage said. "And Cyclops and Rachel are restrained or drugged so they can't use their powers."

"Powers?" Judge Carter said, confused. His face was lined with worry. The crow's feet around his eyes were deeper, and the gray threading through his moustache, eyebrows, and hair seemed more present. She tried to remember how long it had been. "Alison." Her father touched her shoulder. "What are you doing here? What's going on?"

Dazzler glanced around the cell, her mind battling for an answer she could give him.

"Alison," her father said, more firmly. "What is going on?"

She turned back to him. "What are you doing here, Dad?" she asked. "How do you know Sebastian Shaw?"

"I- I've crossed paths with him at the occasional corporate event, but I wouldn't say I *know* him."

"What about Rosenthorpe? You used to defend him." She couldn't help the disappointment and accusation that crept into her voice.

"Rosenthorpe? *Rick* Rosenthorpe? That was years ago," the judge said defensively. "He's involved in this?"

"Yes. And you were his lawyer."

"Years ago, yes. Back then he was just a young businessman. When he started associating with people I didn't think he should, I terminated our agreement."

"So, how did you get involved with them again now?" she pushed.

"Ask *them*!" her father said, anger rising. "They kidnapped me and have kept me here – for what, I don't know. I suspect it's for ransom. Is that why you're here? And what was all that noise I heard before. Fireworks?"

"How did they kidnap you?" she pushed. "Did they just take you off the street?"

"One morning I'm in my car, in the garage, about to leave for work when suddenly there's a guy in my back seat, and the next thing I know, I wake up in here."

Dazzler felt a sense of relief wash over her. Then shame. She knew he wouldn't have been involved with these cretins.

"Now *you* tell me," he demanded, "what are you doing here?

Are the authorities coming?" He glanced at Sage. "And who might you be?"

Sage didn't respond, and instead looked at Dazzler.

"Dad." Dazzler held up her hand to stop the questions. "Just let me think."

"How do *you* know Shaw?" Disappointment now ran through his voice. "How do *you* know Rosenthorpe? Don't tell me you–"

"I don't know Shaw or Rosenthorpe," she cut him off. "But acquaintances of mine do."

"Well, what do they want? I can pay a ransom if it means getting us out of here. I've tried to negotiate with them, but all I got was silence."

"Dad, they don't want your money."

"Then what do they want?"

She stared at him. Memories of her childhood flashed through her mind, of studying, of the good grades, of him telling her she'd make a good lawyer one day. She felt her heart sink, just like it had when she'd been accepted into college. He'd been so proud of her. But she realized she wasn't happy about the acceptance, and instead felt sad. She'd realized that she hadn't wanted to be a lawyer anymore. She'd wanted to be a musician. And when she finally told him, the arguments and shouting came flooding back.

"Alison, what on earth is going on!" he insisted, wanting to know the facts, wanting to cast his judgment.

"I can't tell you, Dad!" she blurted.

He stared at her with those disappointed eyes she'd seen too many times in her life. "What have you got yourself into?"

She glared at him. "I can't tell you, Dad, because it's classified!"

His graying brow furrowed heavily. "What do you mean, *classified*?"

Her mind raced along with her heart. "I- I'm working for a federal agency. I can't tell you what organization or what I'm doing."

"You're working in law enforcement?" The lines of his face seemed to smooth out, his eyebrows raised in surprise.

"In a manner of speaking," she said awkwardly, glancing at Sage.

A sensation of pressure filled her head as Sage's voice sounded inside her mind. "He doesn't know you're a mutant, does he?"

Dazzler shook her head subtly.

"Oh… honey." Her father pulled her into a hug. At first, she resisted, but then she let herself relax. Technically it wasn't a lie. She *was* working for S.H.I.E.L.D. But it still left her with an empty feeling inside. Why could he never be this accepting of her being a musician?

She pulled away from him, uncomfortable with the way he studied her with concern, with curiosity.

"You look different," he said softly. "Not so… *happy* anymore. Not like you used to be. There was sunshine in your eyes, in your smile. Now you look… hardened. Sad."

He pulled his wallet out of his jacket pocket and opened it to stare at a photo inside, then turned it to show her. It was her senior high school photograph, taken not long before her powers first presented at the school dance. She'd been performing at the time, and some thugs had overrun the hall, and she'd inadvertently stopped them with her powers.

But her father was right. She looked so innocent in that photograph. She beamed a sunny smile, and her eyes were alight with stars, so hopeful for what the future promised her.

Dazzler turned away. "That was a long time ago now."

"It was," he said, studying her again. "What's happened to you, Alison?"

She looked back at him again. "Life. It's not always an easy road, you know."

"It doesn't have to be that way."

"Yeah, I know," she said, dismissively, "if I'd just gone to law school everything would've been all right. Well, I didn't, Dad. I went on the road with a band, and I *liked* it, you know? I had fun, and I had success."

"Did you?" he asked.

"For a while!" she said, offended. "My career has had its ups and downs like any other. As I said, life got in the way."

"What life?" he asked.

She looked away again. She couldn't exactly explain how being a mutant and getting entangled in the X-Men derailed her music career from time to time.

"I just want you to be happy," he said, looking at the photo again, then holding it out to her. Dazzler stared at her younger self and felt tears sting her eyes. So much had happened since then. If she'd followed the path her father had wanted her to take, would she be here now? Both of them prisoners, both of them soon to be killed or used for other means. Or would the mutant life have caught up with her anyway, whether a lawyer or a singer? By following her own path, being a musician, she'd at least had moments of happiness, right?

Scenes from her last gig flashed through her mind. She saw the crowd clapping, cheering, and chanting her name. She smiled sadly at the memory.

"I am happy, Dad," she said. "I chose my path. I wouldn't have it any other way."

"Playing in small bars and driving around the country in a beat-up old van?"

Dazzler looked at him, curiously. How did he know that detail? Was it just an educated guess?

"I've kept an eye on you," he admitted begrudgingly, sensing her question. "You sometimes appear in the press. It's hard not to."

Anger surged up, making her wonder how much the judge knew about her life, and thinking how little she knew of his.

"I am your father, you know!" he said defensively upon her angry look.

"Are you?" she blurted. "Then where were you most of my life? I could've used a little support you know!"

Sage cleared her throat, and Dazzler looked around at her, flushing with embarrassment. Caught up in the moment, she'd forgotten her fellow mutant was there.

Sage's voice sounded in her mind. "I hate to break up your family meeting, but we have other matters to attend to. Like getting out of here."

Dazzler nodded, running her hand over her face. "I'm sorry."

"That's OK," her father said, thinking she was talking to him. She glanced at him, then back to Sage.

"Can you reach the others?" she asked Sage in her mind.

"Polaris, maybe," Sage replied. "I think they're in the next cell. Rachel, no, she's drugged. We need her to wake up. She's much stronger than me. Thankfully, because I haven't used my telepathy in so long, Shaw seems to have forgotten I had the skill."

Dazzler nodded and began pacing.

"What do you know about this place?" she asked her father. "Have you picked up any useful information since you've been here?"

"Like what?" he asked.

"Do you know how many guards there are? Do you know where the labs are?"

"Labs?" he asked, confused.

She nodded. "They're producing a steroid here, Dad. It's called MGH, and it's very dangerous."

"I overheard something about that. Thought it might be important. They took me for a bathroom break earlier, and I heard two of the soldiers talking outside. They said something about ramping up production, that mobilization was being brought forward."

Dazzler exchanged a glance with Sage.

"Did they say how soon they were going to mobilize?" she asked her father.

"No. They just said soon. Something about a sudden change of plans. What are they mobilizing?"

Sage's voice sounded in her mind again. "We can't wait. We need to get out and stop them now. Before they can take any MGH from you and use it against us."

Dazzler nodded again.

"What is this MGH exactly?" her father pushed.

Dazzler stared at him, not wanting to say the M word. If she said the M word, it could leave a dangling thread that he could then pull to reveal the truth about who she really was.

When Dazzler didn't answer, Sage answered for her.

"It stands for Mutant Growth Hormone."

Her father turned to Sage. "And that's what he's using Magneto and Cyclops for?" He glanced back at the screens on the wall. "Shaw said something, out on the dock, about using you and others. Are the two women mutants as well? Are you?" Her father turned back to Sage.

Sage looked at Dazzler, unsure how to answer.

"Yes, they are," Dazzler said quickly, wanting to move on. "Now tell me everything you know about the guard movements."

Sage's voice popped into her mind again. "How long do you think you can keep this from him?"

Dazzler ignored her. "Dad?"

He shrugged. "They deliver me three meals a day, and I get maybe four or five bathroom stops. Why?"

Dazzler inhaled deeply and exhaled heavily to calm her nerves. "Just curious," she said, and began to pace. If Polaris and Rachel were being filmed, they would be too, and no doubt one of Shaw's goons was listening to every word they said. She had to go about this carefully. She had to ensure Shaw's Reds did not know their escape was coming.

And escape, they had to. Dazzler had to make a break before they drugged her and started extracting the MGH. She had to warn S.H.I.E.L.D., S.W.O.R.D., and A.R.M.O.R. before Shaw could enact his mutant annihilation on behalf of this New Earth Alliance. She pictured it now. A swift operation where they picked each mutant off, one by one, in a series of coordinated attacks.

But then again, could she trust S.H.I.E.L.D., S.W.O.R.D., and A.R.M.O.R.? How far did Shaw's reach and this New Earth Alliance extend? Had it infected these organizations already? Were its roots already far too entrenched?

Both S.W.O.R.D. and A.R.M.O.R. soldiers had been killed or wounded in the station boarding, but it wouldn't be the first time an organization had scarified its own soldiers as collateral damage. Bennett had made it clear to her that the humans' love of mutants was a slippery slope. Would it erase trouble for all if they turned a blind eye while Shaw wiped all mutants out?

But Shaw would still remain. Was that a risk S.H.I.E.L.D. was prepared to live with? Or S.W.O.R.D. or A.R.M.O.R.? They may not like the power mutants had, but they sure liked calling on them for assistance when their own power fell short on handling certain problems. So long as there existed the vast expanse of space with alien creatures and strange dimensions with other beings, these organizations needed mutants by their side. They couldn't afford to let mutants be wiped out and for Shaw to hold all that power. They needed good mutants to help control the bad. Even Maria Hill knew this.

And that's why S.H.I.E.L.D. had called on Dazzler to help, and why they needed a Mutant Liaison. She was the lynchpin. She was the leader. And it was time she stepped up to the plate and became the strong mutant she knew she could be.

Shaw could not be allowed to succeed. Dazzler had to stop him. Not only to protect the living mutants, but also to protect future mutants born or those whose powers had not come in yet. She would not allow them to be forever hunted down and culled by the N.E.A. And Dazzler was sure all sides of the X-Men divide, whether those led by Cyclops and Magneto, or those led by Wolverine, would not stand for this either. Hell, she couldn't even see Mystique standing for this. Mutants everywhere would come together. So long as Shaw was not granted a head start in his mobilization, so long as he didn't have the upper hand to launch his unsuspecting assaults and weaken their defensive ranks.

"I counted thirty soldiers on the dock before we were taken," Sage's voice spoke in her mind. "Six were killed by the A.R.M.O.R. and S.W.O.R.D. forces. Shaw will, no doubt, have others on the station. Therefore, I predict we could be looking at maybe fifty MGH soldiers to contend with. If we free ourselves, there are six of us including Magneto and Cyclops."

"Two Omega-level mutants," Dazzler added.

"Whose powers may still be recovering from the Phoenix incident," Sage warned.

"They'll find them and make them work," Dazzler thought confidently. "Just like Polaris. They have to."

"And don't discount yourself," Sage's voice said in her mind. "If you focus and tap into your potential, you could be very powerful, Dazzler."

Dazzler stared at Sage, her chest filling with pride at the woman's support.

"The only trouble," Sage thought, "is they've taken your music."

Dazzler nodded, her blue eyes turning to ice. "But they don't know that I can store energy."

A smile curled Sage's lip.

"And I got a *very* big rush from that dimension jump," Dazzler thought.

Sage's smile grew wider.

"But I don't want to use that yet," Dazzler thought. "We don't how long it is back to the dock."

"I do," Sage thought.

"You do?"

She nodded. "When we were on the dock, I calculated the station with my cybernetic glasses. I know the distance from the ship to where Shaw entered, and I used my X-Ray vision to see through the walls and make a crude floorplan map. It won't be a hundred percent accurate, but it will be accurate enough."

"But you don't have your glasses?"

"No, but you forget, my brain is a super-computer. I only need to see things once, and I'll remember everything. I know roughly where we must go. But I don't know how we're going to get out of here if you don't want to use your stored energy to get us out of this room."

"Why are you two staring at each other like that?" Dazzler's father asked. He, of course, could not hear the conversation they'd been having in their minds.

She suddenly realized there was no way they could break out of this cell without him seeing just what she could do. Her confidence wavered like a flickering light. Was she ready to show him? Was she ready for her father to know the truth?

"He's going to find out some time," Sage said aloud.

"Find what out?" her father asked, still looking between the two of them.

Though Dazzler's anxiety shot up again, so did a resignation which quickly stomped that anxiety back down again.

What choice did she have?

There were mutant lives at stake. There was no time for ego, for self-doubt. She had to sacrifice this, her secret, for the sake of others.

Dazzler took a deep breath, exhaled, then looked back at Sage. "What's your favorite Lila Cheney song?"

Sage smiled. "You want a little singalong?"

"No, honey, I want you to shout it out like you're on stage at Madison Square Garden."

Sage got to her feet, cracked her neck and knuckles. "I always wanted to be a rock star."

"Now's your chance," Dazzler said. "How about … 'My Heart Was Made For Destruction'?"

Sage laughed. "Nice choice."

Dazzler moved to the door, raised her hands, and counted in.

"One. Two… One, two, three, four!"

CHAPTER TWENTY-NINE

Dazzler's hands began to glow as her body absorbed Sage's singing. The urge within her to unleash her stored energy was overpowering, but she held it back. She was going to need everything she had to face Shaw and couldn't waste it on something simple like blasting a door open.

"*My heart was made for destruction…*" Sage sang in her Eastern European accent.

"Louder!" Dazzler ordered Sage. "You're at Madison Square Garden, not a dive bar." Dazzler began to sing to demonstrate the volume she needed. "*Your heart don't stand a chance against me…*"

Sage raised her voice to match Dazzler's volume. "*My heart was made for destruction. Your heart is weak at the knees…*"

And the glow at her palms grew brighter.

"Wh- what is that?" her father asked, taking a step back as he stared at the light emanating from her hands. For a moment her powers faltered and receded at the sound of his voice, but she gritted her teeth, blocked him out of her mind, and pushed the energy out again.

"Alison?" he said quietly.

"Quiet!" she barked, needing to concentrate before Shaw realized the flaw in her imprisonment – that although his cell blocked out external noise, it could not stop her from absorbing Sage's singing.

"*My heart was made for destruction...*" Sage yelled louder, commanding her focus.

"Get ready!" Dazzler yelled, surging a wave of light energy from the pit of her stomach, up through her chest, into her arms and hands, and blasted the door right off its hinges.

And she made sure to reabsorb the sonic energy that blast released.

"What the...?" her father breathed. Dazzler quickly glanced around to see him staring at her from where he cowered from the blast.

"Guard him until I get the others!" she told Sage.

Dazzler moved through the doorway to see two Reds running for her. She raised her palms and blasted them with a concussive light burst. They fell unconscious to the floor, and she raced to the next cell door. "Keep singing!" she called over her shoulder to Sage.

"*My heart was made for destruction...!*" Sage yelled, sounding like an Eastern Bloc Lila Cheney metal cover band.

"Get back from the door!" she yelled to the cell's inhabitants, suspecting it was Polaris and Magneto as the door appeared to be plastic. She surged her energy and blasted the door inward.

Laser fire struck the doorway, then scorched the edge of her arm. She gasped in pain, ducked and cowered as she felt a breeze, then looked up to see Magneto in the doorway. Eyes burning with fury and hands raised, he swiftly pulled the weapons from the soldiers' hands and beat them over their heads with them.

"You OK?" Polaris asked, helping her up.

Dazzler nodded. "Keep the guards off me while I get the others out."

"You're hurt," Polaris said, eyeing the burn across her arm.

"I'm fine," Dazzler said.

"Get the others!" Magneto ordered. "I'll take care of these *fools!*"

They saw more Reds running their way and Dazzler quickly ran to the next doorway, soaking in Sage's vocals, and blasted the door open. They moved inside the third cell. Polaris headed straight to Rachel and pulled out her drip.

"Rachel! Rachel, wake up!" Polaris shook her.

"She's drugged," Cyclops said, turning his back to expose his restrained hands to Dazzler. "Get me out of these!"

"Hold still," she told him and placed her hands over the manacles on his wrists. She slowly pushed her light energy through until the manacles melted enough for Cyclops to tear himself free. He instantly rubbed his wrists, then raised his hand to the side of his visor, opened it, and let his laser eyes take care of the manacles on his ankles.

Dazzler looked back at Polaris whose hands rummaged through a medical cart beside Rachel, calling out the contents. She found a vial of something, took a syringe, loaded it, then stabbed it into Rachel's arm, injecting her.

"What are you doing?" Dazzler asked.

"Sage just told me this will wake her up," Polaris said, tapping her temple.

Cyclops, free of his restraints, glanced concerned at Rachel, then moved to the door to see what was happening in the hallway.

More commotion sounded outside, but based on Magneto's insults, he seemed to be doing just fine. In fact, it sounded like he was enjoying himself. Then again, after being kept prisoner for a good part of a week, she wasn't surprised he wanted some payback.

Rachel began to stir and blink her eyes open.

Dazzler moved up behind Cyclops. "She's waking," she told him.

"Good," he said, as they watched Magneto taking care of more Reds that came his way, ripping weapons from their hands, and slamming metal helmets into the walls.

Outside the cells she saw a small guard station and walked to it, searching for her phone and earbuds. Then she spotted a metallic safe placed on a cupboard close by.

"Polaris?" she called. Through the doorway to the cell, she saw Polaris leave Rachel sitting up on the bed with Cyclops, who'd now moved back into the room. Polaris saw the safe, raised her hand, and tugged, but nothing happened. She growled, concentrated, then tried again, and pulled the door off.

There, inside, was Dazzler's phone and earbuds, along with Sage's glasses and weapons.

"Bingo!" she said, pocketing her phone and putting her earbuds in. She looked up and saw Sage at the doorway to their cell. "Nice singing, Lila," she smiled as she threw the glasses to her.

"Any time," Sage said, as she caught them in one hand and

swiftly slid them on, then deftly took the knives, garroting wire, and other strange implements the guards had removed from her person.

"Are you OK?" Cyclops asked Rachel, placing his hand on her shoulder.

Rachel, fully awake now, nodded and shrugged his hand off as she stood. "I'm fine. Let's go."

Cyclops watched her a moment, then moved back to the door and looked down the cooridor to see Magneto at work. He raised his hand to his visor mask and shot his laser down the corridor to keep more Reds back.

"What's the plan?" he asked.

"We get the hell out of here," Dazzler said.

"You got backup?"

"No. It's just us."

Cyclops glanced at her. "And what about Shaw?"

"If we get a chance, we take him out, but I'm not sure how we can do that with his mutant ability."

"No," Cyclops said, moving up behind Magneto, as Dazzler, Polaris, and Rachel followed him. "He's a tricky one."

"Not if we get our hands on a CAP-89," Sage said.

Magneto had managed to push the Reds back to the corridor intersection, allowing for Sage and Dazzler's father to step out of their cell.

"Sage." Cyclops gave a nod. "And who's this?"

"My father," Dazzler explained.

"They're falling back," Magneto said. "Let's go!"

"There'll be more of them," Sage warned.

"Piece of cake," Magneto said, as though they were vermin, "now that I'm not *drugged*." He began to move forward.

"We need to be careful," Dazzler warned. "They're jacked up on MGH. They're fast and strong."

"So are we," Cyclops said, following Magneto.

"They have a small army," Dazzler said quickly, "here on this station, in this dimension, and countless others back on earth. They're about to mobilize and attack. They mean to wipe us out. *All* mutants. Everywhere. Shaw's calling it S-Day."

"We're in another dimension?" Cyclops paused and looked at her. Magneto paused too, quickly glancing back. The two mutants hadn't learned that much before they were taken and had not realized the scale of the predicament they were in.

"Shaw is leading a group called the New Earth Alliance," Dazzler quickly explained. "They're going to use the MGH to wipe us mutants out by jacking up humans with the steroid to compete with us. Did they take any MGH from you?"

Cyclops nodded, concerned. Magneto did too.

"Then we're in trouble if they managed to manufacture that in large quantities."

"Yes, you are," a voice sounded over a hidden speaker. It was Shaw. "Stand down now, and you'll live to see another day. But if you continue with this little uprising of yours, I can't guarantee the outcome."

"We can't guarantee yours either, Sebastian," Magneto said, glancing up at the ceiling, his eyes narrowed in spite. "You want to fight? Come and face us. Out in the open. Not in our cells where you control our powers."

Shaw laughed. "You forget, Erik, I can take whatever you throw at me. Literally."

Dazzler stepped closer to Cyclops.

"If we can get our hands on a CAP-89, we can capture Shaw

inside its bubble-like prison," she whispered. "It won't touch him, and he can't use the kinetic energy against us."

"So where do we get one of those?" he whispered back.

"Hopefully there are still some lying on the dock from our boarding assault."

"You have transport here?" Cyclops said.

She nodded. "And the man who can get us out of this dimension. Provided he's still trapped on the flight deck where Polaris wrapped him in metal."

Cyclops looked back at Magneto. "We push forward!" Then, he looked up at the ceiling. "We're not letting you get away with this, Shaw. *Your* little uprising, this New Earth Alliance, ends today!"

"You can't win. You're outnumbered," Shaw said, his voice dark and dangerous.

"Our mutant numbers might be down," Cyclops said, glancing at Rachel, "but the ones we have left were made to last."

A smile slid across Magneto's lips as he glanced at Polaris. She smiled back at him.

Dazzler looked at her own father. He was terrified and cowering in the doorway, his eyes jumping from mutant to mutant and landing on her, unsure what to make of her.

"Oh, how sweet," Shaw said sarcastically. "Is this like a daddy-daughter day out?"

Rachel snarled. "No, this is the day where we annihilate you!"

Shaw laughed again. "You're not your mother *yet*."

Rachel surged forward in anger, but Cyclops whipped out an arm to block her path.

"Steady, considered actions," he told her firmly. "Rashness will get you killed."

Rachel pushed his arm away but didn't continue her advance.

"Time's a-wasting!" Magneto said, pressing forward. Polaris walked shoulder to shoulder with him, and Cyclops and Rachel followed. Dazzler looked at Sage who stood by Judge Carter. "We do the fighting. Your job is to protect him until we get to the ship. Understood?"

Sage gave a nod. The truth was, with the other mutants present, Sage was best playing bodyguard and letting the others clear their pathway.

Dazzler quickly locked eyes with her father, then looked away, clearing his judgement from her thoughts. She followed the others, blasting her new song through one of her earbuds, while tucking the other away, soaking up the crunching guitars and pounding drumbeat.

"If you try to break me down… I'm gonna take you out…"

CHAPTER THIRTY

Dazzler, music pouring into one ear, moved swiftly after the others, hands glowing and ready to be deployed – to either fight or use as a shield to defend her father and Sage. Magneto and Polaris led the group, having ripped metal doors off hinges to use as their own shields. Cyclops strode after them, hand raised to his visor, ready to fire his laser, and Rachel followed, eyes whitened and head slightly lowered as she channeled her mind to the thoughts around her, while Dazzler led Sage and her father in the rear.

"Ahead, to the right!" Rachel suddenly looked up.

At an intersection of the corridor, Magneto leaned around the corner to the right to face a barrage of laser fire pinging off his door shield. He sent the door flying at the Reds, and Dazzler heard a commotion that she took as the soldiers being knocked down. Then Magneto stepped out into the corridor, raising and waving his hands like he was conducting a chaotic orchestra. Dazzler heard yells of pain and saw weapons fly past the intersection.

"Polaris! Behind you!" Rachel yelled, as laser fire passed the intersection coming from the other direction. Dazzler heard Magneto grunt in pain, as Polaris swung her door shield around to face the second wave. Gripping the door in one hand, she waved her other around viciously, muscles flexing as she inflicted pain on the attacking Reds. More weapons went flying, more groans were heard, and then footsteps as several soldiers rammed into her shield, knocking her over.

Cyclops broke file and raced to her defense, laser streaming from his visor that cut across several of the Reds.

"Get behind me!" Dazzler told Rachel, who didn't argue as Dazzler amassed her energy into another protective shield. They approached the intersection carefully as the mayhem continued. Magneto battled the soldiers on one side, while Polaris faced the other side, and Cyclops was in between fighting with two Reds on his back.

"Sage!" Dazzler called. "Which way?"

"Turn right! Then left, then right again!" she called back over the din.

Dazzler poured into the corridor intersection as Reds rammed and bounced off her shield. They moved in a tight pack, pushing toward Magneto. She maintained the shield with one hand, while aiming the other down the hallway.

"Eyes!" she warned the others, then pulsed a beam of light at a second wave of Reds approaching. The light energy rolled fast and hard down the corridor, knocking them off their feet like a big wave down the beach, stunning each and every one of them and leaving them dazed on the floor.

"Nice work!" Cyclops said, joining them and turning his laser eyes on a new pack of Reds blocking their path and cutting them down. "Magneto! You and Polaris take the rear!"

Magneto fell back, and both he and Polaris sucked their door shields back into their hands and crouched ready, as Dazzler focused back on her light shield with two hands now and pushed forward with Cyclops by her side and Rachel, Sage, and her father close behind.

"You know, your powers are not unlike mine," Cyclops said, glancing at her. "Mine are just more concentrated."

"And deadly," she said.

Cyclops nodded. "You have degrees of capability, you have versatility. That's useful to have. I only have on and off. Not as helpful sometimes. But if you concentrate yours, you can be deadly too."

More laser fire scuttled across her shield as they turned left into a branching corridor, making their way down to another intersection where they would turn right again.

"We must destroy this place as we leave," she heard Magneto say. "Polaris, every room you pass, shred it. Understand?"

"That's going to use a lot of our energy," Polaris said.

"Do it!" he barked.

With the music in her left ear, the commotion ahead, and the sounds of violent destruction behind her, Dazzler was awash in stimulation. More Reds approached, and Cyclops stepped out from behind her shield and blasted the weapons out of their hands.

"The dock's just ahead!" Sage said, tapping her glasses and focusing on the wall between them and it. "And so are a lot of soldiers."

"Magneto!" Cyclops called. "We need you up here."

"Wait!" Polaris called, having ripped a door off its hinge. "I found the lab!"

Dazzler paused, glancing around at her. "Destroy it! Destroy everything inside. Leave no MGH. Destroy it all!"

Polaris gave a nod and set to work. Magneto joined her in a duo of frenzied mayhem and total destruction; metallic objects crashed, glass smashed, electricity sparked, chemicals ignited, and smoke began to waft through the doors. Dazzler noticed Polaris's powers were working just fine now, and she also noticed the mutant occasionally glanced at her father, perhaps for his approval, perhaps to ensure she was keeping up. A little healthy family competition.

"Noooooooo!" Shaw's enraged voice sounded over speakers somewhere, at their demolition.

A group of Reds sprang around the left corner of the intersection, firing at them, and then swarmed in from the right. Cyclops grunted as he caught skimming laser fire across the side of his neck.

"Magneto!" Cyclops called again, as they now faced heavy fire from both sides.

"Coming," he replied, swooping toward them.

As Dazzler edged closer with her shield, she could see the dock beyond to the left. They were close to freedom, to their ship. She just needed to clear the path.

She quickly pooled her light energy into her core. "Eyes!" she yelled, quickly withdrawing her shield, then sending out a pulse with both hands at the doorway. The Reds fell away like autumn leaves on a breeze. Instantly pulling her shield back up, the team shuffled at a quicker pace and spilled out onto the dock, with Magneto and Polaris on either side with their door shields.

Dazzler noticed the dock had been cleared while they'd been

in their cells, the injured bodies removed, the blood mopped up, the weapons stacked and stowed – including the CAP-89s.

"Where's Lenny and the others?" she wondered aloud.

Sage shrugged. "We have to go."

"We can't leave them," Dazzler said.

"We might have to," Sage said, in all seriousness.

The dock suddenly lit up like the Fourth of July as a line of Reds poured through a doorway in the opposite wall and fired upon them. Laser fire sparked everywhere as Polaris and Magneto spread out with their door shields and Dazzler held her light shield firm. Polaris and Magneto waved their arms, doing their best to rip weapons from the arms of Reds, discarding them. But more and more poured out the doorway, amplified on MGH and jetting fast across the dock.

Dazzler scanned the chaos but couldn't see Shaw anywhere. The coward was hiding. But she didn't have time to worry about him right now. She needed to clear the dock so they could get back to the ship.

"Get back!" Dazzler yelled at Polaris and Magneto. "Let me handle this. Protect them!" She stepped forward as Magneto and Polaris fell back using their door shields to cover the others.

Dazzler took a deep breath, then pooled a mass of light energy into her core again, quickly sucking in her shield and instantly pulsing it back out in a massive burst of light that rolled over the dock like a thick wave of lightning. She yelled with the effort it took, tensing every muscle as she surged it outward, ensuring she got them all. When the wave receded, she glanced around to see every single Red on the dock was out cold.

Panting, her shoulders relaxed as Magneto and Polaris lowered their shields beside her.

"Nice work," Cyclops said, surveying the aftermath.

She smiled at him, but then something caught her eye.

Movement.

She turned back to the Reds and saw something shimmering and glowing beneath a pile of unconscious bodies.

Then she heard Sebastian Shaw's laughter.

It was him. The light was coming from him.

Dressed as a soldier and hidden among them, he'd just absorbed all the light energy Dazzler had drenched them with.

"Oh, no…" she breathed.

Shaw's body rose with a bright nuclear glow from the unconscious bodies of the soldiers, beaming a huge smile. "I was hoping you'd do that."

Magneto and Cyclops instantly stepped forward. Magneto extended his arm to an overturned cargo carrier, while Cyclops raised his hand to his visor, but Shaw was too swift. He flicked his hands at them with speed – MGH speed – sending a burst of Dazzler's light energy in each of their directions. The pulse hit them both ferociously, thrusting them backward into the dock wall and rendering both instantly unconscious. As their limp bodies fell to the floor, Shaw aimed his hands at the rest of them.

But Dazzler saw it coming.

She surged her energy into a shield big enough to cover Rachel, Polaris, Sage, and her father. Shaw's burst hit the shield and pushed her backward, but she held strong, tightening every single muscle in her body so that it felt like concrete.

"No!" Dazzler growled at him.

Shaw gave her a glowing smile. "I have your MGH in my blood and your light in every fiber of my being. You're fighting yourself, Dazzler!"

"How do we stop him?" Rachel panicked.

"We need a Cap-89!" Sage said, a worried look on her normally controlled face as she looked around, then spotted one stacked against the opposite wall. "There!"

Shaw walked toward them slowly, confidently, his entire body sparkling and glimmering with Dazzler's light energy. She'd never seen her own power from this angle before. It was both beautiful and terrifying. Mesmerizing and intoxicating. Caught for a moment in the dazzling sight, her mind was soon pulled back to reality as Shaw sent more pulses their way.

Each hit battered Dazzler's shield, as light energy hit light energy, crackling explosively and sending her back. Her muscles strained, and her arms were tiring as she bore the blows and her feet kept skidding backward.

Polaris tried to find things to throw at Shaw, but he swatted them away with his new-found powers and MGH enhancement.

"Rachel," Dazzler said through gritted teeth as more pulses hit her shield, "can you distract him? Can you mess with his mind?"

"Won't he absorb it and use it back on me?"

"We have to try something," Dazzler said, taking another blow that pushed her hands right back, knocking her earbud out, cutting off the music. "He's using the energy in measures, and he'll run out eventually, but I'm not sure we want to test how long my arms can hold him off."

More vicious blasts hit her shield, and she grunted in the effort to hold firm.

"You distract him, Rachel," she said. "Polaris, you get that CAP-89 to us. Sage, when I say the word, I'm going to use all my stored energy and light this place up like I've never done before.

Between Rachel's mind messing and my light distraction, you should get a clear shot. Got it?"

"Affirmative!" Sage said, engaging the dark tint setting on her cybernetic glasses.

Rachel's eyes whitened, and she lowered her head in concentration. Shaw brought down his arms, scowling at them. "You think that's going to work on me?"

Rachel's head moved back violently as though receiving an invisible punch. She groaned, clenched her teeth, bore down, and pushed her mind back at his, an internal struggle taking place between her mind and Shaw's.

"Polaris! Go!" Dazzler said.

Polaris quickly stepped out of the shield, reached out and sucked the CAP-89 in their direction. Rachel's head jerked sideways with another invisible punch, and Shaw raised his hand and fired an energy blast at the CAP-89, destroying it. As the pieces fell to the ground, he quickly turned his hand to Polaris, but she ducked back behind Dazzler's shield in time.

"Rachel! Try harder!" Dazzler said.

Rachel clenched her fists and roared, and this time Shaw's head moved as though he'd been punched. He rubbed his temples, narrowed his eyes, and then snarled at her. Which soon turned to laughter.

"Oh my… I'm being tormented by a *murderer*," he said, looking at Rachel. "You sent an innocent man into the path of that bus. It's your fault he died."

Rachel gasped, and her eyes turned green as she stared at him.

"Don't listen to him!" Dazzler yelled. "Fight him! Fight it!"

Rachel's head jerked back with another invisible mental

punch, then Shaw sent more light pulses their way, sparking off Dazzler's shield, pushing her back and straining her muscles.

"He's the murderer!" Sage told Rachel. "*Not* you!"

Rachel lowered her head again, fists clenched, as her eyes turned white and shone with hatred. Her head bounced back with another invisible punch and blood dripped down from her nose.

Seeing an opportunity, Polaris stepped out from Dazzler's shield again, raised her hand, and tried for another CAP-89. The weapon flew across the room, straight into her hand. Shaw saw at the last minute and fired at her. Polaris yelped in pain as she was struck in the right forearm and dropped the CAP-89.

Rachel yelled now, looking up at Shaw, her white eyes watering, saliva strung between her teeth as her whole body shook with rage.

Shaw's head took a mental punch, and he roared back, firing angry misguided shots at Dazzler's shield as he struggled to concentrate against Rachel's burning fury.

Polaris cradled her blistering arm but, determined, reached out again and sucked the fallen CAP-89 into her other hand then swiftly threw it at Sage, who caught it and pulled the weapon's sight to her eyeline.

"Ready!" Sage yelled.

"Whatever you're planning, I'll absorb it, you *fools*!" he yelled at her. "You can't win!"

"I'm not aiming for you this time!" Dazzler seethed.

Rachel roared now, staring at Shaw like she was possessed.

Moving as fast as she ever had, Dazzler sucked in her shield light, bore down, and purged every ounce of light energy stored in her body. Scraping every cell clean of whatever she had absorbed when they'd crossed into the new dimension, she sent it out through the palms of her hands, which she aimed at the dock ceiling, turning the entire dock white with light – certainly as bright as the dimension crossing had been. She heard an ear-piercing scream and realized it was coming from her as she purged her body of every piece of energy, standing in a room of nuclear light, while smoke began to waft off her skin from the intensity of it all.

Suddenly her father fell unconscious at her feet.

Then Rachel.

She saw Shaw swaying, blinded from the light in the room, and quickly sucked her nuclear energy back.

"Now!" she yelled at Sage.

Sage fired the CAP-89 in Shaw's direction. The glimmering blue bubble of otherworldly origins locked on to its target perfectly, expanding and swallowing Shaw whole, catching him as the mutant fell unconscious.

And there Shaw floated in the air, out cold and contained.

Dazzler, breathless with exhaustion and shock, saw Sage collapse to her knees.

"Are you all right?" Dazzler asked her.

Sage nodded, as tears made their way down her face beneath her glasses, trailing along her tattoos. "I need to upgrade the tint on these glasses," she said, pulling them off to expose her red eyes.

Dazzler managed an apologetic smile as Polaris emerged, cradling her injured arm, from where she'd taken shelter behind the metal door shields she and her father had used. Polaris saw Shaw floating unconscious in his bubble, exchanged a look of relief with them both, then bent down to an unconscious

Rachel. Dazzler looked at her father, then fell to her knees at his side.

"Dad?" She shook him, worried by his motionless form. Had she killed him? "Dad?!"

"He's human," Sage said reassuringly, moving to Cyclops. "I think he'll be out for a while."

Dazzler looked back at the dock, at all the unconscious bodies. Her own body rattled with the enormity of it all. It made her feel a little sick inside, to know that if she'd wanted to, if she'd tried a little harder, she probably could've killed them all.

Was that what it meant to be an Omega-level mutant? To have the power for great destruction? If it was, she never wanted to go there. Today was as close as she ever wanted to get to that.

She glanced back at the unconscious Shaw floating in his CAP-89 bubble. She wondered how long it would hold him, wondered what he would do when freed. Would he keep trying until his competition was wiped out? Should Dazzler have killed him? Shown him no mercy for the sake of mutantkind?

Maybe she should have, but that wasn't her. That was a line she did not want to cross.

Cyclops groaned, and Sage pulled him to his feet, as Magneto began to stir.

"What happened?" Cyclops asked, looking at Shaw. "You did it?"

"*We* did it," Dazzler said.

Sage smiled at her as she collected the CAP-89 again and wiped her eyes. "I guess we better bubble wrap the rest of this vermin, huh?" She checked a setting on the weapon and began shooting at the unconscious Reds, scooping them up, three to a bubble.

Cyclops knelt at Rachel's side as she opened her eyes. "Rachel? Are you OK?" he asked, concerned.

She groaned. "I have a headache the size of Texas."

"Come on," he said, scooping her up. "Let's get you onto the ship and off this place."

Rachel fought against him. "I can walk!"

He sighed and released her, and she walked unsteadily toward the ship, as Polaris stepped in to guide the way.

"I'm not taking my eyes off this one," Magneto said, stepping up to Shaw's bubble. "Not until he's in a cell."

Cyclops bent down and scooped up Dazzler's father. "I'll put him on the ship."

"Thank you," she said.

"You look pretty spent," Cyclops smiled. "Thank *you*, for getting us out of those cells."

Dazzler nodded, and Cyclops walked away with her unconscious father.

Brushing her hair back from her sweating face, she noticed her body still rattling from what had just happened. Feeling utterly spent, she dropped to the floor again, and took in the carnage left on the dock and all that she'd just done.

CHAPTER THIRTY-ONE

Dazzler made sure her unconscious father was strapped in safely, alongside the few remaining injured A.R.M.O.R. and S.W.O.R.D. soldiers, including Aspen, who they'd now freed from their bubbles, as well as Lenny and her surviving team, who they'd found beaten and locked up in another cell. Dazzler couldn't help but wonder how things would've turned out if Aspen had let her go first onto the dock like she'd asked. Would the casualties have been as high as they were? Then again, with her father captive, Dazzler still would have had to concede, and who knows whether Shaw would've killed the remaining soldiers anyway.

"I'll watch him," Rachel said, strapped in opposite Judge Carter. "Go do what you need to."

"Thank you," Dazzler said gently. "I'm sorry I pushed you back there."

"It's OK," Rachel said. "I've never had to fight my own mind attack before. It was … strange." She averted her eyes.

"I bet," Dazzler said. "I don't think any of us would want to face the dark recesses of our own minds."

"No."

"But for the record," Dazzler said kindly, "Reid's death wasn't your fault."

Rachel gave a smile of thanks, and Dazzler moved toward the flight deck. As she passed the ship's entrance, she glanced out onto the dock to see Magneto and Cyclops as they finished bubbling the unconscious soldiers with every CAP-89 they could find.

She entered the flight deck to see Hask still trapped in his chair, as Sage's hands darted around the flight deck controls.

"Do you know how to fly one of these?" Dazzler asked.

Sage nodded. "The ship has a built-in flight manual, and I've downloaded it." She tapped her temple.

Dazzler chuckled tiredly. "Your brain can pick it up that quickly?"

Sage's red eyes looked over the top of her cybernetic glasses. "Super-computer."

Dazzler smiled back. "I'm glad Frost made me bring you."

"She's a smart woman."

With the Reds locked in their bubble cells on the station, and the unconscious Shaw and his bubble squeezed onto the ship with them, they departed Hellfire-Prime Station and made their way back to the location of the dimension portal.

Dazzler braced herself for the transition, all the while keeping an eye on Shaw's bubble. Part of her was too tired to prepare for the rush she knew was coming, but part of her was also glad for it, because she knew it would give her a boost of energy to see the end of this mission through.

Sage began the countdown as they approached.

"I'd close your eyes if I were you," she warned Magneto and Cyclops. "It gets *very* bright."

They looked at her briefly, before Magneto did as instructed.

"My eyes are lasers," Cyclops said plainly, then shrugged. "But OK."

She saw the swirl forming outside, then everything began to turn white, and Dazzler felt the rush commence.

Dazzler entered the flight deck where Sage sat with a now-gagged Hask.

"Something he said?" Dazzler asked, looking at Hask.

"It was that or I knock him out again," Sage said. "I'm giving my knuckles a break."

"Fair enough," Dazzler said, as she put on the comms headset the mutant passed her.

"This is Dazzler," she said into the mouthpiece.

"This is Acting Commander Valdana. What's the status of your mission?"

Dazzler exhaled heavily. "We accomplished our mission. Shaw has been apprehended, the activities on Hellfire-Prime have been shut down, and the MGH found there, destroyed. There have been casualties, though."

"Did you find Cyclops and Magneto?" another female voice sounded.

"Frost?" Dazzler asked, forehead crinkling with confusion.

"Yes. I'm on Alpha Flight. Did you find them? Are they all right?"

"Yeah," Dazzler said. "They're fine. They're on the ship with me."

"You mentioned casualties," Valdana said. "How many?"

"A lot, I'm afraid. Many of your S.W.O.R.D. and A.R.M.O.R. soldiers were killed, including Lieutenant Detson."

Valdana took a beat before speaking but her voice remained steady. "And Aspen?"

"Injured but alive. We're bringing him back along with Lenny and another three wounded soldiers. We left two soldiers on the station watching over the bodies of the others, along with a whole lot of CAPPED soldiers of Shaw's."

"What does CAPPED mean?" another familiar voice sounded, this one male.

"Bennett?" Dazzler asked. If there was one thing she was good at, it was picking out voices, though normally they were singers.

"Surprised?" Bennett said.

"No," Dazzler said, exchanging a glance with Sage. "It doesn't surprise me at all. Has it been twenty-four hours, Valdana?"

"Not quite," Valdana said matter-of-factly and unapologetic.

Dazzler grunted, as she heard Valdana quickly explain the CAP-89s to Bennett.

"Dazzler," Frost spoke up. "How are the other mutants? I know Sage is flying you out of there, so she's fine, but what about Rachel and Polaris?"

"They're fine. Minor wounds. Oh, and my father is alive, too, thanks for asking."

"I was just going to ask about him," Bennett said.

"Sure you were," Dazzler said. "Look, just have some medics on the dock when we land and be ready to take Shaw into custody."

"Will do," Valdana said. "Good job, Agent Blaire."

Sage ended the comms and looked back at Dazzler. "We have quite the welcoming party."

"We do." Dazzler nodded. "I suspect there's going to be a custody battle for Shaw."

"This case started with S.H.I.E.L.D., do you think they'll get him?"

"I don't know. S.W.O.R.D. and A.R.M.O.R. infiltrated the other dimension. But the real question is, can any of these organizations handle a mutant like Shaw?"

"No. But when has that stopped them before?" Sage asked.

"That's what worries me," Dazzler said.

When they exited the ship on Alpha Flight's dock once more, there was a whole swarm of people waiting for them. Valdana, Frost, and Bennett stood front and center with another man that she guessed, based on his uniform, was a senior A.R.M.O.R. representative, while S.W.O.R.D. soldiers readied to take Shaw and medics prepared to receive the injured.

Magneto, who under Aspen's instruction had released a now conscious Shaw from his bubble and sufficiently cuffed the man, escorted Shaw off the ship, while Cyclops accompanied Hask, whom Polaris had freed from his metal restraints. As soon as Shaw laid eyes on Frost, he scowled. Frost, on the other hand, beamed a smile.

"Good to see you, Sebastian," she said, stepping forward and motioning to his hands, "in cuffs like this."

He snarled at her. "This isn't over."

"When will you ever learn?" she said smugly. "You won't ever defeat me."

"Don't be so sure about that," he said, menacingly. "I made

you the White Queen of the Hellfire Club, I can *un*make you, too."

"I'm getting rather bored of your failed attempts, to be honest."

Shaw suddenly elbowed Magneto in the gut with a flare of what had to be the last remains of Dazzler's stolen power. Breaking free of his grasp, he snatched one of the soldiers' guns and fired at Frost.

Dazzler gasped in shock, but as fast as Shaw was, he wasn't fast enough.

The bullet hit Frost, but her body had turned hard as glass, and it bounced right off her, then suddenly stopped midair in the hold of Magneto's powers.

Shaw snarled as Magneto dropped the bullet to the ground and grabbed him again.

"Oh, this is a new enhancement since you saw me last." Frost smiled, waving her hands over her diamond form like a gameshow hostess. Then she tapped her temple. "And I knew what you were thinking before you even did."

Shaw started screaming obscenities at her before Sage stepped up and shot him with another CAP-89. Shaw was taken away in his bubble, beating his fists on the walls as he rolled around like a mouse on a running wheel.

Dazzler stared, impressed at Frost's diamond-like form, and watched as she transitioned back into her normal manifestation. Frost noted her awe and smiled.

"You know what they say, diamonds are forever." Frost gave her a wink, then turned and walked away.

They remained on the Alpha Flight Low-Orbit Space Station overnight. Rachel had some much-needed rest, Polaris had her wounded forearm seen to, Sage got some drops for her eyes, and Dazzler herself had her laser burn dressed. She'd insisted her father remain in the med bay to rest, partly because she was avoiding seeing him. She also wanted to give him time to think about all that he'd witnessed before they spoke. She hoped a little time would inject some rationality into his words. Her father could be fiery at the best of times, and she did not want him shooting from the hip with his initial reactions.

Besides, in a way she actually felt sorry for him. The revelation that his daughter was a mutant would've turned his life upside down, not to mention all he'd witnessed. She'd been hiding the truth for years. The person he thought she was, was a lie.

The bigger problem was, she didn't know how to feel about that. Did she feel guilt for lying? Did she wish she could take it back? Or did she wish she'd told him earlier and unloaded this burden years ago? Was she tired of living the lie? Or did she want to crawl back inside it?

In the morning, Dazzler said her goodbyes to Valdana and the Alpha Flight Low-Orbit Space Station, and traveled en masse back to Earth, with her fellow mutants, Bennett, and her father. Everyone was strangely silent. It felt as though there were several large elephants in the room, but with everyone around, no one wanted to address them.

As they disembarked on a private airfield outside New York City, that started to change. She saw Bennett walking toward Maria Hill, who waited for them. Dazzler felt a mixture of emotions upon seeing Hill in the flesh, but she didn't get time to process them before her father tapped her shoulder.

"We need to talk," he said.

Dazzler nodded then stepped aside with him. Her father stared at her as she waited for him to speak.

"W- why didn't you tell me?" he asked softly. She wasn't sure she'd ever heard his voice so gentle.

Part of her wanted to hug him, but part of her felt angry. Why couldn't he have accepted her for who she was? Why had he let so many years pass like this? She found she couldn't hold her tongue. "Because you didn't accept me as a musician, so why would you accept me as a mutant?"

Her father lowered his face, ashamed.

"Well, now you know," Dazzler said, her voice harder than she'd wanted, but she was unable to lower her guard. "How do you feel about that?"

The judge considered this for a moment, as though he were assessing a case before the court, his eyes analyzing her. "I feel grateful that you rescued me."

"That's not what I asked. How do you feel having a mutant for a daughter?"

Conflict fought its way across his face. "I- I need time to process this."

Dazzler nodded, feeling tender. Did she really think his acceptance would come so easy after all this time? Being a musician was one thing, but a mutant, too?

"I thought so," she said, her voice having lost the power it had moments ago. She began to walk away, but he grabbed her arm.

"It *is* good to see you, Alison… after all these years."

She stared at him as tears pricked her eyes.

"I'm growing old," he said. "Time is short." He hugged her awkwardly, and she flinched, wanting to hug him back, but she couldn't. "I *do* love you," he said, his voice stilted.

She pulled back from his embrace. "I get it. You love me but you just can't bring yourself to approve of who I am… So, nothing's changed."

"I just need time to…"

"I gotta go." She walked away, heading straight to where Hill and Bennett were speaking to Frost and the recently arrived Logan.

"S.W.O.R.D. and A.R.M.O.R. will clean up Hellfire-Prime and keep an eye on the dimension to make sure no one starts up production of the MGH again," Hill told them.

"What about the MGH left here on Earth?" Logan asked, arching that eyebrow of his, like he did. "And Shaw's N.E.A. supporters?"

"We're still extracting information out of Rosenthorpe and Walsh. S.H.I.E.L.D. will keep an eye on things and stamp out anything or anyone we find."

"As long as any MGH is out there," Dazzler said, "or any other humans sympathetic to the N.E.A., everyone is at risk."

"I know," said Hill. "So, I trust if we need your help again, we can call on you."

Dazzler stared at her, considering her options. But she knew there wasn't really a choice. She relented with a nod to Hill.

"Good," Hill said. "Now, I'm sure you understand, but we need to have a word with your father and make sure he understands the classified nature of everything he's seen."

Dazzler nodded, and Hill walked off toward her father.

Bennett stepped forward. "You did a good job, Agent Blaire. It's a shame you didn't trust us more."

"Well, trust has to be earned," she replied.

Bennett nodded. "It does. And you earned mine." He

extended his hand to her. Dazzler looked at the proffered hand, then shook it, before Bennett followed Hill over to her father.

Magneto and Cyclops ventured over to join them with Rachel, Polaris, and Sage. Dazzler felt Logan's shoulders tense as they did.

"Keep me posted," he said gruffly to Frost, before locking eyes with Magneto and Cyclops. His gaze lingered on Cyclops, seething. Cyclops stared back, defiant.

Logan motioned to Rachel and Polaris. "Come on. I'll give you a lift back to the school."

Cyclops turned to Rachel. "Thank you for coming to get me," he said to her.

Rachel glanced at him, then at Frost. "I didn't have much choice."

Cyclops gave a subtle sigh and placed his hands on his hips. "Well, you did well. Very well," he told her.

"Yes, you all did," Magneto said, seeming to want to cover their awkwardness. He turned to Polaris. "We worked well as a team. I thought you were going to come by more so I could teach you how to harness your power more efficiently?"

"Yeah, I was," Polaris answered. "I just…"

"What?"

Polaris looked her father in the eye with a steely stance. "I'm training fine with Logan."

"He can't show you what I can," Magneto said. "You know that. I encourage you to visit and learn from a true master of magnetism." He turned to Cyclops. "Now, I don't know about you, but there are some people in New York that I'd *very* much like to pay a visit to," he said as his face hardened.

Cyclops and Frost nodded, and together, they began to walk away.

"Frost!" Dazzler said, pulling her aside. The ice queen raised a manicured eyebrow. "I… just want to say you were right. About everything. I should've trusted you."

Frost smiled at her. She wasn't smug, wasn't catty – it was actually a friendly, warm smile. "And *you* were right, you are more powerful than I gave you credit for. Sage told me what happened up there. What you did." Frost stepped closer and whispered in her ear, "Tap into your power, and you'll be an Omega in no time."

Dazzler felt humbled by Frost's praise, but also terrified by it. She suddenly found herself thinking about being in that hallway at the New Charles Xavier School, and not knowing how she got there – the gap in her memory that the mutant had intentionally put there. She remembered, though, the conversation beforehand in Frost's office. Frost had failed to wipe that part, the part that left a clue. Frost had wiped her memory of Cerebra to keep the finer details out of S.H.I.E.L.D.'s hands. She didn't know why it hadn't occurred to her earlier, but perhaps it was because her attention was too caught up in her mission at the time, too caught up in paranoia and mistrust.

Strangely enough, she wasn't angry about what Frost had done. She realized that Frost had been trying to protect Cerebra. It proved to Dazzler that Frost was loyal to her students, loyal to mutants, and she might've realized that sooner if she'd just allowed herself to trust.

She was impressed that Frost had the power to wipe memories. And it made Dazzler wonder… Could Frost erase her father's memory of all that he'd seen?

"C- can you wipe my father's memory of what he saw up there?"

Frost looked at her as though trying to solve a puzzle. "Do you really want that?"

Dazzler nodded. "I don't want him to know I'm a mutant."

"You've been holding it in all these years, now it's out, you want to hide again?" Frost challenged.

Dazzler felt uneasy. She struggled to supply an answer. She didn't want to hide, but she didn't want her father's disappointment either.

Frost's eyes pinned hers. "A mutant should never hide. Wear your power with pride."

Dazzler watched Frost walk away, following Magneto and Cyclops. Maybe she was right. Maybe it was time Dazzler stopped running and own who she really was.

As Dazzler pondered this, she saw Hill and Bennett escorting her father into their vehicle.

"It was good working with you," Sage's voice sounded behind her. Dazzler turned to see Sage, Rachel, and Polaris waiting for her. Sage's hand was extended in a fist. "The four of us, we made a good team, yes?"

Dazzler smiled and bumped Sage's fist with her own. "We did."

"We did," Polaris agreed, as Rachel nodded.

In the distance, Logan honked the horn of the car he waited in, waving them to hurry up.

"I guess we'll see you around sometime, Blondie," Rachel said.

As Rachel and Polaris headed toward Logan's vehicle, and Sage toward Frost's, Dazzler felt a sudden, strange pang inside, of loss, watching the mutant ferries leave her solitary island, and head back to their mainland. Their separate lives.

"Hey!" Dazzler blurted to them.

They paused and looked back at her.

"There's a cool band playing this weekend that I think you might like."

"Oh yeah?" Polaris smiled, folding her arms. "Anyone we know?"

Dazzler grinned. "Maybe."

"But it's rock, right?" Rachel said. "'Cause I don't like pop."

Dazzler grinned. "Oh, it's definitely rock, honey."

"Sounds like a plan." Rachel smirked, before they continued to Logan's car.

"Do you need a ride?" Sage asked.

Dazzler shook her head as she saw her transport arriving. She spotted Tommy's pink mohawk from where she stood.

"I'm good. My band just arrived. We've gotta rehearse."

Sage laughed. "You don't need some rest after what we've been through?"

Dazzler shook her head. "Nah. Music gives me the energy I need."

CHAPTER THIRTY-TWO

Dazzler sat backstage, putting the finishing touches on the glittery blue wing over her left eye.

A knock on the door sounded, and she looked up to see Benedict poke his head in. "Ten minutes, love," his Cockney accent announced. "The guys are just about set up."

"Sure thing," she said.

Dazzler looked back into the mirror as Ben left. She stared at her reflection, studying the blue wing, studying her face. She looked normal. There were no signs of anything that she'd been through in the past week, not her battle with the Reds, not her battle with Shaw, her near-Omega output, or even the dimension jumps. Though she still had the energy she absorbed from the second dimension jump in her system.

She thought of her father and the photo he'd shown her, thought of what he'd seen and what a shock it must've been. The truth was out there now. It would take some time, but she hoped it was something that both of them would be comfortable with eventually, something they could move on from.

She pulled out her phone, not the new S.H.I.E.L.D. one that Bennett had sent her, but her personal phone, and she opened her stored photos from years ago, from her first gigs. She studied herself, her smile so innocent, her eyes so fresh and inspired. She'd seen so much since then. But as she looked at herself, she realized that girl, Alison, was still inside her. The young singer with the two blue wings over her eyes, comfortable with who she was and eager to face her future.

Dazzler looked back into the mirror and studied the glittery blue wing. She'd started wearing only one after the Mystique incident. After she'd lost part of herself and no longer felt whole.

But now?

She'd stopped Shaw and his MGH trade, and she'd released her mutant secret to her father. She'd released some of her baggage, had healed some of her wounds.

Now, she felt different. She was starting to feel whole again.

Now, she felt as though maybe she could trust again.

Dazzler put her phone away and finished getting ready. As she made her way to the side of stage, ready to perform, Ben caught sight of her face and grinned at her.

"I always liked you better with the two wings," he said.

"Yeah," Dazzler said, as her band began to play the opening riff. "Me too."

With a huge smile on her face, the music pulsing through her veins, and amid some *dazzling* light effects, she danced her way on to the stage.

And there in the front row of the audience, Sage, Rachel, and Polaris cheered her on.

ACKNOWLEDGMENTS

Thank you to Aconyte Books, and my editor Gwendolyn Nix, for giving me this opportunity, and to Marvel for allowing me to write in your glorious X-Men universe. It's an absolute privilege to write Dazzler and this magnificent cast of X-Men characters. I hope the fans love reading this story as much as I loved writing it. Thanks also, as always, to my family and friends for all their support, understanding and patience.

ABOUT THE AUTHOR

AMANDA BRIDGEMAN is a versatile writer who enjoys working across both original and tie-in worlds. She is a two-time Tin Duck Award winner, an Aurealis and Ditmar Awards finalist, and author of several novels and short stories, including the *Aurora* series, *The Time of the Stripes*, Scribe Award-winning novel *Pandemic: Patient Zero,* and the Salvation series consisting of *The Subjugate* and *The Sensation,* which is currently being developed for TV by Anonymous Content and Aquarius Films.

amandabridgeman.com.au
twitter.com/bridgeman_books

MARVEL SCHOOL OF Ⓧ

AMAZING POWERS
DARING EXPLOITS

SOUND of LIGHT
AMANDA BRIDGEMAN

THE SIEGE OF X-41
AN ORIGINAL X-MEN NOVEL
TRISTAN PALMGREN

MARVEL XAVIER'S INSTITUTE
SCHOOL OF
EDITED BY
GWENDOLYN NIX

MARVEL XAVIER'S INSTITUTE
TRIPTYCH
A PROSE NOVEL FROM THE PAGES OF X-MEN
JALEIGH JOHNSON

MARVEL XAVIER'S INSTITUTE
FIRST TEAM
A PROSE NOVEL FROM THE PAGES OF X-MEN
ROBBIE MacNIVEN

MARVEL XAVIER'S INSTITUTE
LIBERTY & JUSTICE FOR ALL
A PROSE NOVEL FROM THE PAGES OF THE X-MEN
CARRIE HARRIS

MARVEL HEROINES

POWERFUL STORIES
ICONIC HEROINES

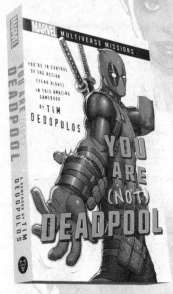